RAGE

NIA MYST

CONTENT WARNING

Dear readers,

This book contains themes of dark romance, including violence, murder, torture (of the bad guys), explicit sexual content, and plenty of profanities. The book is recommended for 18+ readers.

<u>Potential Triggers:</u>

- Description of Sexual Assault in the past
- Conversations on marital rape, child abuse and domestic violence (not of main characters)
- Murders and torture of the abusers
- Violence and Gore
- Castration (of abusers)
- Gang rape
- Pedophilia
- Mention of Acid attack

<u>All intimacy between the main characters is consensual.</u>
<u>Kink List:</u>

- Breeding kink
- He spits in her mouth
- Cum play
- Impact Play
- Breath Play
- Light Degradation Kink
- Light choking
- Unprotected sex

DEDICATION

To all the women who had to build themselves back up.
Who came out stronger and deadlier.
The world bows down to you.

GLOSSARY

Appa: a Korean term for Dad

Didi: a Hindi/Gujarati term for elder sister

Eomma: a Korean term for Mom

Hyung: a Korean honorific term used by a male to address an older male who is his brother, a close friend, or a mentor.

Maa: a Hindi word for Mom

Oppa: a Korean honorific term used by a younger woman or girl to address an older male she has a close bond with, such as a brother, male relative, older male friend, or romantic partner.

CHAPTER 1

DOMINIC

ine missed calls. All from my sister Sophie.

I walked down the hallway of my office toward my cabin, checking the timing of the calls. Two calls from around eleven in the evening and seven calls from about half an hour ago. It was one in the morning, and my meeting with some Korean clients had run later than expected. My phone had been on silent the whole time. The entire office floor was empty, except for the evening cleaners, who were quietly tidying up the open kitchen area.

My sister was attending the Manhattan Center for Healing for Survivors' charity event, which aimed to provide support and shelter for abused women. Our parents were also at the gala, representing our company, Park Real Estate Group, the largest real estate business in the US.

Ever since Dad retired, he had been going to these events with Mom to pass the time. I preferred working in the comfort of my own office over talking and schmoozing with Manhattan's elites. They rarely cared about a gala's cause and gossiped worse than my mother and her five sisters on a phone call.

I stepped into my cabin and closed the door behind me, wondering why Sophie would've called in the middle of the party. Something dark and threatening churned in my gut at the seven successive missed calls from merely half an hour ago. Just as I was about to return her call, my phone rang again, her name lighting up my screen.

I picked up the call, worry sitting heavy in my gut.

A panicked voice—not Sophie's—screamed on the phone. "Dominic, it's Sophie. I've been trying to call you for the last half an hour."

My stomach dropped, and my hand clenched into a fist as Ashley, Sophie's interior design firm partner, cried on the damn call.

"Ashley, what's going on? What happened to Sophie? Where are you?" I barked, whirling around and marching toward the elevator.

A tearful, broken sound escaped her. "Hospital. We're at the hospital."

My feet halted as a tremor of bone-chilling fear raced down my spine.

"What the fuck happened, Ashley?"

My heart pounded in my chest, and my hands trembled as a sinking sense of impending doom washed over me. I wanted to end the call. I wanted to go back five minutes and freeze time, anything to avoid hearing what Ashley had to say. Some part deep within me knew I wasn't ready to hear it.

"Raped. Sophie was raped. We've just arrived at Mount Sinai Hospital. They say it's critical, Dominic."

Every word from her mouth dropped like a grenade at my feet. My chest caved in as my legs gave out, and I collapsed to my knees in the middle of the office hallway.

My baby sister.

Raped.

Critical."

My stomach revolted as bile rose in my throat, and I threw up right on the floor. Terror, unlike anything I've ever experienced, raced through my veins. My vision blurred, and all thoughts left my mind. It felt like I was caught in a free fall of disbelief and sheer horror. My eyes stared at the blurry hand streaked with drops of water, the other still clutching the phone.

Somebody touched my sister.

I wanted to scream and break something, but my throat had closed up, and my body felt like it was being torn apart from the inside. As if someone were digging into me and sucking out every ounce of happiness and joy and heart I'd ever experienced in this life, leaving behind nothing but agony and rage.

I stared at the phone in my hand as I leaned on the floor, my body shaking. Slowly, I raised it back to my ear. Ashley's crying pulled me out of my spiral as she said, "Your parents are here, and they're inconsolable. We need you, Dominic. Please hurry."

"I'm on my way."

My next call was to Maxim, my driver who's been with me for the last fifteen years.

I ran to the elevator, my feet slipping slightly on my own bile, and hit the elevator button.

"Dom," he said, his voice sharp and attentive as always.

"It's Sophie. Get the car ready. Mount Sinai Hospital."

"Fuck. What happened? Is she okay?" His voice rose in panic.

My voice shook as I felt wetness on my cheek. My throat closed as words refused to surface.

"Dom!" Maxim barked.

"Critical."

The elevator dinged, then opened, and I stepped in. I

stared at my reflection as the doors closed and the elevator started to go down.

A shell of a man—an utterly defeated man—stared back at me. Cheeks streaked with tears, jaw clenched tight, suit completely rumpled, and eyes completely devoid of light. He kept holding the phone to his ear even as the call cut off.

I looked back at those eyes—my eyes—and they stared back at me, full of accusation and anger. If I'd just picked up the phone the first time she called, would she have been okay? Did my neglect lead to her rape? Would she be alive when I got there?

A numb mist was pulling me under, refusing to let go of me, when a tight slap rang in my ears. My face jerked sideways as I slammed into the elevator wall. I was hauled by the collar of my shirt, and another slap rang in my ears as pain burst across my cheek.

Clarity burst through my vision as my eyes met Maxim's.

"Snap out of it, Dominic. Everybody needs you."

Right. My legs shook as I walked, but somehow, Maxim pushed me into the passenger seat and ran to the driver's side. He drove like a madman, while I managed to get some words out and update him on what Ashley had told me.

My baby sister. Raped. Critical.

The car screeched to a halt right outside the front door of the hospital. I jumped out, uncaring of everyone and everything around me.

I was rushed to the top floor, thanks to Dad being there with Sophie. The moment the elevator doors opened, I ran.

The first person I saw when I reached the waiting room was Mom. She sat on a metal chair in a corner, holding her head in both hands as her shoulders shook with her sobs. My eyes met my father's devastated ones as he held Mom in his arms.

My father looked broken. Devastation and heartbreak

were etched in every angle of his body. For the first time, he looked defeated.

Tears freely flowed down his cheeks. This man, this strong man whom I'd never seen shed a tear, never break down, crumpled right into my arms the moment I stepped closer to him.

"Dominic," he cried, his hands shook in mine as I clutched them, holding him up as the urge to break down at the knees overwhelmed me.

"What did the doctor say?" My voice broke as I asked the question, petrified to hear the answer.

Mom sobbed louder at my question, and I instantly regretted asking it.

Just then, a doctor, followed by a nurse, walked into the waiting area.

"Mr. Park?" she asked.

"That's me," I said, not wanting Dad to take on any more burdens.

As she approached us, I noticed the strain and worry in her eyes.

"How is Sophie, Doctor?" I asked.

Her lips pursed, and she sighed in defeat. "Let's step into my office, please."

I was tempted to shake her to get some answers right now, but Mom and Dad rushed behind the doctor. As soon as we were seated in her office, she looked at all of us. "I can only imagine the pain and shock you have been through. I'm sorry about what has happened. Sophie was conscious when she was brought in. She was able to give us as much information as she could. She also gave us her consent to share all the information about the incident, as well as her physical condition, with her immediate family."

My fists clenched as she talked, the need to know what happened to my baby sister colliding with the need to put my hands over my ears and scream into oblivion. "How is she, Doctor? Tell us everything."

Her eyes met mine, and her throat bobbed before she uttered, "Sophie was raped by three men."

My soul shattered.

"She had vaginal and anal tearing."

My mom wailed.

"Trauma to the uterus."

Dad's shoulders shook as he sobbed.

"A fractured cheekbone. Severe concussion."

My baby sister, my little Soph, who'd followed me around as a toddler and made me have tea parties with her.

"Cracked ribs."

Every word out of the doctor's mouth wrapped itself around my heart, weaving an impenetrable wall of raging, hot wrath and bone-deep guilt. The need to slam my head into the wall to relieve some of the agony threatening to burst from my body had my limbs shaking.

"Internal bleeding in the abdominal cavity, caused by punches to the stomach."

My chest heaved, and tears streamed down my face as the doctor continued listing every injury Sophie had sustained. I sat there, listening to and committing every single one of them to my memory.

Whoever did this to her was going to pay.

Guilt tried to drown me, but my parents' cries kept me rooted to my seat.

I looked at the doctor and asked the question I was dreading the answer to. "Will she be okay?"

"We've performed the necessary surgery. We have her sedated and on a ventilator to allow her body the time it needs to rest and heal. Her injuries were severe but we're hopeful she'll make a full physical recovery. It is going to take time. But she is out of critical danger. However, it's her emotional trauma that is of utmost concern."

"We will hire the best psychiatrist to help her, Doctor. But I need my sister to be alright."

"I understand, Mr. Park. But these things require time and understanding. All you can do is be there for her and help her feel safe."

My dad nodded. "We understand, Doctor."

She looked at all of us with a kind smile, maybe trying to put us at ease. She shouldn't have bothered. Nothing was going to revert the harm that was done to Sophie. Nothing was going to change the fact that I'd failed to protect my baby sister. Nothing would help except finding the bastards who dared to harm my sister.

The doctor's next words pulled me out of my spiraling thoughts. "Would you like to see her?"

"Yes," I said, needing to hold Sophie's hand and tell her everything would be all right.

I turned to Mom and Dad. "You guys are coming to see Soph, right?"

Dad started to shake his head in denial when Mom snapped at him. "Don't you dare, Michael. Our daughter needs us, and if a few minutes are all we get with her right now, we're going to be there. Don't you dare be a coward."

With that, Mom wiped her tears and turned to the doctor. "Take us to Sophie, Doctor."

I held Mom's hand while Dad rested his hand on her shoulder as we walked down the hallway.

Nothing could've prepared us to see the woman lying on the hospital bed.

My baby sister—her face swollen from someone's punches, a black eye, bruises on her arms, and dried blood at her lips—had a ventilator helping her breathe.

Mom stepped toward Sophie first. She placed a soft kiss on her forehead, her tears dripping on Sophie's cheeks. "You'll be alright, baby. Eomma is here."

My dad dropped onto the chair by her bed, his chest

heaving as he sobbed. He held Sophie's hand in both of his, chanting a million apologies in a whisper.

Nine missed calls from Sophie.

Guilt so sharp burned through my veins that I wanted to stab myself to let some of it out. I should've picked up when she called.

Nine fucking missed calls.

The overwhelming need to apologize to my sister tore open my chest. I put one foot in front of the other and walked to the other side of the bed.

Gently, I ran my hand along her head. "Wake up, Soph," I whispered, my voice breaking.

"Please, Sophie girl. Open your eyes." Tears blurred my vision when she didn't. I was distantly aware that she was heavily sedated but my heart screamed at me to wake her up, to see her eyes shining with that light, to make sure she was all right.

Mom's sniffles were another dagger to my bleeding heart.

"I'm so sorry I wasn't there for you. I'm so, so sorry I didn't protect you."

Sophie didn't even stir.

I gently took her hand in mine and pressed a soft kiss to her bruised knuckles. My sister had put up a fight.

I was going to find the fuckers who did this to her. I'd scorch the earth or tear apart the world if I had to.

I didn't know whether Sophie could hear my voice, but I made her a promise. "You have to wake up fast, Soph. You need to tell your big brother who did this to you. I promise you. They will pay. For every cut, every bruise, every punch, every despicable thing they did to you, they will pay for it a thousand times over. You have to wake up to watch them suffer, Soph. I'm right here."

I looked at the despair in my mom's eyes, the defeat in my dad's shoulders, and I met their eyes even as I clutched

Sophie's hand in mine, feeling the pulse in her wrist, and made a promise. "I'm not going to let anything happen to Sophie. Whoever did this to her just made the biggest mistake of their lives."

CHAPTER 2

"Crimson Tiger, you copy?" Sloane's voice crackled in my earpiece.

"Copy," I muttered, focusing my gaze on the four pathetic fucks lounging near the swimming pool of one of their summer houses, smoking pot.

"Now remember, we only want them injured and unconscious to transport them with the least resistance. Minimal bloodshed. You can have your fun later."

I hid in one of the neighbor's giant trees, staring at my targets.

Anger coursed through my veins at the thought of these rich, entitled assholes getting away with the most horrendous crimes and then lounging in their daddies' summer houses without a care in the world. A total waste of human life.

"Will try. Let me know when it's all clear." I cracked my knuckles, impatience clawing at me from the inside as my rage and violence waited to burst free.

"All clear. You have ten minutes. Once they're immobilized, Shadow Panther will help load them up. Clear?"

"Clear."

I jumped off the tree and swiftly landed right beside the first piece of human trash.

Before the other three could comprehend what happened, I backhanded the first guy, and he instantly dropped unconscious. *Pathetic.*

The other three immediately scrambled out of their lounge chairs. They tried to come at me, but I was stronger and quicker.

I kicked one of them in the ribs, grabbed the arm of another, twisting it sharply to dislocate his shoulder, and punched the last one in the head, knocking him unconscious.

"Who are you?" the guy whose shoulder I had dislocated whimpered.

"Your worst fucking nightmare," I said, cocking my head and moving closer to where he leaned against the lounger.

He scrambled back, eyes wide with terror at the sight of me.

I stood clad in black tactical gear, stretched taut over thick muscle. My biceps strained the sleeves, and powerful thighs tested the fabric's limits. A predatory crimson-and-black tiger mask with gold lining hid my face. At five feet, nine inches, I was coiled with power and menace.

I advanced a step. The two weak shits practically tripped over themselves falling back.

"Stay back," the guy with the broken ribs shrieked.

I chuckled. "Did you stay back when Mary asked you to?"

Without waiting for his response, I lunged at them, knocking them both out with a punch to one's head and a backhand to the other's face.

"They're all unconscious. Get the van ready," I informed my team via comms.

"Copy. Shadow Panther reaching you in ten seconds."

I was tying up one of the unconscious dudes when Shadow Panther landed beside me.

"Took you long enough," she said.

"Needed to at least get in a few punches before I incapacitated them."

I lifted one of the guys and dropped him onto Shadow Panther's shoulder, then hoisted the second one onto her other one. Grunting with the weight, she said, "Damn, these rich kids are heavy."

"Fucking pigs," I muttered.

She snorted as I lifted the remaining two onto my own shoulders.

"Exit via the east backyard. Coast is clear."

With a grunt, we moved quickly. We were inside the van within twenty seconds and speeding out of that shithole town fifteen minutes later.

I removed my mask and met the eyes of my fellow Wildcat, Tara, who did the same.

I cracked a smile. "Now, the real fun begins."

———

One precise snip and I sliced that tiny dick clean off the fucker. He bucked, shrieking like an animal caught in a trap, his shouts echoing off the walls. *Pathetic*. Blood spewed down his legs as his shrieking dissolved into agonized wails. Fucking music to my ears.

"Relax." I chuckled, admiring my handiwork before flicking the blade clean. "It was a clean cut. It won't kill you." I tossed the shriveled little trophy in a tiny box.

He cried harder, terror amplifying as he stared at the snarling crimson tiger that hid my face. We never showed our faces—standard op for plausible deniability if things went sideways. "Help! Somebody, help me."

"Cry, you little fuck. Cry harder." I laughed in his face, knowing no help was coming for him.

"You can't do this. Help!" he shrieked, spit flying. Blood

dripped down his cracked forehead, his swollen eyes staring at me with abject horror and that primal fear that I loved to see. Oh yes, I knew that look. If he could shit himself, he would. He'd already pissed himself ten kicks and five punches ago.

He lay in a spreading puddle of his own piss and blood, one hand clamped uselessly over his mutilated groin, sobbing and thrashing in pain. Behind him, the other three guys were already whimpering and clawing at the walls of the small room, making me that much more excited.

"Stop moving so much, or you'll bleed out," I mumbled, tapping my boot impatiently and looking at the clock.

"I'm sorry, I'm sorry. I shouldn't have hurt Mary."

A harsh, barking laugh ripped out of my chest. "*Hurt* Mary?" The sheer understatement of their act made me see red. "Is that what we're calling it these days? *Hurt?* See, that's why entitled fucks like you don't deserve to have that tiny little part I just cut off." My boot slammed into his gut with a *thud*, making him fold over and start gagging on the floor.

"I'm sorry we r…ra…raped Mary," he finally choked out between harsh breaths.

Too fucking little, too fucking late. They hadn't just raped her; they had brutalized her and damn near killed her. She had to stay in the hospital for three months just to be able to go to the bathroom on her own. And if that wasn't enough, when she pulled herself together, gathered the courage to speak her truth, and complained to the police, their rich dads had just waved their money. They made the whole thing disappear, making her a laughingstock in their little town.

Yes, I loathed bastards like these, and if I had to be the one to serve them karma and take them out, good fucking riddance.

My kick arced down, aimed to hit his bleeding groin, but Naomi's sharp voice cut through my earpiece, "Careful, Tiger. You don't want to kill him just yet." *Dammit.*

My boot halted barely a millimeter from his bleeding hand

clamped around his groin. With a grunt, I left him bleeding on the floor and whirled around to face the remaining three.

The moment my gaze locked on them, the three of them dissolved into pure panic. Screaming, they clambered along the walls, pushing each other in front. They raised their hands in surrender as snot and tears ran down their face.

I stepped closer, and they flinched in sheer terror. Amusement trickled down my spine at the view. "How does it feel to be on the other side, boys?"

They all whimpered when I snatched the guy closest to me by his designer shirt and drove my fist deep into his gut. He slammed down on his hands and knees, blood spewing from his mouth.

He raised his arm in defeat as he tried to breathe through his mouth. "Please! Please don't cut my dick off. I told them it was a bad idea. I told them we shouldn't do it," he cried.

I leaned down until my mask was inches from his face. He flinched and pushed himself deeper into the ground, trying to escape me. "Yet you did," I whispered. "You raped her. You didn't actually stop anyone. You didn't even get Mary to the hospital." Driven by the dark red rage running rampant in my veins, I slammed my forehead against his. The loud, satisfying crack echoed in the room as his eyes rolled back in his head and rendered him unconscious.

Or maybe he was just faking it to delay the inevitable. Who cared.

I straightened and turned around to the other two, their faces white with terror. My chest heaved with anger, and I roared like a fucking tiger, making them squeal like the pigs they were. My mask only fueled their terror, and I relished in watching them piss themselves.

A mad, unhinged laugh escaped my throat, and I bellowed, "RUN!" The two of them shrieked, scrambling over the walls, dashing around in the tiny room, and pushing each other toward me.

Neither of them dared to try to attack me. Not that it would do anything. They'd just piss me off, and they all knew instinctively not to push the biggest predator in the room.

Just as I was deciding who to grab first, Tara's bored voice droned through my earpiece. "Here we go again. Stop playing with your prey, Samaira. The bar's filling up, and the boss needs you upstairs. Now."

Fuck, playtime was over. I sighed and lunged at the boys.

———

I stormed out of the torture room, a box full of four severed dicks in my bloodied hand, ready to lay it down at Mary's feet. Naomi, in her black-and-silver jaguar mask, stood right outside the door. Her arms crossed at her chest, she was furiously tapping her foot. "Couldn't you be quicker? A little more careful? Do you know how difficult it is to keep these fuckers alive when you toy around with them *after* chopping off their dicks?"

I shrugged, my mask hiding the huge smile stuck on my face while waving the box of their dicks in front of her.

She sighed and entered the room, where all four unconscious men lay in their own blood.

I walked down the hallway. Both sides were lined with smaller rooms, each soundproofed so no noise could escape. These were where we occasionally kept the culprits. Our operation was three floors below ground level. The ground level itself operated as a bar and restaurant. I walked up a hidden, wooden staircase to the floor directly above, entering our private space, which we called our Den.

The moment I entered, I removed my mask. Facing the entrance was a twelve-foot-tall black wall etched with our emblem—a giant lunging gold panther right beside the word WILDCATS in bold gold letters. Painted directly underneath it was our tagline: *When the law doesn't work, WE do.*

A bit overdramatic? Sure. But we called ourselves Wildcats, and we were proud of it.

Five black lockers were affixed to the same wall.

I hung my black-and-crimson tiger mask on the door of my locker. The tiger on my mask looked ferocious, its eyes narrowed as if its gaze was stuck on its prey, ready to launch, its jaws slightly open to reveal its canines. It demanded respect and submission. It was a representation of what I truly felt from within when I hunted down predators.

Powerful. Deadly. Invincible.

Our masks not only hid our identities from the world, but they also gave strength to the women who came to us.

A lot of women and families who came to us for help didn't have the heart to order an assassination. Most of them wanted justice without taking a life. Our job was to deliver.

We were the ones whom women hired when everything else had failed to bring them justice. Be it rape, domestic violence, abuse, attacks, or any form of violence committed against women, we were their vengeance. We were the monsters they hired to slay the *real* monsters in their lives.

We did whatever they wanted us to do. Find their attackers? Done. Make them suffer? Of course. Chop off their dicks? With pleasure. Make them disappear from their lives? On it. Kill them? No problem.

They named it, we did it.

Gladly.

Proudly.

Without. Any. Hesitation.

I'd just removed my holster and placed it in the locker when I was thrown off balance and pushed against my locker —courtesy of our team's hyperactive rookie.

Shadow, Tara's big black Doberman, jumped up onto my chest, almost licking my face. I was pretty sure it was the blood sprayed on my hands and chest that had him going crazy.

"Down, boy." I giggled as I tried to get away from him.

"Auntie needs to wash herself before petting you. C'mon, go back to Tara. Go back to your mama."

I glared at Tara, who was busy laughing at Shadow as he tried to get a taste of the disgusting blood on my skin.

"Shadow baby, come to Tara. Come here. Here's a treat, boy," she cooed. The moment the word *treat* came out of her mouth, Shadow jumped off me and ran to her.

Even though he was Tara's, Shadow was all of our baby. He went wherever Tara did. She was our hacker, our stalker, our very own Shadow Panther.

Once Shadow was busy chomping down his treat, Tara turned her gaze to me. "Samaira, you need to chop the penis at the end of your torture session. Fuck, girl. Naomi was pissed."

I snorted and started to remove my tac gear. "The fucker deserved it."

She sat at her massive desk, her three computers open in front of her, the light from them illuminating her face, the left half of which she covered with a black mask. Tara sighed, rolling her eyes at me. "Bitch, they all deserve it. But you must admit, you were a little extra today."

Grunting, I dropped the box of dicks beside her computer. "Here's the package. Give it to Sloane. She'll want to make it pretty. And ask Mary if she wants to keep them alive or not."

Tara made a disgusting face and placed the box on the top shelf along the wall to keep it out of Shadow's reach. She visibly shuddered. "Only she thinks decorating the box in glitter and shit might cheer up the girls."

I snorted, untying my braid. "And you call *me* crazy."

I made my way to the washroom but turned around at the last minute and asked, "Where are Sloane and Lena?"

Tara popped her gum and, without moving her eyes from her screen, answered, "Upstairs. The bar's packed. A bit of a rowdy crowd today."

"I'll freshen up and join them."

After a scalding shower to wash away the blood, piss, and tears of those fuckers, I changed into my usual black tank top and cargo pants. I put on my choker and two gold necklaces, the longest one resting between my breasts. I put in all my usual earrings—my daith, orbital, industrial, forward helix, helix, and the hoops on my lobes. I fucking loved seeing my ears all blingy and pretty.

I blow-dried my hair quickly since it was getting a bit too long to air-dry properly. Once I felt ready enough, I put on my black combat boots, went to the kitchen of our den, and opened the fridge.

I grabbed my berry milkshake jar that I always kept stocked in bulk. Beating and torturing men made me hungry and hot, and nothing cooled me down and pulled my mind out of the crimson rage it got lost in better than my cold berry milkshake.

When I noticed one was missing, the wave of crimson rage surged back to the surface. Immediately, I clicked the picture of the empty space on the shelf and posted it in our group chat.

> Me: Who the fuck stole my milkshake jar? You know I need them to cool off.

> Me: Tell me now.

> Me: You know I'll find you.

> Sloane: Here we go again.

> Me: Was it you, bitch?

> Sloane: Pssh. I'm not crazy.

> Me: Sloane, you absolutely are batshit crazy.

> Me: Tara? Was it you?

Immediately, she shouted from across the room, "Hell no."

> Me: Whoever stole my milkshake, I'm coming for you.

> Lena: Samaira, if you're done with the hissy fit, come upstairs. NOW. It's rush hour on Saturday.

A growl escaped my lips at having to let it go—for now. They knew I needed my milkshakes, and I did not share them. I *would* find whoever did this after my shift upstairs. Lena wouldn't use all caps in her text if she didn't genuinely need me upstairs, especially after my torture session. I either needed to fuck or sit in a warm bathtub for an hour with a dildo and my ice-cold milkshake—possibly both—to burn off the adrenaline still pumping through my system.

> Me: Yes, Boss

I quickly gulped down my milkshake and was just about to head upstairs when Tara called out to me.

"What's up?" I asked, pausing at the foot of the hidden staircase that led up from our Den to the basement level. Our Den was located directly under the basement and could only be accessed via a secret floorboard known only to the five of us. All our client meetings were held in the basement.

We handled most of our dirty work either down under the Den or from our safe house farther outside the city. We definitely did not kill people here. That was strictly reserved for our safe house.

She popped her gum and rearranged the items on the screen. "I just sent Mary an update. She's coming to collect the box tomorrow. She asked for a night to think over what she wants to do with the boys."

"Cool."

The moment I stepped onto the main floor of the Thunder Claw, one of Brooklyn's happening bars and restaurants, a cacophony of deafening noises engulfed me. Lena, the leader of Wildcats, owned Thunder Claw, which acted as a front for our other…uh…activities. The rest of us worked here as employees, handling day-to-day operations alongside our regular staff.

For obvious reasons, I was an excellent bouncer. As I walked from the back of the bar toward the entrance, several pairs of eyes followed me. In my black sleeveless tank top, my arms—showing a stunning tiger tattoo sleeve on my right one—looked massive and strong and intimidating. I had muscles on top of muscles, and I flaunted them with abandon. Women usually stared at me with a sense of awe, whereas men looked at me with a mix of challenge and surprise.

"Yo, Big Sam!" a dude yelled, raising his glass at me. Most regulars knew me as *Big Sam,* for obvious reasons. Not exactly the most original name for a bouncer.

"Yo, Doug!" I waved back. "Have a fun night."

I waved at Sloane, who was operating the bar with our hired bartender, Zoey, and was in her signature bold makeup and the cutest short skirt and tank top. She single-handedly brought in more tips than all the other bartenders and servers combined.

Lena came up right beside me as I stood near the entrance, where I got an uninterrupted view of the entire bar. "Tough crowd?"

She rolled her eyes. "A typical Saturday."

She leaned closer to me and muttered, "Next time, you chop the dick at the end. Naomi is going to chop your hair off in your sleep one of these days."

I snorted. "I'd like to see her try."

She playfully rolled her eyes and bumped my shoulder. "Nice work today, though. I'll let you out early."

I grunted. As satisfying as the work felt, it sucked that it was actually necessary. The system was so rigged that we women had to take basic human rights, like our safety, into our own hands. As if fighting for our rights day-to-day wasn't enough, as if constantly worrying about our safety wasn't enough, we were often denied even the basic decency of justice. When the entire world seemed designed to stomp down on women, it really left us no choice except to rise up and roar back. To snatch back the justice we deserved. To tear apart the egomaniacs and assholes who thought it was okay to abuse women and then get away with it. Not under my fucking watch.

"By the way," Lena continued, pulling me out of the hazy fog of anger. "There seems to be some chatter about an increasing number of missing women."

"Chatter where?"

"More missing persons reports have been filed on women in the past six months than in the past four years before that. Also, I've heard some talk around the bar."

The abundance of access to "chatter" and news of underhanded activities in the area was one of the few genius reasons for opening a bar as a front.

"Are we gonna do something about it?" I asked.

Lena shrugged. "Not yet. We don't have much to go on. If something big happens, I'm sure it will land in our lap."

We had our methods to allow people who needed us to find us.

And find, they always did.

CHAPTER 3

DOMINIC

Four excruciatingly long months passed with no justice for my baby sister. She used to be a strong and talented interior designer who ran her own firm, but now she was a mere shadow of her former self.

Every day that passed without knowing who the fuck raped my sister, my mind slipped further into darkness and despair. The world around me had lost all its color, the blood in my veins constantly strumming with violence and a need for vengeance. The burden of guilt for failing my sister grew heavier as the days passed. But the rapists were fucking ghosts.

I pinched the bridge of my nose as Robert, the private detective I'd hired, droned on and on about the lack of evidence, the charity being a masked event, no significant input from Sophie, and every other obstacle preventing him from finding the criminals.

"I'll try to talk to Sophie." I cut him off, absolutely done with his bullshit. "See if she's able to talk about it. Until then, I need something concrete from you. And if you can't do your job properly, tell me now. Stop wasting my time. You have twenty-four hours."

I had barely spoken the last word when he practically fled out of my office.

I tapped the intercom button that connected my line to Kai, my assistant and my younger cousin. "Yes, Mr. Park."

"Kai, do I have any appointments or anything that requires my immediate attention today?"

"No, Mr. Park. I stopped scheduling anything after five, per your instructions."

I looked at the clock, and it was 6:15 already.

"Alright, let's head out. I need to punch something. Or someone."

A pitiful moan came over the line. "Hyung, I'm really not in the mood to get beaten up today."

I scoffed. "Then block better and focus on attacking *me* for a change."

I cut the line before he could respond, knowing that the little shit would be ready to head out by the time I was out of my office. I sent out my last email, shut down my computer, and walked out.

"I'm not holding back today," Kai said, falling into step beside me as we headed to the elevator.

"Good. Can't wait."

Maxim had already reached the building's front door when we stepped outside.

"The Serpentine Manor," I told Maxim as we slid into the car.

The Serpentine Manor, like the name suggested, was an exclusive club for the city's elites. The widow of a billionaire entrepreneur established it as a way to remind everyone how none of the elites had supported her in her time of need. Regardless, every single millionaire and billionaire salivated over a membership at her exclusive mansion, which promised seduction, privacy, and entertainment. The richest snakes of

Brooklyn hung out here, brokering deals, building empires, and getting richer and more corrupt by the day.

One good thing about the manor being exclusive to elites was that they loved their pretty faces and pampered asses. Hence, the boxing ring was always empty.

Maxim looked at Kai through the rearview mirror, quirking an eyebrow with a teasing smile. "You ready to get beaten up again, kid?"

Kai was in his late twenties, a decade younger than me. He simply groaned at Maxim. "Not today, Maxim. I'm not gonna hold back this time."

I shook my head, a small smile pulling at my lips. Kai was one of the few who managed to do that these days. He'd really stepped up in the past few months, taking up the majority of the workload and handling the company while I tried to track down Sophie's rapists.

Once we'd changed into gym wear and walked into the boxing ring, we found Maxim waiting for us in the ring to be our referee.

"Don't hold back now," I teased him.

He was actually a very good boxer. That was why I always sparred with him. But it was fun to see him get riled up before a match. He always punched harder that way.

With a sharp whistle from Maxim, the round was on. I didn't wait around or circle Kai. I didn't have the patience, nor was I aiming to win. All I needed was to beat the shit out of someone or get beaten myself. I threw a punch at his jaw, which he easily blocked, landing a quick jab to my stomach in return.

I grabbed his arm and threw him over my shoulder, then slammed him on the mat. He gave me a ruthless smile and swept my ankle, causing me to stumble. He immediately took advantage, landing a solid punch to my nose.

Pain exploded through my nose, my vision blurring as I felt the warm trickle of blood on my upper lip. Adrenaline flooded my system, my pulse hammered, and I bounced on the balls of my feet.

Finally, I felt fucking alive.

I kicked him in his stomach, and not even his block could stop him from stumbling.

"Fuck, you're in a mood today," Kai grumbled, shaking his head and circling me, looking for an opening.

"Quit dillydallying and attack. You're boring me."

This time, he laughed and launched himself at me. We were a blur of punches and kicks and jabs until blood and sweat ran down our faces, and my vision turned hazy.

All my frustrations, my desperation, my bone-deep terror, and my feverish need for revenge were poured out in every punch and every kick. And Kai took it all and gave it to me harder. I took it all with relish, needing the pain and the punches to assuage the constant guilt haunting me.

He knew I could've blocked over half of the jabs I let through. He knew I needed to feel just as much pain as I needed to inflict. He fought me till I no longer could pick my arms up, till my knees gave out, and I dropped on the mat, bruised and bloodied.

Kai offered me his hand to get back up. When he pulled me to a stand and we made our way to the shower rooms, he slapped me on the arm, making me wince. "Fucking block, man."

"I do. You're a good fighter."

He snorted. "I'm good. But I'm not blind."

I remained silent as we jumped into the shower stalls and cleaned up.

Once we were done, I changed into a pair of pants and a black shirt, rolling the sleeves up to my elbows. I stood in front of the mirror and inspected the injuries. A red bruise bloomed right under my eyes, which I was pretty sure would be purple tomorrow. Aside from that, I looked fine.

Once we were both ready, we silently made our way to the

manor's bar. The mansion hallway was lined with rich emerald tapestry as intricately threaded gold serpents seemed to slither across the walls, while sparkling chandeliers illuminated our way.

The bar itself was a display of extravagance. Only the best liquors lined the shelves. The walls continued the same emerald-and-gold theme. The two of us took a seat directly at the bar. The entire space was large enough to fit about a hundred people.

The two bartenders at the bar already knew us and our usual orders.

"The usual, Mr. Park?" Juliet asked.

She wore a gold dress that wrapped around her body like a second skin. It stopped right above her knees. The spaghetti straps of the dress showcased the colorful rose-and-thorn design tattooed over her arms. She was pretty and delicate, but that did nothing for me. It had been a long time since anybody had done anything for me.

I gave her a polite smile. "Yes, please."

"Mr. Kai, the usual for you as well?"

He gave her a flirtatious smile and winked. "You know it."

"On it, gentlemen. Let me know if you need anything else."

Once she left us to serve the other patrons hanging out around the bar, Kai turned to me and asked, "Any progress in finding those fuckers?"

My jaw clenched. "Nope. They're fucking ghosts."

He nodded. "How is Sophie?"

Kai was only a year older than her, so he had been close to her since they were kids.

Juliet placed the drinks in front of us. An old-fashioned for me, and a Macallan neat for him. "Thank you," I told her.

I took a sip of my drink, the whiskey burn warming my throat, before answering Kai. "She's the same. Silent. Tortured. Doesn't look at anyone. Hasn't smiled at anyone.

She's staying with Mom and Dad for the time being, but they're worried."

"You think it would help her to go back to living at her own place?"

I shrugged. "I don't know. I don't know who raped Sophie. Don't know if they had an ulterior motive. Don't know if they intended to kill her. I'm not sure if they plan to finish the job. At least the security at Mom and Dad's is top-notch. None of us wants to risk putting Sophie in any more danger or stress. Mom is the only one she's talked to properly, so I don't want to take that away from her."

He nodded at Juliet as she placed our food in front of us and turned to me as he cut his steak. "I still can't imagine the cops not finding anything."

A wave of violent rage flooded my veins at the thought of the cops. "They've done jack shit. Every time I ask them for an update, they seem to have problems. Evidence disappearing. The officer assigned to our case has been transferred. No leads. At least they made an effort early on. But now that it's been over four months, it's radio silence from them. They've called it a cold case and moved on. They're waiting for a new lead to appear as if it's just gonna drop out of thin air."

I cut into my filet mignon, still burning in anger.

Kai swallowed a bite of his food, strumming his fingers on the bar table. "Do you want me to ask around and see if anyone has a better private detective?"

Robert's face popped into my head, and I immediately took Kai up on his offer. "Yes, please. The detective we've got right now is incompetent as fuck."

We ate our food in silence for a while, still recovering from our boxing match.

We were quietly nursing our drinks when Juliet stopped in front of us. She bit her lip and tapped on the bar top as if hesitating to speak.

"What is it, Juliet?" I asked, encouraging her.

"Umm, Mr. Park, I wanted to say that…uh…I'm really sorry to hear about your sister."

My eyes widened, and when I turned to Kai, his expression matched mine. After Sophie was raped, the rapists had thrown her body in a darkened alley behind the venue. It was only after Ashley had found her missing and alerted the security that they'd found my sister's broken body. My dad had bought everyone's silence, so the whole ordeal was kept under wraps. We'd managed to avoid the press and the word of mouth, and we wanted to keep it that way.

So if Juliet knew about my sister, I intended to find out who let it slip. "How did you know about Sophie?"

Juliet turned red at my question and stammered, "Um… sorry, I overheard you talking to Mr. Kai."

We weren't exactly quiet, and the staff are strictly ordered to keep things to themselves here. Still, I needed to remind her. "It's okay, Juliet. But I need you to keep this to yourself. If not for me, then for Sophie."

"Of course, Mr. Park. Um…I also overheard that the cops haven't made much progress?"

"Nope," I answered, taking a sip of the drink.

She was again biting her lip, clearly fretting over something.

"Spit it out, Juliet."

She nodded and, taking in a deep breath, said, "Umm. I might know someone who could help you out." With that, she slid a business card across the bar toward me.

My eyes met Kai's as I picked it up. It was a plain black card with a golden silhouette of a tiger or some other wild cat drawn in the center. Underneath, in bold gold letters, was one word. WILDCATS.

I flipped the card over only to find a phone number on it. No names, no address. Absolutely nothing else.

"What's Wildcats?" I asked, flipping the card over in my hand before handing it to Kai.

"Shh…" Juliet put a finger to her lips. She looked around quickly, then leaned across the bar. Kai and I mirrored her motion, meeting her midway.

She took another surreptitious look around before saying, "Wildcats are the ones you go to when you can't get justice through the law. A lot of women contact them when men, as well as the justice system, fail them."

It sounded like some ridiculous amateur vigilante bullshit, but I kept that thought to myself.

I took the card from Kai and placed it in my pocket. "Thanks for this."

"I'm sure they'll be able to help you."

I nodded, not letting her see the doubt on my face.

As soon as we left the manor and were back in the car, Kai piped up, "You believe her?"

I shrugged. "Not really."

Yet the card felt like it was burning a hole in my pocket.

Once I was home, I called Mom to check in on Sophie. We talked for a bit about how they had a quiet movie night. I checked in with the security at their place, ensuring nothing was amiss.

When I retired to bed, it was around ten. I plucked the Wildcats' business card from where I'd placed it on the night-stand and stared at it. I ran a search on them on the internet but found absolutely nothing.

Again and again, I flipped the card in my hand, wondering if I should approach them. I didn't want to risk sharing what happened to Sophie until it was necessary. But the sheer number of dead ends we'd encountered so far had me fucking downright desperate.

"Fuck it," I muttered and got my phone out.

It wasn't exactly business hours, but given the ominous look of the card, I made the call.

The phone rang merely twice before a woman's voice

came on the line. "Hello, please let us know the name of the person who gave you the card."

Wow. Deciding to humor the person on the call, I said, "Juliet from the Serpentine Manor."

"Identity confirmed. You've reached the Wildcats. How may we help you?" the woman said, her voice significantly warmer and more approachable than before. It didn't escape my notice that she didn't state that they were the Wildcats before confirming the reference.

I sat up on the bed and decided to just give the mysterious woman the essential details. "My younger sister was gang-raped by three men a little over four months ago. I've tried everything, but those rapists are fucking ghosts. And I need help to find those men. To bring my sister justice."

There was silence for a beat, and then she said, "Be at Thunder Claw tomorrow at 9 a.m., Mr. Park."

Before I could agree, the line went dead.

Quickly, I searched Thunder Claw on the phone, and it appeared to be one of the popular bars in Brooklyn.

Well, that wasn't all that reassuring. Who invited a potential client to a bar at nine o'clock in the morning? Were we meeting to discuss something extremely sensitive or to cure a hangover?

I was debating whether I should go when a text message notification pinged on my phone, displaying the time and address of the location.

And suddenly, I remembered what the lady told me. *Be at Thunder Claw tomorrow at 9 a.m., Mr. Park.* How the hell did she know who I was?

CHAPTER 4

When I told Maxim where we were going and who I was meeting, he burst into laughter. When he'd asked me if I needed him to come along to save me from the "wild cats," I'd politely declined using two of my favorite fingers.

So he'd left me at the doors of the Thunder Claw. The bar was in one of the shadier parts of Brooklyn. From the outside, it was a two-story brick structure. The ground level was part glass and part dark wood front with a large "Thunder Claw" sign overhead. The second story featured three large stained-glass rose windows, giving the bar a Gothic vibe.

The first thing that hit me upon entering was the smell of freshly brewed coffee. The place had a decent crowd of patrons in various corners, eating and chatting. Not for the first time, I wondered if meeting in such a public space to discuss something so confidential and sensitive was a good idea.

I approached the woman at the small reception counter near the front and gave her my name.

I was about to ask her if the *Wildcats*—I mentally rolled my eyes at the thought of saying it out loud—were waiting at some table. But the woman simply said, "Please follow me."

She started toward the back of the establishment, and I quickly followed, taking in the hustle and bustle. A solid black bar dominated the left side of the restaurant, with about fifteen barstools arranged along its length. Every one of them was occupied at the moment.

The entire decor was Gothic industrial, with black chandeliers hanging from the ceiling. It clearly wasn't a dance club but more of a sit-and-relax lounge bar. It actually looked like the kind of place Kai and I would come hang out at.

The woman went through the curtain at the back and opened an ominous black door.

"The Wildcats are waiting for you downstairs. Would you like some coffee? Tea?"

"No, thank you," I said and made my way down the stairs. The door shut behind me with a click.

The dark wood handrail of the staircase glinted under the yellow lights of the ceiling. The staircase itself did not have natural lighting. I reached another ominous door at the foot of the stairs. I rolled my eyes at the amount of mystery these *Wildcats* were trying to create.

I turned the knob, pushed the door open, and halted at the doorway. The sight that greeted me could have been pulled straight out of a Hollywood sci-fi movie.

Five women stood inside a large, open room, each wearing a black-and-gold mask representing a different feline. The woman in the center wore a sharp black suit that rivaled mine and a black-and-gold lioness mask.

Faint light streamed from the small windows near the basement ceiling, casting sharp shadows across the women. The entire room, which was as large as the bar above, was nearly empty, with a boxing ring in the far-right corner and rows of strength training equipment along the opposite wall.

It looked more like a training center than a formal meeting room.

In the center of the room stood an ordinary brown table, where the woman in the lioness mask waited. An empty chair sat across from her, most likely for me.

A shiver raced its way down my spine as I made my way to the chair, taking in the four other women in the room.

Two women flanked the lioness. The one on the left with a cheetah mask hiding her face wore a half-sleeve black T-shirt and cargo pants, her pink hair bunched in a high ponytail. To the lioness's right was another woman dressed in long-sleeved black gear just like the cheetah, her face hidden by a black-and-gold panther mask.

The fourth woman, dressed in all-black clothes and wearing a black-and-silver jaguar mask, stood beside the panther.

But it was the last woman who held my attention in a choke hold. She wore a sleeveless black tank, showcasing her bulging muscles that rivaled my own, and her right arm featured a long-sleeved black-and-crimson tiger tattoo. She sat in another chair set slightly farther away from the table, one foot casually crossed over her knee. Her mask was a black-and-crimson tiger with intricate gold lining. She looked, by far, the deadliest of the group.

My heart hammered against my ribs at the stillness with which the tiger's head tilted slightly as she stared at me.

"Mr. Park," the lioness greeted me from where she stood.

My gaze moved away from the tiger as I reached the table and shook the lioness's offered hand. Her grip was firm and professional, her hand covered by black leather gloves.

"How did you know who I was?" I asked.

The lioness's head tilted slightly—it was disconcerting to see the expressionless faces of the masks—as she said, "We wouldn't be very good at what we do if we couldn't figure out who was calling us."

I nodded. "And the masks? Do you need to scare your clients?"

Again, the masked head tilted. "Depends on who's sitting in front of us. We do dangerous work here, Mr. Park. We can't reveal our identities to just anyone, especially not to public figures such as yourself. Besides, some people find it comforting to share their story with masked people. Gives them a sense of anonymity. Some prefer a more…human connection. What is your preference, Mr. Park?"

I shrugged, feigning indifference. The thought of five women staring at me as I talked about my sister made my skin crawl. I guess I did prefer them in masks after all. Made what I wanted to talk about a little easier to share. But it also didn't make me trust the unknown masked faces. "Can I see one of your faces?" I asked, my voice tight. "I need to know who I'm really talking to."

To my utter shock, it was the tigress who reached up and pulled off her mask, only to reveal the face of a warrior goddess.

The first thing I noticed was her chocolate-brown eyes, then her golden-brown skin, which seemed to glow when the sun's rays coming from the small basement window hit her form just right, and the sharp line of her jaw. God certainly took his time creating this woman. She reminded me of one of those Greek god statues in the Met. I couldn't take my eyes off her.

The woman's long, jet-black hair was pulled into two thick braids, though a few curls escaped, falling over her cheeks, giving her a touch of softness. Her neck was adorned with a choker and two thin gold necklaces, but my attention was drawn to the cluster of piercings decorating her ears. She had an industrial barbell through her upper cartilage, and at least six other earrings glinting from her lobes and helix—hoops, delicate chains, diamond studs.

She raised her eyebrows at me, a small, knowing smile

playing at the corner of her full lips. Clearly, she was amused at my ridiculous, slack-jawed reaction.

"Haven't seen a strong woman before, pretty boy?" the tigress asked. What else was I supposed to call her when I didn't even know her name?

My cheeks heated at being caught staring, and definitely *not* at being called *pretty*.

"Strong? Yes. Jacked like a warrior? No."

That got me a savage smile from her as she gave me a wink. "Thanks."

A throat cleared, and my attention moved back to the lioness. "So, Mr. Park, how may we help you?"

The tigress got up and moved closer to us, dragging her chair behind her and sitting beside the lioness. Guess she didn't want me to move my face back and forth between the two.

For some reason, I certainly felt more comfortable talking to her.

Speaking of my sister, the familiar rage flooded my veins. I looked the tigress straight in her eyes and said, "I want my sister's rapists. Alive."

It was the lioness who spoke. "You mentioned in the phone call that you have no idea who they are?"

With a clenched jaw, I nodded. "I've been trying to find them for four months. But they left no evidence. They were at the gala that my sister attended and grabbed her from outside the venue. They threw her out of their car in the back alley once they were done."

The tigress's lips curled in disgust, and her muscles bunched around her shoulders as if she were ready to attack the rapists. But she stayed silent.

So I turned to the lioness when she asked, "What about the cops? How long did they work on your case?"

My blood boiled at the mere thought of the cops. "A

month, month and a half at max. The level of competence in the cops is a fucking joke."

The lioness and the tigress looked at each other. It was merely a glance before they both turned their eyes to me. "Or maybe they were protecting the person who raped your sister."

A harsh chuckle escaped me. "Do you know the amount of money I offered the cops?"

This time, the tigress shook her head at me in pity. In *pity*. "If your exorbitant amount of money couldn't make the cops do their job, who do you think they're protecting?"

My head buzzed, my mind spinning in circles, looping through every conversation I had with the detective—more like detectives—assigned to Sophie's case. The numerous delays in reporting progress, the lack of evidence, the inadequate thought put into interviewing people, the excessive number of excuses for not working the case, the cold trails, and the conclusions reached without any proof. Their incessant blame on Sophie for not being able to provide them with much made her and, in turn, me feel guilty for not doing enough to help them. What I thought was mere incompetence on the part of the cops might actually have been sabotage.

Fury raced through the blood in my veins. The need to destroy every person responsible for making Sophie's life miserable was a living, beating thing inside my chest. I wanted to find every single fucker responsible and kill them all with my bare hands.

"Mr. Park..." The tigress's voice infiltrated my spiraling mind, and my eyes snapped to hers as she said, "We'll take on your case."

CHAPTER 5

SAMAIRA

he words escaped my mouth before I could stop them. This wasn't the normal protocol. Lena talked to the clients. *She* asked the questions. We decided whether we could take on the case together *after* the client left.

I did not make decisions on the spot. *I* did not take over the conversation with a client. *I* certainly never repositioned myself just so I could take a better look at the client's pretty face.

I did not find men's faces pretty. As a general rule, I hated the species and didn't trust a single word out of their mouths. They were shallow, self-serving egomaniacs.

According to Tara's research last night, he was the CEO of Park Real Estate Group, the largest Korean American real estate company in the US, which should have automatically put me off.

If I hated men, I loathed *billionaire* men.

But *this* man. Fuck. This pretty man seemed to be carved out of the finest marble in the world. He wore his suit like armor for battle, showing off his bulging biceps and broad chest. I'd nearly drooled behind my mask when I first saw him walk into the room. With his hair styled to perfection and his jaw as sharp as a blade, he made the blood in my veins pump faster.

His dark blue eyes reminded me of angry and volatile thunderstorms. Something was magnetic and so insanely captivating about him that I couldn't take my eyes off him. Even when he'd stepped inside the room, he hadn't faltered—*much*—at the sight of the five of us in our gear and masks.

He had walked in, taking us in, first with disbelief, then mistrust, and finally, with intrigue.

He'd talked about his sister with the kind of strength that I admired. It wasn't easy to describe something so barbaric and inhumane happening to your loved one. Most people clammed up, and some felt the disgust so strongly they refused to say it out loud.

But Dominic Park was out for blood, and I respected that.

The moment I said that we'd take on the case, a breath whooshed out of him.

He turned to me, and his eyes were filled with genuine gratitude and hope. "Thank you."

I nodded, but Mr. Park wasn't done. "And I would like to work with you personally on this case."

"No." My answer was immediate. But for the first time, it wasn't because I didn't trust the man. Just thinking about Mr. Park putting himself in danger and possibly getting injured had a violent storm surging inside me. *Pull yourself together, Samaira. What is the matter with you?*

When I didn't expand on my answer, Mr. Park gave me what seemed to be his harshest glare, which probably had his employees do all his bidding. But this wasn't his office, and I wasn't his employee. I was the tigress of this empire.

My own glare must not be reaching him clearly because he scowled right back, fury causing a nerve to pulse on his forehead. "I will pay the Wildcats fifty million dollars if you let me work with you and find the rapists."

"Done," Lena said before I could give this Richie Rich a piece of my mind. "You can work with us directly. We'll draft the contract and send it to you by the end of the day. Crimson Tiger will be in touch with you for further steps."

A victorious smile came over his pretty face, and fuck, the way that smile completely transformed his expression. Two deep dimples appeared on his cheeks, turning his face down-right angelic. *What the fuck!*

I didn't even realize when Tara came closer to me and jammed her knee into the back of my chair, jerking me out of my stupor. Quickly, she bent closer to my ear, pretending to share something important with me. "Bitch, what are you doing? Pull it together."

I could feel Mr. Park's eyes on me as I gave a serious nod to Tara as if I wasn't having a personal fucking meltdown right in front of my girls.

I looked at Mr. Park, who now stood shaking Lena's hand.

My eyes zeroed in on the way their hands touched and how she wrapped her fingers around his palm. My anger surged, a red haze blooming behind my eyes. A sudden, inexplicable jealousy wrapped itself around my throat, squeezing me so hard I wanted to scream. As soon as Lena let go of his hand, the strangling ceased, and I could finally breathe again.

Before I could stop it, my body—out of nowhere—stood from the chair. I straightened my shoulders and stepped closer to Mr. Park. I extended my hand, offering it to him. As soon as his fingers wrapped around my hand, a current of electricity surged through my veins. It was only through sheer will that I didn't let him see how much he was affecting me, and my voice came out strong. "We'll be in touch, Mr. Park."

He simply nodded, his tone polite and respectful. "Please call me Dominic."

"Dominic," I said, the name rolling around my tongue like a delicious treat.

With one more nod, *Dominic* turned and walked out of the room. I went to the monitor that Tara had set up on our property and watched him leave the restaurant.

A loud pop of bubble gum had me glaring in its direction. I didn't even realize Sloane had come up right beside me, but the way she was looking at me funny had my temper flaring. I just knew they were all gonna be up my ass about this. "What?" I grumbled, not meeting anyone's eyes as I headed to the rack of boxing gloves.

Sloane chuckled and followed me. "Umm, Lena," she shouted, turning around for a second, then looking at me with downright amusement.

"What?" Lena asked, pulling off her lioness mask, a teasing smile on her face as well.

I rolled my eyes, but Sloane quickly raised her fingers, chiding Lena. "You know, don't ever touch Dominic's hand again. Otherwise, Samaira here will eat you."

"Fuck off," I grumbled, knowing that this wasn't the end of it.

Tara chuckled. "Did you see how she kept staring at him?"

"Very subtle," Naomi chimed in.

"I must say, he looked *yummy,*" Sloane piped in.

"Don't—" I said.

"Touch him. I know," Sloane finished the sentence that I was *not* going to say, making the rest of them laugh.

I put my boxing gloves on and went to the punching bag, just realizing that I didn't deny her words. I *couldn't* deny her words. Fuck.

The only way to get out of this conversation was not to get involved at all.

"And what was up with removing the mask, Sami?" Lena asked.

I punched the bag hard.

"Ooh, someone's mad," Sloane teased.

And this was a fucking tough question to answer. But I ground out the words anyway. "I just wanted to see him better."

Tara and Naomi joined in with Sloane in ridiculous hooting and laughing as Lena said, with a teasing smile on her face, "And you wanted to see his face because…"

I did a three-punch combo at the bag and sighed as hot blood rushed my cheeks. I raised my hand in a fighting position, and without meeting anyone's eyes, I muttered, "He was pretty," and punched the shit out of the bag, listening to the obnoxious cackling from my four best friends.

"Sami found a new toy," Naomi teased.

I kicked and punched at the bag, pouring out all the pent-up energy, purging myself of the ridiculous thoughts that had taken over my brain. What the fuck was wrong with me? Staring at a pretty man with googly eyes? I punched the bag again and again and again until all thoughts of Dominic Park and his dimpled smile, his razor-sharp jaw, and his fucking three-piece suit disappeared from my mind.

And I kept punching because every single one of those thoughts seemed to have taken up residence in my deteriorating brain.

Lena suddenly appeared on the other side of my punching bag, grabbing it to a stop, daring me to punch it again. Only she could get away with doing that. "Why'd you agree to work on his case so impulsively?"

I could still see the fury in Dominic's eyes, not just for the rapists but at himself. I knew that anger. Knew the way it burned through your organs, your very sense of self, the way it destroyed your soul.

The look of utter destruction that he wanted to inflict on himself and the world made me react on instinct. I looked at

Lena, and instead of explaining all that to her, I said, "He needs us. If there are rapists who could rape a powerful billionaire's sister and get away with it, can you imagine what they have already gotten away with? We need to find those bastards and eliminate them."

She knew I was right, but she also knew me enough to know that wasn't the only reason I had accepted the case. Not that Lena would've refused to help him. We'd never refused anyone who was telling the truth and genuinely needed our help. Ever.

After staring at me until she could probably see my soul through my eyes, she let go of the punching bag. "Fine. Now let's get serious and set up the case."

That reminded me. "Speaking of serious, how could you agree to Dominic's idiotic demand to work together?"

"Fifty million dollars, Sami."

I rolled my eyes. "He could get hurt. Who's going to give you fifty million dollars if something happens to him? We're probably dealing with powerful people here. Dominic is a public figure. What if he gets himself killed? What if we get exposed while working with him?"

Lena's eyes turned challenging. "Then you better protect that man like your life depends on it, Sami. You and I both know how many lives fifty million dollars would affect."

Why was everyone hell-bent on driving me insane?

The moment Lena stepped away from the punching bag, I kicked the damn thing until it punctured.

It was during my post-workout shower when I realized I would be working on the case with Dominic Park. I'd be seeing him on multiple occasions. I wiped the fog from the mirror after getting out of the shower, only to find a stupid smile etched across my face staring back at me. In the next moment, I immediately smacked myself hard on the cheek, wiping off the idiotic smile.

I *did not* get infatuated by a pretty man. I definitely did not get infatuated by a pretty *billionaire*. And I most definitely did not get infatuated by a pretty billionaire who was also a public figure, whose mere association with us could risk the secrecy of the Wildcats and destroy everything we had built.

CHAPTER 6

DOMINIC

was scrolling through my emails that I'd missed during the day when a notification popped up on my screen.

> Unknown number: I need to meet your sister.
> Crimson Tiger here.

I shot upright on my bed, my heart kicking against my ribs.

A rush of excitement raced down my spine. The thought of *her*, the tigress, messaging me sent downright flutters in my stomach. But the message itself hit me like a bucket of ice-cold water.

My sister was a mess. It had taken weeks before she could even get out of bed. She still slept with her lights on, hadn't stepped outside our parents' house since it happened, and was tired of answering the same questions over and over again.

Every failed attempt by the cops had chipped away at my sister's hope for justice until nothing was left. For the life of me, I couldn't bear to give her any more hope in case the Wildcats failed too.

Not having the strength to put it all into a text message, I hit the call button.

The phone rang three times before the call connected.

"Dominic, hi," a breathy voice said with a sharp exhale. It sounded like I'd caught her doing something strenuous.

"Tigress, hi. Is this a bad time to talk?" It didn't seem too weird to think of her as Tigress in my mind, but calling her that out loud almost brought an embarrassing smile to my face. Every time I closed my eyes, all I could see was the light shining down on her muscular arms, the way her earrings sparkled, the anger in her eyes like a raging volcano, and those full, pouty lips that had smirked so beautifully when I'd called her jacked. She truly was a Tigress.

"Nope. What's up?"

"I actually called to tell you that it won't be possible to talk to my sister about the matter. I've given you all the files, all her statements, and all the recordings of her interviews with the cops."

"I started going through them. But I still need to talk to your sister myself."

"Miss…uh…Tigress, my sister is in an extremely delicate condition right now. She hasn't left our parents' house in the past four months. She hasn't smiled a real smile since the fucking incident. Her physical condition has just barely recovered, and her emotional recovery will still take time. I haven't told her that I've hired your team. I don't want to give her any false hope or stress her out any further by making her answer the same questions over and over again."

Silence greeted me from the other end, followed by a soft sigh. "Dominic, I admire your care and concern for your sister. I understand what you're going through, what she's going through. However, I still need to speak with your sister. You have to trust me on this. I don't want to stress your sister any more than you do. But I need to meet her."

Just the thought of telling Sophie about the Wildcats and

asking her to talk to one of them was making me rethink my decision to work with them. "Do you genuinely believe you could find her rapists?" I asked, needing to know the answer. Not for me, but for Sophie's sake.

There was no hesitation from Tigress, just pure, unwavering confidence. "Yes. I *will* find the rapists."

For some insane reason, I believed her. Believed in the surety of her tone, the way she didn't follow up with any explanations or assurances. Just thinking about the strength she exuded, her unflinching gaze when she'd heard what happened to Sophie, and the crackling fury in her eyes made me want to put my faith in her.

I sighed, running my hand through my hair. "Fine. I'll talk to my sister tomorrow. When would you like to meet her?"

A loud slurping sound came from her end as she said, "The sooner, the better. The trail's cold already."

"Are you drinking something?" I couldn't help but ask as another loud slurp hit my ears.

She gave a low chuckle. "Yep. I need my berry milkshake."

I lie back down on my bed, resting my head over my folded arm as something inside me—that playful, innocent feeling buried deep under the weight of the constant guilt and violent need for justice—slowly unfurled and compelled me to tease the big, bad Tigress. "You know, drinking sugar so late in the evening is not good for your health."

A loud bark of laughter crackled in my ears. "You've seen my muscles, right?"

I stared at the mirrored ceiling and found my lips stretched in a wide smile. "Yep, smaller than mine."

I bit my lip, bracing myself for implosion.

"Are you fucking kidding me? No way, motherfucker."

I burst out laughing. "I don't lie about the size of my muscles, Ms. Tigress."

She scoffed and slurped into the phone in a deliberately

loud and obnoxious manner. "I saw you in your suit today. No way you're packing that much."

"If that's what you want to believe to help you sleep better."

"Oh, I sleep just fine." I could just imagine her rolling her eyes.

I stared at my reflection in the mirror, and there was a lightness on my face that wasn't there before. I couldn't understand it, but talking to her made me feel like I was floating in the air. I desperately wanted to know more about the mighty Tigress. "Can I ask you something?"

"You can ask me whatever you want. Doesn't mean I'll answer." Her voice was gruff but not dismissive, which made me keep going.

"I really don't want to keep calling you Tigress. Could you tell me your name?"

It was as innocent a question as it could get, yet my heart raced in my chest.

She snorted, but I knew in my bones that she was smiling. "But I love it when you call me Tigress. Makes me feel mighty."

My chest expanded as a smile—a downright obsessed, crushing-over-a-girl kinda smile—stretched across my face. "You only need to look in the mirror to feel powerful."

"Don't need a mirror for that."

Yep, she certainly didn't. Just the thought of her muscles flexing had blood rushing straight to my cock. It had been a while since I'd felt *and enjoyed* the familiar pulsing. What about her was making me so fucking hard and so unreasonably talkative?

"Have you been a part of the Wildcats for long?" I asked, a loud yawn following my question, even though I felt like I could talk to her all night.

Tigress—who still hadn't told me her name—gasped. "Are you getting tired of talking to me, Dominic?"

If the playful gasp didn't wake me up, my name on her lips in such a playful tone certainly woke *every* single part of me fully and excitedly up. I bit my lip hard to suppress the groan that wanted to escape my throat as my hips flexed with need. Biting my groan, I turned my body to lie flat on my stomach, just to give my achingly hard cock *some* friction.

My voice was a gravelly rasp as I said, "Certainly not. It's just been a long day, and I'm usually asleep by ten."

I looked at the clock to see that it was nearly midnight.

"Hmm. I've been with Wildcats for about thirteen years now."

My eyes widened. *Thirteen years?*

"So you're telling me that the Wildcats have been operating for over a decade in New York City, and nobody knows of their existence?" I asked, incredulous. "How have you all kept it a secret for so long? Doesn't the family of these abusers, the cops, the lawyers ever wonder where these men disappear to? Haven't any police investigations been launched to find these missing individuals?"

My mind poured out more and more logistical questions, my thoughts spinning and wondering about all the mysteries the city of New York might hold in its underbelly.

Her breathy sigh through the phone pulled me back from my spiraling thoughts. "First, we do far more than just *find* the rapists. Nobody knows about our existence because nobody even understands what they should be looking for. We've taken hundreds of precautions to ensure our anonymity. And we've made damn sure that the people who truly need us can find us."

"Through people like Juliet, who gave me your card," I mused, a pleasant warmth pulsing through me as sleep began to tug me under.

She hummed quietly on the other end as my breathing deepened and the pull of sleep became stronger, my eyes refusing to stay open.

"You can call me Samaira." Her soft voice infiltrated my mind, hovering on the edge of unconsciousness—that one name stretching my lips into a drowsy smile.

I whispered, "Samaira," and drifted off to sleep with her name on my lips.

CHAPTER 7

SAMAIRA

The files that Dominic gave me on Sophie were quite thorough. There were transcripts from Sophie's conversation with the cops, the medical reports of her injuries, and the tiny morsel of findings from the private detective he'd hired. There was also information on Sophie's life before the incident.

The Park family was among Manhattan's richest. Per my quick search on the internet, Dominic's father had passed on his mantle to Dominic eight years ago, right after Dominic turned thirty. He'd built the company into the billion-dollar establishment it is today.

I sat in the Den, spreading all the papers and the laptop on the large couch with Shadow lying at my feet on the floor. We'd gone out for a little walk when I woke up since both of us needed some fresh air.

I'd started researching and surfing through the materials as soon as we were back, which was still pretty early in the morning.

Tara and I were working out last night when I received

that call from Dominic. I worked out twice a day and preferred the quiet of the night. Tara also preferred as few people as possible around her when she exercised because of her scars.

I was in the middle of my deadlift set when Dominic called.

Tara's eyebrows reached her scalp, and a smile tugged at the corner of her lips when I dropped my weights right in the middle of my set and grabbed the ringing phone. I was so lost in conversation with him that I completely lost track of what I was doing. One minute, I was giving Tara the finger for laughing at me, and the next, I was sprawled on our couch in the Den, sipping my milkshake.

As if that wasn't enough, my mouth just chose to whisper out my name to him before my mind could grab the reins of the conversation. To top it all off, I'd drifted off to sleep on this cursed couch and woken up with my phone plastered to my cheek.

I blamed the couch for last night's malfunction. It was like sitting on a cloud. Anybody would fall asleep on it after they'd exercised like a machine.

It was definitely *not* the soothing, gruff timbre of Dominic's voice that put me in a dreamlike state. Absolutely not.

I shook my head, pulling myself back to the present, and focused on going through the file while sipping my coffee right on this *cloudlike* couch.

I was reading through Sophie's medical report—the sheer number of injuries that had been inflicted upon the woman made my skin blaze hot with rage—when the door to the Den pushed open.

Shadow immediately jumped up and ran to the door to welcome Lena with his barks and kisses. She laughed and dropped to her knees to give him cuddles.

Lena was the founder, leader, and mother of the Wildcats.

I was the first person she took in as a member—more like, I hounded her to the point of extreme exasperation until she agreed to train me and let me help her save other women. She gave purpose to my life when I'd lost everything. She was not just my savior but also my best friend and was currently sporting deep frown lines between her eyebrows.

Once she'd given Shadow a sufficient amount of love, she plopped on the couch next to me, dropping her purse on the coffee table.

I looked down at the file in my hand and pretended to read. "You better stop frowning like that, or you'll have that line permanently etched between your eyebrows. FYI, it ain't pretty."

"Fuck you, bitch. I'm the hottest shit out here."

I scoffed. "Sure you are."

She truly was. In her bold red suit over a black lace corset, her matching red pants, her short hair styled to perfect waves, and her six-inch high heels, she was a lethal beauty. Her Japanese heritage endowed her with the skin of an angel and the discipline of a ninja. She was one of the fittest women I knew and could beat any of us in a fight despite being nearly a decade older than the remaining three Wildcats. She was almost six years older than me.

Her parents own a fighting gym in downtown Manhattan, a thirty-minute subway ride from our bar in Brooklyn. She grew up learning how to fight—karate and the naginata being her strength—and boy did she give us hell while training us.

She also dressed like a boss. Her shirts and pants never had a wrinkle, her accessories were always on point, and her custom-tailored suits could rival Dominic's. She kept her hair at shoulder length and always wore makeup that was applied to perfection. She was a powerhouse all by herself.

She pulled out her thick notebook and started clicking her pen, a telltale sign of her gearing up to talk about something unpleasant.

"Just spit it out, Lena."

She rolled her eyes and looked at me. "I know you took on Sophie Park's case, but I want to make sure you're okay handling it. It's a bit too close to home for you. We help people but not at the cost of our own trauma."

I looked down at my calloused hands. They once belonged to a girl who dreamed of dancing and acting on a stage. A girl who had soft hands, shiny black hair, and dreams bigger than the ocean. A girl who died thirteen years ago when she turned nineteen. "We help and fight for women *because* of our trauma. Every punch I land on a fucker's face, every dick I chop off, every life I take, it's *because* of my history. Does this case hit a little too close to home? Yes. But that just makes me more determined."

Lena nodded. "And it isn't because of a certain smoke show in a suit?"

I snorted at her description. "He is pretty. But no. A pretty face doesn't make me rash."

Her lips curled at the corners, her eyes shining with mirth. "So only impulsive, then?"

I sighed. No denying that. I was impulsive when I accepted the case, just like I was impulsive last night. I could have ignored the call. I could have kept the call short and professional. But both times that Dominic Park had talked to me, my brain had melted into a puddle of illogical goo. I needed to get myself sorted.

With a loud groan, Lena got up from the couch and shouted out loud, "Team meeting, ladies. Conference room, stat."

She bent down to give some more love to Shadow, cooing at him. "You like that, baby? Yes, you do. Now, go call your mommy Tara, and I'll give you a few more rubs. Yes, yes, I will."

Shadow gave an excited yip and ran toward Tara's room, now barking loudly.

Our Den occupied two subbasement levels, complete with three bedrooms, a large conference room, a kitchen, a large yet cozy living room, an interrogation room, and a fully equipped medic room. If we all chose to leave our own places, we could just all live here.

For a while, we actually did.

But we all needed sunlight and windows, as well as some personal space. Now, we just slept here when we were too deep into a case, too drunk, or simply too lazy to go home. Which, I suppose, meant we ended up sleeping here most days of the week.

I grabbed myself a fresh cup of coffee and carried it with Sophie's files to the conference room.

Lena had already taken a seat and was looking through her thick notebook. Naomi entered the conference room looking as fresh as a daisy. Her dark skin glowed under the warm light of our conference room, and she wore a maroon vest with white pants. She seemed to have even gotten a haircut because her curls were freaking bouncing.

"Anything special today, Doc? A date, perhaps?" I asked, placing my coffee and the files on the table and taking a seat beside her.

She scoffed. "Nope. After the long-ass procedure of getting those four losers to survive, I treated myself to some self-care. No more bloodshed today, Sami. I'm not ruining my cute vest. I'm going to organize my clinic today, see some patients, then treat myself to a nice bottle of wine in the evening."

Lena instantly piped in, "Noted, Doc. You deserve it."

Tara and Sloane arrived with their coffees and took a seat. Tara was still in a black sweatshirt and was half asleep, her half mask in place covering her scarred side, while Sloane wore loose blue denim with a cute yellow crop top.

"Looking good, Sloane," I said. That girl loved to have her

efforts appreciated. And I made sure to do it as often as I could.

A bright smile lit up her face, and she pressed a finger to her cheek in a cute manner. "Thanks, Sami."

I shook my head at her antics and sipped my coffee.

"All right, everyone. Let's get started," Lena said. "Tara, please pull up the schedule and our database."

Everyone turned serious, and Tara went from drowsy to alert in the blink of an eye.

The screen displayed a list of our clients, sorted by the person who had taken the lead on the case, the crime committed against them, the date they came to us, and important dates to note, such as whether they have an ongoing case or a pending police hearing.

"First up, Monica." Lena turned to Tara for the status update.

Tara leaned forward in her seat, dropping her elbows on the table as she looked at the screen. "The perpetrator, also her husband, is roaming free. Monica wants him out of the picture since he also started beating their young daughter. He threatened to kill the daughter if she ever involved the cops. So this is going to be a quick and silent affair."

"Does the guy have any family we need to be worried about?" Lena asked.

Tara shook her head. "A deadbeat father who lives in California. I went through the phone records and emails, and there's been no contact between the two in the past eight years."

"Perfect. How many of us do you need for the extraction and execution?"

"Sloane and Sami for extraction. Sami, I'll let you chop off his dick. Fucker has been raping his wife for three years now. It was only after Monica caught him touching their daughter inappropriately that she chose to speak up. So you've got free rein. And then, I'll be torturing the fucker. He's been giving cigarette burns to Monica and their daughter for years. See how he likes being burned."

One side of Tara's face—the one not hidden by the mask—turned up in a vengeful, ruthless smile. As an acid attack survivor, half of her face had been burned off. When I first met her, her left eye was missing, her nose and half an ear had melted, and third-degree burns covered her cheek and parts of her scalp and neck. Even her left arm was burned by the splashes of acid that had hit her.

Once she joined us, and as the years passed, she started getting facial reconstruction surgeries. With every surgery, her self-confidence grew. Obviously, the surgeries didn't make her burns and scars magically disappear, but they were more manageable and less painful. As much as she tried to appear strong and unaffected in front of us, she still struggled some days. While she always kept her scarred face covered in public, she had started letting go of the mask when it was just the five of us in the Den.

Tara was fucking beautiful. Her golden-brown skin, her hazel eyes, and her perfectly bow-shaped lips made it difficult for a lot of people to look away from her. Losing her beauty, a part of her identity, to a monster of a man had broken her. If I could kill the fucker who did that to her all over again, I would. She still hadn't reached that *fuck the world* mentality that some of us lived by. But she was getting there. Slowly. I was waiting for the day she embraced every part of her, the day she would hold her head high and proudly and unashamedly look the world in the eye.

We next moved to Mary. Sloane jumped in since she was the lead on her case. Since I'd been the one to chop off her perpetrators' dicks, she turned to me. "Mary doesn't want them dead"—she rolled her eyes—"she just wants them to disappear from her life."

That was more of a hassle than just eliminating the fuckers. Thankfully, I didn't have to do much in this step except scare them for life. I'd probably done that already, but a little one-on-one session would do the trick.

Tara piped in, "I'll create new identities for those guys and find a house for them in Florida where we have a few eyes and can keep track of them."

Sloane nodded and took notes on her phone. "Sounds perfect. We can wrap this up in three days. I'll make the transport arrangements. And feed them, I guess."

They were currently locked in our perfectly soundproof interrogation room downstairs.

We moved down the list, and it was Sophie. I instantly opened her file. When the case was this new, and especially when the perpetrators were unknown, we all needed a brainstorming session.

I began to provide a brief overview of the file. "Listen up, ladies. Sophie Park was invited to the Manhattan Center for Healing for Survivors' charity gala. Usually, many of these charity events were by invitation only. However, the gala had also extended invitations to two additional guests. So she'd taken her firm partner, Ashley, and her junior employee, Anna, with her. Her parents were also invited and had arrived separately. It was a crowded party with over three hundred guests. Also, if that wasn't enough, it was a masked event."

"Great," Tara muttered.

I nodded and continued, "Sophie had an altercation with one of the masked men when she saw him spiking Anna's drink. She slapped him and tried to claw off his mask. But he got away before she could succeed. She did get him thrown out of the party by security, though."

Sloane chimed in, "Atta girl. I love a fighter."

I grunted, knowing what came next. "Around midnight, she went outside the event space to see off Anna after the girl was spooked by the whole incident. She asked her driver to take Anna home in her car. She had just turned to go back inside when a man picked her up from behind and threw her in a big SUV. She was raped and assaulted by all three men in the car. None of them removed the masks at any point. She has no idea who the men were. It took over three months for all her physical injuries to heal."

All four of them sat in silence. Hearing about these assaults never got easier. They made me want to find every man on the street and blow their brains out. Every single one of us had suffered at the hands of men. We'd all lost something to their cruelty and inflated egos, and none of us had any mercy left in our hearts for monsters like them.

Tara cleared her throat, breaking the silence. "Any street camera recordings? It was a big event, so surely the event was recorded."

"Very limited footage was released to the cops. According to the Manhattan Center and the gala's organizers, a glitch occurred, and most of their footage was destroyed. The police couldn't verify any identities because all the people in the footage were wearing masks."

Naomi picked up the medical reports and started reading through them. "It wasn't just about sex for these men. Seems like she was punched and kicked a lot. Punched hard enough to crack her cheekbone. Guess the rapist didn't like that she hit him and got him thrown out of the event."

I shook my head, disgust roiling through my body. "Anyway, we know that the rapists were among the three hundred people who came to the party. It's also safe to assume that it's someone more powerful than Dominic Park, which is saying something. So it's the process of elimination in figuring out who the perpetrators are."

I turned to Tara, and before I could say anything, she made a note in our database. "I'll hack into the servers of the Manhattan Center as well as of the Healing for Survivors' database and find an invitation list. We would also need a list of all the people who actually came to the gala. I just hope they collected the information about the guests at the entrance. Otherwise, that's a huge blind spot for us."

I nodded. "Agreed. I've asked Dominic to set up a meeting with Sophie as soon as he can. I'll wait for him to send me a date and time, or else I'll follow up tomorrow."

Lena quickly nodded. "Sounds good," and turned to Tara. "Moving on."

However, Tara apparently had other ideas. She gave me a devilish smile as she typed in Dominic Park on the internet.

I had barely rolled my eyes before hundreds of pictures of Dominic appeared on the large monitor. Sloane gave a loud, teasing moan. "The man can wear a suit like a God."

He did wear a suit like a God. I'd seen Sloane binge-watching the Korean dramas, and this man could give any of those actors a run for their money. He had a razor-sharp jawline and not a hint of a beard. His eyes were dangerous and lethal, and it just made me want to lick him up like an ice cream cone. Not to mention the way his suit hugged his thick arms and stretched over that wide chest. Dominic was very indecently checking every single one of my boxes.

"Enough with the scrolling already." I tried not to look at the screen like an obsessed fool while hating the girls' greedy eyes on him.

Tara rolled her eyes and was about to close out the window when my eyes fell on a picture of him with a woman.

"Wait," my mouth stupidly and very, very recklessly blurted out. I could've just as easily searched for the image later. But my eyes narrowed on a certain image.

A devious smile came over all their faces as Naomi said, "Yes, Tara. Wait a minute. Who's this bombshell hanging off Dominic's arm?"

Lena groaned. "Is it gonna be another milkshake situation? He's not yours, Sami. Keep the crazy to a minimum. He's our biggest client."

The moment she clicked on the picture, a few hundred

more images of him with other women opened. "And who are these women?" Sloane piped in, leaning forward on the table, fake trying to get a closer look.

I knew he wasn't mine. I'd met him *once*. Yet a plethora of ugly emotions threatened to rise to the surface of my mind. I sat still as a statue, trying my damnedest not to let them see how it affected me. "What do I care about that? Clearly, he's a player."

Lena and Tara exchanged irritatingly amusing smiles, and Lena jumped in. "Were you expecting the young, hot billionaire to be a virgin, Sami?"

I started closing my files and, without looking at any of them, I grumbled, "Since when is thirty-eight young?"

Lena gasped. "Bitch, I'm thirty-eight."

I gave her a wink and walked out of the meeting room, done with their antics.

Once I was back on the couch, I allowed myself to search for Dominic's pictures with women. The more I scrolled through the search page, the more images I found of women in their gorgeous gowns, holding Dominic's arm. They could just be his dates for the evening, but I did not like it one bit.

If these were the kind of women he preferred, he would definitely not be into me—brown, bulky, and badass.

I slammed the laptop screen shut, scolding myself for getting caught up in petty, jealous emotions. I stomped upstairs to go to our training area and jammed my hands into my boxing gloves.

With a light jog on the spot, I took my stance in front of the boxing bag, imagining the boxing ring to be Dominic's pretty face. Then I slammed my fist into it.

I'd already decided he wasn't for me. *Jab, jab, cross. Kick.*

I had no space in my life for a man. Especially someone so out in the public and so gorgeous. *Double kick, five-punch combo.*

I didn't have the time or the need to fawn over a pretty man. *Punch. Punch. Punch. Punch.*

Sweat dripped down my back as my arms burned with the impact.

I breathed in the leather of the boxing bag, the sweat that dripped down my nose as I continued hitting the boxing bag for the next half an hour.

I only stopped when my hands started shaking with every punch, and my mind finally emptied of all thoughts except for the rhythm of my breathing. I took several deep breaths, centering myself, reminding myself of my purpose in life.

Hunt down the monsters of this world. Show them that there were even bigger monsters ready to eat them alive and spit them out. To remind them that no one could save them from the wrath of a woman wronged.

CHAPTER 8

DOMINIC

I walked back and forth across Sophie's room as she watched me from her bed. It was the weekend, and like every weekend for the past four months, I had come to my parents' place in Connecticut to be with my sister. She hadn't set foot in her apartment since the attack. I worried that with every day that passed without finding her attackers, Sophie was spiraling deeper into her fears and nightmares.

She always had a short fuse, but these days, all she did was hide in her room, watch mindless television, and snap at me if I asked her to go for a walk. As much as I wanted to shield her from the world and keep her under strict protection, I increasingly worried about her mental state.

And now, I had invited Samaira—such a beautiful name—to meet Sophie. I also might not have talked to Sophie about the Wildcats yet, and Samaira—I finally knew the tigress's name—was arriving in thirty minutes. Clearly, I had more than enough time to say two sentences to Sophie.

What worried me was the time Sophie might need to

prepare herself emotionally and mentally to retell the events of that evening to a total stranger.

"Dominic, if you have nothing to say and are just getting your steps for the day in, please do it in the gym. You're making my head spin," Sophie snapped, stopping my feet with her glare.

I ran a hand through my hair, pulled out the rolling chair from her desk, and took a seat. Rubbing my palms together, I met her eyes. "So I might not have stopped looking for the fuckers from that gala."

Sophie instantly turned her eyes away with a sigh. "Dominic."

My jaw clenched at the hopelessness in her voice, the lack of fire in her eyes. "You know I can't stop. I *won't* stop."

She shook her head in defeat. "You heard the cops. You heard the lawyers. They've all got nothing. *I* have nothing to help you."

I nodded, willing her to meet my gaze again. "That's why I've hired the Wildcats."

Her eyes snapped to mine. "Wildcats?"

My lips curved in a smile. "You wouldn't even believe me if I told you about them."

She shook her head at me, but a hint of a smile touched her lips. "Are they a gang or something?"

That pulled a chuckle out of me. "More like super badass women who are vigilantes," I said. "And one of them is coming to meet you and talk to you about that evening in about twenty-five minutes."

That had her jumping off the bed. "What?" she screeched, stalking over to tower above me from where I sat. "You want me to talk about that day all over again? Wasn't once, twice, ten times enough? Every single day, I try to put that day behind me. Every day, I try to forget what happened. To wake up and find the will to leave this house, go back to my apartment, go back to work, and start fucking *living*. And now, you want me to talk about it again?"

I knew how much it would cost my sister to talk about that day, but I had to try. I clutched her hand in both of mine and gave her a pleading look—a look that had always gotten me my way ever since we were kids. "Just this one last time. Please, Soph?"

Her eyes glistened with tears as she shook her head defeatedly, as if pitying me. "One last time."

I jumped off the chair and pulled her into a hug, swaying her in my arms. "Thank you, Soph."

Her voice came muffled as she spoke in my arms. "Don't get your hopes up."

Leaving her to freshen up, I walked into the living room but didn't find my parents. They had to be somewhere in the house. I hadn't told them about the Wildcats yet and was still debating whether it was a good idea. I didn't want to give them false hope, only to disappoint them later. Yet I also hated seeing the defeated look on their faces, the hurt and betrayal knowing their daughter hadn't received the justice she deserved, that everyone who should have been fighting for her had given up. Perhaps knowing someone was out there trying to bring her justice could alleviate some of that pain.

I settled on the couch to wait for Samaira, but my mind kept drifting to the night before last. I hadn't stopped reliving that late-night phone call ever since I'd fallen asleep listening to Samaira's voice. That was the first time after endless nightmares, circling what-ifs, and an ever-present guilt that I actually had a full night of sound sleep.

I had slipped into that blissful darkness with a whisper of her name in my ears and woken up with it escaping my lips. I was obsessed with the way her name rolled off my tongue. I had been sure she wouldn't disclose her name when I'd asked her, especially when she hadn't outright answered. I could just imagine her weighing the pros and cons of revealing her name to me. The thought of her arriving at a decision in my favor made me unreasonably happy.

My phone pinged with a loud ding.

Samaira: I'm outside your house.

I jumped off the couch and pressed the button by the door to open the front gate of the house. I opened the main door and stepped onto the covered porch to greet her. An average-looking black sedan entered the driveway—certainly not the kind of car I expected the tigress to drive.

The car door opened, and she stepped out, planting thick, mid-calf black boots on the pavement. A short-sleeved black T-shirt stretched taut over her powerful arms, showing off her sharply defined muscles and a vibrant red and black tiger tattoo sleeve that seemed ready to pounce right off her skin. Loose cargo pants hung on her frame. Her hair was pulled back in a thick ponytail with some loose curls hugging her face, giving her hard and lethal expression that hint of soft-ness, which tightened something in my chest.

She gave me a simple nod in greeting. "You tell Sophie about the Wildcats?"

There was no smile on her face, no softness in her eyes, and no hint of acknowledgment that I'd fallen asleep while talking to her. She was cold and aloof, as if creating a hard line of professionalism between us. "Samaira." I nodded back at her, giving her a smile anyway.

A hint of warmth reached her eyes, but she didn't return my smile. She simply waited for my answer. Did something happen between the night before last and this morning?

Putting that thought aside, I walked inside the house, with her right beside me, leading us to Sophie's room, silently thanking my lucky stars that my parents weren't around. "I did talk to Sophie about hiring your team to work her case. Clearly, she doesn't have much hope right now."

We were almost to her room when I stopped walking, making Samaira look back at me. "Samaira, I need you to know that Sophie's physical injuries might have healed, but she's still extremely sensitive. I just want to make sure that you'll tread carefully."

Her steady gaze remained fixed on me as I spoke. As I finished, her shoulders seemed to have released some hidden tension, dropping slightly. She took a step toward me, her eyes kinder than I'd seen today, and placed a reassuring hand on my shoulder, her touch flooding that spot with warmth. "Dominic. Sophie's safe with me. Our whole purpose is to take care of women just like Sophie. To bring them justice. To give them a voice when the perpetrators and the justice system have snatched it away. You need to trust me and let me do what I do."

My heart calmed at her words, and I took a deep breath, her scent of orange blossoms flooding my senses. Everything within me yearned to trust her. I nodded, listening to my instincts. "Understood."

I took the lead to Sophie's room and gave a quick rap on the door. Instantly, the door opened, and Sophie stood ready in a sweatshirt and jeans. That was far more put together than she'd been in ages. Hiding my reaction, I stepped inside, Samaira following.

Before I could make the introductions, Samaira stepped around me and stood in front of Sophie. "Hey, Sophie, I'm Samaira. I'm here to find the motherfuckers who dared to touch you."

Sophie's eyes widened as she took Samaira in, her jaw dropping at the picture she painted in her all-black outfit, looking like she could take down ten guys in under a minute. It took Sophie a few seconds to snap out of her awe and close her mouth. I hid my smile as a red blush rose along her cheeks. "Uh, hi, Samaira. Pleased to meet you. Dominic said you have some questions for your investigation."

When Samaira just nodded politely, Sophie turned around and sat on her bed, hugging a pillow to her chest. Samaira took a seat right across from her on the bed, while I tried to give them space and leaned against her desk a few feet away. Sophie chewed her lip. "I don't know how much more I can help. I honestly told the cops everything I knew."

Samaira's voice was remarkably gentle. Her tone was so soothing that she not only put Sophie at ease but also put me at ease. "I know you did. You were very thorough. But I had to meet you and ask you a few questions to get a better understanding. I need some specifics in your story, so if you could fill in those parts for me, it could be beneficial for the case. Does that sound good?"

When Sophie nodded, Samaira pulled out her phone and opened something, maybe her notes. I couldn't see it from where I stood. Samaira placed her phone on her lap and turned to Sophie. "So during the gala, did you first see the attacker when he was attempting to drug your employee, or did you notice him around her prior to that?"

Sophie thought for a second before saying, "I saw him approach Anna and talk to her for a good five minutes at the bar. She'd turned around to talk to my business partner, Ashley, when I caught the masked guy spiking her drink. I immediately rushed to her and pulled her away. If only…"

She stopped talking at that, biting her lip and staring at her lap.

Samaira whispered, "If only what?"

Soph shook her head, her shoulders tensing and giving a defeated shrug. "If only I'd just pulled Anna away and walked off. But I was so mad I just couldn't help hitting the guy. I tried to pull off his mask, but he was quite tall, and he quickly walked off. Anna and Ashley were quick to stop me from following him, but I called security to get him thrown out of the gala. I was worried he would attempt to spike some other girl's drink, you know."

Samaira nodded sympathetically as Soph continued, clutching her own arms as if holding herself together. I so badly wanted to wrap my baby sister in a hug and save her from the horror. "Maybe if I had left him alone, he wouldn't have caught me a…and r…r…raped me."

I quickly stepped toward Samaira, afraid she would ask something further and upset Sophie more. I'd barely made contact with her shoulder when I found myself flung in the air and landing sharply on my back. Samaira's eyes glared daggers at me, her hand clutching my neck, her face pulled in a mask of violent rage that had me going absolutely still. Her jaw was clenched tight as she bent her head down slightly, and she spoke in a tone that sent shivers down my spine. "I did not give you permission to touch me."

CHAPTER 9

We all had baggage and issues that we silently—or violently—dealt with. Mine was approaching me from behind and touching me without permission. Add in the conversation that we were having, and my mind wasn't in a cool and receptive place. It was a barely contained storm of rage and revenge.

So when I felt that touch on the back of my shoulder, my body reacted in reflex, and before I knew it, I had Dominic pinned to the floor, my hands at his throat. My mind knew that he meant no harm, that he was one of the good ones, but my body was trained to react first and think later.

The moment he raised both hands in surrender and nodded at my words in understanding, I loosened my grip on his throat. I lightly grazed my fingers on his chest as I got up and extended my hand to him as a show of friendship and apology. He only hesitated for a second before grabbing my hand and pulling himself off the floor.

I, then, turned back to Sophie, who had just watched her

big, bad brother get knocked on his ass in under a second, staring at me with eyes wide open and her jaw on the floor.

Her eyes were still glued to me as I took my seat on the bed. "So, Sophie. Where were we?"

When she didn't respond and kept staring at me with starry-eyed awe, occasionally glancing at her brother, who I knew had an identical starstruck expression, I continued, "Yes, you were thinking of what-ifs and if-onlys."

With those words, she shook off the shock and slowly nodded. "I just wonder," she said with a slight shrug.

"From here on out, no more wondering. There is no point. We are going to find those fuckers and show them that they messed with the wrong woman. Are you with me?"

Her jaw hardened at that, and she gave me a single nod that was far more confident than before.

I braced myself for what I was going to ask her to do. "Now, Sophie. I'm going to ask you to do something really difficult, but just know that I'm right here with you."

When she nodded, silently asking me to continue, I said, "I need you to go back and recall the events that transpired in the car after they grabbed you from behind."

Dominic growled in protest. "Absolutely not. There's no need for her to recount those events, Samaira."

I paid no heed to his noise and continued to look at Sophie. "You don't need to describe every single thing they did to you. But I need you to try to pull yourself out of your body at that moment and focus on your surroundings if you can. Was there a landmark where your car passed? Were there any tattoos, anything noteworthy in any of the men's features? What were they talking about? Were they all in agreement with what was happening? Were any of them panicking? Did they stop the car somewhere along the way?

"I know you were only trying to survive in those moments, and you didn't care about any of those things at that time, but our mind is a potent tool. Our subconscious records far more details than our conscious mind remembers. I need you to close your eyes and try to focus on the things that I asked. If talking out loud helps, I'm here."

For a second, Sophie's eyes met Dominic's, and an unusual, uncomfortable moment passed between the two of them. She bit her lip nervously as Dominic shifted on his feet, his face turning red. And something dawned on me. I looked between them and landed on Sophie. "You haven't talked about what happened in front of Dominic, have you?"

Dominic ran his hand through his hair as Sophie shook her head. "I couldn't get the words out. It was too painful and embarrassing."

I nodded in understanding. Most women felt too embarrassed to share the details with the men of the house. "I understand. Do you need him to step out of the room?"

Sophie turned to look straight at Dominic. "Are you going to hold it together?"

His eyes blazed. "What do you mean, am I going to hold it together?"

She narrowed her eyes at him. "I mean, are you going to blow up?"

His eyebrows reached his forehead as he straightened up and towered over us. "Of course I'm going to blow the fuck up. What, you want me to silently listen to you talk without wanting to put my head through the wall?"

"Yes," Sophie and I said it together.

"It's difficult to talk as it is. I don't need to worry about your reaction and how you feel when I'm barely holding myself together."

I was so proud of Sophie for standing up to her brother.

He shook on his feet and bent down so his face was on level with hers as he pointed at his head. "You see these stupid gray hairs popping up on my head?"

Sophie's eyes narrowed to slits. "Yes. You're getting old."

I snorted. Dominic's eyes widened in shock as he spoke

through clenched teeth. "I'm not getting fucking old. It's the stress you put me in when you say shit like this. You think I'm dramatic now? You just wait till we find those motherfuckers. I'll show you fucking *holding it together*."

I couldn't help but smile at his dramatics. Well, it wasn't dramatic, and the moment was totally inappropriate with us discussing the most traumatic event of Sophie's life. But a smile slipped across my face.

Sophie noticed my smile and gave me a smile in return, rolling her eyes at her brother. "Fine. You can stay. But sit quietly in the corner facing the wall. I can't do this with you looking at me like that."

"Like what?" he asked, dragging his chair to a corner.

"Like you blame yourself."

He sighed at that, a world of hurt and defeat crossing his face, if only for a second, before he pulled himself together and nodded. He turned the chair and sat facing the wall.

When I gave Sophie an encouraging nod, she gulped and started talking. "So the main guy was wearing a black wolf mask and was about six-two since he towered over me at least half a foot when I hit him. He also wasn't an old man. He was Caucasian, and his hair was dark brown and wavy. I only saw one of his friends at that time, who grabbed him and dragged him away when I attacked him. He was an inch or two shorter than him, also Caucasian. He, too, wore a black wolf mask.

"It was the friend who grabbed me from outside the building. He dragged me around the side of the building where they had an SUV waiting. He threw me in the car, and before I could make a run for it, the masked guy I'd attacked had already got his hold on me. The guy who'd thrown me in the car had then rushed to the passenger seat, and the driver had immediately gotten the car on the road."

With every word Sophie spoke, my own past kept trying to rear its ugly head in my mind. She had no idea how close her experience was to mine. I needed to hear what came next just as much as I wanted to shut my ears and scream into oblivion.

I could feel the helplessness and rage bubbling in Dominic even though he was behind me. I could feel the tension rising in the air, in the swift breath he took, in the way his feet bounced on the floor, the *tap-tap-tap* of his shoes giving away his bubbling wrath.

Sophie bit her lip as she hesitated. "And then…uh…then, obviously, there was a lot of fighting, resisting, kicking, biting, screaming, slapping." Her eyes widened as she stopped at slapping.

"What is it?" I asked her.

She quickly looked at where Dominic sat before turning her eyes to meet mine. "When he'd first slapped me, I remember wishing he wasn't wearing such a big ring because it had hurt so much. I don't know if his wearing a ring helps in your investigation or not. A lot of men wear rings, or maybe he only wore it for the occasion."

I quickly reassured her before she started to doubt her intuition. "Sophie, this is exactly what I'm talking about. Every little detail helps when it comes to narrowing our search. Now, can you tell me on which hand he was wearing the ring?"

She closed her eyes for a few seconds, thinking things through. I quickly looked behind to check on Dominic, only to find him sneaking a glance at us. Our eyes met, and his were brimming with bottomless agony for his sister. They were rimmed red and shone with unshed tears, and my entire being wanted to walk to him and pull him into a hug. Instead, I gave him a quick nod in reassurance, trying to convey through my eyes that I was here. The deep line that was etched between his eyebrows smoothed a bit as his eyes softened. He gave me a jerky nod back and quickly turned to face the wall.

I looked at Sophie, who was still deep in thought, her hands clutching the pillow in her lap as if her life depended on it. I was about to call her name, just to tell her not to stress too much about it if she couldn't remember when her eyes snapped open. "Right. It was his right hand."

"Very good, Sophie. This is helpful. Can you recall if they were talking about anything? Any name that they uttered? What did they call each other?"

She closed her eyes again, but instead of remaining silent, she started to talk. "I don't…I don't recall much." A tear leaked from her eye as her lip trembled. My mind kept throwing my old wounds back to the surface, knowing the terrors that Sophie was recollecting. I wanted to apologize to her for putting her through this pain all over again, a pain that still managed to haunt me even after thirteen years.

Sophie frowned with her eyes closed as she said, "Uh…the driver kept saying 'This will mess up the plan,' 'You're messing up the plan,' and the guy in the passenger seat got into an argument with him. I was, uh…busy resisting and fighting off the masked guy above me, when he'd yelled at me, saying, 'This bitch is the one who messed up the plan,' and well, he'd shouted at the guys in the front to shut the fuck up and drive if they wanted a chance at me."

She opened her eyes as we heard a loud crack behind me. We both turned to find a hole in the wall with Dominic's fist in the hole. He didn't turn back to face us but mumbled, "I didn't say anything."

Sophie grumbled and closed her eyes, either trying to ignore a raging-mad Dominic or to recollect more clues that she thought could help. "Umm," she said, "the guy in the passenger seat had really sharp incisors. Uh, at one point, I remember thinking how he reminded me of an actual animal. And…uh…and the driver guy was suffocatingly hairy."

Another loud crack snapped Sophie out of her memories with a sudden gasp. "Dominic, you scared me," she shrieked, her eyes flooding with tears.

Dominic's shoulders were bunched as his head hung in

defeat. He was trembling, and I was torn between needing to hold Sophie and the man who was trying to hold himself together but failing miserably.

The moment he heard Sophie's sob, he flung out of the chair and turned around. His cheeks were streaked with tears, his knuckles bleeding in several places. He rushed to Sophie and pulled her into his arms.

"It's okay, Soph," he whispered, holding her head against his chest. "I'm here. I'm here. I'm so sorry."

She clutched his shirt as tears created a wet patch on the fabric. He only pulled her closer as I watched his heart breaking for his sister all over again. His eyes met mine over her shoulder, and everything within me wanted to reach over and wipe the tears from his cheeks. I wanted to take him in my arms and tell him everything would be okay. I wanted to promise him that I'd slay all his demons and bring him the heads of the monsters who did this to his sister.

I promised myself that I would.

I let the siblings grieve. It was sheer torture to watch a man as strong and powerful as he crumble with so much guilt and agony. It was my personal nightmare appearing right in front of my eyes, to watch a woman as strong and beautiful as Sophie, a woman with dreams and passion, a woman with a loving family, be crushed and tormented all because of men's bruised egos.

Sophie's eyes and nose were swollen red, yet she held her head high as she straightened and let go of Dominic. I was in a far worse headspace when I was in her position. And I was so proud of her, so insanely proud of her, for surviving. "Can I hold your hand?" I asked her.

When she nodded, I clutched my hand around hers. "Believe it or not, I understand what you went through better than most. I'm so sorry I made you go through this pain all over again. You did so well, and I know it doesn't feel like you gave me many clues, but you did. And you were very brave."

She gave me a small smile, and after a glance at Dominic, she turned to me. "It's okay. Your specific questions helped me stay out of the more traumatic moments better."

I squeezed her hand. "That's all I need from you for now. Would you like to be kept in the loop about things we find or any progress? Or should I just stay in touch with Dominic?"

Even Dominic looked at Sophie for an answer. She cleared her throat and said, "Honestly, I'd rather you just keep Dominic posted about the progress. I don't really have much hope. Being involved with constant updates would just rack up my anxiety."

I nodded. "Makes sense."

Our hands were getting clammy as I continued to hold her hand—probably more for me than her at this point—when she said, "If anyone can find those three men, it's you."

That brought a smile to my face as I gave her a confident wink. "Damn straight."

"One last thing," I told her, very deliberately not looking at Dominic. "Do you want to learn to fight like me?"

Before even Dominic could react, Sophie said, "Fuck yeah."

"Atta girl. Training begins tomorrow at 6 a.m. sharp. Be at Thunder Claw Bar & Restaurant. Basement. Your brother knows the place."

Dominic's eyes were wide with shock at, I guess, my offer as well as Sophie's immediate acceptance.

I met his eyes and gave him a nod. "You wanna walk me to my car?"

He quickly closed his gaping mouth. "Uh. Yeah."

We stood from the bed. I patted Sophie on her head in goodbye. "See you tomorrow."

She gave me an excited smile that had my heart feeling slightly lighter than before.

Whoever decided to mess with Sophie had just started their countdown to fucking hell.

CHAPTER 10

DOMINIC

Sophie's words kept ringing in my ears even after we left her room. Every word, every moment, every punch and kick, and the abuse she endured felt like hot coals being raked down my chest. The blood in my veins roared and kicked and screamed with the need to avenge my baby sister and bring her the heads of the rapists and lay them down at her feet.

My muscles bunched as my vision kept tunneling into red, my body needing to beat something to a pulp. That little voice in my head roared at me that I was a failure, that I couldn't protect my sister. It showed me the heartbreak in my mother's eyes and the helplessness in my father's hunched shoulders. The deepest voice from the darkest recesses of my mind kept whispering in my ears that my parents, too, were disappointed in me for not saving my sister, for not finding the rapists, for not bringing her the justice she truly deserved.

"Oh, Dominic, who's this with you?" the voice from my mind suddenly transformed into my mother's.

A sharp jab at my ribs drew my attention to the two

people in front of us that I really, really did not want to encounter right now. My mom and dad.

"Uh, Eomma, I didn't see you there."

I quickly looked at Samaira, and for the first time since we met, I saw a hint of panic on her face.

Mom and Dad sat on the couch, drinking tea. We were among the wealthiest Korean American families in New York. But thanks to my mom, who'd come to the States from Korea after marrying Dad, we lived a relatively grounded lifestyle.

She wore a casual blouse and long, flowy pants, while Dad was in his usual polo shirt and slacks. With glasses perched atop his head and a newspaper in hand, they both looked back and forth between Samaira and me.

I mentally chided myself for being lost in thought, shot Samaira an apologetic glance, and led her toward the living area. For a moment, she hesitated but then followed.

Mom placed her teacup on the coffee table and looked at us expectantly. "Eomma, Appa, this is Samaira." I had been debating all morning whether I should tell Mom and Dad about who Samaira really was, but after actually listening to Soph talk about everything, I couldn't stay quiet. We all needed a little hope in our lives, and Samaira was that ray of light. "She is working on finding the men who hurt Sophie."

My mom gasped and clutched the little golden pendant of her necklace, her eyes as wide as saucers. Even my dad straightened on the couch, putting down his newspaper.

Here we go.

"Dominic, what are you up to? Didn't the cops tell us that the case was closed?" Dad asked, his hands shaking as he removed his glasses, rubbed his eyes, and put them back again.

I led Samaria to the couch, and we sat side by side across from my parents.

"Dad, you know I could never stop looking for those bastards."

I never cursed in front of my mother, but even she never

chided me for my choice of words when it came to those fuckers.

"But how? How would you find those men?" Mom's voice shook as she looked at Samaira, now scrutinizing her, starting from her chunky black boots to her build to the confident and authoritarian expression on her face. Samaira had appeared nervous when my parents had called us, but the moment I told them who she was, she'd assumed the identity and responsibility of a true Wildcat.

Before I could even utter a word, Samaira met my mother's eyes with a confidence that even I lacked sometimes. "Mrs. Park, I'm a member of a secret vigilante group. We are called Wildcats. We avenge women who don't find the justice they deserve from the people who are supposed to help them. No matter who the criminal is, whether they come from a small family or an affluent one, whether they're rich or poor, young or old. We don't care. We find criminals who've gotten away with abusing and raping and murdering women and dole out whatever punishment the women want."

Then she bent forward, resting her forearms on her knees and lacing her fingers together in front of her as she continued, "I promise you, Mrs. Park. I will find those three men who dared to touch your daughter, and we will show them that they don't mess with us and get away with it."

And I knew my mom had just fallen in love with the tigress. She moved toward her and clutched her hand with both of hers. "What was your name again, dear?"

"Samaira, Mrs. Park."

Mom picked up the teapot and poured the tea into an empty cup, filling it to the brim, and handed it to Samaira. "Well, Samaira. Let me tell you. We're going to be great friends."

A loud laughter burst out of Samaira, and she gave my mother an honest-to-God smile. "Sounds great, Mrs. Park."

She waved a hand at her. "Oh hush, now. Call me Hana-eonni."

Samaira's face turned red, and she blinked rapidly as if she were having a nervous breakdown. But she quickly recovered and nodded. "Hana-eonni."

That brought a proud smile to my mother's face as she raised her cup in cheers to Samaira and took a sip.

My dad's jaw was on the floor as he watched my mother be so animated. His eyes met mine with that ray of hope I was talking about—Samaira truly was the one to shine that spark of light on my small family. Looking at the awe and wonder on my dad's face, I knew he would pour every resource he had into whatever Samaira asked for.

Once Samaira finished her tea, she bid my mother goodbye with a promise to keep her posted, *and* they exchanged phone numbers.

We were both silent as we made our way to her sedan. I couldn't help but ask, "Why the sedan?"

One side of her lip curled in a smile. "Why *not* the sedan?"

I looked at her, then at the car, then back at her, and shrugged. "Doesn't exactly match your vibe."

She bit her lip and nodded. "It doesn't gain any attention. Easy to blend into the traffic. Helps me stay incognito."

I nodded, words escaping my mind. I wanted to ask her a billion questions about our next steps—if she needed anything from me, how she would find them, and what she gained by talking to Sophie again—but nothing came out of my mouth. I placed my hands in my pockets, barely holding on to my sanity. My mind was a churning mess of agony, darkness, and fury.

"She's strong, you know." Samaira's words pulled me out of the dark vortex I was spiraling into.

It took everything within me to move my lips and get the words out. "I know."

Samaira looked at me with a kind of intensity that made

me feel as if she could read every single one of my depraved, violent, rage-infused thoughts. Like she could see the storm rising and rioting within me, consuming my very soul.

"What?" I asked her, not being able to stand her unnerving silence and the way she looked at me.

She jerked her head toward her car. "Get in."

Then she promptly opened the driver's door and slid in. My feet were moving before I could even ask where we were headed. I just knew I'd follow her anywhere she asked.

I'd barely buckled in before she reversed her death machine of a car and tore out of the driveway.

We were both silent as she drove along the streets of Manhattan. I watched the buildings pass by, the people on the streets lost in their lives, each haunted by nightmares of their own, yet time kept moving and the world kept spinning. Some just learned to live with the horrors, while a rare few chose to fight back. Sophie was a strong woman, and she had chosen to smile today, chosen to revisit her nightmares, chosen to learn to fight.

She'd told her story in my presence and chose to let me in. And I only had one person to thank. I turned to the woman who looked so fierce and ruthless yet had been so gentle and protective of my sister. "Thank you for today," I said, making her glance at me.

She nodded, focusing on the road ahead. "I'm sorry for what you and your family are going through. It's not easy, but you're all a strong bunch. Sophie has the spirit of a fighter. I could feel it. That's why I offered her the option to train."

As much as I'd loathed the idea of Sophie learning to fight, I knew it was the right step. Sophie's immediate accep-tance had sealed the deal. If she wanted to learn to fight, she was going to fight. And it had been good to see some of that old spirit return in her eyes. "Would she be okay, though? Not from the fighting, of course, but from the external threat of the rapists? You think they'll be waiting for her to appear and finish their job or something?"

Samaira nodded. "That's a possibility. But it's been four months since the incident. They might have become confident that they're safe and that the situation is under control. They might have forgotten about Sophie altogether. But even if that weren't the case, and if they're waiting in the shadows, they'll be just that much easier to catch."

I nodded, but my mind was busy arranging the logistics of letting Sophie go for training every morning. I'd have to assign Maxim to take her and maybe have a car or two following her. If she agrees to have two bodyguards accompany her in the car, even better. I'd have to talk to Soph about it, convince her to be on board with my bodyguard idea.

Another thing had been circling in my mind. The way Samaira had slammed me on my back for merely touching her shoulder. The inferno mixed with panic in her eyes had frozen me to the spot. She'd looked like she could skin me alive if I dared to move. Something must have happened in her past for her to react in that manner.

I cleared my throat, my heart beating abnormally fast at the thought of talking to her about this. "Umm. I also wanted to apologize to you for touching you without your permission."

If I hadn't been looking at her, I wouldn't have caught her cringe. She bit her lip, and after a few seconds of saying nothing, she sighed. "It's not your fault. It's a trigger point for me. And with the kind of conversation we were having with Sophie, my mind wasn't exactly in a cool and calm space. Sorry I slammed you like that."

"No, it was fair. I promise you, it won't happen again."

She gave me a small smile and nodded, turning her eyes back to the road.

What caused her the trigger? Did something happen to her? Who would dare do something to this fierce woman? And how fucking dare they?

Questions bombarded my mind like a freight train. The way she pointedly stared at the road told me that the topic was closed for further discussion.

I pulled out my phone and texted Maxim to set up the security detail for Sophie. I was in the middle of replying to Maxim's text when the car stopped, and I found us parked right across from Thunder Claw.

"Are we getting started with work?" I asked as Samaira unbuckled her seat belt.

She looked me dead in the eyes. "We're here to fight."

She got out of the car, making me run after her. She entered the bar without pausing, and I caught up as we walked to the back, toward the basement staircase I now recognized.

We stepped into the basement where I'd first had a meeting with all of the Wildcats, and the view was slightly different today. The intimidating desk and chair setting was absent, transforming the vibe of the place from secret society to a large training room.

We walked in on two women mid-workout—or rather, frozen mid-rep. One held a hundred-pound lateral raise on a cable machine, while the other was stuck in a sumo squat holding a giant kettlebell. Their eyes tracked us, their jaws slack in shock.

Paying them no mind, Samaira headed past them to the fighting ring beyond. Their gazes were stuck on us, and I was still wondering about their reaction when a pair of gloves hit my chest.

I quickly caught them before they dropped on the floor as I watched Samaira step out of her boots. She was putting on her gloves as I said, "Um…I'm not dressed to fight."

I didn't care about my clothes. I just didn't want to fight Samaira.

I heard two snorts from behind me as Samaira looked at me pointedly. "Are you going to wear special clothes to beat up your sister's rapists?"

"Fuck you," my lips uttered before my mind could put a leash on my mouth.

A vicious smile stretched across Samaira's face, and then, she fake yawned.

Keeping my eyes trained on hers, I placed the gloves on the ring and removed my shoes and socks. The belt went next, the watch after that. At last, I rolled the sleeves of my shirt to my elbows, not pulling my gaze off her.

Fire danced in her eyes as she climbed into the fighting ring, hitting her hands against each other to warm up.

I shook my head and started to put on the gloves. "You know, I've been boxing for a few years now."

She smirked. "Good to know. I'll go easy on you then."

A laugh escaped my lips at her confidence.

"Don't go too easy on him," one of the two ladies shouted from behind. I turned to look at who shouted and found the two of them resting against the machine, all prepared to watch the fight. The woman with pink hair winked at me as she chewed on gum while the woman with the short hair gave me a small smirk and a thumbs-up.

The moment I climbed into the ring, Samaira continued to hit her gloves and jump on the spot, warming up her body. I followed suit, then asked, "You ready?"

She stood in the orthodox stance, her left foot and hand in front. "You need to step closer so we can begin."

Once I mirrored her stance, she said, "It's not going to be a traditional match. We're just letting off some steam. So don't hesitate to tap out."

I scoffed. "Just start the fight."

Her smile widened, and she counted down, "Three, two, one. Fight."

And she was on me. She came for my face, and I blocked

the punch. Then came stomach, ribs, face again, all of which I blocked. She circled me as I kept my guard up, loving the way her entire focus was trained on me. Only me.

She lunged at me again, her hand flying at my cheek. I raised my hand to block, and she landed a solid punch to my stomach. The moment my body bent down in response, she had her arms around my neck. I tried to get her arm to loosen, but it was like a band of steel across my throat, blocking my airflow.

Pleasure unfurled in my veins as the blood flow started to get restricted in my body, and it became more and more difficult to get a breath in. Her skin was hot against mine, her sharp exhale against my throat making my body hum with need. I still didn't tap out. A quiet, pleasurable burn was starting to rush through my system. I was near delirious when she growled in my ear, "What the fuck are you doing?"

She let go of my neck a little, causing me to gasp for breath. Air rushed through my lungs, and blood rushed to my brain. "What do you mean? Getting choked by you?"

She threw me away from her and came at me with a five-punch combo at my ribs and stomach, all of which I blocked. "Why aren't you hitting me?"

She got me there. "You think I'm not trying? I've never hit a woman in my life. Not even while playing with Sophie, not in fun, and not while boxing. My body wouldn't let me."

She scoffed and landed a punch to my cheek so fast, I couldn't even block it. The hit threw my head sideways, and a zing of pleasure hit my bloodstream, thrumming and writhing and begging for more.

"Not the pretty face." The pink-haired woman groaned. She now leaned against the ropes of the fighting ring.

"Screw you, Sloane," Samaira grumbled and turned her eyes on me. What I saw in them had me rethinking my words because fury blazed in her eyes like a bubbling volcano at the brink of an eruption. "You," she rumbled and held me by the collar of my shirt while her other hand clutched the shirt at my abdomen. Before I could comprehend what she meant to do, she picked up my two-hundred-pound body and slammed me down on the ring. Hard.

Pain raced across my back as my body jerked from the hard impact. I groaned as every organ in my body shuddered, my brain rattling in my skull. But she was not done. She came down on me, her muscular legs on each side of my chest. She pressed down on my chest with a gloved hand and looked at me. "You think you're showing me some kind of respect by not hitting me?"

Pain and pleasure wreaked havoc in my body. This glorious, powerful woman had trapped me between her thick thighs, her gritted teeth and sharp eyes trained on me with so much intensity, she completely enraptured me. I would only have to grab her hips and pull her mere inches closer to me, and I could drown myself in the scent of sweat, fight, and sex.

But one thing I couldn't do was throw a punch at her. "I could hurt you, and I don't want to hurt you."

Two loud scoffs came from the side.

She raised her eyebrows at me, not acknowledging the scoffs. "You think you can hurt me? You think you can get a single punch in? You think I'm giving you my hundred percent? You not giving me your hundred percent is the kind of disrespect I won't tolerate in my ring. If you want me to give you my all, you better bring your all. Or get out of my ring."

With that, she got back up, waiting for me to follow suit. She wasn't wrong, not one bit. To gain her trust, I had to give her my everything. If she said she could handle it, I'd just have to trust her.

I stood and twisted my neck from side to side and jumped on my feet, loosening my body after getting slammed on my back. Which reminded me, I removed one of the gloves with my teeth, and then another. Her face tilted a little, watching me with curiosity.

I put the gloves on the floor and started to open the buttons of my shirt. Her eyes tracked my fingers as I popped the buttons open one after another. When she looked at my face, her cheeks were flushed red. I gave her a wink. "Don't need to give you that easy of a hold to slam me back down."

Two loud woots came from the sidelines as one of them catcalled, "You want me to hold your shirt, sweetheart?"

A loud growl came from Samaira as she glared at Sloane. "One more word from you and you're in the ring next."

Sloane let out a loud, ringing laughter. "I'm good with Lena. She actually cares about my face."

"Eyes on me, Dominic." Samaira growled my name, and I hadn't realized my eyes had strayed. Her eyes slowly traveled down my body, starting from my shoulders to my pecs, down to my abs. My core tightened at her perusal, heat spreading everywhere she looked.

She started to circle me. But this time, I circled back.

Our eyes met. Challenge and attraction spun a weave of magical violence in the air between us. My eyes tracked the light falling on her arm, the roar of the tiger in her tattoo stirring an inferno of heat inside me. Her eyes glowed with challenge. Her lips curled up in so much confidence that I wanted to slam her on the ground and devour her mouth. Taste the danger that poured out of her in waves.

Where the hell did that thought come from?

She was driving me to the brink of insanity.

This time, when she came at me with a punch, I blocked and punched back, aiming for her ribs. She easily blocked the punch. In fact, she grabbed my outstretched hand and landed a solid kick to my stomach, hitting me so hard that I bent over with a loud "oomph."

She tried kicking again, which I blocked. I pushed her with my shoulder, putting all of my weight into it, causing her to let my hand go. I circled her and rained down combinations of punches and jabs. She blocked them all, landing a sharp uppercut on my chin, bashing my teeth into my tongue.

This time, I laughed as I tasted blood at the back of my throat. Pain lanced through my entire face, and adrenaline rushed through my veins as I finally felt alive.

Blood trickled down my chin as I met the tigress's eyes and licked my blood-stained lips, giving her a wink.

She rolled her eyes at me, but a wide, challenging smile tugged at her lips. "Thought you were good at it."

A laugh burst out of my chest, and my body pumped with the need to defeat the tigress. Samaira was a fucking beast at fighting. Any restriction and hesitation I had about hitting her evaporated with every jab she blocked and every drop of blood she drew. With every twenty punches I threw at her, I landed one, causing her to merely stumble a little. It didn't even take her a second to pull herself back.

With every punch I managed to land in her ribs or stomach, she punched me ten times harder. I was sure my chest would be black and blue. My entire face was throbbing, and my abs seemed to have been kicked inside my stomach.

I'd never felt more alive and in the moment. Every kick, every punch released that ever-growing knot of guilt from my chest. My body begged for mercy, while my mind embraced the pain, begging for more.

My muscles screamed with agony as I shuffled closer to her and sent a high kick flying toward her face. Instead of ducking, the crazy woman grabbed my calf in her hand and swiped my other leg from under me, dropping us both to the ground. While I landed flat on my face, my breath coming out in a whoosh, she landed gracefully in a motherfucking side lunge like a ninja. Before I could even get up, she jumped on my back and had my throat in another chokehold, her biceps and forearm crushing my windpipe. No matter what I did, her grip on me didn't loosen.

An inferno rushed through my body, my mind floating between pain and pleasure, all the blood rushing south.

"Tap the fuck out, Dominic," she growled in my ear, knowing I was losing consciousness. Her breathy voice, so close to my ear, had my cock throbbing.

Realizing that the game would be over if I actually passed out, I quickly tapped out. Instantly, she let me go, and I dropped down face-first on the floor of the ring, wheezing and shaking.

"Had enough?" she asked, back up on her feet and circling me, almost looking bored. Her hair was coming out of her ponytail, her body was soaked in sweat, and I'd never seen someone more magnificent and powerful.

"Never," I panted, beating at my chest, trying to get air in my lungs.

A wicked smile came over her face as she stood above me. In the next moment, her leg came flying at my ribs. Thanks to the adrenaline and my body's survival instinct, I rolled away as her feet slammed right where I had been a mere second ago.

I quickly jumped up to stand and flew toward her, sending punches flying at her with all my strength. Her blocks were solid like a wall, but instead of looking where I punched, I stared at *her*, the way her face was red from exertion, the way the tendons in her shoulder were taut, and the way the veins in her arms and biceps were pumping.

She instantly noticed the change in my punches. As soon as her eyes met mine, something electric zipped through my body and straight into my heart, causing some tight knot in my chest to unravel, to soften, to yearn for more. And I knew Samaira felt something too because her block faltered. If only for a moment. And I grabbed that opening and swiped her legs.

Her eyes went as wide as saucers as she felt herself go down. Being the gentleman that I was, I broke her fall by putting my hand at the back of her head and climbing on top of her, my legs on either side of her waist. She immediately had her guard up. I grabbed both of her hands and, to her utter surprise, pushed both of her hands above her head.

I bent closer to her face, my hair falling over my eyes, my breath coming in harsh pants, sweat rolling down my chest, and pain blooming in every part of my body. I could see the perspiration dotting her face as her breath fanned my jaw. I focused very, *very hard* on not getting *hard* on top of the tigress. She'd probably claw my face off. Holding her gaze, I could see small specks of light brown and gold in her eyes as I whispered, "I win."

Two sets of heavy claps and whistling broke the moment as both of us turned to look at our audience of two very excited women with maniacal glee on their faces. Samaira let out a growl, and I quickly anticipated her next move—rolling me down and raining hell on my face—and pushed myself off her body. "You did not win."

I looked at our very own audience of two, then met Samaira's eyes. "I dropped you on your ass after taking about five hundred punches and kicks. Feels like a win to me."

"Yep, Dominic wins," the pink-haired woman, who Samaira had called Sloane, chimed in.

"Nope," the other woman, Lena, said, giving a wink to Samaira. "He needs to get her to tap out for him to win. He barely landed ten punches on her."

Sloane looked at Samaira and Lena with a teasing smile. "He could've been holding back."

When Samaira turned her eyes on me, I raised my hands in surrender. "I promise, I wasn't holding back."

She jumped back to her feet and shook her head. "Then you suck at boxing. Might want to find a better trainer."

I looked at her and cocked my eyebrows. "Seems like I already did."

She scoffed, and before responding to me, she turned to

the two women who were staring back and forth between us, as if regretting not bringing popcorn. "Leave us alone. Now."

"But you're just getting to the fun part," Sloane whined. "Lena, order them to let us stay."

Lena rolled her eyes and dragged Sloane away from us.

Samaira let out a relieved sigh and met my eyes. "I don't have the time to teach you how to fight."

I didn't think I could ever spar with anyone else. "How about I come tomorrow morning with Sophie?"

She instantly shook her head in denial. "Nope. That's the ladies' batch. No men allowed in this space."

Shock traveled through my body. "Am I the first man you've brought here to spar?"

She rolled her eyes and turned away from me. "Don't make a big deal out of this."

I would not make a big deal out of this *out loud*. Inside, I was doing fucking backflips and kicking my feet in the air. Despite her warning, I couldn't wipe the stupid, proud smile off my face. "Fine, I won't come with Sophie. Speaking of whom, I must mention that I am extremely glad that she gets to learn to fight from an expert like you."

When she turned her face to look at me, I continued, "Trust me, offering to teach Sophie to fight, giving her an outlet to deal with her emotions, I can't thank you enough. Even if we can't find the fuckers, just helping Sophie get back on her feet is worth everything to me."

Every time I mentioned Sophie, Samaira's eyes softened, and an air of warmth and protectiveness poured out of her. Her eyes were fierce and jaw sharp as granite when she said, "We *will* find those fuckers. No question about it."

I nodded, my once-wavering belief solidifying with every confident word from Samaira's mouth. I could fucking hug her right now. But I didn't dare take a step toward her, knowing she'd punch my throat before getting hugged by me. At least that's the energy she was projecting.

"Now, off you go," she said, jumping down from the ring and removing her gloves. "I have work to do. See that you bring Sophie tomorrow."

"Maybe I'll see you tomorrow," I shouted at her retreating form.

"Maybe," she shouted back without turning around.

I texted Maxim to come pick me up as I went upstairs to the bar area, which was currently operating as a diner. I took up a seat at one of the corner tables and nursed a smoothie as I waited for Maxim.

The entire time that I waited for him, throughout our entire ride back to my parents' place, all through the dinner with my family, and as I lay on my bed staring at the ceiling for hours, only one thought, only one question looped through my mind.

What did Samaira mean when she told Sophie, *Believe it or not, I understand what you went through better than most?*

CHAPTER 11

The next day, Sophie arrived at six o'clock sharp, tagging behind two other regulars at the gym. Sloane and I ran the self-defense and training program for women every morning. We offered a special class for our clients who wanted to learn to fight, get stronger, and have a physical outlet. We also held Muay Thai training sessions three times a week.

While I was strong in boxing, Lena taught us all Muay Thai. None of us were limited to specific fighting techniques. In our line of work, most of our time was dedicated to honing our skills, training, fighting, and researching.

Our regulars knew their warm-up routines and jumped right into it. Sophie slowly made her way to me, her steps faltering as she moved closer. I gave her a quick smile and closed the gap between us. "Hey, Sophie, I'm so glad you joined us."

She wore athletic leggings and a long-sleeved gym top. Her hair was in a tight braid, and she looked ready to get to work. She gave me a small smile in return. "I'm glad I came.

Dom's face after he returned to our parents' place was an even better motivator."

I chuckled. "Soon, you'll be just as good at kicking his ass."

That got a laugh out of her.

"Who do we have here?" Sloane came around from where she was talking to two women and stood between us. She wore pastel-pink leggings and a matching athletic crop top with straps at the back that showcased her biceps and muscular back.

Sloane tended to put people at ease, so I turned to her. "Sloane, this is Sophie, Dominic's sister," and then looked at Sophie. "Sophie, this is Sloane, one of the Wildcats. She's our undercover expert."

The moment Sophie accepted Sloane's handshake, Sloane pulled her by the hand and led her away from me, shouting at the ladies. "Meet our new bestie, everyone. This is Sophie."

"Hi, Sophie," everyone cheered.

The next hour-and-a-half-long session went by quickly—with a lot of stretching, kicking, swearing, sparring, getting beaten by me, and practicing each self-defense move over and over again.

By the time we were done, every single woman, including Sophie, had sweat running down their body and a smile on their face. Every single woman in this early morning batch was a survivor. Every single one had suffered at the hands of men, and each of them had a burning determination in their soul to never be powerless again.

We—they—all pushed each other to do better, fight harder, and always get back up. We didn't pull punches here. We didn't bitch about each other. We only uplifted and supported each other. There was no room for a bitch among the Wildcats.

That was who every single woman who fought here was. A Wildcat. We rose above the abuse and violence thrown at us.

We not only learned to fight with our bodies, but we also learned and helped each other fight the stigma associated with the abuse and rape. We carried each other's pains and nightmares, we held each other on rough days, we fought for a better life, and we fought *for* each other.

I saw Sophie talking and exchanging numbers with a few other women. Dominic would be happy to know that not only was Sophie a good fighter but she was also opening up to other people.

When our eyes met across the room, I gave her a warm smile. She bid the other women goodbye and walked to where I stood, arranging the gloves in the cubicles.

"You were great, Sophie. How do you feel?"

An honest-to-God, genuine smile lit up her face. "Really good. I'm glad you asked me to come."

"So I take it you're going to come regularly, then?"

"Every single day." She looked around at the dispersing crowd with awe on her face. "Sloane told me every woman in this batch is a survivor. They're all so inspiring. As much as it hurts to know they all went through something horrific, it gives me some hope that I'll be alright."

I clutched her shoulder. "You will be. You're a fighter."

She nodded, her eyes fueled with determination. "Yes. Yes, I am."

I placed the glove that I was holding in its cubicle and decided to ask her something that I'd been wondering about for a while. "So, Sophie, I hope you don't mind me asking. But are you seeing a therapist?"

A frown appeared between her eyebrows. "Umm…Not really. I don't have the words to talk about it to someone I don't know. Talking to the cops and detectives was difficult enough. I don't know if I can handle talking about it even more, day after day, week after week."

Every woman who had come to us said the same thing. "Sophie, my girl, it is extremely harmful and self-destructive to keep everything bottled up inside. We all need to deal with our emotions without feeling judged. And that's what good therapists do. They listen, they support, they help. *I* go to a therapist. Every Wildcat here attends therapy. With the things we see and do, with the trauma we've all faced, we all need help dealing with our emotions."

Her eyes were wide with disbelief. "You go to a therapist?"

I nodded. "Once every two weeks. And if you don't know any, I'm happy to recommend my therapist. I've known her for over ten years now. I really, really need you to consider it."

She stared at the floor, shuffling her legs and biting her lip like her life depended on it. "Can I think about it?"

"Of course. Think about it. Do some research. We also have monthly group sessions here where all the ladies from this fighting group just get together and have a sleepover."

A smile came over her face. "I'd be down for that."

I chuckled. "I knew you would be. Now, off you go before your brother rushes downstairs looking for you."

Her mouth hung open. "How'd you know he's upstairs?"

I couldn't help but roll my eyes. "If I've learned anything about your brother since I met him, it's that he's protective as fuck, and he wouldn't dare let you out of his sight for a long, long time."

She giggles. "He's always been that way. Uh…do you wanna come up and say hi?"

I should've said no. I even said it in my mind. *No, I'm busy. No, I have a class to run. No, say hi to him for me.* I recited each of these lines in my head. But my feet betrayed my mind as they started walking by her side, carrying me upstairs, all the while my brain screamed at my legs to halt immediately. But all they did was just walk faster.

"I'll handle it here, Sami," Sloane shouted behind me. I absolutely did not respond to her teasing. And I definitely did not show her the finger behind my back.

What was wrong with me? I didn't focus on men. I didn't

even like men. I was happy with my vibrators, my fingers, and an occasional hookup if I missed dick. But this? Looking forward to seeing a guy's face? Getting jealous of seeing a woman with him in a photo? Wanting to kill for him? Needing to comfort him? Bringing him to Thunder Claw and beating the shit out of him to help him let off steam? Letting him see the Wildcats' faces?

With every passing day, I was crossing every boundary I'd set for myself.

The moment we entered the restaurant, we found him working on his laptop with a cup of coffee and a croissant on the side. My feet stumbled, and I barely caught myself as I took him in. As if Dominic in a suit already wasn't my kryptonite, the man was determined to make me lose what little mind I'd left by coming here dressed in fucking gray sweatpants and a white T-shirt. Add in the light green and purple bruising at the top of his cheek, marks that *I'd* put on him, and every pore of my body burst into flames.

My blood felt like it was consumed by lava, and my heart raced a mile a minute. I could feel heat rushing to my cheeks and need unlike anything I'd ever experienced coursing through my veins.

Pretty sure I was being punished by the universe right now for chopping off dicks like a sport.

This was not the plan. I would not let a man make me act like an idiot.

Not wanting to come off as an obsessed fool, I schooled my expression a mere second before he sensed our presence and turned to look at us. A warm smile came over his face as he saw his sister.

But the moment our eyes met, his lips stretched into an even wider smile, flashing me his ridiculous dimples—right beside a fading yellowish bruise that *I'd* given him last night—that threatened to break my resolve of keeping my distance, staying professional, and not getting him too close to the Wildcats. I had half a mind to grab his face and lick those damn dimples right off. *Fuck him for being so gorgeous.*

I gave him a small smile because it was impossible not to return a smile when he looked so warm and inviting. Sophie took a seat right across from Dominic, while I took a seat between the two on the empty stool. She grabbed the croissant and bit into it with gusto. "God, I'm starving."

"I take it the first day went well?" Dominic asked her, his face bursting with joy at seeing his sister smiling and eating. I could feel his relief in the way his shoulders instantly relaxed, the way his eyes lit up, and he looked between the two of us with so much excitement. I couldn't help but smile at him.

Sophie launched into narrating the session when I met the eyes of Tammy, one of our servers. When she reached us, I asked her for my usual smoothie, and Sophie ordered a cappuccino to go.

Once we placed our orders, Dominic looked at me. "So how's the case coming along? Would you like me to stay put? Anything I can help with?"

"We'll be working on some recon today. I'll update you if I have any questions or need your help."

He got super serious as he stared me down. "You do know that you're supposed to involve me in the case, right?"

I leaned on the table and stared back at him, my temper slightly flaring. "You do know that you're paying us to work this case, right? Don't you have a billion-dollar empire to run?"

"Oh, I run it just fine. This is top priority."

I understood that he was worried, that he was in pain, that *he* needed to be the one to bring down the culprits, but he needed to trust us. "You need to have faith in me, Dominic."

I could see Sophie's eyes jumping between us as we stared each other down.

With a sigh, he unclenched his jaw, as if it cost him a great deal. "You're right. Just let me know if you need me. Day or night. I'll be there."

As snappy and passionate as he got, I knew his reaction was reasonable. I *knew* these responses. Every burst of anger and helplessness came out of a place of hurt, that bottomless pit of guilt that never abated, no matter what you did to assuage it.

"I know," I said softly.

He looked at me as if my two words meant something to him. His Adam's apple bobbed as he gave me a nod, and it took every ounce of my strength to pull my gaze away from it.

The moment broke when Tammy arrived with my smoothie and Sophie's cappuccino. I quickly jumped off my seat, not needing to expose myself to the increasingly deteriorating effect that Dominic was having on me.

I grabbed my smoothie and turned to the siblings. "You guys carry on. I'm needed downstairs."

Both had similar smiles on their faces as they bid me goodbye. I nearly ran to the back of the restaurant. I didn't. I kept my cool till I was out of sight from Dominic's view, after which I literally sprinted down the stairs, all the way down to the Den, and jumped into the fucking shower.

I took a freezing shower that had my teeth chattering and my mind numb, which was exactly what I needed. As soon as I stepped out of the shower, Shadow was on me, jumping up to try to give me kisses.

I bent down and rubbed his head, showering him with affection.

I knew Tara was at her computers, digging through Sophie's case. "Yo, Tara, did you get Shadow out today?"

She shouted from the other room. "Yeah. We went an hour ago when you guys were in the class."

I rubbed Shadow's head as he gave me excited nips. "You love going outside, don't you? Don't you? Did you see any butterflies?"

I got up from my knees and walked to her side of the Den, which was basically four monitors, a big-ass rolling chair, and mood lighting. Shadow was ahead of me as he ran to Tara and jumped around the chair where she sat. Tara's hair was in a bun on the top of her head, and for a change, she was without her mask.

"Stop looking," she muttered, petting Shadow as he gave her licks on her scarred side.

Just to keep things normal and not make her feel awkward, I joked, "You want me to talk to you with my eyes closed?"

The unscarred side of her lips turned up in a smile. "Fuck you. You know what I mean."

Grabbing the smoothie from where I'd left it on the coffee table, I dragged one of the chairs from the dining area and sat beside her. "You know, we never stare at you with pity or disgust. I look at you the same way I look at Sloane or Naomi or Lena."

"I know," she said, her face buried in Shadow's neck.

I ruffled her bun at the top of her head, causing her to shriek and curse at me as she redid her hair. "Stop doing that to break the fucking tension. There are more subtle ways."

I chuckled and sipped at my smoothie. "Nah. This was more fun."

She grumbled about an impossible and rude bestie as she clicked through her screen.

"You find anything from the gala?" I asked, seeing various invitations she was surfing through.

"I found a lot of things. Here, check this out," she said, turning the screen slightly so I could look at it. "Since the people at the gala had somehow *lost all the data and backup*, I had to do a little more digging. Seems they'd just been paid off by someone because their data, including all the invitations, the security footage of the gala, who came, who didn't, is all available."

"No shit." I whistled. Tara scrolled through hundreds of

invitations. Thankfully, the gala had a barcode on the invitation card for entry, and all the entries were digitally recorded.

"Did you find anything of importance? Or do you want me to go through these?" I asked, polishing off my smoothie.

Tara scoffed. "You'll need to go through the invitations, who they were sent to, who arrived, and the guests they arrived with. Fortunately, we have video footage of the entry point to the gala. It's tedious work. I would do it, but I have to work on another case."

I nodded. "All right, send me all the files and videos. I'll work on this today."

She started transferring everything to a USB drive, and we watched as hundreds of gigabytes worth of files were transferred.

"What's the other case you're working on?" I asked her.

She turned to me, scratching at Shadow's neck, who didn't waste a second before climbing onto her lap as she moved, making her giggle. "Shadow, baby. You're too big."

He only cuddled further into her lap, licking her face and causing her to shriek.

We'd rescued Shadow from a dog-fighting ring. But it was Shadow who'd brought Tara back to life. His body was heavily scarred on one side where he didn't get much fur. The day we went to shut down that ring, Tara was the one who'd found Shadow. We'd given all the dogs to a shelter, but Shadow had refused to leave Tara's side. Tara hadn't hesitated in adopting the giant dog who'd snapped and barked every time we came within three feet of Tara.

It had taken a few months of training for Shadow to see us as his family too. But he still became ragey when a stranger came close to Tara.

She kept petting Shadow as she talked. "Remember, I need to create fake IDs and jobs for the four fuckers locked up downstairs? Sloane and Lena are working on getting them shipped to Florida tonight."

Since it was Sloane's case, she handled keeping them fed, and Naomi handled keeping them alive just enough.

Once I had all the files, I took a seat on the couch, retrieved my laptop, and began reviewing the invitations and videos. With each invitation email sent to a person, I verified whether the invitation had been scanned. The scan was thankfully time-stamped, so I verified whether the person who arrived at the time stamp was actually the one who had received the invitation. I also verified if the person was a tall white man in a black wolf mask.

And lo and behold, I'd already come across five black-wolf mask-wearing men. I started copying over their video time stamps for later. The more I went through the files, the more suspects I started to gather.

By the time I was done, it was late in the evening, and I was starting to see double on the screen. Thankfully, I didn't have a shift at the bar upstairs today. We had enough employees to handle the weekday crowd.

Tara was still at her computer, whereas Sloane and Lena had dragged the unconscious men up to the basement to get them transported.

I had gathered enough suspects and was confident it had to be someone among them.

Knowing Dominic was waiting for an update, I picked up my phone and opened his contact.

> Me: I have some things that I'd like for you to look at before we involve Sophie.

I didn't even have to wait fifteen seconds before he responded.

> Dominic: I'll be there in 45 minutes.

> Me: I didn't mean you had to rush right away.

Dominic: Is that a problem? I can come tomorrow.

Yes, it was a problem. I'd been staring at the screen and working for the past twelve hours. I wanted to eat something greasy and then go home to sleep. I was so brain-dead and so hungry, I was afraid I'd drool at the sight of him and crave a bite of those stupid dimples on his face. I stared at his message and tried to type *Come tomorrow.*

But to my utter mortification and disbelief, my fingers betrayed me as I read the message I'd typed and sent.

Me: It's no problem. See you soon.

See you soon! Fuck!

"What happened?" Tara bent sideways to look at my face from behind her screen.

I raised my eyebrows at her.

"You yelled fuck. So loud it spooked Shadow."

I threw my phone on the couch and got up, pointing an accusing finger at the stupid device. "I did something stupid," I said, and instantly corrected myself and stared down at my fingers in betrayal. "Not me. My asshole fingers did something stupid."

"Sami, what did you do?" Tara asked in a teasing tone.

I shook my head and pulled off the hair ties holding my braids and started untangling them. "I asked Dominic to come look at the suspects I've gathered."

"Right now?" Her eyes were as wide as saucers. "It's ten o'clock."

I had my long, wavy hair free of the braids as I combed through them with my fingers. "I know," I whined, something I *never ever* did. "He even said he could come tomorrow. I even said *Come Tomorrow* in my mind, but my stupid fingers asked him to come right away. It typed *See you soon, Tara.* See. You. Soon."

Tara laughed so loudly it actually got Shadow to start barking and circling her. She laughed so fucking hard she literally slipped out of her rolling chair and sprawled on the floor like a lunatic as Shadow licked the tears streaming down her cheeks.

She pointed her finger at me from the floor, her laughter making her gasp out her words. "And is that your stupid fingers making you remove your braid and finger-comb your long hair? Are you prettying up for Dominic?"

Horror washed through my brain as I looked at my fingers, now in my hair, combing through the tangles. I shrieked and let them go. Running to the sink, I turned the tap to the coldest setting and submerged them in freezing water.

Tara laughed harder as I heard a click.

"What are you doing?" I screamed at her.

She was clutching her stomach as she continued to laugh. "Need to send your face to the group chat. This moment needs to be preserved forever."

"Don't you dare, you bitch," I seethed. I so badly wanted to go to her and snatch her phone away, but I was more terrified of what my fingers would do if I removed them from the freezing water.

"Get it together, Sami. Or I'm gonna pee my pants." She howled with laughter as she typed something on the phone. I knew she'd sent the picture to the group when I heard the ping of the notification on my phone.

"You bitch. I'm gonna ruin you."

She showed me a finger. "Pull it together, Samaira Sharma. When is he coming?"

I turned off the tap and slapped both my cheeks. Hard. "Probably in thirty minutes now."

She barely contained her laugh as she ran her eyes from my head to my toes. "You want to change for him?"

I threw the nearest thing I found—Shadow's chew toy—at her, which she easily caught, and started laughing. She got back to her chair and said, "Go change, Sami. You do look like shit."

Just because of that, I absolutely did not want to change. But then Dominic's face popped into my mind. What if he came in his stupid three-piece suit, and I was sitting in my tank top and shorts? I then looked at my thick-ass thighs and smirked. Maybe not changing wasn't a bad idea after all.

Was I trying to impress him with my body? Had I stooped so fucking low so fast?

I could feel Tara's gaze boring into me as I walked back and forth, trying to decide on my fucking outfit. When I turned my helpless eyes to her, she bit her lip as if trying not to laugh at my pathetic state. "You've already lost, babe. Just change if you want to look presentable and stay put if you want to make him bite his tongue off."

I sighed in defeat, disappointed at myself for being so… so…obsessed over a guy.

Fuck it. He wouldn't make me change into a new pair of clothes. I was going to stay put, and if he found my thighs sexy, then it was his problem. Not mine.

And that was exactly how I opened the door to the basement level when he arrived thirty minutes later. He was not dressed in a three-piece suit like I'd thought—secretly hoped. Because the universe was out to get me and bite me in the ass, he, too, was wearing his workout gear. Unlike some dudes who wore long-sleeved T-shirts and joggers, this man wore a loose sweatshirt with giant holes for sleeves, showing off his thick arms with bulging biceps, while holding what looked like three large boxes of pizza. It was obscene, really. His suit and this morning's T-shirt really didn't do enough justice to his chest.

It was wide, his shoulders popping from the sleeves, and that just made me want to climb him like a tree.

I was so lost in checking him out that I didn't realize that he was busy with his own perusal. Thankfully, I was the one who pulled myself together before him. I watched his Adam's apple bob as his eyes were glued to my legs.

I cleared my throat, snapping his attention to my eyes. I gave him a quick quirk of my eyebrows in a *caught you* gesture, making him shake his head. "Come in." I turned around to walk to the desk I'd set up with my laptop and a few prints of the suspects with basic information on them. Considering they were all some kind of public figure, I was guessing Dominic might recognize at least a few of them.

I heard a low growl behind me as he followed me. "I brought pizza," he said, placing the boxes in the empty space on the desk.

A loud gurgling sound came from my stomach, startling us both. His eyes narrowed. "When did you last eat?"

I looked away from him and sat down, pretending to think. "I had the smoothie."

His eyes widened and turned into a storm of worry and anger. "That was in the morning after your workout. What the hell, Samaira? You haven't eaten the whole day?"

Before I could answer him, he opened the box, grabbed the biggest slice of pepperoni pizza, placed it on a paper napkin, and handed it to me. "Pepperoni okay? Do you eat meat?"

"Should've asked me before handing over the pizza," I grumbled, biting into the slice with gusto.

He opened another box. "I got veggie pizza too."

"Pepperoni is fine," I mumbled between the bites. Something warm tugged in my chest at the way he was looking at me right now. Like me not eating hurt *him*. Like he genuinely cared.

"Aren't you going to eat?" I asked him after he kept glowering at me, his hip leaning against the desk, his arms folded across his chest.

He rounded the desk and sat on the chair next to me. He grabbed a veggie slice for himself, biting into it. "*I* didn't starve myself."

He kept looking at me as he ate, the intensity of his gaze unnerving me. I rarely, if ever, allowed a man close enough to me for him to bring me food. The only people I'd ever allowed to be there for me were my Wildcats.

It might just be that I'd never had a real connection with any man before, which was making me so mushy for just getting a pizza from a guy. Even friends bring pizza for each other. Considering he was a billionaire, he would've looked stupid if he'd come empty-handed. Yep, that was it. There was no need to feel so soft for him.

He was our client.

Just. A. Client.

Then why was my heart fluttering around my chest like a fool?

CHAPTER 12

DOMINIC

She forgot to eat. My temper flared the moment she said that the last thing she had was that smoothie that she'd ordered in the morning. How could someone just forget to eat?

I looked at her as she demolished the entire pepperoni pizza. I had the veggie pizza box turned toward her before she could even ask. "Just one more slice," she grumbled.

I shook my head, glaring at her. "You will not skip a meal again, Samaira."

She rolled her eyes. "Are you this bossy with your girl-friends?"

Oh, how I loathed someone rolling their eyes at me. If she were mine, I'd have put her across my knees. My gaze turned to the obscene shorts that she wore, and the thought of those tiny shorts riding up the back of her thick thighs, exposing the perfect curve of her cheeks, had my cock stirring in my sweats. My hands tightened into fists as I restrained the urge to say something inappropriate and scare her off.

The moment I'd seen those short shorts, her thick quads,

the golden-brown skin shining under the yellow gym lights, her hair falling down her back in messy waves, that choker around her neck, I'd not only lost my train of thought, I'd forgotten my own name. The way she sat on the chair beside me, folding one of her legs onto the seat, had my eyes betraying my senses as they got distracted.

It took me a minute to comprehend the words she'd just spoken, and an excited flutter raced across my stomach. Was Samaira…fishing…for information? My lips instantly curled into a smile as I looked at her, and she quickly turned her gaze away from me, a dark red blush coating her cheeks.

I cleared my throat so she met my eyes and said, "First, I don't have a girlfriend. Second, I *am* this bossy."

She flushed and shook her head, getting back to the pizza.

Not wanting to make her uncomfortable, I pulled us back into familiar territory. "You find something in Sophie's case?"

I caught a small, amused smile on her face—her eyes thanking me for the shift in the conversation—before she quickly swallowed the last bite of her pizza, wiped her hands with a tissue, and opened her laptop. "Now you're asking me the right questions."

I wiped my hands and sat up straighter, looking at Samaira as she laid down a stack of photos and pulled up what appeared to be a security camera recording of the gala on her laptop.

"How'd you find the gala footage? They told the cops that all their footage was lost in some server damage."

Her lips curled in disgust. "That's what they say when someone doesn't want you to look at the footage. It's either the people at the gala or it's the cops who're hiding something from us. Thankfully, we were able to hack into their server and get all the footage. We also got the recordings from the cameras across the street and at the side alley."

My chest burned with rage at whoever hid so much vital information from us. I moved closer to the screen, staring at people entering the gala one after the other, as Samaira continued, "Since Sophie mentioned that the guy was in a black wolf mask, I've separated every Caucasian guy with a black wolf mask. I reviewed all the invitations that were sent out and all the ones that were scanned at the gala entrance as well. Each scan was time-stamped, so I was able to verify whether the name on the invitation matched whoever entered the gala."

My mind was reeling with the information coming at me. I kept up with Samaira as she spread out thirteen pictures on the desk. When I looked at her in question, she said, "These are all the men who arrived at the gala in a black wolf mask. I was able to verify the invitation and the person who arrived."

She crossed out nine of them. "I've verified the identities of these men using their names and the video footage. They're all over fifty, and since Sophie also mentioned that the men who raped her were young, I suggest we exclude them for now to narrow the initial search. The remaining four identities are questionable. One arrived as a regular guest, and the other three used invitations issued under different names. They might be connected to the original invitees, something we need to confirm. I also have the names listed on the invitations those three used. I called because I hoped you might recognize someone personally. This way, we can potentially rule anyone out or prioritize them."

She'd achieved more in a week than the cops and my PIs had in over four months. For the first time, I felt genuine hope. Before diving into the identities, I turned to Samaira. When our eyes met, I almost reached across the desk for her hand resting there but quickly stopped myself. "Thank you, Samaira. This…This is great work."

She gave me a small smile and a nod. "We'll get them, Dominic. I promise."

I actually believed her.

I glanced at the crossed-out photos just to see if I recognized the men. Samaira had written their names on the picture, considering every single one of them was in a mask. Most of the crossed-out names belonged to businessmen in various industries, but they were well-known enough for me to recognize them.

I moved to the remaining four pictures. The one who'd arrived as a guest was a mystery to me. But the person he'd arrived with was Sheila Bastion. I picked up the picture of the masked man with a petite woman's arm in his. "Sheila Bastion. She's a recent widow of one of our rival companies. Anthony Bastion, her late husband, left her everything when he passed, and she spends her days going to galas with various boy toys by her side. He might be her latest companion. I can call her tomorrow and ask her about him."

Excitement lit up her eyes. "Great. One less person for us to dig through. Keep going."

Even at a time like this, when I was trying to identify my sister's rapists, Samaira managed to tame the violent rage bubbling inside me. She looked like she could slam ten guys twice her size with no effort. But when she smiled at me, when she reassured me with that surety in her eyes, she looked like the warmest person to ever exist. She made me want to snuggle her in my arms and absorb all that warmth into me, to melt the bone-chilling guilt that constantly consumed my soul.

I picked up the next photo when the voices of two women reached us, just before the door to the basement opened, and Sloane and Lena walked in. I'd seen them working out during our little fighting match, but right now, they were in all-black tactical gear, their respective masks pulled up over their heads.

Sloane had a black-and-pink cheetah mask, whereas Lena had a black-and-golden lioness mask. The moment Sloane noticed the two of us, a brilliant, mischievous smile lit up her face.

"Here we go," Samaira muttered from beside me,

pinching the top of her nose. I bit my lip to stop the laugh threatening to escape my chest.

Sloane winked at me and jabbed Lena, who was looking at her phone. The moment Lena raised her eyes, her gaze stopped on us. She immediately exchanged a teasing smile with Sloane as they quickly changed paths and made their way to us. "Hey, guys, we didn't know Dominic was coming tonight," Lena said.

"Good evening, ladies. You want some pizza?" I greeted them when Samaira simply gave them a grunt without meeting their eyes.

They each grabbed a chair from the stack of chairs in the corner of the room and took a seat right across from Samaira and me. "I would love some. I'm starving," Sloane said, grabbing a veggie slice. She quickly texted on her phone and said, "I've texted Tara to come upstairs if she wants pizza."

Lena grabbed another slice and looked at the photos strewn across the table and the open laptop. "You make headway in the case?"

Samaira sighed. "You both are just going to sit here?"

Sloane had a delighted twinkle in her eyes as she turned to Samaira. "You don't want us to stay here, Sami?"

Sami. It suited her. Especially when she turned bright red like right now. "I don't care. We were just going over the list of suspects that I narrowed down. I asked Dominic to come by to see if he recognized any, or if he had any personal connection or animosity with any of them."

As Samaira talked to them, both the ladies turned serious, nodding along. Right then, a hatch on the far side of the room opened, and another woman climbed out. Well, that was a surprise. How many more floors did they have beneath the basement?

She had half a mask covering the right side of her face. The other half of her face was just as eye-catching. This woman was stunning in her own right. Her features were almost too perfect, with her bow-shaped lips, her golden-brown skin, and her hazel eyes. I could make out some burn marks where the mask touched her skin, but I quickly ignored them. Instead, I got up and extended my hand. "Hi. We meet again."

She gave me a firm handshake and a small nod. "Tara. Thanks for getting us pizza."

"Of course. It's the least I can do for you all."

While Sloane and Lena removed their masks from their heads and placed them on the desk, Tara's mask seemed to be custom-designed so she could eat with half her lips covered by the mask.

"So who're the suspects?" Lena asked, biting into the pizza, bringing everyone's attention back to the topic at hand.

I picked up the photo of the next suspect—the one who didn't match the name on the invite—and read the name under the image. "Thomas Cooper Sr. Obviously, the state attorney. And if he didn't arrive at the gala, this could be his son, Thomas Cooper Jr."

I raised my eyebrows at Samaira at the fact that she'd put the state attorney's son on the suspect list. She simply shrugged. "It's just tentative. But there's a reason you couldn't catch the guys. They're either above you in the food chain or they're extremely smart."

I nodded. "We can set up an appointment with the state attorney and go talk to him. See if he reveals who came to the gala."

The three of them nodded, and I made a note to ask Kai to send out an email requesting an appointment. I spoke as I typed the note. "I'll make an appointment under the pretense of needing his opinion on a real estate project we're working on. I can casually slip in the conversation about the gala."

Samaira nodded. "I'll come with you."

Sloane's, Tara's, and Lena's gazes snapped to her, whereas Samaira pointedly kept her eyes on me. I nodded when

Sloane piped in, "I mean, I am our resident undercover, Sami. Are you sure you don't want *me* to go?"

When Samaira glared at Sloane, I couldn't hide my smile anymore. Especially when Samaira said through her clenched teeth, "I'm sure. I can be his fake assistant."

Lena gave a thoughtful nod, her lips twitching in a smile. "Of course. Let us know when you need us to get involved."

Samaira averted her eyes and picked up the next photo, handing it to me, and nodded. "Sure."

I stared at the man in a black wolf mask, a lady on each of his arms. "Brian Montgomery. Steel industry mogul. I can reach out to him as well to find out who came in his stead."

I picked up the last picture and stared at the masked man with one man and woman behind him. "Looks like the invitation is under Zarine Blackwood." I turned to Samaira and shrugged. "I don't know who Zarine Blackwood is."

She nodded and flipped through her notepad. "She's the founder of Lustre Diamonds. It's an up-and-coming jewelry line, mostly based in Manhattan."

Sloane chimed in, "I'll find out who came to the gala using her invitation. If it's an up-and-coming venture, she must be going to other galas and parties. Tara and I can work together to figure out where she plans to make an appearance."

Tara swallowed her pizza and nodded. "I'll look into her."

Sloane gave a wicked smile to Lena and flicked her hair. "Time to bling it up, boss. I'm gonna need a nice dress, and of course, a diamond necklace."

"Put it all under your invoice for me, Ms. Lena," I said, giving a nod to Sloane. "Bling it up, Ms. Sloane. Whatever it takes."

Sloane's lips stretched into the biggest grin I'd seen on her face. She turned to Samaira and gave her a pleading look. "Can we please keep him?"

While Samaira gave her an exaggerated eye roll, I burst out laughing.

She instantly turned to me. "Don't you start too."

I quickly zipped my mouth shut and threw away the key, making her smile.

"Aw, she's got him whipped already," Sloane crooned. I had to clap my hand over my mouth to stifle the laughter that threatened to burst out at how red Samaira's face became.

Lena and Tara quickly got up, each grabbing one of Sloane's arms. "Alright. Let's go before Sami kills you."

They dragged her away. As they did, Sloane flashed us both a heart sign from behind Lena's and Tara's backs, and Samaira immediately threw her pen at her.

It felt like some teenage antics, but I loved how riled up Samaira got. I couldn't stop staring at her. Her tank top and those fucking shorts were driving me crazy, and if Sloane's teasing had even a hint of truth in it, I wanted to strut like a fool knowing that I was being teased with the hottest woman on the planet.

But because it seemed that Samaira was very much like a tigress—spooked quickly and turned angry even quicker—I didn't mention Sloane's teasing.

Silence ensued as Lena opened the trapdoor at the corner of the room and walked downstairs. I turned to Samaira. "How many more floors have you got downstairs?"

She cringed. "Forget you saw that."

"Alright."

"So you ready to become my assistant?" I asked, collecting the pictures of the suspects and stacking them.

She scoffed. "Fake assistant."

I closed the empty pizza box and collected the stray napkins. "Potato, potahto."

She shook her head in mock exasperation, but I definitely caught a hint of a smile in the small tilt of her lips. "Let me know the date and time of the appointments you get with Thomas Cooper and Brian Montgomery. Don't forget to talk to Sheila Bastion about the man she came with. And I'll keep you posted about Zarine Blackwood."

It seemed like our conversation had come to an end, and I was being booted out of the basement.

Every step we took toward the door leading to the bar upstairs felt like wading through cement. What was it about her that made me just want to keep talking to her, to prolong any moment we shared? Time seemed to race when she was with me, as if every moment was rushing by and all I could do was try to hang on to them tighter.

Her smile, her voice, just her mere presence seemed to keep my monsters at bay.

But Samaira had walls around her so thick, they made me want to chip and chip and chip at them until I knew every little thing about her. I wanted to know what made her become a Wildcat, where she came from, what her family did, if she had siblings, what made her happy, and what terrified her.

When we reached the door, it took me by surprise when she started climbing the steps right behind me. "You're going to the bar?" I asked, turning around to look at her.

She shook her head. "I do have a home, you know."

I ran my hands through my hair. *Get it together, Dominic.* "Um, of course. Would you like me to drop you off?"

She grabbed a helmet that hung beside the door and banged her knuckles twice on it. "I have my ride."

No fucking way.

The moment we set foot into the bar, a low hum of music engulfed us as conversations flowed around us freely. The bartender shouted at Sami, waving at her. Samaira gave her a big smile and waved her goodbye.

A few other patrons, especially some guys, yelled, "Yo, Big Sam," to which she gave a classic two-finger salute and a shout, "I'm watching you, Doug."

My gaze zeroed in on the douchebag who had the

audacity to call her Big Sam. As if she were his fucking dude bro. Something ugly churned in my gut as she smiled at the guy like they were friends. What was up with that exchange? And how many people knew her here?

"Who the fuck was that?" The words slipped from my mouth before I could stop them.

She gave me a cocky are-you-kidding-me look and grabbed a jacket from the receptionist, who also bid her a good night. I waited for her as she put it on before we stepped out of the bar into the crisp night air.

"That was Doug, one of our regulars," she said, taking a step in the opposite direction from where I'd parked my car.

"Why'd he call you Big Sam?"

She raised her eyebrows and then raised her arm, flexing her biceps. "You see these big guns? You meet a jacked, five-foot-nine woman who works as a bouncer in a club every day?"

I kept my eyes locked on her. "Never."

Her eyes softened, and she bit her lip as she stopped walking. She stared at me, her gaze moving to my lips, making my heart pound out of my chest. Blood roared through my veins at the desire I saw in her eyes. I took a step closer so I stood mere inches from her. Her breath came out in a rush as our eyes held.

Her fingers raised, and she lightly grazed the bottom of my lip, my breath freezing in my chest. That singular touch had my blood turning into an inferno. Every pore of my body yearned to pull her into my arms. But just as quickly, she pulled her fingers back and shook her head. "I don't mix business with pleasure, Dominic."

I met her eyes, the sharp sting of disappointment just as evident in her eyes as I knew it was in mine. Every logical thought about the consequences of kissing her evaporated from my mind as everything within me begged and screamed for just a touch. Just a taste. Just fucking once. I clenched my hands into fists, restraining myself from pulling her lips to mine, and whispered, "That would be disastrous."

She nodded, her gaze still stuck on my lips, her eyes burning with a dark storm of arousal. I held still, waiting for her to do something. *Anything.*

She stepped back. A rush of cool wind replaced the warmth of her presence, and disappointment churned in my gut like bitter acid. She took another step back, and one more, as she murmured, "Disastrous."

She then turned, put on her helmet, and climbed on her motorcycle—a Harley 883 Iron.

"I knew the sedan wasn't your vibe." My heart hammered in my chest as I looked at the woman who was pure sin and danger incarnate. She sat astride the black beast of a motorcycle as if it were an extension of her.

A wicked gleam shone in her eyes as she gave a loud chuckle. "Of course the sedan isn't my vibe." She caressed the engine of the bike—just the way she'd caressed my lips—scrambling my brain and making all my blood rush to my cock. She started the motorcycle, the rumbling roar of it fueling the crackling tension between us, making my cock weep. "Good night, Dominic."

"Good night, Tigress."

I stood there on the sidewalk, my hands jammed in my pockets as I watched her drive off, leaving my heart pumping and roaring with the kind of fire and passion and need I hadn't felt in a very long time.

CHAPTER 13

SAMAIRA

Dominic worked fast when it came to contacting the suspects. Considering his influence in the city and the number of investments the Park Real Estate Group made in the government, his words carried weight.

He secured appointments with both our suspects just two days after our meeting.

Our first appointment was with Brian Montgomery, the steel industrialist. I was meeting Dominic in the lobby of Montgomery Steel's office building at two o'clock. Since I would be pretending to be Dominic's assistant for the day, I wore a brown turtleneck blouse tucked into matching brown wide-leg pants, with pretty, lace-up, chunky office heels. My hair was tied in a professional ponytail. I'd removed all my jewelry except for the gold necklace that rested on my chest.

I looked extremely professional and exactly like someone who worked for a man like Dominic, if I do say so myself. Sloane had been hell-bent on making me wear a blouse and a pencil skirt, but I'd put my foot down. I loved dresses and skirts just as much as the next girl, but a pencil skirt showed off my legs a bit too well and didn't project the professional, innocent image I needed for the role.

The moment I entered the lobby, my gaze collided with Dominic's. He was back in his three-piece black suit and charcoal shirt, his hair styled so a single lock fell perfectly over his forehead, giving him a lethal edge. A dangerous aura seemed to swirl around him. The man was a personification of power and sex.

My heart took flight in my chest as his lips curled into a smile, his deep, lickable dimples popping on his cheeks. One day, I was going to eat those damn things for dessert. His eyes raked over me, starting from my eyes all the way to my heels, leaving sparks of electricity racing down my body.

"Hello, Samaira," he greeted me the moment I reached him.

"Dominic." I nodded at him. "Do I look the part of your assistant?"

"You look perfect." His eyes smoldered as they met mine. Time seemed to stop as I looked at him, the world around him becoming a blur as my eyes only saw him.

A loud ding of an elevator brought the world back into focus. "You ready?" I asked him.

He nodded and led us to the reception area, where he got us the guest passes.

I noticed the exit stairways on the west side of the lobby. Once we were in the elevator, he pushed the button for the top floor. As the elevator moved up, I stood beside him, his large presence and sinful cologne pushing my senses into overdrive. I wanted to step even closer to him and run my nose along his throat, lick his Adam's apple, and fucking drown in his scent. So I deliberately took a step away from him and said in a low voice, "Remember, we're only here for your business meeting. The party is just an afterthought. Do not lose your cool."

He simply nodded, his jaw clenched as he righted the shirt at his wrist.

The elevator dinged open to reveal a massive office space with another reception area on the side. The office was a bustling space with all-glass walls separating the different spaces. There was only one exit aside from the elevator.

A petite woman in a pretty, pink, knee-length dress led the way to Brian Montgomery's office. She opened the door for us as Dominic entered first, with me following. I could feel the way she looked at me, something between awe and fear. I gave her a quick smile as I entered the office, without waiting for her response.

The door shut right behind us as a man with a small potbelly sat behind the desk in a blue suit. He got up as we reached his desk and shook hands with Dominic. He sent a quick, dismissive glance my way but did a double take when he actually saw me, his eyes deliberately moving over me.

Dominic let out a sharp cough. "Brian, how are you?"

"Surprised to hear from you, actually," he said, taking a seat in his chair as we did the same.

I opened my handbag and pulled out a small iPad, ready to pretend to take notes. Dominic's gaze fell on the iPad as he talked to Brian about a project of his, but I could feel his amusement at my pretense.

I continued to take notes as Dominic and Brian discussed the bylaws and building codes that would affect the building, the steel quantities he would need, the demand and supply timelines, and so on. I remained silent, occasionally looking up between the two of them.

At one point, I "accidentally" dropped my iPad pencil. Both of them turned to look at me, and I waved my hand for them to continue. "Please continue. I'll just quickly grab the pencil."

I bent down to pick it up. As I straightened, I surreptitiously stuck a small recording device to the underside of his wooden desk. We could listen to the live audio feed through this device. It would also automatically upload the audio recordings to the cloud every hour.

We sat with him and talked for another half hour. As the meeting came to an end, Dominic said, "Oh, by the way, my father was at the gala for the Healing for Survivors charity and was hoping to meet you there. But he didn't see you."

Brian waved a hand. "Oh man, say hi to your father on my behalf. I had a meeting in Abu Dhabi and couldn't go. I gave the invitation card to my younger brother."

"Ah. Did he have a good time? I hear these gala events could get wild toward the end," Dominic said, his tone casual as he leaned back in the chair.

Even I stopped taking notes and pasted a polite smile on my face as if his answers meant absolutely nothing to me.

Brian guffawed. "Eh, he said the event was a dud. He'd taken two bombshells with him, so I think they left early to party at his bachelor pad."

My lips threatened to curl in disgust, but I kept the polite smile on my face as Brian winked at me.

Dominic was quick to pull Brian's eyes off me. "Yeah, I didn't go either. I'm not a big fan of these galas."

He glanced at his watch. "Anyway, I should be on my way. I have a meeting at four. Right, Daisy?"

It took me a second to realize he meant me, but I quickly looked up and nodded.

As soon as he rose, I was out of my seat too. After he and Brian shook hands, we left the office, walking side by side out of the building.

"Did you drive?" he asked, already typing something on his phone.

"Took the subway. Parking downtown is impossible."

"Right. We can just head to the senator's office together, then. I've texted Maxim that we're ready."

He started walking toward Park Avenue, and I hurried to keep pace. "By the way," I said. "Sloane is going to an exhibition next weekend. Zarine is going to be displaying her jewelry there."

"That's good. Let me know if she needs additional funds to catch Zarine's attention."

"Sloane doesn't need anything to catch anyone's attention. She's skilled at making people notice her."

He gave a soft chuckle at that. "I noticed. By the way, I also contacted Sheila Bastion. She said that the man she hired was from an escort agency. She also confirmed that he'd been by her side throughout the party."

"That's great. Could you ask her to send you the details of the agency and the guy she hired? I would like to have Tara confirm her story."

He gave me a small smile, his eyes shining with a hint of pride. And why did that just make my knees weak? "I'll give her a call."

A light breeze of wind blew some of his hair over his forehead, and my fingers ached with the need to push them over his head. I clenched my fingers into a fist, afraid they'd form a mind of their own. "Thank you. I really appreciate it."

I had barely finished my sentence when Dominic suddenly stopped walking. My body went fully alert, trying to figure out if there was a threat somewhere.

But I stopped breathing when he dropped down on his knees in front of me—hold the fucking reins—and started tying up the lace of my heels. When the hell did the lace get untied? And what the fuck was going on with my heart? Something extremely warm was exploding in my chest at the way Dominic's large hands were holding the thin, delicate laces of my heels in his fingers, uncaring of the fact that a crowd of people was passing by us. We were literally in the middle of a New York City sidewalk and getting dirty looks from people around us.

No, the man did not care about any of it.

His sole focus was on tying up the delicate lace of my

heels. My hand trembled with the need to run my fingers through his thick, lush hair. I tightened my hands into fists, my nails digging into my palms. My stomach was twisting and turning as if I had indigestion. But this wasn't an acidic burn. This was the glowing warmth of a million butterflies fluttering and taking flight in my stomach, making me feel as though I were flying. My heart was gushing, and my cheeks were on fire. Has anyone ever done something like that to me before?

When was the last time I felt this way? So soft on the inside, I feared all my organs had decided to melt out of my body, leaving me in a pile of goo in the middle of the sidewalk.

I felt…special. That was what this was.

His fingers barely brushed my heels, but just that minuscule touch reverberated through my bones. Every cell of my body screamed at me to grab his hair, pull his head up, and slam my lips against his.

As if Dominic Park hadn't just shifted my entire world on its axis, he casually rose from his knees and gave me his killer dimpled smile. "There you go. Can't have you stumbling on your lace."

My cheeks blazed, and for the first time in a long while, my words stumbled. "Uh…yeah. Uh…thanks."

Right then, an SUV stopped right in front of us. "That's us," Dominic said, opening the car door for me. I felt his hand hovering an inch away from the small of my back as I moved to get into the car. Every pore of my skin yearned to feel that large hand graze across my back, that tiny amount of distance seeming like a hundred miles.

The fact that he didn't just touch me, that he remembered the boundaries I'd set, that he respected my words, my wishes, just made me trust him even more. It made me want to *remove* all my boundaries for him and give him the right to take that liberty with me.

I was in so much trouble with this man.

With a quick thank you, I climbed into the car, the car behind us honking like a menace, having absolutely no manners or patience. Dominic quickly got in behind me, and we were on the move as soon as he shut the door.

The moment we hit the first stoplight, Dominic turned to his driver. "Maxim, meet Samaira. Samaira, that's Maxim."

"Please to meet you, ma'am," Maxim said, turning back to look at me.

I gave him a quick smile. "Likewise. And please, call me Samaira."

Once the traffic light turned green, we were on the move. I'd never sat in the back seat of a car with a man like Dominic before. Sex and sin swirled around in the air between us, the heat radiating off him warming my arm close to him. Even the car smelled just like his cologne.

"Did you actually bug Brian Montgomery's office?" Dominic asked, breaking the silence and managing to pull me away from my horny thoughts.

My face broke into a wide smile as I gave him a happy nod. I loved listening in to people's secrets, especially when it came to powerful men with low morals. "And I'll also bug the state attorney's office."

He gave me a wicked smile in return. "Good girl." A breathy gasp escaped my chest. Those two words. Two fucking words spoken with so much genuine pride in his voice for me that I wanted to melt on his seat. Blood flowed like lava through my veins as I pressed my legs together to relieve some of the pounding ache in my core.

A rough squeak rushed out of me. "Uh…Thanks."

This was so not part of the plan. He wasn't supposed to say things like that. *I* wasn't supposed to be affected by his words. He was my client. Nothing more. I had to stay within a professional fucking boundary. The man was paying us fifty fucking million dollars. I couldn't mess this case up, no matter how badly I wanted to climb on his lap and claim his fucking lips.

I was in the middle of hyperventilating from his proximity and his scent when the car slowed to a stop.

"That's us," Dominic said, who'd surprisingly stayed quiet and busy on his phone after dropping those two panty-melting, mind-bending words.

I tightened my ponytail and pulled myself together. After exiting the car, we followed protocols similar to the last building, making our way through the lobby to the state attorney's office.

The moment we stepped into his office, Dominic shook Thomas Cooper's hand and then introduced me. Unlike Brian, Thomas extended his hand to me. He appeared to be in his sixties, with graying hair and a receding hairline.

As he shook my hand, he turned to Dominic. "Is she your assistant or your bodyguard, Dominic?" he boomed, laughing as if he'd made the most original joke in the world.

Before Dominic could respond, I tightened my grip slightly and offered Thomas a sharp smile. "What good is an assistant if she can't protect her boss?"

He let out an uproarious laugh, patting my hand. "Well said, my dear."

Ugh. I wanted to wash my hands.

Once we were seated in front of him, I took out my iPad and the tiny recorder, hiding it in my hands as I started to take notes. Thomas Cooper Sr. was a large man, his belly protruding from his suit. He knew he was powerful, and it showed in the way he took a few seconds before answering any questions that Dominic asked.

Again, I dropped my iPad pencil while taking notes and stuck the recording device under his desk.

When the meeting concluded, Dominic once again brought up his dad and asked, "Mr. Cooper, my father was hoping to meet you at the gala that happened around four months ago. Now that he's retired, those are the only events he prefers to attend. But he didn't see you there."

Something minuscule shifted in Thomas's eyes. "Oh, uh, I didn't go to the gala. Who has time for such nonsense?"

He did not volunteer any information on who went on his behalf.

"Oh really?" Dominic asked, acting genuinely surprised, showing a hint of worry and confusion in his tone as he continued, "I was talking to Anthony, the organizer of the gala, and he mentioned your invitation being scanned. You know how he is. Always boasting about the influential people attending his events."

"He said that?" Thomas asked.

When Dominic nodded, looking genuinely confused, Thomas gave something between a scoff and a chuckle. "Ah, my son went in my place. Since it was a masked event, I figured there wouldn't be much conversation anyway. Tommy offered to go, and I told him, 'Better you than me, son.'"

He chuckled again, grating my insides.

Dominic waved off his answer with a smile, acting as if he couldn't be bothered one way or another, and stood, buttoning up his suit. "Never mind. You should visit our place in Connecticut. Catch up with Father. He might be retired, but he isn't out of new project ideas if you know what I mean."

Thomas's eyes gleamed as he shook hands with Dominic. "Of course. Let's set something up soon."

We were out of the office and in the car in under five minutes. Once Maxim got the car on the road, Dominic turned to me. "You got the recorder set up properly?"

I nodded. "Yep. The device uploads the recordings every hour. I'll start going through whatever we gather tomorrow."

Before Dominic could say something, Maxim jumped in. "Miss Samaira, where do I drop you?"

"Thunder Claw, please."

He gave a quick nod and took the next turn to the right.

When I looked back at Dominic, he asked, "Did something seem off about Thomas? I got a different vibe from him than Brian."

"Yep, I felt the same way. Brian was just obnoxious, whereas Thomas actually seemed to think before speaking. Still, I wonder…if his son *was* the culprit, why would Thomas offer up his name as the one who attended the party? Wouldn't he try to hide that? If this Tommy actually raped Sophie, surely he thinks you were trying to figure something out, wouldn't he?"

"Maybe he's trying to appear nonchalant. Perhaps he thought that by giving out his son's name, I would find him innocent. Maybe he's trying to apply reverse psychology on us."

"Maybe," I said, still in thought. "We'll figure it out soon enough. Men like these often tend to take care of personal business in their offices themselves. It's that ego that always fails them. One minor indication in the recording, one tiny slip of a word, and we'll be one step closer."

His fist clenched on his thigh, a low rumble vibrating in his chest. "You have *no* idea what I'm going to do to those bastards."

The raw violence radiating from him sent a thrill through me, my blood pounding and pulse accelerating. The predatory gleam in his eyes had my mouth watering. "Oh, I have *some* idea."

His ruthless smile met mine, and he nodded in understanding. "So what's your plan for today aside from going through these recordings?"

I tightened my ponytail, breaking eye contact. "Oh, I'm not going over the recordings today. I have another assignment with my girls."

"Anything I can help with?" he asked. I thought he was just being perfunctory, but when I looked at him, the honesty on his face took me by surprise. Why would he want to help with someone else's problems?

"I don't think so." I genuinely had no idea how he could be of help, aside from pouring money into our accounts, which he was already doing.

When the car stopped at Thunder Claw, Dominic stepped out, ever the gentleman. We stood facing each other, the sensible part of my mind screaming at me to step back, to bid him goodbye. But the naughty, reckless, obsessed part of my mind pushed that sensible part aside, taking complete control over my mouth. "You wanna come watch?"

Blood rushed to my cheeks as warning bells started ringing in my brain, the sensible part of my mind bellowing at me to take back my words. But to my utter relief—and shock—Dominic did not hesitate for even a second. "Yes."

My face broke out in a stupid smile as my naughty brain danced around in manic glee, thinking of all the ways we were going to show him my raw power, my ruthlessness, my violence. The sensible part of me was downright panicking at the thought of the four Wildcats who were going to bust my balls at seeing Dominic by my side at the safe house.

At the fucking *safe house*. Safe. Fucking. House.

Fuck my life.

Fuck my idiotic brain.

Fuck Dominic Park and his stupidly handsome face, his charming smile, his fucking dimples, his warm eyes, and his stupid, sinful suits.

On second thought…Do. Not. Fuck. Dominic. Park.

CHAPTER 14

DOMINIC

Samaira had been driving us out of the city for about an hour in her sedan. By now, we were far enough outside New York City that I hadn't seen another car for over half an hour. With every turn she took, we moved deeper and deeper into what felt like a dense forest. The road had turned to dirt, flanked by trees on both sides—so close that branches scraped across the windshield and scratched against the car's sides.

It was so lush I couldn't see anything in the side-view mirror except for the dense growth of trees and the rays of the setting sun glimmering through them.

When Samaira asked me if I wanted to watch her on a mission, I'd been equally surprised and elated. To watch this woman do *anything* felt like a treat in itself. I'd have agreed if she'd asked me to come watch her file her taxes.

But watching her work? I wouldn't have missed it for the world.

I'd said yes to her before she could even blink. Before she could rethink her offer and retract it. I had sent away Maxim before she'd even turned around to walk to that ugly sedan of hers.

With the way she kept glancing my way and pursing her lips, I was pretty sure she was rethinking her decision. "You think your friends will be mad at you for bringing me along with you?" I asked her, wondering if she might be worried about that.

Her eyes flashed at me for a second before she turned her gaze back to the road. She shook her head with an arrogant smile. "Nobody gets mad at me, Dominic. They'll be surprised, for sure."

"Because you haven't brought a man to your safe house before?" I asked, prodding the beast.

"*Nobody* has brought a man to our safe house before. It's too risky, and none of us trust men enough to show them our back, let alone something that could destroy everything."

The gravity of her action was starting to dawn on me, and I felt compelled to reassure her. "I promise, I would never speak a word of it to anyone. Wildcats' secrets, locations, existence, everything is safe with me."

She looked at me with a genuine smile and nodded. "I know. For some reason, my mind has decided to put my trust in you. So don't make me regret it because neither of us would like it if you do."

A sliver of fear and danger slithered down my spine, making me hard as a rock at the warning in her tone. Something was insanely attractive about the way she threatened me. Her threats, her words, her warning seemed to wrap around my cock and squeeze it to the point of losing my sanity. I took in a deep breath to tamp down the roaring arousal I felt in her vicinity. "I won't."

Her lips curled in an excited smile as she banged on the steering wheel twice. "Great. Now, let's have some fun."

With that, she turned a corner. The dirt road and the trees opened up to a large, two-story house, surrounded by about a hundred yards of open space, with trees sprawling across the area. Four cars lined the parking space toward one side of the house. Two of them were huge trucks, one was a large van, whereas the last one was a smaller sedan. We parked our car right beside it and got out.

Just as we reached the entrance of the house, the main door burst open and a large black form jumped on me, almost pushing me to the ground.

"Shadow," Samaira screamed. "Down, boy. He's a friend."

The huge figure was pulled off me, its growling sound chilling me to my core, only to discover that it was a large, muscular Doberman, currently trying to get out of Samaira's hold on its leash.

"Tara, you need to come get your child," Samaira shouted.

She looked at me as she tightly held the leash of the giant dog currently eyeing me like a piece of meat. I usually loved dogs, and I was sure I could befriend him. I was gonna have to bring some treats with me next time.

I was about to extend my hand to let him sniff me when Tara, dressed in all-black tactical gear—just the way I'd seen the Wildcats dressed the day I met them for the first time— came rushing to the door, half of her face covered by a mask. She grabbed the leash from Samaira. "You're late. Where have you been?"

Her voice tapered off the moment her eyes fell on me. Her lips curled into a teasing smile, and with her eyes trained on Samaira, she shouted, "Lena, look who's here."

Samaira grumbled low in her throat, "Watch it, Tara."

She gave Samaira a delightful smile and turned around. "C'mon, Shadow baby, let's go."

Samaira led the way inside the house as I followed her, taking it all in. The entrance was like any other two-story house, with a small foyer and a staircase going up, and two rooms on either side of the foyer.

The moment Samaira turned to the room on the right, my feet froze on the spot.

Rows of large machine guns hung on one wall, another row of large, deadly knives and axes directly underneath the guns. All the Wildcats, except Samaira, stood around a large wooden table, their eyes trained on us.

I met each of their eyes and gave them a small smile. "Ladies. Good evening."

Sloane, with her pink hair tied in a braid, snorted loudly.

All four women turned their heads to look directly at Samaira, who actively avoided eye contact with them. Instead, she walked to the large lockers lined along the opposite wall and started pulling out her gear. When her ignoring didn't work and all four ladies kept staring at her, she turned around with her gear in hand and huffed. "He was curious to see what we did and wanted to come along. Stop acting strange."

I absolutely did not tell them that it was Samaira who had offered to let me join them.

Lena gave me a quick smile and, with a sass that only a leader of the group could exude, looked at Samaira. "Oh, didn't know *we* were the ones acting strange."

Samaira muttered something under her breath and turned to me. "Make yourself comfortable. I'll be back in a bit."

Before I could respond, she turned and ran to another room, disappearing out of my sight.

Sloane, also dressed in her gear, walked over to me, holding a pink-and-black cheetah mask. "Dominic, how was your interrogation with Thomas and Brian today?"

"Pretty productive. Samaira installed the recording devices under their desks, so we should be able to listen to them. Big job today?" I asked her, looking around at the way all four of them were ready.

She gave a tiny shrug. "Not too big. Pick up a guy, torture him, get a confession. Easy peasy. You coming with us?"

"To kidnap a man? Sure," I replied.

"Absolutely not." Samaira cut in simultaneously.

My attention snapped to her, and all coherent thoughts left my brain. She stood there in all-black tactical gear, the material clinging to the hard lines of her muscles. Black leather gloves covered her hands, and my mind instantly flashed an image—those gloved hands working my cock. My heart hammered against my ribs as arousal surged, a hot tide rushing through blood and muscle, tingling along my skin, as she moved closer. Raw power and strength radiated from her. She was a tigress, poised to hunt.

"Isn't that why you brought him here? To join us on our mission?" Sloane asked, shattering the spell Samaira held over my thoughts and my body.

I pointed my thumb at Sloane and looked at Samaira. "What she said."

Samaira stood between the two of us, her arms folded across her chest. "No. I brought him *here* so he could watch us handle our operation from *here*, with Naomi and Lena. He could stay and watch us get the confession from the two scumbags. He doesn't need to join us in the kidnapping. He's a public figure."

"C'mon, let me join you guys. I could stay in the car and be the lookout," I argued.

A deep V formed between Samaira's eyebrows. "Sloane is going to be our lookout."

"Even better. I can stay with Sloane."

Sloane instantly piped in, "I don't mind the company."

Samaira turned to Lena, who was watching us argue.

Lena raised both of her hands. "He's your guest. It's your call."

"You'll distract me," she said, turning to me.

"How?"

"I'll be worried about you."

I bit my lip—hard—to stop the idiotic smile from

surfacing on my lips. I was almost forty, dammit. A woman being worried about me shouldn't please me so much.

"I'll stay in the car and not even talk to Sloane. You won't even know I'm there."

"Oh, I'll know."

I was ready to beg more, but she sighed. "Fine. You can come with us."

Then she turned to Sloane and looked at her with such authority that my blood turned to molten lava. "Not one scratch on him."

Even Sloane lost the gleeful smile she had on her face. "I promise, Sami."

Samaira nodded and turned to walk to her locker. My eyes were hooked on her as she opened the locker and pulled out—no way—another mask just like hers. I heard a sharp intake of breath beside me, but all my attention was focused on the tigress walking toward me, a determined look on her face and fierce protectiveness gleaming in her eyes.

Nobody had ever been protective of me before. I'd always been the protector of the family. The way Samaira looked at me, as if she would hate if something were to happen to me, tightened something in my chest.

She stood in front of me and held out a black-and-crimson tiger mask to me. "Wear it during the mission. We don't want anyone to catch your face."

As I took it, my fingers brushed against hers, leaving behind electric sparks where we touched. Her eyes darkened, a dark red flush rising to her cheeks. I loved that my touch affected her as well, because the slightest touch from her shot ecstasy through my veins.

She cleared her throat, gazing around at the others. "Everyone ready?"

The atmosphere shifted. The women's expressions hardened as they formed a huddle around Samaira. Banging their masks together in the center with a sharp clap, they shouted, "Go Wildcats."

While Naomi and Lena stayed at the safe house, I walked out, following Samaira and Tara, with Sloane right behind me. Sloane climbed into the driver's seat while the three of us climbed into the back of the van, taking a seat on the bench seats. Samaira and I were on one side, whereas Tara sat across from us.

"Remember, Sami, no playing around. We have only one target. We knock him out and carry him to the van. I'll knock him out. You carry him. Quick and easy."

Samaira rolled her eyes. "Fine," she said and looked at me with excitement in her eyes. "The interrogation is more my jam."

Tara scoffed and turned to me. "You're in for a treat."

We drove out of the woods, passing through several small towns I didn't recognize. Sloane navigated the van and parked it behind an abandoned warehouse. By then, the sun had set, and it was nearly dark.

She climbed over the front seats and into the back of the van, then turned on the monitoring screens. Then she retrieved a drone from a suitcase and launched it out of an open window. The drone made very little noise as she guided it remotely. Activating the small screens mounted overhead, she instantly brought up the drone's video feed.

As Sloane worked the drone, Samaira and Tara pulled on their masks. They looked like superheroes come to life. My heart pounded erratically in my chest, knowing that I was in the middle of a kidnapping mission. Samaira knocked on the mask that I still held in my hand, demanding I put it on. Not wanting to argue—and secretly wanting to match her—I put the mask on.

"Crimson Tiger, Shadow Panther. You're good to go."

"Go get 'em, Tiger." The words slipped out of my mouth, making her pause, her hand clutching the door latch. She turned around, her eyes shining from behind her mask, and she gave me a quick salute.

"Subtle," Sloane muttered right beside me in a low enough volume so Samaira couldn't hear.

"Save it," I muttered back, making her chuckle.

They opened the van's door and jumped down, quietly closing it behind them. My eyes followed Samaira's retreating form until it disappeared when she climbed over a fence, Shadow Panther right behind her.

Turning quickly to Sloane's monitor, I watched them move through the trees separating the various houses spread throughout the area.

"What did this guy do?" I asked as we watched them. They were as agile as cats as they climbed over fences, jumped on trees, and kept making their way.

"The guy was already beating his wife. He's started to beat and burn their daughter. The wife asked us to take him out."

Now, I definitely didn't feel bad for kidnapping the guy. He deserved it, and I was going to relish every moment of torture that Samaira doled out to him.

I stayed quiet as the women reached what looked to be a small house. Samaira seemed to have hidden in a tree, whereas Tara seemed to be checking the perimeter of the property. My heart was in my throat as I watched the two women in action.

Beside me, Sloane kept a live commentary going, letting them know when their way was clear or if a resident was out and about somewhere. Tara made some movements and noise outside the house, causing a man to open the door to his backyard. It didn't take more than five seconds for her to knock the guy out. He didn't even stand a fighting chance.

Upon Sloane's go-ahead, Samaira jumped down from the tree and ran to Tara. My body automatically moved closer to the screen as my leg kept bouncing. She easily lifted the guy on her shoulder, her muscles bunching, while Sloane guided them out of the property through a different way. Once she'd given them instructions, she quickly climbed into the front of the van, and we were on our way.

We made a few turns around the empty streets and parked under a cluster of lush trees. In the next few minutes, the van door slammed open, and Samaira dropped the unconscious guy at my feet. The moment my eyes met Samaira's, and I saw that she was unharmed, I felt like I could finally breathe again. Once Samaira and Tara climbed in, we were on the move.

"You good?" I asked Samaira, who sat right beside me, the heat exuding from her body bringing me the kind of comfort I wouldn't feel in the middle of a kidnapping.

Her masked face turned to mine. "Of course. That went perfectly. You ready for the next part?"

"Absolutely."

Except my jaw was at my feet as I watched Samaira lift the two-hundred-and-fifty-pound man and slam him on the floor, his groans echoing in the basement of their safe house.

I stood outside the *torture room*—basically, a large cage—in the basement, watching Samaira "interrogate" the sobbing man. With every punch, she broke the guy's teeth. Every kick made him scream. My body thrummed with adrenaline and need as I watched her muscles bunch and contract as she viciously punished the man.

My stomach clenched as she pulled out every single fingernail from his hands without hesitation. The sheer beauty in her violence riveted me as she relentlessly tortured the guy until he started to confess.

"Yes, I beat my wife. I promise I won't do it again."

"No, I don't have a job."

"HELP!! Someone, help me!"

"She needed to learn her place."

"Who are you?"

"Yes, I did threaten to burn my daughter with cigarettes."

Blood sprayed over her mask as she punched him in the face. Something inside me turned feral at her ruthlessness. Her gloved hands dripped with blood from where she held the man's bleeding jaw, shaking him to get him to confess every sordid, horrifying act in detail. My blood boiled with every sick act he revealed, vindication thrumming through my veins at the punishing blows that Samaira dealt the man. She was a monster come to life, making the man bleed and suffer for his atrocities.

But she felt very much like *my* monster. I desperately wanted to feel those unforgiving, powerful hands around my cock.

She was the goddess of death, delivering her justice to the worst of humanity. I wanted to pray at her altar, fall on my knees, worship her till all her rage, all her violence seeped out of her. My cock throbbed in my pants as she slammed her knee on his back, making him howl in pain.

My eyes were glued to her when I felt a presence beside me.

"You might want to look away for what comes next. She's at the end of her torture," Tara said, standing beside me.

"I need to watch the kind of justice the tigress will dole out for my sister."

I didn't move my eyes away from Samaira even for a second—not even to blink—as she removed her mask and spat on him. I realized I was smiling as arousal was roaring and thrashing through my body like a wild beast trapped in a cage.

"She only removes her mask if she's going to kill the man," Tara said.

My hand tightened into a fist, my heart hammering with adrenaline, my mind throwing questions at me I had no answers to. How many people had she killed? Did she get affected by these kills? Did she relish them, or was it a chore?

Samaira pulled out her knife, grabbed the tiny dick of the squealing man lying in his own piss and blood, and chopped it right off in one single slice. Goose bumps broke out along my spine as she climbed over him, stuffed the dick in his mouth, and sliced his neck in another swift move as the man gurgled to death.

She got up and turned around. Her face stretched into a feral, victorious smile—a smile so bloody, so fucking beautiful —I couldn't help but smile myself. I'd never seen her smile so wide before. Not even when we were sparring or when I'd gotten her that pizza.

She walked out of the cage to come face-to-face with Tara and me.

With her gaze locked on mine, she said, "Tara, he's all yours. Get rid of the body. Sorry I didn't save him for you."

Tara chuckled. "I knew you wouldn't, especially today."

With that, Tara stepped inside the cage, leaving just the two of us. Samaira stood there, dripping blood, sweat plastering her unruly hair to her face, that wide, manic smile still in place. She took a step closer, and my cock wept in my pants, aching to get closer still. "You watched it all, huh?"

I took a step toward her, the metallic scent of blood thick in the air around us. "Didn't even blink."

She chuckled, closing the remaining distance. "Didn't scare you, did I?"

I mirrored her movement until our chests brushed, the heat radiating from her enveloping me, her brown eyes dilated, almost black with adrenaline and the residual violence. "I'd marry you right now."

A loud laugh burst from her chest, and I was utterly lost. She was a total paradox with her blood-soaked clothes. Sweat and blood dripped down her cheeks, yet a delighted smile lit up her face, her eyes twinkling with the purest of innocence. I wanted to drown in her, push her against the wall and feel her wrap around me, wanted her to sit on my face and squeeze my throat with her thighs. There was no question about it. I was maddeningly obsessed and violently attracted to every ruthless inch of Crimson Tiger.

"I'll wash up, and we'll get out of here."

I simply nodded at her as she walked past me, her finger softly grazing against mine, leaving a hint of blood and electricity in its wake.

I walked back into the room upstairs where Lena and Sloane were sitting, having a drink.

"You alright, Dominic?" Lena asked, a kind—almost motherly—smile on her face.

"Was it your first time watching a man get killed?" Sloane asked, getting Lena to scowl at her.

I turned to both and answered, "Yes," and "Yes," to each of them. "It was my first time but not the last time watching a man get killed. Men like that fucker need to be put down."

"That they do," Lena said, sipping her drink.

"By the way, what would happen to the woman and the daughter he left behind? Would they be okay? Do they need any funds?"

Lena gave me a small smile. "That's kind of you. But they're both taken care of. They've been moved out of the house just tonight and into an apartment in Brooklyn. And we've received ten million dollars for your initial payment. Believe me, that's going to go a long way."

"Trust me. It's not nearly enough for finding the culprits of my sister."

Right then, Samaira walked in from behind me in a loose pair of sweatpants and a white tank top, her hair wet from the shower. She stood right beside me, the smell of fresh oranges in a summer garden flooding my senses. I wanted to press my lips to the side of her neck and bask in her delicious scent. Her arm grazed mine, and heat flooded down my body. Her lips were stretched in a wide smile, her eyes still holding that adrenaline-fueled excitement. "We would've done it for free."

I shook my head. "The only way I can help your organization is by providing funds. Be it for my sister or anyone else. Consider me your bank for life."

Sloane had just opened her mouth to say something, but Samaira beat her to it. "Let's go, Dominic. Before Sloane starts robbing you." She looked at the ladies next. "You all good? Need me for anything?"

"We've got it. You rest up now," Lena said, waving us off.

We were quiet as we got into her sedan, and she started driving us back to the main road. The air in the car was charged with something potent, something on the edge of volatile that made me want to brace for impact. Samaira's hands squeezed the steering wheel so tightly, her knuckles had gone white.

My own skin was stretched too tight. The adrenaline from the mission, the high from watching Samaira kill a man, the vision of her bathed in blood and sweat, the power still pouring out in waves from every pore of her body, had my cock pounding in my pants.

I wanted to devour her, wanted to make her submit in the bedroom. My jaw ached with the need to take a bite at her throat and feel all her strength underneath me, around me, molding into me.

I turned in the seat so I sat facing her, my throat dry, and my heart racing in a gallop.

"You're staring," she said, her voice a breathy whisper.

"Tell me to stop." I didn't think I could even if she did. But something told me she enjoyed having my eyes fixated on her, relished in being admired, and being the center of my obsession.

A wicked smile crossed her lips, her face shaking back and forth. "That fucking mouth of yours. You have no idea what you're dealing with right now."

Her tongue swiped across her lower lip as she kept her eyes on the road. Her chest rose and fell with how heavy she was breathing.

"How do you feel after killing a man?"

Her eyes met mine for a brief second, and I found dark pools of hunger and bloodlust and adrenaline coursing through them. She wanted to devour and *feast*. My own body responded in kind; the need to consume her coursed through my veins and hammered from deep inside my skin, begging to be let out, yearning for a taste.

She cleared her throat, as if it were too difficult to form words right now. "I feel like the judge, jury, and the executioner. To take a person's life, especially the life of a creature so vile and monstrous, I feel like a god. I feel like I'm flying on the highest of the highs."

My voice was scratchy when I asked, "And what do you do to get down from this high?"

Her lips turned into a smile. She bit her lip, and I wanted to suck that little dent her teeth made on her lip. My cock was weeping, precum sliding down my erection, making me dizzy with the way I ached for her.

She shook her head, tapping her fingers on the steering wheel. "That's need-to-know information." Her gaze turned to me, and her eyes were talking to me in a very different language than her words. "And *you* don't need to know the information, Mr. Dominic Park, my client."

"What if I were Dominic, your friend?"

A chuckle escaped her lips, the sound a welcome reprieve from the electric intensity thrumming between us. "Are you? My friend, Dominic?"

My mind screamed a big, fat no. If only she could read my thoughts or feel my cock right now. I turned to her and, with a voice like gravel, said, "Definitely not, Samaira. I'm not your friend. Not even a little bit."

By the blush coating her cheeks and the smile playing on her lips, I'd bet my entire empire on the fact that she really liked not being my friend.

CHAPTER 15

SAMAIRA

I parked the car at the side of Thunder Claw, and the silence that ensued was deafening. My heart pounded in my chest, and the adrenaline coursing through my veins had me teetering on the sharpest edge. I was on the verge of slamming Dominic against the window of the car and jamming my tongue down his throat.

The fact that he was a public figure, that he was my client, that he could very well be my ruin, seemed entirely inconsequential right now. All I wanted, all I *needed*, was his rock-hard body rubbing against mine. To feel his cock stretching me and fucking out the high of killing a man.

The high of killing a despicable piece of human garbage was otherworldly. It was sharper than any drug that I'd tried. The effects of it lasted for days. With each kill, the high got sharper and easier to manage. I knew what I needed.

A stiff drink, a rough fuck, and a warm bath. In that fucking order.

I knew I could find the first two things at Thunder Claw. I always did.

But today, my body wasn't craving an anonymous, rough fuck. It was the man sitting beside me with an aura of danger and sin, wrapped in a suit that had me soaking my panties.

You cannot fuck him. He could put the Wildcats at risk. He could make you fall for him. He could destroy you.

Despite the warning bells ringing in my head, my heart was one stubborn, horny bitch in heat. My fingers tightened around the steering wheel as I met Dominic's eyes. "Do you wanna grab a drink?"

"Yes." His answer was immediate, as if he were waiting for the offer.

He quickly unbuckled his seat belt and got out of the car.

"Fuck me," I said in the empty car, knowing damn well I was screwing myself over this man.

With a defeated sigh—even though my heart was downright fluttering like a hummingbird—I climbed out of the car.

We stepped into the bar, and instantly, the soft music and the chattering of the patrons engulfed us. Thunder Claw wasn't a dance bar. It was a place where people came to catch up with friends or drink in peace.

I made my way to the bar, needing that stiff drink to get myself under control. I could feel Dominic's eyes trailing down my body as he stayed right at my back. My body was floating on the highest of highs, arousal and excitement roaring through my blood.

My hands tightened into fists as I tried to gain back some sense of control over my senses. As soon as I took a seat at the bar, Dominic sat on the barstool beside me, his sinful scent of amber and sandalwood flooding my nose. His warm presence beside me was overwhelming and comforting, making me want to curl up in his arms and also run away screaming and hide under my blanket.

Zoey approached me from across the bar. "Hey, Samaira, what would you like to have?"

"A Negroni for me."

She turned to Dominic. "And you, sir?"

I turned to find Dominic's unwavering gaze stuck on me. He gave Zoey a glance. "Whatever she's having."

Zoey got a twinkle in her eyes, the same as the Wildcats got every time Dominic was near me. I shook my head and turned in my stool so I sat facing him. He mirrored my stance, and the proximity of his legs to mine was minuscule. If he really wanted to, he could've enclosed my legs between his. But he didn't.

And the urge to feel his body against mine was downright maddening. I fucking yearned to close the tiny little gap between us, but I didn't. The fact that the man hadn't touched me *once*—even accidentally—ever since I'd slammed him on his back was as frustrating as it was arousing.

The more he kept his distance, the more I wanted to close it.

"What are you thinking, Samaira?" Dominic's voice was a gravelly rumble, and it made me want to purr. His eyes were as dark as thunderous clouds, and the crackling heat in them had my heart pounding.

I shook my head. "You don't want to know."

His hand on the bar top moved closer to mine, his fingers clenching tight as if he was stopping himself from covering my hands. His eyes were a storm of need and arousal as he looked at me with so much desperation. "Believe me, I do."

Right then, our drinks arrived, and I was saved by Zoey.

He raised his glass to toast. "To powerful women saving the world."

If I hadn't been ready to worship his cock before, I was now. I clinked against his glass. "Cheers."

The first cool, bitter sip of the drink burned down my throat. I chugged the whole glass down, and fire danced in my blood. Dominic's eyebrows were up to his forehead, his glass still almost full. "Thirsty much?"

Without moving my gaze away from him, I swallowed the last sip. "Very."

He took a sip of his own drink and handed me his half-full glass. "You want mine?"

Arousal pooled low in my belly, and I could feel the wetness coating my pussy. The need to push my fingers in my core to relieve the ache sharpened to a painful extent. I clutched the glass he was offering, lightly grazing my fingers against his, and took it from his grasp.

His breath hitched, and he bit his lip. His chest heaved as he kept his gaze trained on me and watched me sip his drink from the same spot where his lips had touched. He straightened on his chair and leaned toward me. "You're playing a dangerous game, Tigress."

I handed him his glass back, keeping my eyes trained on him. "Am I?"

He *did not* touch his fingers to mine when he took the glass back. Like me, he drank from the same spot I did. My gaze moved lower, and the evidence of how much our dangerous little game was exciting him was very, very hard to miss. I bit my lip and watched his Adam's apple bob as he swallowed the drink. "Delicious."

I needed to pull myself off the horny train. Stat. "Tell me something that makes you angry."

That should make me focus on things to get angry about.

His brows scrunched into a frown. "You want to know what makes me angry?"

I nodded, ending our little game of kissing on the glass—because that's exactly what we were doing.

Dominic shook his head and gave a soft chuckle, probably at the abrupt change in direction. He gulped down the remaining drink and met my eyes, his own shining with amusement. "Let's see," he hummed. "Hmm. Incompetence. Yes. Incompetence makes me angry."

He looked like someone who needed things done right. I

nodded at him and was about to think of something else when he continued, "Also, dishonesty. I'd definitely take a bitter truth over a sweet lie. Laziness annoys me too. Don't forget tardiness."

Well, would you look at that? Dominic had a list. He placed his empty glass on the bar top, and boy, he was getting comfortable. His eyes were lost in thought as if trying to recount *everything* that made him angry. "Hmm. People who walk slowly on the sidewalk. Hate them."

He literally had stopped in the middle of the sidewalk to tie the laces of my heels.

I bit my lip to hide my smile, nodding along, as he continued, "Don't even get me started on people asking to borrow shit from me. Especially Kai. I buy myself stuff because *I* want it. Not so you can borrow it and never return it. Or worse, return it in a worse condition."

"Who's this Kai, again?"

He rolled his eyes, but a fond smile stretched across his face. "He's my maternal aunt's son, and also my office manager at work. He's about ten years younger than me and is an absolute menace."

"Seems like you love him."

A twinkle lit up his eye as he ran his hand through his hair. "He's not so bad. He's been managing the office pretty well in my absence. Don't tell him, but I'd actually be lost without him."

Fucking hell. How was I even more turned on by this man than before? The only thing that could probably stop my gigantic crush on this man was scooping out my eyes. Considering the man had a voice that made my panties melt, I'd have to shoot my head off to get rid of this massively irritating obsession.

Dominic looked at me with such puppy-dog eyes and a shy smile. I couldn't help but play along and give him a wink, enacting the motion of zipping my mouth shut. "My lips are sealed."

"Can I ask you something?" His face turned serious.

"Sure."

Zoey came at that time and replenished our drinks.

Dominic took a sip of his drink and asked, "Who was your first kill?"

That was one way to crash my adrenaline and spike my anger, all at the same time. I took a sip of my drink. "Pass. Ask me something else."

He gave me a kind, understanding smile. "Alright. Do you enjoy killing men?"

The memory of killing a man, of taking a life, was still very fresh in my mind. I shrugged. "The act of killing itself doesn't bring me any joy. But knowing that by killing those monsters, a woman could finally be free of the abuse, finally get the vengeance she deserved, could finally shed that constant anxiety and panic, that she could finally start living, that brings me joy. I'd kill those monsters a thousand times if a woman got to live the life she wanted. No regrets."

He raised his glass in another toast at that. "To keeping women safe."

I raised mine in return. "To eliminating the monsters who endanger them."

We sipped our drinks in silence for a while after that. I knew I wasn't getting any fucking today, rough or otherwise. So I'd have to make do with booze and a bath. I finally started to feel my adrenaline slowly leaving my system after two more drinks. The alcohol finally started to spread that pleasant buzz through my body, relaxing me and loosening my muscles.

"You wanna get out of here?" Dominic asked.

I gave him a wide smile. He looked so adorable with his face scrunched up like that. "Aw, I'd love to. But remember what I told you? I don't mix pleasure with business."

He snorted. "Yep. Remember it very clearly. But that's not what I meant. You're drunk. I'll drop you off at home."

"That's probably a good idea. Let me ask Zoey to put everything on my tab." I should head home before I get too drunk to even walk.

"I already paid the tab. Maxim is waiting outside."

I clutched my heart, totally impressed by his take-charge attitude. "You've thought of everything, huh?"

A laugh escaped him, and those sexy-as-sin dimples popped on his cheeks. And I fucking couldn't resist. I leaned forward and pressed my fingertips into both. They were so soft, my heart gave a sharp ache in my chest. Every pore of my body urged me to lean forward even more and lick those damn things up. "I love these," I crooned.

His chest heaved, and a loud groan vibrated in his chest. "Dammit. I hate myself right now." With that, he took a step back and led me out of the bar.

He held the car door open as I climbed in, only to find Maxim in the driver's seat. "Hey, Maxim. How are you doing?"

He gave me an amused smile. "Samaira. I'm good. You?"

"Fucking great. I feel great."

Once Dominic closed the door behind him, they both looked at me. "What?"

"What's your address, baby?"

Aw, he called me baby.

Dominic chuckled, exposing those deep dimples again, making me swoon and my heart just pure giddy. "Address, baby."

Oh, yes. I rattled off my address, and we were on our way. I probably dozed off on the way because the next thing I knew, we'd stopped right outside my brownstone apartment.

"Let me walk you inside."

Nobody ever entered my apartment. Even in my drunk state, I remembered that. "Absolutely not."

"I'm worried you'll fall or hit your head." His eyes were narrowed, and he looked really stressed.

I ran my fingers between his eyebrows, smoothing the vein popping up. "There, there."

I heard Maxim chuckle from the front.

"Samaira." Dominic's warning tone had my pussy fluttering.

"I'll be fine. See you later."

"Call me when you get inside. If I don't get a call within five minutes, I'm coming in."

"Yes, sir," I moaned, making him growl under his breath.

I giggled and jumped out of the car, only lightly stumbling.

As soon as I was inside my apartment, I stepped to the window overlooking the main road, only to find Dominic's car waiting across the street.

I dialed his number. "Look up at the fourth-floor window," I said as soon as he picked up the call.

"Good girl," he growled. "Now, take a shower, drink some water, and go to sleep."

Something loosened in my chest at the way he was caring for me. It made me want to obey him. Curl into a ball in his lap and lick his throat. "Yes, sir."

He growled again, making me giggle.

I dropped the call and did exactly as he instructed. I went to sleep with the image of Dominic's wide smile and his deep dimples.

CHAPTER 16

woke up to the thoughts of stormy eyes and a sharp jaw, eyes that reflected a similar darkness and violence that I saw in the mirror. Four drinks didn't give me a hangover, but last night's dry spell definitely had me waking up with an excruciating need pushing through my veins. Need for one man.

I stayed in bed, completely naked, relishing the soft sheets against my back and the cozy comforter enveloping me. Visions of Dominic were on a constant loop in my mind, every inch of my body still feeling the sweet and sharp burn of his gaze from last night. My pussy throbbed with bone-deep need and excruciating emptiness, my thighs soaking wet with arousal. My body was an inferno of longing, desperate to feel his large hands on my throat, holding my choker and feeding me his cock.

My pussy pulsed with sharp arousal, soaking the sheets beneath me. My nipples were pebbled to the point of pain, my entire body thrumming with the need to be filled. I'd never felt this desperate, this hungry for a man before. With a broken moan, I turned on my stomach, got on my knees, and grabbed the dildo from my nightstand. With a wild edge that had me clutching my pillow in a deadly grip, I dragged the thick cock-like vibrator between the drenched lips of my pussy, causing a million sparks of pleasure to rush through my veins.

My hips arched up with the agonizing need to be filled, to feel Dominic's hands holding me down and thrusting deep inside me, fucking me into the mattress, taking complete control of my body. My ears strained to hear *good girl* from his lips as he grabbed my hair, pulling me up on my knees so his massive chest brushed my back. His sweat soaked my skin, his heat setting me on fire as I screamed his name, all the while coming on his cock.

My mind flashed to the moment when I'd walked out of the torture room soaked in a man's blood, to the way he'd looked at me with so much pride, so much lust, so much wonder. It was those eyes—those dark, sinful, wild eyes—that had my body pulsing and pleasure rushing through my veins, electrifying every nerve in my body, paralyzing me as a blinding-white orgasm raced through me.

I dropped onto my back, panting as thoughts of Dominic swirled around in my mind, and the sensible part of my brain tried to put a stop to it all.

There was no future with Dominic. He had his own empire to rule, a life in the public eye, and a family who loved him. My life was riddled with murders, torture, and violence.

While a part of me was thrilled that he found my torturous, gruesome, murderous ways attractive, the question was, *for how long?* I was a Wildcat. Wildcat was me. I had dedicated my entire existence, my whole purpose of living, to giving women justice. I wouldn't quit for anything or anybody.

I was also completely aware that a day would come when we'd be caught. We'd be punished, put behind bars, or worse.

It was a choice all five of us had made very consciously, very happily. But I couldn't put that cross to bear on Dominic. On *anyone*.

Once all my morbid thoughts had successfully wiped away all that glorious post-orgasm bliss, I got up with a tired sigh and jumped into the shower. I got dressed in sweatpants and a hoodie since I was staying home till my evening shift at the Thunder Claw. For now, I planned to listen to the recordings from Thomas's and Brian's offices from the comfort of my cozy two-bedroom apartment.

I was in the middle of preparing chai, one of the few routines I had from my earlier life, when the doorbell rang. Only four people in the world knew my address. So when I looked into the peephole, I wasn't surprised to find the girls.

I loved my ladies, but showing up on my doorstep without warning should be all kinds of illegal. There was only one person on the other side of the door for whom I was opening the door with a smile. "Oh, hello there, little Callum. How are you, kiddo?"

"Auntie Sami," the little guy, Lena's five-year-old son, shouted and lunged into my arms.

I instantly scooped him up, twirling him in my arms as my four best friends and one big dog burst into the apartment. They swept through it like a hurricane, filling the place with commotion before collapsing onto the couch with a flourish.

My living room, kitchen, and dining area shared an open-plan layout. While I held Callum, Tara and Shadow claimed a spot on the floor near the coffee table, whereas Sloane and Naomi made themselves comfortable on the couch, promptly turning on the TV.

I looked at the little man in my arms. "What brings you here, little man? You want some pancakes?"

"Yes, please. Will you put chocolate chips in them?" he asked, holding my face in both his hands.

"Of course. I'll also add some strawberries on top. How does that sound?"

"I love it. Will you teach Mom how to make your pancakes?"

Lena, who'd been standing at the kitchen counter listening to our conversation, scoffed. "Callum, don't you like my pancakes, baby?" She put her hands on her chest and pretended to be hurt.

His tiny little mouth dropped into an O, and his eyes widened with worry. He wiggled down from my arms and hugged Lena's legs. "I love your pancakes, Mommy."

This little guy was Lena's little protector and her entire world. A family she protected with the ruthlessness of a lioness. She gave him a little kiss on the head and ruffled his hair. "Go play with Shadow and keep an eye on your other three aunties while I help out Auntie Sami with preparing your pancakes. Okay, baby?"

He gave her a little soldier salute. "Okay, Mommy." Then he ran off, calling Shadow.

Shadow's loud barks, Callum's squeals, and the Wildcats' chatter made my little house come alive. Made it feel like a home, a place where family came together.

"You're moping, Sami," Lena said, cracking twelve eggs in a big bowl.

I put a pot of coffee on for the ladies as I poured my chai in a cup with a sigh. "It's one of those days."

She stood beside me as she prepared the batter for pancakes. "Sami, you have been with me more than anyone here. You've seen me at my worst. You're here with me as I'm *living* my worst. But do you know what makes my life worth living? My little boy. You. Tara. Sloane. Naomi. My parents. You all are my family."

I clutched her shoulder and pulled her into a side hug, resting my head against hers. Given the kind of work we did and our past, we didn't have many people around us to make new friends. These women were my everything—my sisters, my best friends, my family. "You all are my family too."

"You need to get back in touch with your parents, Sami. They need you. They need to see their daughter."

A sharp breath escaped my chest. "You know I can't, Lena."

"I would do anything, *anything*, to see my daughter. Trust me, your mother, your father, your siblings, they would want to see you."

Five years ago, Lena's daughter was kidnapped. She was the one person we hadn't been able to find. For that entire year, all we did was look for her. Sadly, Tara wasn't a Wildcat back then. She would've been able to use her hacking and technology superpowers to find Ava. The four of us had searched through every corner of New York, followed every minor lead we had, beat up a hundred people to get them to talk, but nothing. We still had searches for her running. We still had our eyes and ears open for just a sign. Tara had constant facial recognition running through her satellite system, but that had only been set up a year after her kidnapping. Most of us were losing hope of ever finding Ava. She was only nine years old at the time. A kid.

I pulled Lena into a hug as I felt the eyes of the rest of the girls on us. Besides Lena, none of the other girls kept in touch with their families. We all knew the consequences of having a family around. "I know they would want to see me, Lena. I'm staying away to protect them. They can't get involved in our world. You have no idea the harassment they faced thirteen years ago. I can't pull them into my lifestyle and make them always worry about my siblings' lives. You, of all people, know how dangerous it can be to have a liability. To have someone you care about."

She gave a quiet nod, easing out of the hug. As she started preparing pancakes, I began chopping some fresh strawberries. "Is that why you're keeping your distance from Dominic?"

That one word had Sloane jumping up from her seat and dragging Naomi with her to perch on the barstool right across from us. "We heard Dominic."

I popped a piece of strawberry into my mouth, focusing on chopping them into perfect little slices. "He's a complication."

"He's hot," Sloane declared.

"And rich," Naomi piped in.

"And seems like a nice guy," Lena chimed in, not wanting to be left out.

"And makes you act like a fool," Tara shouted from the floor where she lay beside Shadow.

"Tara's not wrong," I admitted, sighing. "He *does* make me act like an idiot. You all see it, don't you? He's affecting my work, making me act on impulse, making me reckless. And he's a *client*. A fifty-million-dollar client who not only knows about our den but also our safe house location because *I* revealed it all. What if he went to the cops? We'd be locked up and charged as serial killers."

Sloane flicked her hair dismissively. "Are we *serial killers* if we're vigilantes?"

I couldn't help but roll my eyes. "Get real, Sloane. Just because we're cleaning house doesn't mean we wouldn't be put behind bars if we got caught. How could I put the Wildcats at such risk?"

Lena finished preparing the pancakes and started plating Callum's. "Sami, just because we're Wildcats doesn't mean we don't have the right to lead a normal life. I never intended for that to be the case when I agreed to let you join me. When I asked you all to join me. You're allowed to put your trust in people. You're allowed to fall in love. You're allowed to bring in new people."

Tara mock-coughed, muttering, "Dominic," under her breath. Obviously, I threw a piece of strawberry at her.

We put the coffee pot, pancakes, strawberries, maple syrup, and chocolate chips on the coffee table as each of us grabbed a plate and prepared our pancakes.

I played around with the food on my plate as my mind drifted to the possibility of crossing that professional boundary with the only man who's made me so irrational and impulsive. "You know," I said, garnering everyone's attention. "When I went to his parents' place, I was talking to Sophie, and he touched my shoulder from behind."

All of them cringed—knowing it was my trigger—as I continued, "Yeah. It went as you would expect. I slammed him on his back and told him that I hadn't given him permission to touch me."

"Good for you, Sami. No harm in setting those boundaries," Naomi said, biting into her food.

I turned to all of them and whispered, "He promised he wouldn't touch me again without my permission. And he hasn't ever since. Not even accidentally. Not even a graze of our shoulders. Not even a handshake."

"Are we supposed to be happy or sad about it?" Sloane asked, looking around at each one of us.

Lena hid her smile behind her fork. "We're supposed to be happy. The man knows the meaning of boundaries. I think."

"But…" Naomi waggled her eyebrows.

"She wants him to touch her so bad. Sami is hard up for Dominic," Tara finished her sentence.

Lena coughed loudly, but it was too late. Callum's little ears were entirely focused on our conversation, even though he was sitting a little farther away from us, near Shadow, eating his pancakes. "What's hard up?"

I threw my couch cushion at Tara's face, making her shriek and causing Shadow to rush to her. Callum all but forgot his question as he jumped to get Shadow back.

I put my face in my hands, giving up. "He didn't even get scared of me when he saw me yesterday."

"I thought that man was going to drop on his knee right there." Naomi's words had my heart rattling against my rib cage, as if ready to jump into Dominic's palm.

I quickly gulped my chai to try to stop that ridiculous smile threatening to cross my face. What was it about Dominic that had my entire being so wholly focused on him? Why was I so overly trusting of all our secrets? And why the fuck did he make my chest tighten all the damn time? It was irritating and inconvenient, and it made me want to grab him by the shirt and slam my lips on his.

Lena looked at where Callum was feeding Shadow some strawberries and turned to us. "You know," she said softly so only the four of us could hear. "You can just play with him." She mouthed, "*Fuck him.*"

I rolled my eyes. "Glad to have your permission, boss."

"You're very welcome, Sami. You know we all want the best for you."

I had no words. And thankfully, the four of them stopped talking about Dominic for a while as we ate in peace.

Once they all left, my fingers twitched with the need to text Dominic. I had absolutely nothing to say to him—and I would never ever admit it out loud—but I wanted to hear his voice. Wanted to know what he was up to, figure out what made him laugh aside from being beaten to a pulp by me. I wanted to figure out every little thing that made him the man he is, gather every little morsel of his life and hoard it all in my heart. With each passing moment, I stopped thinking about *why* I was so affected by a man.

I'd always relied on my instincts. They had never let me down. And my instincts were screaming at me to trust Dominic, to grab him by his suit and kiss him, to drop to my knees for him and own him. Mark him. Take him. Claim him for myself. My heart screamed that he wouldn't let me down.

Because as much as I seemed to need him closer to me, a tiny part inside me believed that he needed me just as much as I needed him, if not more.

The faster I found something on those culprits, the faster I could ask him to meet me. I got my laptop out and started going through the recordings, determined to find those rapists.

CHAPTER 17

DOMINIC

Sophie and I got out of the car after I parked it on the street beside Thunder Claw. Maxim's shift started at eight in the morning, so it was just me taking Sophie for her training here. Well, Maxim would drop Sophie off at four in the morning if I asked, but that was just an excuse to see Samaira.

Sophie stared at me from top to bottom. "What's up with the suit? It's six in the morning."

I love how Samaira looks at me in my suit. "I have to go to work directly from here."

As we neared the bar, we encountered other women walking into the entrance. Two ladies noticed us and gave Sophie a big smile. She instantly smiled back and joined them. Ever since she had started learning to fight, Sophie had begun to smile again. She'd set up a huge boxing bag at our parents' place, and according to Mom, she had taken to hitting it at all hours of the day.

Her posture had improved significantly, and her arms were starting to develop muscle definition.

I followed the ladies through the entrance. There, grabbing a coffee at the bar, was the woman who tortured my every waking and sleeping moment. She was smiling as she chatted with the server when her eyes met mine. They widened, and her lips stretched into an even bigger smile, sending my heart galloping in my chest. I moved closer to where she stood. "Good morning."

Her gaze made a slow sweep over my body, from my shoes to my neatly styled hair. I was tempted to flex my muscles in the suit, but I knew she'd just laugh at me. "Good morning to you as well."

I ordered my coffee and turned to Samaira. She was in her sweatpants and a dark red tank top, showing off her tattooed tiger sleeve. One day, I was going to thoroughly worship that tattoo with my mouth. "I'm surprised you're not teaching the class today."

Once I got my coffee, she led me to one of the booths at the back of the restaurant where she'd set up her laptop. "Sloane and Tara can handle it today. I actually found some pretty damning evidence that I wanted to show you."

Excitement shot through my system. The darkness and the ever-simmering rage to tear apart those scums bubbled through my veins. "Show me."

We took a seat on the bench against the wall, and she opened her laptop. "So I decided to go through the voice recordings of Thomas Cooper Sr. first since he sounded a bit too sketchy. And you wouldn't believe how loose his tongue got after we left. In the time that we placed the recording device, he's had three extremely incriminating phone calls."

She had wired earbuds connected to a laptop. She gave me one earbud as she placed another in her ear. She leaned closer to me, making it more comfortable to share the earbuds, her scent of fresh oranges and honey flooding my senses and soothing my frayed edges.

As soon as she hit Play, the voice in my ears crackled a

little before I heard the one-sided conversation that Thomas seemed to be having on his phone. "Boss, we might have a problem. I thought the matter was resolved months ago, but it seems the problem has resurfaced. We couldn't have taken care of the problem then. It was too risky. Yes, boss. I agree it was Tommy's responsibility. I'll take care of it, boss."

My hands were clenched into a fist as blood roared through my ears at the phone call. While it didn't provide much confirmation, it didn't sound good. Samaira must've sensed what I was thinking because she jumped forward to the next flagged conversation. "This could be anything, but listen to this conversation with Tommy."

She hit Play, and Thomas Cooper's voice rang in my ear. "You idiot. You had one job, and you couldn't do that right…I don't want to hear it, Tommy. Do you know how much trouble we're in? No, *you're* in? I don't care if she raised a hand on you…"

My eyes snapped to Samaira as Thomas continued to speak. "No, you stay in Amsterdam. People are starting to ask questions and inquire…I'll handle it here…I'll let you know when it's safe for you to return…I don't know, dammit, probably a week or two."

Samaira paused, and I instantly pulled off the earbuds. "It is him, isn't it?"

She chewed her lips as she nodded. "Seems that way to me. Now, this is the last recording that seems relevant. He's again talking to the boss."

I put the earbuds back in. "Boss, I've talked to Tommy and asked him to stay put in Amsterdam…He'll handle the delivery there, and I'll have one of my trusted men handle the shipment here…He does regret the insubordination, boss…I understand…Understood, boss."

She hit Stop, and silence ensued as I tried to get my breathing under control. I handed her the earbuds and ran my hand through my hair. "Tell me we're going to Amsterdam to handle him."

She rubbed her eyes and took a sip of her coffee. "As much as this conversation feels like they're talking about Sophie, we don't exactly have a confession or clear proof of what he did. I'll ask Tara to track Tommy in Amsterdam. We need to get some visual confirmation that he's indeed in Amsterdam. Let's give it a week to figure out his location, see if it's better to wait for him here or grab him there."

I nodded, but waiting wasn't one of my strong suits, and the urgency to get Tommy and exact my revenge on him was tearing me up from the inside. Despite not having a confession or concrete proof, my gut told me it was Tommy. Something in the way Thomas Cooper Sr. looked at me, his gaze boring into me to figure me out, had put me on edge.

As easy as it might be to grab him in the city as opposed to Amsterdam, I needed Samaira to know that we didn't lack in resources. "Samaira, if it's about the resources, you will have whatever you need to get him from Amsterdam. Private jet, security passes, hiring a team in Amsterdam. Whatever you need, you got it."

"Oh, I know. But it's not just money and logistics. We can figure that out. It's about whether he is indeed your culprit. While we don't mind bringing in a person for questioning, Tommy is the son of the state attorney. Are you ready to make an enemy of such a person? He would certainly have more people in his pockets, and he could prosecute you without much proof, given the threat you pose to him and his son."

My mind spun at the risks that I'd be putting my family under by going head-to-head with the state attorney. But what choice did I have? I needed Tommy to be buried and wiped from the face of the earth, no matter the consequences.

My eyes burned with resolve as I looked at Samaira. "Whatever it takes, Samaira."

Her eyes softened with understanding, and slowly, as if she

were afraid I'd move away, she reached out her hand toward mine, the one that was resting on my thighs. I sat still, not wanting to spook her but needing to feel her skin against mine.

My heart thudded in my chest with the raw need coursing through me, the need to feel her closer, to find that support in her. Her fingers merely grazed my knuckles, and just that slight touch shot an electric zing through my body. She quickly pulled away, clenching her hand in a fist. My heart sank at the loss, and I nearly whimpered.

I barely held myself in check as her breath hitched, our eyes meeting. Something akin to disappointment shone in hers, which I was sure reflected in mine. Not wanting to spook her further, and knowing I didn't have the permission to touch her, I took a sip of my coffee, swallowing the ever-growing urge to hold her.

I cleared my throat, trying to steer us toward a safer topic. "So if we're waiting for Tommy to return or for more concrete evidence, what are your plans?"

She shrugged. "Get some training in. Help the girls with their missions. The usual."

I wanted to ask her more about her missions when the door leading to the basement opened, and women from the classes downstairs started to make their exit. "Guess they're done," Samaira muttered.

Sophie appeared at our booth in the next minute, sweat running down the side of her face and a bright smile lighting up her eyes. "You guys are still busy?"

Samaira quickly shook her head, a soft smile on her face. "We were just finishing."

Need screamed inside me as she started to get up from beside me. "How about we grab some breakfast?"

One side of her lips tugged up in a smile. "We do serve pretty good breakfast here, you know. We could've ordered it."

Sophie met my gaze, and by the mirth in her eyes, I knew

she understood what I was trying to do. "Samaira, Dom and I have a really special place where we usually grabbed breakfast together when I lived in the city. We would love to take you there."

Her eyes widened. "Uh…now?"

Sophie gave a soft chuckle. "Yes. Of course now. C'mon, Samaira. Please? It would be fun."

Knowing that there wasn't a person on earth who could refuse Sophie when she got all cute, I let her do her thing as I hid the smile that was threatening to slip on my face. I kept my eyes innocent and hopeful as Samaira looked between the two of us, her conflicted expression nearly undoing me. Before I could say she didn't have to come, she sighed. "Fine. Let's go."

She closed her laptop and gave it to the woman at the reception desk, asking her to hand it to Sloane. We walked to the car, with me leading the way. Sophie talked to Samaira about the moves they had learned that day, a few steps behind.

As soon as I unlocked the car and got in, I saw the two of them shuffling around outside. I was hoping against hope that Sophie would do right by me. My wish came true when the front passenger door opened, and the tigress slipped into the seat right beside me.

I bit my lip hard to stop the foolish grin threatening to break free. I would definitely have to get Sophie something nice for this.

Once we were all buckled up, I drove us to the diner in Downtown Brooklyn that Sophie and I usually went to. Her office was close to the place, so Kai, she, and I usually met there before we went to work.

Just like in the car, Sophie maneuvered the seating arrangement so that Samaira and I sat directly across from each other, while Sophie sat beside Samaira. Our knees met under the table, and despite my need to pull her legs between mine, I pulled my legs back, immediately regretting the move. I had vowed not to touch Samaira without her permission.

We were perusing the menus when there was a sudden movement beside me. "Sorry, sorry. I'm here, you guys. Let the fun begin."

I looked at Sophie, my eyebrows raised in accusation.

She quickly raised her hand as Kai took a seat right beside me. "He's been dying to meet Samaira. I had to invite him."

Samaira looked between the three of us, her lips curved in a wide smile.

Kai extended his hand to her. "I'm Kai. Dominic Hyung's younger and much more handsome cousin. And this big guy wouldn't be able to survive without me." He then turned his head to me and said, "Go ahead, Hyung. Tell her how invaluable I am to you."

Samaira shook Kai's hand with a chuckle. "I see. Great to meet you, Kai."

I immediately removed Kai's hand from Samaira's. Here, I was using every ounce of my will not to touch Samaira, and this idiot wanted to hold her hand. *Fuck no.*

Kai jabbed me in my ribs, knowing what I did there. It also didn't escape Samaira's notice because she had a very delightful twinkle in her eyes.

Kai had that same awestruck look in his eyes that Sophie —and I—had when we each met Samaira for the first time. He leaned forward on the table, making Samaira do the same. "Is it true you defeated Dominic Hyung in boxing?"

Of course that was the first thing he'd ask.

Samaira laughed and looked at me with that soft look in her eyes, as if remembering that evening. "Damn right, I did."

"Fuck yeah. You're going to have to train me. I've never once defeated him in a match."

Like fuck I'd let him train with my Samaira.

I grabbed the back of his collar and pulled him back. "Absolutely not. She's only going to train me."

Sophie immediately pointed at herself. "Hello, she's already training me."

Samaira nudged her shoulder. "Damn straight."

Kai dramatically held his chest, as if his heart was breaking. "So only I don't get to train with you, Miss Samaira?"

She shook her head, smiling fondly at him. "We'll see. Are you any good at it?"

Kai bit his lip. "Definitely not as good as Dominic Hyung."

Samaira scoffed. "He's not good."

I pinched the top of my nose. "Brutal. And totally uncalled for."

Samaira kicked me lightly under the table, almost asking me to meet her eyes. "Honest. And totally called for."

While Samaira, Kai, and Sophie talked, my eyes were glued to the woman across from me.

Every time she was in my vicinity, the world around me blurred, the sounds got muted, and all I saw was her. All I heard was her voice. Her presence grounded me and also made me soar. Something was so powerful, so maddening about her that it made me want to leave everything behind just so I could spend all my time admiring her.

I didn't even realize when our server arrived, but I felt the slight touch of her fingers along my arm. I would've made nothing of it, but Samaira banged her fist on the table, the glassware clattering as she stared down the server and pointedly looked at where she still had her fingers on my arm. My cock turned rock fucking hard at the lethal edge in her gaze, her jealousy brewing up a storm of savage want deep within me, making a million butterflies erupt in my stomach.

The server instantly took back her hand and quietly took our orders without meeting Samaira's or my eyes.

My lips stretched into a wide smile, making Samaira roll her eyes at me. "She was totally inappropriate."

Kai and Sophie coughed but gave her a supporting nod. "Totally."

I couldn't stop smiling even if I tried. "Of course. That was what that was. You were protecting me."

Her cheeks flushed red as a smile overtook her face. "You're welcome."

Sophie caught my eyes and mouthed, "So jealous," as she discreetly pointed at Samaira.

We were all quiet once our food arrived, and we started eating. Sophie and Kai told Samaira stories about our childhood, including how the two of them would get together to play pranks on me and how I was always so serious.

Sophie also told her about her work, her passion for it shining through her eyes, and the way she became animated while describing her projects.

"When do you plan to go back to work?" Samaira asked, swallowing a bite of her breakfast burrito.

Sophie twirled her fork in her scrambled eggs. "I actually started working on some designs from home. I'm hoping to at least visit the office occasionally starting next week."

I didn't know that. Pride washed over me at every step Sophie took forward with her life. "That's amazing, Soph. I'm so proud of you."

Red coated her cheeks as she bit into her eggs. "Thanks, Dom. I was going to tell you."

"It's okay, Soph. But no going to work alone. I'm going to have Maxim join you."

She pressed her lips together, thinking over my words, but I knew she wouldn't refute. Especially considering her rapists were still out there.

Putting that thought out of my mind, I focused on enjoying the meal with two of the most important ladies in my life, and my young cousin, who was truly the one who kept me sane on some days of the week.

My eyes drifted to Samaira, who was attacking her burrito

with gusto, her dark, wavy hair pulled into a ponytail that spilled over her shoulders. What I wouldn't give to see her hair down, flowing across her face, her eyes hooded with arousal, her lips swollen and red from hours of kissing.

I couldn't pinpoint when she'd become the only woman I thought of last thing at night and first thing in the morning. She occupied every single one of my thoughts—her fiery gaze, her powerful body that made me hit the gym twice a day, her manic laugh when she slaughtered that penis, and that powerful stroke of her hand when she landed that killing blow. She was vengeance incarnate and my all-consuming obsession.

Before I realized, to my utter disappointment, we had polished off the food, and I'd paid the bill. We slowly got up, making our way out of the restaurant.

As we walked toward where I'd parked the car, I kept thinking of all the ways to prolong our time together. With the way we had to wait up to two weeks for Tommy to resurface, my mind spun, desperately thinking of reasons—excuses—to see Samaira again. As I neared my car, I turned around to meet Samaira's eyes, who was walking beside Kai, slightly behind Sophie and me, when her eyes suddenly widened.

What happened next probably took only two seconds, but my mind cataloged every millisecond as Samaira flew to where Sophie and I stood and lunged at us as a deafening gunshot erupted, shattering my car window.

Samaira shoved Sophie away as she dropped over me. Her eyes had gone entirely black, a snarling, vicious rage swirling in their depths. She clutched my cheeks, her eyes scanning my face and checking me for injuries.

Before I could process what was happening or tell her I was unharmed, she let out a guttural roar that shot shivers down my spine, jolting my mind the fuck up. Then she screamed in my face with the ferocity of a tigress. "Take care of Sophie and Kai. Get the fuck out of here!"

She launched herself off me, spun around, and sprinted toward a building across the street, leaving me behind.

No, she fucking didn't.

She did not just jump in front of a bullet for me.

She absolutely wouldn't dare put her life in danger to protect me.

But she fucking did.

My vision turned red. Blinding panic and uncontrollable rage tore through my mind as I watched what felt like my heart being ripped out of my body, the dark emptiness swallowing me whole and pulling me under.

She was so fucked.

CHAPTER 18

One moment, I was walking behind Sophie and Dom, smiling at Kai's constant commentary on Dominic and the way he tortured him. The next, I saw a red dot on Dominic's head as he turned around to look at me, a soft smile on his face that threatened to melt my heart.

The last time I'd felt a similar bone-deep panic was thirteen years ago when I was a helpless young girl. Only one word rang loudly in my head as I saw that red dot threatening to destroy the very thing that was filling my life with excitement and color and fucking giddiness.

Protect.

Protect.

Protect.

It was only my years of experience and pure adrenaline spiking through my body that had me pushing Sophie and Kai to the ground and flying at Dominic to protect him from the bullet. I'd just pushed us down when the bullet shattered his car's window, glass raining on us as I fell on top of him.

The wave of crimson fucking rage tore through my body, consuming every one of my senses.

Someone had dared to touch what was *mine*.

Someone had dared to harm the man who was all *mine*.

Someone had tried to kill Dominic Park, and they were going to fucking pay.

Every single thought evaporated from my mind except one.

Revenge.

Once I quickly checked for injuries and verified he was unharmed, I jumped off him and whirled around to where the shot came from. I saw the tiny movement of a man retreating from the roof of a brownstone. My body shot across the road, my senses zoned in on my target, my legs pumping harder to get to the man who had just signed off his death at my hands.

I jumped over a brownstone fence to find him running across the opposite street. I ran faster, my legs burning, my vision sharpening. I crossed the street, following the guy who had the sniper case slung over his shoulder.

He kept running, but I knew I would catch him. It was only a matter of time. He didn't know he'd woken up a beast. He *would* know. He would know what happened when someone tried to mess with a tiger.

They hunt you down and tear you apart. Limb by fucking limb.

People moved out of my way as I chased the guy. I pumped my legs faster as I almost caught up to him, just a few feet of distance separating us. The thought of losing Dominic to the man in front of me had rage pouring out of me, my need to tear apart the man overwhelming my senses and narrowing my vision.

Luck wasn't on his side because the next turn he took into an alley led to a dead end with a tall fence separating the other side of the road. While his own fear had him clambering up the tall metal fence, it took me a mere moment to follow him. Before he could turn around to climb down, I grabbed his shirt and threw him on the ground from about fifteen feet high, dropping on him with my knee landing in his stomach.

A loud oomph escaped him, but I had no patience to let this man live for another breath. He took a shot at the one man who made my heart flutter. And this motherfucker would pay with his life for trying to take him away from me.

I punched him over and over again. My knuckles slammed into his cheek, making him cough up blood and a tooth. With every punch I landed on his face, my skin coated with his blood, the proof of the life I was draining from his body for trying to harm what was mine.

"St…Stop…pl…please," he whimpered, his voice a wet rasp.

Wrath, unlike anything I'd experienced, pumped through my blood, my mind failing to form words. I pulled out my knife from my boot and slashed across his chest, blood instantly seeping through his shirt, his painful cries fueling my rage.

I clutched my knife, ready to plunge it into the center of his chest when a loud voice—a voice that made me smile, a voice that made my heart sing, a voice that belonged to *me*— shouted my name.

My narrowed vision expanded as my gaze landed on the car at the end of the alley about twenty feet away from me. My eyes landed on Dominic, his lips curled in fury, his eyes blazing like wild thunder, his voice booming. "Get in the car, now. Hurry the fuck up."

Everything within me wanted to grab the little head of the man at my feet and twist his tiny neck. My mind roared at me to just do it when another thunderous roar came from Dominic. "Now, Tigress. Or I swear to fucking God."

With a frustrated growl, I backhanded the guy, rendering him unconscious. I lifted his limp body onto my shoulder and ran toward the car. As soon as I neared the car, the back door opened, and I dropped him on the floor of the car, his head colliding with Kai's feet, and got in, slamming the door behind me.

Dominic floored the car as I kicked the guy lying at my feet, red-hot rage slamming against my skin, wanting to tear the guy apart with my bare hands. My chest heaved as I tightened my fists, resisting the urge to pound into him, my mind dizzy with the overwhelming emotions coursing through me.

The car swerved, and Dominic's hard-edged voice hit my ear. "Where to, Samaira? We need to hurry."

"Safe house."

Since he already knew the location, I sent a quick message to the Wildcats, informing them about the attack and our intended destination. In the next few seconds, I received several pings from them, letting me know they were headed to the safe house and would meet us there.

I stared at Dominic, cataloging his body, his arms, his shoulder, his chest, and his beautiful face. Everything looked unharmed. "Are you okay, Dominic?"

Because I was sitting behind Sophie, he turned his head to look at me. His eyes were narrowed into slits as he stared at me with so much anger and disbelief, I was taken aback. "Look down at your fucking arm, Samaira. You are shot. I am one second away from driving you to the nearest hospital."

My eyes widened as I looked at the streaks of dark red blood streaking down my arm. My body was pumping with so much adrenaline, so much anger, that I couldn't feel a thing. When I looked closer, the bullet hadn't hit me. Otherwise, I'd probably be having a stroke from all the blood loss. "I guess the bullet managed to slightly graze me. No need for a hospital."

"You stupid, stupid girl," he growled, his hands clenched tight around the steering wheel.

Sophie simply looked between her angry brother and then

at me, not saying anything at all. Whereas Kai's wide eyes were glued to the trickle of blood running down my arm. I looked down at the unconscious body and kicked him once more in his stomach. This time, for managing to graze his bullet on my arm, which was now starting to burn.

"Do you have a handkerchief or something?"

Kai quickly pulled it out from his pocket, and with a shaky voice, he asked, "Umm…can I?"

I grunted and extended my arm.

He moved quickly, wrapping the cloth tightly around the injury. Turning to Sophie, he asked, "Do you have any extra? I think we should add one more."

My mind was clouded with so much anger, but the way Kai's hand shook and his voice trembled, a hint of amusement trickled down my mind. "It's fine, Kai."

He gulped. "I'd prefer it if we could wrap it up in one more layer."

Before I could protest, Dominic barked from the driver's seat, "Don't you argue, Samaira."

Sophie handed him a large napkin, her eyes shining with tears as Kai wrapped it around my arm.

Dominic drove like a madman, constantly looking behind at me, getting madder and madder with every passing minute.

I kept my eyes trained on him, nothing else holding any importance to me at the moment. Had I been looking elsewhere, I'd have lost Dominic. Had he been even a little farther away from me, I'd have lost him to a fucking bullet to his head. How long had he been followed? Was he the aim, or was the kill meant for Sophie? Who hired this fucker? How many more would they hire? What if I wasn't around to protect him? What would happen when he went to work?

Each and every scenario brought me pain that was far worse than the graze of a bullet. Anger and panic collided in my chest, sending jolts of violence and darkness to creep at the edge of my vision, the need to protect Dominic suffocating me from the inside.

Nothing and no one should be able to reach Dominic Park. They would have to go through me first.

I looked at the man lying in his own pool of blood and bent down to inspect his pockets. I unmercifully turned him around, deliberately banging his head, as I found a burner phone in his back pocket.

It was a very old model and was easy enough to unlock. Idiot didn't even have password protection. Looking through the phone, he had zero contacts. A few unknown callers in the history. I put the phone in my pocket to give it to Tara later.

"Do not fucking carry him," Dominic growled at me as he parked the car in the same spot we'd parked it last time. I was just going to drag him by his arm, but whatever. I'd let him have this.

He opened the opposite side of the door. Kai quickly got out of the car, and Dominic leaned over the seat to look at the unconscious body. "Is he alive?" he asked, pulling the guy out from the small space.

I looked at the pathetic excuse of a human, his chest rising and falling slowly. "Unlucky for him, yes."

With that, I left the car, slamming the door behind me. I needed a drink.

CHAPTER 19

DOMINIC

My vision was dark red as Kai and I carried the limp form of the motherfucker into the safe house, Sophie silently tagging behind us. I heard her mumble, "It's all my fault," as she walked behind us, but I did not have any words that didn't include raging and screaming at Samaira for stepping in front of the bullet.

I had never experienced the heart-stopping panic that I felt as I heard the gunshot with Samaira on top of me, streaks of red blood dripping down her arm as she ran away from me.

Samaira, the stupid girl, had gotten herself injured. The wild Crimson Tiger almost took a bullet for me. The strongest, the most powerful, and the prettiest woman I'd ever met had just saved my life.

So fucking reckless.

So fucking foolish.

So *fucking mine*.

I dropped the body on top of the large table where the Wildcats had sat discussing their strategy the last time I was here. My eyes met Samaira's. She had a bottle of alcohol beside her as she sat on one of the chairs, her feet kicked up on the table.

I saw the rows and rows of weapons hanging on the wall behind her. I turned to Sophie and Kai. "Pick a weapon. Keep a watch on him. If he moves, stab him. Can you do that?"

Sophie pursed her lips while Kai nodded, looking at Samaira, who looked relaxed—relaxed as if her entire arm wasn't coated in blood—as she raised her eyebrows at Sophie.

Sophie nodded, and I didn't wait around for the two of them to grab their weapons.

I rushed to Samaira and snatched the bottle from her hand. "Up. Medical room. Now."

Adrenaline fueled my blood, anger so visceral coursing through my veins that it was downright impossible to form a full fucking sentence.

Samaira got up without any arguments and started walking to the back of the house. We passed the kitchen and turned into the hallway. She walked to the end of the hallway and opened the door, my eyes tracking her every moment, every step she took, monitoring her body.

A fully equipped medical operating room was set up here, rows and rows of medicines, supplies, oxygen tanks, and several machines and cables that I didn't understand were hooked to the wall.

Samaira walked to a shelf and grabbed a big box. "Supplies."

I jerked my head toward the bed. "Hop on."

She kept looking at me as if checking on me, as if *I* were the one who got shot and could drop dead at any moment.

I opened the first-aid box, pulled out all the supplies I needed, and looked at her as she sat on the bed. "Do I have your permission to touch you?"

Her eyes widened, and she nodded, extending her hand toward me.

I stepped closer to her so the side of her leg touched my hip. I didn't move away, needing the contact, and neither did she. Gently, I loosened the towel wrapped around her arm, and then the bloody handkerchief, unwrapping it slowly so as not to distress her wound.

Instantly, drops of blood pooled at the injury. I retrieved the antiseptic solution from the kit and started cleaning it. With every drop of blood and debris that I cleaned, my blood roared in my veins, anger finally erupting out of my body. "What the fuck were you thinking, Samaira? How could you fucking jump on us like that?"

She flinched as I poured more antiseptic solution, and I quickly blew over the wound. Every time she flinched in pain, an invisible wound slashed through my heart, making it bleed with so much hurt and panic I couldn't breathe. Despite blowing on her wound gently, I couldn't fucking hold back my tirade. "Did you even think for a second what would happen to *me* if something were to happen to you? Who in their right mind jumps in front of a bullet? What if it had hurt you even more? Or fucking worse?"

She kept staring at me as I screamed at her wound, needing it to disappear. Once the wound and the area around it were cleaned, I grabbed an antibiotic ointment and started to apply it on the wound, causing her to hiss out a breath, her hands clutching her pants in a tight grip. "You know what? I don't even want to entertain the thought of the bullet actually hitting you because I am about ready to walk back out and kill that motherfucker with my bare fucking hands."

Her lips tilted up in a small smile, and if that just didn't make me angrier. I grabbed the sterile bandage and started to wrap it around her arm. "Don't you fucking smile at me after the shit you've pulled, Maira. I am so tempted to spank the fucking shit out of your ass. I hired you to find Sophie's rapists. Not to put your life at stake, you hear me? You do not stand in front of a bullet coming at me. You fucking let me take it. You have no idea what you've done by pulling off this stupid stunt."

My voice rose higher and higher as I started to tie the ends of the bandages in a knot. "And because jumping in front of a bullet wasn't enough, you ran off like a fucking fool while your arm bled like a motherfucker. What, you think you're so badass that you can't bleed out? You think you would've saved me by jumping in front of me? You would've destroyed me. You would've obliterated my will to live a life where you're not in it. Stupid fucking girl. I'd rather be hit by a hundred bullets than watch a hair on your head be harmed because of me. You had no right…"

My words were suddenly cut off as Samaira grabbed my face and slammed her lips on mine. Her taste flooded my mouth. So fucking sweet with a sharp bite of lethal danger.

So fucking mine.

She took deep pulls of my lips as if her life depended on it and grazed her tongue against mine.

A needy moan escaped my lips as she pulled away. Her eyes were wild and glazed over as she licked her lips. Her sharp breath touched my lips, and I grabbed the back of her head, my fingers tangling in her beautiful, lush hair, pulling her head up so her eyes met mine. "Not fucking enough."

I slammed my mouth on hers, all my pent-up rage and panic and worry turning into a storm of thundering arousal that threatened to devour me whole. I sucked on her full lips and pushed my tongue into her mouth, tasting her, feeling the warmth of her tongue against mine, the sharp bite of danger dipped in honeyed sweetness. If I were to be shot right now, I'd happily die with her taste on my tongue.

Her fingers pulled at my suit and pushed it off my shoulders, dragging me between her legs. I deepened my kiss, the need to feel her heartbeat overpowering everything else. With my one hand clutching her hair, I dragged my palm up her waist and flattened it between her breasts, feeling the pounding *thump, thump, thump* of her heartbeat against my hand.

"This needs to always be pumping for me. You fucking understand?" My chest heaved at the feel of her body against mine, and I growled against her lips, biting the bottom lip in warning. Pleasure and arousal rode my body hard as I waited for her answer.

Every part of my body shook with the need to claim this woman, to slam my cock deep inside her, just to remind myself that she was here. In my arms. Alive.

I took a deep inhale at the side of her neck, breathing in the scent of her sweat, her strength, her power. She was a tiger, a powerful protector, a predator so threatening, her enemies trembled with fear. Yet she *melted* in my arms.

She arched her neck further, asking for more, and I gave it to her. My cock ached at how hard and stretched tight it was, my balls heavy and full. I sucked hard at the part where her neck met her shoulder, making her writhe on my aching cock, and bit her hard, knowing I'd leave my mark on her. "Promise me. Promise me you won't step in front of danger for me."

I stopped everything—my body begging and screaming at the sudden loss—and looked at her, waiting for her to open her eyes and meet mine.

"Dominic," she gritted between clenched teeth, her breaths coming out in pants.

"Promise me, Samaira," I growled.

She grabbed my shirt and pulled me closer, wrapping her legs tight around my hips, dragging my hard cock between her legs. My mind blanked out, my vision turning white as her sharp eyes met mine. "Danger would have to get through me first before it ever touches you. I promise you *that.*"

Her words crashed into my heart like boulders, my soul wrapping itself around them, embedding her in my heartbeat.

Her eyes burned with challenge and arousal, fueling my rage and terror and so much need, it made me want to drop to my knees to worship her and tie her to my bed and fuck her into oblivion.

Despite her stupid declaration that managed to tie her soul to mine, I would never fucking let her. "Like fuck it will." I slammed my mouth on hers, biting her lip hard.

She grabbed my hair and pulled me. "Try to stop me."

I grabbed her *injured* hand that she'd used to hold my hand and pulled it off me, thunderous rage clouding my vision dark. I grabbed both of her arms and pulled them behind her back, holding them in my one hand, pressing her chest further into mine. Her eyes hooded with pleasure as she moaned, grinding against my cock.

Her nipples poked through her tank top, and I was so tempted to put my mouth on them and suck them till she cried. I bent lower so I grazed my jaw along her neck, my words rumbling in her ear. "You have no idea who you're dealing with here, baby. I am so fucking tempted to tie your rebellious little ass to my bed and spank you so hard, you wouldn't be able to sit for a week, let alone run in front of a bullet."

She whimpered as her back arched and she writhed on me with a wild abandon, pulling my hips deeper into her by squeezing her legs tighter. "You want that, Samaira?"

She bit her lip, refusing to utter a word, but tightened her legs around me, tempting me to get rid of our clothes and push into her. Knowing that my filthy words and my dark promises were making her so wild with want, my cock pulsed with the need to consume her and fulfill every one of her desires. "I'm going to keep you tied to my bed, completely naked, spread-eagled, entirely at my mercy, until you promise not to put yourself in danger for me."

She moaned loudly, arching her head back, lost in the fantasy. I let go of my hand from her hair and clutched her choker, pulling her up. Her eyes opened wide as her gaze darted to my hand that held her by her choker. I gave her a vicious smile as I tightened my hold on it, pulling her so close to me that my lips grazed hers. "You like this, baby? Is that why you wear a choker? You want me to put a leash on the end and fuck you as you ride me?"

I thrust my hard, pulsing cock between her legs, the friction of our clothes only making me harder. She whimpered into my mouth and dragged her teeth against my lips as her eyes closed and she surrendered herself to the pleasure. "I would keep you bound and gagged and not let you come until you promise to…" *Thrust.* "Not." *Thrust.* "Put." *Thrust.* "Yourself." *Thrust.* "In." *Thrust.* "Danger." *Thrust.* "For me." *Thrust.*

She shattered in my arms, her back arched, eyes rolled back in ecstasy, writhing on my cock, her lips whispering only one word. "Dominic."

It was by pure miracle that I kept myself from coming right between her legs. I let go of her hands and wrapped her in my arms, tucking her head into my chest, breathing in her hair, and feeling her heart softly beating at my chest.

CHAPTER 20

SAMAIRA

One moment, my mind was filled with visceral, burning rage and a need to destroy everything. In the next, Dominic was screaming his heart out at me while patching me up and blowing softly on my wound, worrying about me, and looking so, so cute, and so devilishly handsome with a severe frown on his face. I couldn't stop myself from grabbing him and shutting him up with a kiss.

For the first time, someone had managed to cool down my wrath merely by shouting at me, taking charge, and just fussing over me. I'd forgotten how much I enjoyed being fussed at, to be cared for.

I snuggled closer against his warm chest, feeling his heartbeat, his huge hands moving up and down my back. I'd just come on his cock, simply by the way he talked about what he'd like to do to me, and God, how much I *needed* what he was offering. How much I craved for it, how my mind yearned for it. I'd never found a person I trusted enough to let go of control, had never found a man whom I respected and craved with an intensity that took my breath away. But Dominic had managed to push me to the peak and made me feel alive, merely by his words.

And here I was, cozying up in his arms as if he were my boyfriend.

I quickly pulled back, reminding myself that he was my client, a client whose life was in danger, whom I was going to protect.

But Dominic, being Dominic, glared at me for pulling away. "What do you think you're doing?"

My throat dried as I met his eyes. "Umm…The girls will be here soon. And we should check on that guy."

"Sophie and Kai have it under control, and we'll leave once the girls are here. You're staying right here in my arms." With that, he dragged me back against his chest, his arms wrapping around me.

I breathed in him, and he smelled like aged whiskey and sandalwood, like a cozy night under a warm blanket in front of the fireplace. I bit my lip as I tried to pull back and put some walls around my heart. "I think we made a mistake."

His chest rumbled as he pulled me even closer into his embrace, running his hand through my hair. "Stop thinking. You fucked up. You saved my life. You almost took a bullet for me. Clearly, you like me."

I was about to refute, but he continued over my sound of protest. "Hush now, baby. I like you too. You sealed our fates by putting your life on the line for me. Now, you're stuck with me forever."

I pulled away from his chest and looked at him. His eyes burned with determination, as if he'd already made up his mind and there was no arguing with him. But he lived in a land of dreams where he wasn't a billionaire with a public profile, and I wasn't a vigilante who had killed over a hundred men. I was about to bring him to his senses when a loud commotion in the hallway had me turning toward the noise.

Dominic did not move an inch as the noise descended

closer and closer. I glared at him, warning him to move away before the girls caught us in a compromised position. He simply kissed me and bit my lip. "I'm done pretending I'm not obsessed with you."

The door to the medic room slammed open with all four ladies rushing in and immediately halting at the sight of Dominic between my legs.

Dominic, the bossy asshole, simply turned to them with his hand around my waist and a soft smile on his face. "Ladies, thank you for rushing out here."

Without giving them the time to process, he continued, "Naomi, I believe Samaira must've skipped out on mentioning that the bullet grazed her arm." He stopped to glare at me and hear the gasps from my friends. "I've tried to patch up the wound, but I would really like for you to look at her."

Naomi raised her eyebrows and crossed her arms over her chest. "Dominic Park, you'd have to get out from between her legs for me to take a look at her."

His lips curled in a smile at that. "You'd have to ask Samaira to unwrap her legs from my waist first. Although I'd be happy to stand here all day."

My eyes widened in horror. I didn't even realize I was still clinging to him like a fucking possessive monkey. Immediately, I pulled apart my legs, letting go of Dominic as Sloane cheered loudly, bouncing on her toes. "Tell us you banged on Naomi's operating table."

Naomi's eyes narrowed at the two of us. "Tell us you didn't."

Dominic chuckled. "We're fully clothed."

Her gaze softened as she noted my banged-up arm. "Everybody except Sami, out." Dominic unashamedly dropped a kiss on my forehead and murmured so only I could hear, "Be good."

Puddle. My heart was in a puddle.

Once everyone shuffled out of the room, Naomi came to

stand by me, a teasing smile on her face. "He's so smitten with you, Sami." She opened the bandage carefully and whistled. "And not so bad at patching you up. But it's a slightly deeper flesh wound than what I'd like. So we're gonna have to glue this together."

Naomi was quiet as she did her thing, rubbing enough anesthesia on my skin to numb the pain as she patched me up. She was wrapping my arm in a bandage when she turned her eyes to me. "Did you throw yourself in front of a bullet to protect him?"

I glanced at my arm. "My body just moved, Naomi. I would've done the same for any of you. You know that."

She clutched my hand. "Exactly my point, girl. You've started to care for him. Probably as much as you care for the four of us."

I scoffed. "Never. Nobody can replace you all."

She looked at me. Her eyes glistened with so much kindness I wanted to run out of the room. "You're allowed to care for more than four people. You're allowed to let him care for you too. We would all be happy if you find that someone who loves you to death."

I couldn't think about it right now. As much as I claimed that Dominic was mine, as much as he felt like he belonged to me, *only me*, deep in my soul, I couldn't risk his life. Couldn't tie him to my secrets and my lifestyle. I jumped down from the table once Naomi was done and had me take some meds. "Let's go. We gotta interview that fucker. Also, I sliced his chest with my knife. So you might want to patch him up a little. On second thought, leave it. He's dead anyway."

Naomi simply rolled her eyes at me. "You go ahead. I'll clean up around here and join you all."

I walked into the main living room to find the unconscious guy still on the table, Lena, Sloane, Tara, Sophie, Kai, and Dominic sitting in the chairs around the table. Dominic was the first to see me, and he was instantly out of his chair, dragging me to sit beside him.

"You ready to wake this fucker up?" Lena got a bottle of water in her hand.

I smiled at her, ready to start. "Let's do it."

She uncapped the bottle and poured it on the guy's face. Instantly, his eyes flashed open, and his body jerked, sputtering water out of his mouth. We were all out of our chairs. Before I could even attempt to climb over the guy and interrogate him, Lena was on top of him, landing a solid punch on his cheek that had him spitting out his tooth.

I pulled his phone from my pocket and handed it to Lena. She slapped the guy hard. "Who hired you? Who was your target?"

The guy's eyes widened at the six of us. He lay there, trembling on the table. "You…You don't want to cross these men. They're powerful people."

Lena scoffed and spread her arms. "Look around, fucker. One of us could handle twenty of them. So think very, very carefully before you say another word."

She pulled out her knife and put it to his throat. "Now, you harmed one of my girls. You targeted someone innocent. So give me a name. Who hired you?"

"I'm just a hit man. I don't know who exactly hired me. We only communicated through the burner phone. He used a voice modulator to make it unrecognizable. I just knew he was powerful because he offered five million dollars to kill Dominic Park. Seven million if I managed to kill his sister as well."

Lena passed the phone to Tara. "Keep it. Whoever hired him will contact him for an update sooner or later. You can track the line then."

She was the only one who wore her half mask right now.

The guy was still trembling with an angry Lena looming

over him like death incarnate. "Are…Are you going to let me go?"

A dangerous smile spread across Lena's face, a smile that looked very, very similar to the one I got on my face. "You, Mr. Hit Man, have already seen all our faces. You attempted and nearly killed Dominic Park and his sister. Had it not been for my girl here, they would've been dead, and you would've walked off happily with your seven million dollars. So no. You don't get to walk away."

Lena only had to give me a look. By the time she jumped off the guy, I grabbed a gun from the wall behind and climbed over the guy on the table. Standing over him, I pointed the barrel at his forehead and looked straight at Dominic. His eyes were burning with an intensity that had my heart slamming against my chest. This writhing tide of protectiveness surged through my body, the need to eliminate anything that tries to harm him overpowering any rational thought. "He shouldn't have taken a shot at you."

With my eyes trained on his, I pulled the trigger. Dominic didn't flinch—didn't even blink—at the booming noise. He simply kept his gaze locked on mine, his lips turned up in a proud smile. "Good girl."

Had I ever been more turned on right after shooting a man in the face before? Fuck no. Right now, all I wanted to do was jump into his arms and claim his mouth.

A loud retching noise had me pulling my eyes off Dominic and onto Kai, who was leaning over against the window, on the verge of puking.

"If you puke on the floor, I'm going to make you clean it," Lena's voice boomed.

Instantly, Kai had both of his hands sealed over his lips, his body heaving. From behind his hands, he muttered, "I've never seen someone get shot."

I rolled my eyes and looked at Sloane. "Can you take care of this?" I asked, hitting my foot to the side of the dead guy.

She sighed and dragged him down the stairs—loudly and carelessly—to settle him in the basement. At the same time, Lena made a call to the cleaners to come and take care of him. Once Sloane returned, I turned to Lena, who sat on her chair, one leg crossing over another, sending some message on her phone.

Dominic quietly talked to Sophie, his arm rubbing soothing circles on her back. She was clearly shaken and blamed herself for the entire debacle. She was worried that she'd now put her brother's life in danger as well, and that he should be moving to their parents' place.

Having heard enough of their conversation, I cleared my throat and sat cross-legged on the now-empty table, meeting everyone's eyes and then landing on Sophie. "Nothing will happen to your brother. I'll make sure of it. I'll be his bodyguard until we find the person who put a hit on both of you and deal with them."

"Sounds perfect," Lena said.

"Makes sense," said Tara.

"Thank you, Samaira," Sophie chimed in.

At the same time, Dominic shot to his feet, his eyes fuming. "Absolutely not. I should be the one protecting you two. I can protect myself."

I raised my eyebrows at him as my four best friends scoffed, which only resulted in him clutching his hair, his eyes blazing. "I don't have eyes in the back of my head. I also didn't have any idea that there was a hit on us. Now that I know, clearly, I'll be hiring a team of bodyguards for all of us."

He looked right at me, his jaw clenched tight. "Like I told you a few minutes ago, you will not put yourself in danger to protect me."

I crossed my arms at my chest and stared him down, fury coursing through my body. "And like I told you a few seconds after that, danger would have to get through me first before it ever touches you. *I* will be the one taking care of your safety. Not some random, incompetent team of men."

"Absolutely not, Samaira. That's not happening."

"You know I would be the best person to protect you."

His eyes were wild as he looked at all the women gathered around the table, who were looking back and forth between us. "Are you all not hearing this? You cannot possibly think it's a good idea."

Lena raised her eyebrows. "You know she's the best fighter we have. She's lethal. She's powerful. There's no one else I would trust to keep you safe. Seems completely logical to me."

Tara's lips tugged in a smile. "She's also been in far more dangerous situations than being a bodyguard to a billionaire who spends the majority of the day in his office, working behind a desk. I'd say she's slacking off here."

Dominic's face was turning redder by the minute. He turned to Sophie for support. "Tell me you think it's a crazy idea. I can hire a whole team of bodyguards."

Sophie bit her lip, her gaze moving from him to me and back at him. "Dominic, just from what happened today, I trust Samaira with your life. With *my* life. I don't think anybody else would protect you as well and with as much care as Samaira."

My heart fluttered in my chest as my cheeks turned hotter at the way Sophie implied that I cared for Dominic. Of course, I cared. But a proud feeling burst in my chest knowing that his sister saw it and that she seemed to like having me by Dominic's side. I gave her a warm, reassuring smile, appreciating her unspoken support.

Dominic paced the room, his fingers clutching the bridge of his nose. "Samaira, baby, if you become my bodyguard, I'd be constantly worried about any threat coming your way. I know I'd jump in front of a bullet rather than risk having it touch you. You're not getting shot under my watch."

His words landed on my chest like physical blows. Deep in my mind, I knew he trusted me to protect him. He believed me to be strong, and he was only saying this because he cared about me. But his doubt about my ability to keep us both safe felt like a slap in the face.

This was why I could never date a man like Dominic. If he couldn't trust me with something like this, how would he handle me being out for bigger, more dangerous missions? My life was the Wildcats. And if push came to shove, I would always choose Wildcats. I would always fight for women. If Dominic couldn't let me protect *him*, how would he ever let me protect other people?

He had to get over it if we had any chance of being together. "How about we fight it out? If you beat me in even one round out of five, I'll let you hire a team. You fail, you accept me as your bodyguard."

All the women chimed in with their support, along the lines of "Seems fair," "Sounds good to me," and "This is the only way to solve it."

Dominic stood leaning against the table where I sat. His hands were on his hips, his hair was completely disheveled, and he looked hot as fuck. His eyes were tight with worry and frustration, and it only fueled my anger at him. How dare he feel so conflicted about letting me protect him.

When I kept glaring at him in a challenge, he gritted out, "You're hurt. You just got grazed by a bullet."

I raised my eyebrows. "It's an advantage you desperately need, *baby*." My *baby* was condescending as fuck.

His eyes narrowed. "Fine. If I win a single round, you'll listen to me."

Oh, I'll show him. I looked around at my girls to find half of them hiding their smiles behind their fists, while the other half were outright grinning at Dominic's misplaced confidence.

"Let's go, pretty boy." I jumped down from the table, pointing outside.

"What, here?" Dominic frowned. "I thought we'd go to the ring at Thunder Claw."

I gave him the most patronizing smile I could muster. "You afraid the ground would hit your back too hard?"

Kai snorted as the Wildcats tried—and spectacularly failed—to hide their snickers.

"Let's go, Tigress," he growled. Walking around the table, he started to unbutton his shirt.

Dominic led the way, walking out of the house. I turned to the girls, a challenging grin on my face. "Five minutes. Bet on it. If it takes longer, I'll give you all my milkshakes."

Sloane cheered. "Let's go. Things are finally getting interesting."

When we walked out of the house, Dominic was wearing a white undershirt, which showed the outline of his abs. His golden skin was glistening in the morning sun, and his arms were looking jacked. My body wanted to pull that undershirt up and lick those abs, but my mind was ready to slam him to the ground. Repeatedly.

I tied my hair in a high ponytail as I walked up to him. Lena stood between us, a whistle in her hand, becoming our referee.

We took our stances and waited for Lena's sign to begin.

The moment the shrill sound of the whistle came, I flew toward Dominic before he could even raise his hands in a blocking stance. With a sharp kick to his knee, causing him to buckle, I picked him up and slammed him on his front. Before he could brace for impact, his face licked the ground. Capturing both his hands under my knees as I dug them into his back, I wrapped my arm around his throat. He was completely immobilized. I held him in position for the next few seconds. "Did I forget to tell you, *baby*? I was being *very* easy on you the last time because I like your pretty face."

I let him go at Lena's whistle, his breath coming in deep pants as he took in gulps of air.

"Let's go, Dominic. We don't have all day." I got into position as Dominic stood, his body coiled in anger, ready to strike.

I gave him a wink.

With the next whistle, Dominic was ready to block. But you didn't win by blocking. You won by attacking. By *faking* and attacking and catching your prey by surprise. I slammed him on the ground once again, my legs wrapping themselves around his throat, as I grabbed his legs with my arm, curving his spine backward, and once again, immobilizing him.

His hands tapped the ground, and I let him go.

The next three times went pretty much the same way, and I became Dominic Park's bodyguard in four minutes and thirty-five seconds.

Dominic didn't look as defeated as he should have. His chest heaved, and rivulets of sweat glided down his abs, mixing with the sand sticking to his skin. His eyes were dark, and he had a euphoric smile on his face, blood dripping from the corner of his lips as we stood across from each other. I could feel the eyes of the women around me, but I ignored them all.

I walked up to him, held the side of his throat, and wiped his blood with my thumb. "Say hi to your new bodyguard, Dominic."

His eyes were dark pools of lust that had blood roaring through my veins for entirely different reasons. "Hi, baby." His voice washed across my skin like threads of silk wrapping around me in a sinful embrace.

"I can't watch this." Sophie's voice penetrated my senses from somewhere far away. "Me neither," Kai added.

There was a shuffling sound as my eyes stayed glued to Dominic's, and we were completely alone.

I pulled him closer by the back of his neck and bit his lip hard, causing him to hiss out a breath. "If you *ever* doubt my strength, my ability to keep us both safe, you will lose all the respect I have for you. And I don't work with people I don't respect, let alone fuck. Are we clear?"

He pulled me closer to him by my waist, his large hand sending warmth through my skin as I felt his cock throbbing against my hip. "I never doubted your ability, and you know it. I just worry because I care about you."

I pushed at his cock, drawing a grunt from him, and I remembered how he hadn't come before. "If your worry stops me from doing my job, then it's a problem."

He bent closer until our foreheads touched. With his eyes closed, he nuzzled my cheek. "You're right." His words washed over me, soothing the jagged edges that his doubts had left behind.

My eyes remained closed, feeling his sharp jaw rubbing against my cheek, leaving behind a thousand fiery needles that sent jolts of sharp need through my body and filling my heart with the kind of warmth that I wanted to drown in. Why did this man affect me so much?

I couldn't comprehend this savage kind of protectiveness that burned within me for Dominic, but I knew in my bones that I'd let no harm come to him and that he was someone who belonged to me. No matter how hard I tried to ignore it, this obsessive, savage possessiveness threatened to burst from me.

Once we stepped inside the house, the women thankfully ignored the moment I'd shared with Dominic. Instead, every single one of them pointed out Dominic's idiocy in taking up my challenge and failing so spectacularly.

Kai was very proud as he pointed out, "Even I lasted longer against you than you did against Samaira."

Dominic had the biggest smile on his face as he rolled his eyes. "You wanna fight Samaira?"

"Fuck no. I'm not stupid."

And I couldn't help but laugh at that, bumping my fist with him.

Dominic had a ridiculous smile on his face as he took all the ribbing in stride as we sat planning our next move.

Since someone had eyes on Dominic, we didn't want to let it show that he had hired a bodyguard. So, we unanimously decided that I'd act as his personal assistant.

Dominic got an unhinged smile on his face. "If I'd known you'd be spending every waking moment with me, I'd have never objected to you being my bodyguard."

I rolled my eyes at his delighted expression, and I knew I had a similar smile on my face.

Dominic turned to Kai. "Have a desk set up for Samaira in my office on Monday, will you?"

He gave him a salute. "Yes, boss."

I raised my eyebrows at Dominic and said, "And don't you give me any fake tasks that make me step away from you for too long."

This time, *he* gave me a quick salute. "Yes, boss."

Dominic turned serious as he saw Sophie laughing at his joke. "I need someone to protect my sister as well. Whoever put that hit on me also put a hit on my sister."

Sloane wrapped an arm around Sophie's shoulders. "I'll take care of your sister."

Lena piped in, "Sophie, if you want, you could move into the Den for a while. It's the safest space, and you'll have more than just Sloane's eyes on you."

"The Den?" Sophie, Kai, and Dominic asked at the same time.

Lena's lips tugged in a smile. "The Den."

With that decision made, Naomi and Tara decided to stay at the safe house to wait for the cleaners to arrive to take care of the hit man's body while I took his phone with me.

Lena and Sloane headed to Thunder Claw, along with Sophie, while I got into the car with Dominic as his brand-new bodyguard.

We sat in silence as he drove us back into the city to his

home, the air between us charged with such intensity that it made the hair on my skin rise and my heart beat a mile a minute.

Now that I had tasted Dominic, I was starving.

Add in the high from defeating him five times in a row, remembering the feel of his muscles, his throat, his sweat-soaked skin under my palms, and I now wanted to feel his hard cock in my hands.

I was drowning in the heady scent engulfing the inside of the car, the proximity to his body threatening to crumble me.

We made occasional conversation about the logistics of the next day, but every word from Dominic's mouth, the way his Adam's apple bobbed, the way the dark baritone of his voice washed over my skin, had my panties soaking wet.

"So your den is under the basement of Thunder Claw?" he asked.

I swallowed, my throat parched. "Yeah. Sophie will be safest there."

He nodded. "I'll let my parents know and get her stuff so she can live there for a while."

I met his eyes and nodded.

Fire danced in his eyes, and in a slow movement, he moved his hand that was resting on his thigh and brought it toward mine, waiting for me to grab it. And because he waited for it, waited for me to touch him, I clasped his hand in mine, searing my entire body with the heat of his touch.

"Thank you for doing all this for my sister," he said, squeezing my hand in his large palm.

I moved my thumb over his, and a breath hissed out of him. I shook my head and looked at him. "You don't need to thank me."

He gave a jerky nod, and slowly—so I could stop him if I really wanted to—placed my hand on top of his thigh and covered it with his own, keeping his eyes on the rough stretch of road as if he hadn't just sent my world into a tailspin.

Did he not know that I'd never done this? Never had a man hold my hand? Never had him place it on his thigh, the thin material of his pants doing nothing to hide the strength of his muscles there? Never had my heart beating like a caged butterfly not knowing how to be set free?

I wanted to sit with him in the car forever, surrounded by his scent, the feel of his thick, muscular thigh under my palm. On the other hand, my mind wanted to bolt, hide myself from the pain that might shred me to pieces if I lost him.

I kept my hand still as he kept driving, every cell of my brain and nervous system trying to redirect it a little above, an excruciating need thrumming in my veins to feel his hard cock against my palm. I wanted to bend across the car and open his pants, feel the rough glide of his thick cock along my tongue, swallow him so far down my throat, I'd gag. I needed to see him lose control over me, watch him completely unhinged and thoroughly wrecked for me.

As my body waged war against me, he kept silent, occasionally brushing his thumb along the back of my hand, making my panties melt merely by that soft touch. How long had it been since I'd last had a good fuck? Probably ten months ago?

Too soon, we arrived at a tall, glass-and-steel building, one of Manhattan's most iconic skyscrapers. I gave him a side glance and found him already looking at me.

"Welcome to my humble abode."

"Humble, my ass," I muttered, causing him to break out in laughter.

I kept a glance at the side-view mirror just to see if anyone followed us down into the parking lot.

The building had seven stories of underground parking. Once we'd parked the car, Dominic led me to the small lobby space. "Maxim usually picks me up from the ground-floor lobby. It's only when I'm driving myself that I use this lot. I'll get you access to the building by tomorrow morning."

Once the elevator arrived, he pressed a fob onto the small device at the elevator and hit the penthouse button. "So only you can access the floor using this fob? Nobody else can access your place?"

He shook his head. "Not without approval from me. I told you that you didn't need to check through my building and my apartment for any intruders. The security in my building is top-notch."

"Your building?"

He gave a small smile and nodded. "My building."

Fuck me. I shrugged my shoulders. "I had to make sure. You never know when someone could try to attack you. The parking lot, the lobby, all of them are accessible to other people. It's my job to get you home safely."

The elevator dinged open to a doorway. Dominic unlocked the front door with his fingertips, leading us directly into a massive vestibule, the view of the entire city of Manhattan welcoming us into the obnoxiously large living room beyond. A loud whistle escaped me as I took in the sheer magnificence of Dominic Park's "humble" abode.

We were on the 120th floor, and I felt like I was watching the city from the clouds. Despite the stark glass walls and massive open space, his house felt surprisingly homey and welcoming. A large, dark green, L-shaped couch with over a dozen throw pillows strewn across it faced a massive TV hanging from the ceiling over an electric fireplace. Potted and hanging plants graced every corner of the house, flooding the space with life and lush greenery. Soft, expansive carpets transformed the entire space into a warm, cozy cocoon, making me want to spread-eagle on the floor and get thoroughly fucked in front of the fire.

I turned to Dominic and found him watching me, eyes blazing with heat. Maybe he was having the same thoughts as me. My throat was dry as I asked, "Do you have any other exit aside from this elevator?"

He tried to walk past me, and I immediately stopped him. "I go first."

He sighed, clearly displeased, and pointed to the right. "There's an emergency exit door when you cross the kitchen and go to the pantry."

"Stay here."

I quickly crossed the kitchen area, and it looked like it was picked straight out of a magazine. Once I reached the door that Dominic mentioned, I went through and checked the door that led into the stairwell. Everything was silent, and I made sure the door opened only from inside.

With that being done, I crossed to where Dominic waited for me in the living room, now sitting on the barstool in his kitchen. "Do you need me to take you upstairs? Want to see my bedroom?" His voice was rough, his eyes hooded. I was so tempted to walk up to him, stand between his legs, and jam my tongue down his throat.

Instead, I stood a few feet away from him, afraid my temptations would overpower my senses. "Yes, please. But I step through the doors first."

He gave me a single nod as I led the way. We climbed up the massive, helical staircase leading us to the next floor, the light from the huge central chandelier washing him in golden hues. He'd lost his suit jacket as soon as we entered the house, so he only wore a shirt and pants, his sleeves rolled to his elbows.

I inspected every room, with him opening the doors for me, and me walking in and looking under every bed, through every closet, behind every shower curtain. They were all designed similarly, with king-size beds, work desks, side tables, and lush carpets.

"You ready for the last room, Samaira?" he asked, walking to the end of the hallway. An eight-foot-high, dark wood door loomed in front of us.

Slowly, he opened the room, and without him having to

tell me, I knew it was his bedroom. It looked like a lived-in space. The walls were a rich black color. You'd think that black color on walls would make a room drab and weary. But his room looked lethal and cozy. The slight pops of color came from the green plants and the polished-wood work desk in the corner. Another wall was lined with floor-to-ceiling black bookshelves, brimming with books and vinyl records. Warm yellow and orange lights brought warmth to the dark space. His bed sheets were charcoal gray, with black pillow-cases and a black comforter. And the ceiling over his bed was covered in a large mirror.

My gaze flashed to his, and the man simply placed his hands in his pockets and shrugged. My mind flooded me with the thoughts of all of his pale, golden skin stark naked on the dark sheets, the mirror on the ceiling capturing all of his glorious beauty as he jerked himself off.

Fuck that mirror.

Just great. Now I'm jealous of a fucking mirror.

I turned around and found him leaning against his bedroom door, his eyes tracking my every move. "Can I enter my room, Tigress?"

I loved it when he called me *Tigress*. It made me feel powerful and, at the same time, somehow cherished and admired. It made me want to show off my strength to him, made me want to lick him and bask under his attention.

His question reminded me of why I stood in his room. I checked his closet, which exuded wealth with its neatly lined rack of suits and about a hundred shirts and pants.

His bathroom was the size of my bedroom, with a glass partition separating the shower space. A large clawfoot tub was placed along another glass wall, looking down upon the endless stretch of the city, but I was *not* tempted to get into it at all.

Not finding any intruder in the washroom, I walked into the room and nodded at Dominic. "All clear."

He stepped inside the bedroom, and I realized how close I stood to his bed. If he wanted—if *I* wanted—he could easily cover the distance in five steps and push me down. This man did something to me, something so primal and carnal, it made me lose all my sense of self. He made me feel raw and flayed open, needy and desperate for his touch, hungry for a single taste. He made me feel strong and powerful with just the way he glanced at me but also made me shy and downright giddy when he smiled at me with those dimples.

I was a riot of a hundred emotions, trying to get them under control but constantly failing.

My throat went dry as he took a step closer, the scorching heat in his eyes sending hot sparks of electric pleasure coursing through my body. Sharp arousal surged through my core, making me lightheaded for a second as I felt the sticky wetness glide through my folds. My core throbbed as he took another step closer to me, and I just had to rub my fucking legs together to assuage the ache. "I should go."

Knowing there were no intruders in his place, I really had nothing to do.

He kept walking toward me, his steps measured, his eyes rooting me to the spot, my heart hammering against my ribs. He removed his hands from his pockets and slowly, so I could stop him, took my hand in his. I looked down at the softness with which his fingers wrapped around mine, the rise and fall of his chest giving away the fact that he was just as affected by my touch as I was by his.

Softly, he put a finger to my chin and pushed it up so my eyes met his. "Have you fulfilled your duty of being my bodyguard for the evening?"

Blood raced through my veins, my heart pumping faster as his words washed over me. He looked at me with so much desire, so much hunger, so much *need*, words escaped me. So I nodded, lost in his delicious scent, in his dark, hooded eyes, in the way his nostrils flared as he bent his head slightly and breathed me in.

Keeping his finger under my chin, he growled low in his throat. "Good girl. Now, it's my turn."

My pussy pulsed with an ache so sharp that wetness coated my thighs. I tightened my hand into fists to stop my fingers from pushing between my legs. "Your turn for what?" My voice was a whisper, my words falling over his lips.

I didn't know how it was possible, but he moved even closer into my body so his chest brushed against my nipples, shooting sparks of biting pleasure to my already aching core. He brushed his soft lips along mine, his thumb delicately tracing my jaw as he rumbled, "My turn to fulfill the duty of a man dying to taste his woman. My duty to worship her. To pleasure her. To have her sit on his face until she's coming down his throat."

My brain instantly fried and short-circuited, sending every signal down south as he brushed his thumb along my lip. "Would you let me fulfill my duty, Maira?"

My neck arched involuntarily, need so sharp flooding my body, my knees weakened. I had to clutch his shirt to stay upright. Instead of the *fuck yes, yes please,* trying to escape my throat, the words that actually came out of my throat were, "Nobody calls me that."

His hand wrapped around the side of my neck, his thumb pushing into the silver ring of my choker, pulling a whimper out of my lips. He bent his head lower and ran his nose along my jaw. "Good. Only I get to call you that. Now, Maira, baby, you're killing me here. Say yes. Let me worship you."

With one word, with three letters, I turned a deaf ear to my brain and listened to my heart, my body, and my soul. "Yes."

CHAPTER 21

DOMINIC

One word from her lips, and I pulled her lips to mine by the ring on her collar. One day, I was going to put a leash on it and ask my tigress to crawl for me. Hopefully in her mask.

Her soft lips brushed against mine. My mind flashed white, and ecstasy flooded my blood as her taste exploded in my mouth. I clutched her closer and pushed my tongue in deeper, fucking her mouth the way I wanted to fuck her sweet, sweet pussy.

I wanted to lick and bite and taste every inch of her glorious skin. Considering she was only in her tank top and sweatpants, every inch of her curves and her well-honed muscles molded against mine, making my cock strain against my pants, weeping with the need to be buried deep inside her.

I moved down her throat, pulling the little slip of her sleeve aside, baring her shoulder to me and arching her neck by the back of her head to get better access, causing her to whimper. "Dominic."

My name coming from her lips had my cock pulsing and

precum spurting from my tip. "What is it, baby?" I asked, nipping across her shoulder, tasting her skin.

Her fingers tightened on my shirt, and I all but threw her on the bed. But instead, she pulled back and asked, "Can… Can I take a quick shower?"

My cock throbbed with the thought of a naked Samaira in my shower. And I slammed down on my knees, kissing and licking every inch of her covered body, nuzzling between her legs like a man starved for an eternity. I looked up at her from down on my knees, lowering her sweatpants slightly to lick at her abs, pleading with her with my eyes. "Tell me to join you."

Her cheeks flushed as her lips parted. Her chest heaved as she clutched the collar of my shirt, her eyes burning me with hunger and desire. "Join me."

I jumped to my feet, carrying her in my arms, making her shriek and giggle. "Oh my god. You can't lift me, Dominic."

Her legs wrapped around my hips as I supported her ass in one hand while I held her waist with the other, kissing her. "Clearly, I can."

She licked the side of my throat, moaning my name. Her eyes shone with mischief. "I'll break your back. I've heard bones weaken with ag…"

"Don't you dare finish that sentence, Maira."

"Age."

A harsh chuckle escaped my lips as I stepped inside the shower and put her down. "You're going to get punished for that."

She trembled as I stepped closer to her. I loved how she responded to my words. "Arms up."

Her eyes darkened, and her chest heaved. But she obeyed.

My cock jerked at her obedience, releasing so much precum I could feel it sliding down the length of my cock. I knew it in my bones that if I asked her to drop to her knees, she'd do it without question. But I didn't need her on her knees today. I needed her taste on my tongue.

Silently, I grabbed her thick tank top and removed it.

My eyes tracked every inch of skin that she revealed. She wasn't soft and dainty. She was all hard edges and bulging muscles. She had abs that glistened with sweat. She had swagger and confidence that made my dick hard. She had hair that I wanted to wrap around my fist when I fucked her. She had dirt streaking her skin from our fight. She was raw and honest; she was powerful and vulnerable; she was protective and stubborn.

She was everything my heart desired and my soul needed to feel complete.

My fingers traced every single line of her well-defined muscles, committing them to memory. I unzipped the front of her sports bra, my heart beating out of my chest in anticipation. The moment her sports bra pulled open, her glorious tits pushed out, and I nearly crumpled to my knees. "You're fucking stunning, baby."

"Touch me, Dominic." Samaira leaned against the wall of the shower, her neck arched back, her tits pushed up to me, desire flushing her cheeks red.

"Your wish is my command." I wrapped my arms around her waist and leaned down, nuzzling at the softness of her breasts, breathing in her scent. She smelled of oranges and a hint of sweat, adrenaline, and raw power, of the woman who took a bullet for me.

I looked at the bandage covering her arm where the bullet had grazed her. I pressed soft kisses around the covered area, trying to take the pain away. "You have no idea how much I hate seeing this."

"It's okay. Doesn't even hurt all that much." Her voice was soft as she trembled in my arms. "Just make me feel good, Dominic."

Her words were my undoing. I pulled her nipple between my lips, my mouth watering at the way her soft skin melted over my tongue. Her dusky-brown nipple pebbled in my mouth, and my precum soaked my briefs. Her moans spurred me on as I pushed my leg between hers, giving her my thigh to grind on.

She was a writhing, beautiful mess in my arms and very close to coming. Quickly, I stopped, needing to feel her come on my tongue. She whimpered at the loss of my mouth on her tits. "Soon, baby. Need to see all of you."

I dropped to my knees and removed her sweatpants and underwear in one go, leaving her completely naked.

Her golden-brown skin shone under the warm light, high-lighting every cut of her muscles. The black and red tiger on her arm undulated as she flexed her biceps, the bandage from her wound giving her that striking, badass edge. The veins on her forearm popped as she raised her arm over her head, showing off every inch of her lethal beauty. "Stop flexing, Maira. I'm already obsessed with you."

Her lips were curved in a smile as she winked at me and proceeded to put her foot on my knee. She arched her spine even further, pushing her tits up and flexing her thighs. Her pussy was entirely bare, and my mouth watered at the way her juices coated her entirely, also running down her thighs.

I held her foot and slowly moved my palm over her calf. When I reached the back of her knee, she let out a loud moan, the sound echoing around the room. "Let me watch that pretty pussy." I lifted her knee and wrapped it over my shoulder, moving closer to her pussy.

"Dominic." She whimpered my name, writhing on top of me, her hands pushing at the walls of the shower. She was completely naked while I was fully dressed. The vision of us only managed to make me harder, need hammering through my body to devour my tigress whole.

The inside of her thighs glistened with her wetness. I looked up to meet her eyes, and her cheeks were flushed as she bit her lip. Keeping my eyes on her face, I spread her lips, and her eyes rolled back.

"Eyes on me, Maira."

Her eyes burned with need. "Good girl."

She shuddered, and I looked at her spread pussy, and what I saw had me almost coming in my pants. I had to squeeze the base of my cock through my pants to stop myself from ejaculating. "Fuck, baby," I exhaled. "Look how wet you are. Is this all for me?"

I spread her juices all over her pretty little pussy with my thumb, making her moan and whimper. Her scent was all woman and earthy musk, all power and submission rolled into droplets of fucking heaven. I brushed my nose along her seam, breathing in deep, my chest thundering with blinding need.

I nuzzled into her crotch, soaking my face with her wetness, coating my face in the proof of her need. Need for me. I wasn't kidding when I told her I needed to worship her. To drown in her. She was my goddess of vengeance, and I was a dying man at her altar.

"I'm glad I didn't turn on the shower right away." I pressed my lips to the apex of her thighs, dragging my tongue all the way from her little rosebud at the back to the top of her clit, her thighs tightening around my shoulder. "Fuck, I would've never forgiven myself if I'd missed out on this."

"You're making me crazy, Dominic. Please, please, please, give me more." Her hand moved from the wall of the shower to the back of my head, clutching my hair like her life depended on it.

I licked her pussy again, her taste exploding on my tongue, making me dizzy with want. "What were you saying about my age, baby? I'll show you how strong my knees are for my age."

"No, please." She pulled my hair hard, trying to push me deeper into her.

I moved away from her and gave a sharp slap to her clit.

Her shriek rang in the room, echoing off the walls and

wrapping around my cock. "You might be in control outside, but here, I'm the one in charge."

I gave her another sharp slap on her wet cunt, and she shuddered above me, a sob escaping her lips. Her pussy gushed so much wetness. I latched on to her to capture it all on my tongue, not wanting to waste a single drop on the floor.

She went to putty in my arms, her body going lax at my tone. Her obedience, her response to my every touch, her shuddering body every time I dragged my tongue around her clit, had blood pounding through my veins. I looked up to find her eyes drunk on submission, her chest heaving with the strain of holding herself up on one leg.

"I need you to come in my mouth, baby. Need to feel your taste exploding on my tongue."

My mouth was back on her pussy as I pushed my tongue in her opening, drowning myself in her taste. My body shuddered as she gushed in my mouth, my hands tightening on her thighs, knowing I was going to leave my marks etched on her skin. My balls were so full, so fucking tight and heavy, and I was dying to jerk myself. My cock throbbed and jerked and ached. It ached so fucking much that I was on the verge of madness. The need to stroke myself, to relieve the sharp ache, had me moaning into her opening.

The vibration from my mouth had her writhing on my face, her thighs threatening to squeeze my throat. I had to hold her steady by pushing my hand against her hips. I fucked her with my tongue, licking around her clit in a rhythmic motion, thrusting into her opening at every upward stroke.

Her hand clutched my hand that held her hip, her nails digging into my skin, sending pinpricks of pain shooting down my arm. It only added to the pleasure pounding through my veins. She was so fucking wet. I inserted two of my fingers in her dripping opening as I continued to lick around her clit.

The moment I moved my fingers in a come-hither motion in tandem with flicking her clit with my tongue, she tightened around my fingers as her body arched into an orgasm. Pleasure slammed through my veins as I watched her back arch in pleasure. Her eyes rolled back into her head, tears sliding down her cheeks. Her mouth dropped open in a small O, and she moaned so brokenly, her juices sliding down my fingers.

It was when she pushed my fingers into her even deeper, holding me inside her as she cried beautifully over me and shuddered around me, that my balls tightened and my cock exploded into a blinding rush of pleasure. My mouth latched on to one of her fingers at her pussy, needing to feel her in my mouth as my hips jerked and rolled as my orgasm rocketed through me like an earthquake, shifting and realigning my life, drowning me in pleasure like I'd never felt before, utterly ruining me for any other woman.

I panted on my knees, my face covered in her sweetness, as I caught my breath. Slowly, I got back up on my feet, licking and tasting her sweat-soaked skin. I took in her face, the streaks of tears on her cheeks making her look wrecked and ruined. A beautiful mess. A debauched goddess. I licked her tears, and they tasted like mine.

I brushed her hair behind her ears and pressed a kiss to her forehead. "Let me get the shower started."

She nodded, and I moved around to turn on the knobs of the rain shower, setting the temperature to high. Water rained down on me, soaking my clothes. But I didn't give a fuck.

I turned on several knobs along the wall that started to spray warm jets of water on our bodies. Her moan had me turning around to find her face turned up to the water, wearing a soft, relaxed smile. Water sluiced down her body, making me want to follow the droplets with my tongue.

"This is heaven, Dominic."

I watched the gentle smile on her face, and my lethal tigress looked as soft as a kitten. I wanted to wrap her in my arms and run my fingers through her beautiful, dark hair. I simply couldn't take my eyes off her. "It is, sweetheart."

She opened her eyes and looked down at me. A smile tugged at her lips. "Are you planning to take off your clothes?"

"You only had to ask, baby." Slowly, I removed my shirt, one button at a time, enjoying the way her eyes followed my fingers. Loving the way they lingered on my chest.

I clicked open my belt and dragged it out of my pants, relishing her heated gaze on me.

My cock stirred in my pants, and her eyes heated as she noticed the effect she had on me. But it was when I pulled off my briefs that her eyes went wide as she took in the evidence of what her coming in my mouth did to me. "Is that…?"

Her chest heaved as she placed a hand on the wall beside her. I couldn't help but chuckle at her reaction. "I was barely holding on when I tasted you on my tongue. But I couldn't hold back when you came on my fingers."

Once I was completely naked, I let her continue her perusal. She was tall and muscular, but I was taller and wider. From a woman who'd honed her body to be a deadly predator, her admiration for my body had me preening on the inside.

Her eyes followed me as I plucked the shampoo from a rack and stepped behind her. Gently, I washed her hair, and she all but melted into me. All of her soft curves lined up with my hard body, my now plump cock slipping between her tight, round cheeks, flooding me with warmth and that soft churning of arousal.

Once I'd washed her hair, I softly washed her body, suds of soap slipping between our bodies as we kissed each other. Hot water washed away the entire day as I kept reminding myself that she was all right. My hands roamed over her body, feeling her strength. I clutched her hair and turned her face so she looked at me. Water rained down over us, and I traced the droplets on her cheek, running my thumb along her lips. "You're breathtaking. And you're mine."

She ran her fingers over my chest and stared back at me with just as much possession. "And you?"

I brushed my lips over hers. "Only yours."

She pulled me down and took my lips in hers, sealing her fate with mine. I bit her lip and nipped her jaw, whispering in her ear, "I'm going to show you how much all through the night, baby."

She giggled as I grabbed the towel from the rack outside the shower stall. I quickly wiped myself and helped her pat her hair dry. I wrapped her in a big, fluffy robe and grabbed the hair dryer from under my sink, dragging her to the bed.

I took a seat along the headboard and plugged in the hair dryer. I widened my legs and patted the spot between my thighs.

Her eyes moved to my slightly open towel, giving her a glimpse of my cock. I pulled her by the hand and got her seated between my legs with a big smile on my face. "You'll get my cock after your hair is dry. Can't have you falling sick."

She lightly wrapped her fingers around my knee, her voice soft as an angel as she whispered, "Thank you."

"For what, baby? Drying your hair?" I turned on the dryer and started to dry the strands.

Her voice was barely audible under the noise of the dryer, but I heard it. "For taking care of me."

I shut off the dryer for a second and pressed a kiss to her head. "Always."

Her head shook slightly as her fingers tightened around my knees. Before she could try to put any walls between us, I turned on the blow-dryer to the max and kept drying her hair.

I dried them until every strand of her beautiful, dark brown hair slid through my fingers like silk. One day, I was going to wrap them around my fist and feed her my cock. I put away the hair dryer and brushed her hair with my fingers for a few minutes, giving her a massage on her shoulders.

I gently tilted her head and pressed a kiss to the side of her neck, only to find her already dozing off.

My heart gave a painful squeeze against my ribs while simultaneously gushing with so much fucking warmth that I had to clutch my chest, struggling to fucking deal with the softest ache I'd ever felt. I pressed another light kiss, this time to the back of her head, and gently helped Samaira settle more comfortably. I turned off the lights, placed a glass of water beside her, then walked to my closet.

I dressed in a pair of sweatpants, got on the other side of the bed, and instantly smelled my shampoo in her hair. I couldn't help but stare at how peaceful she looked sleeping. Samaira's soft snores filled the air, and it almost had me chuckling. She was so adorable and loud as she slept. I moved slightly closer to her so I could see her better and feel the soft heat of her body.

I so badly wanted to pull her into my arms and sleep wrapped around her body, breathing in her scent. My arms ached to do just that, but I didn't want to without her permission.

But something magical happened as her light snores stopped and she moved in her sleep.

She turned around and shuffled closer to me, as if her body was yearning for the warmth of my body. I stayed still, not breathing even a little as she slowly wrapped one of her legs over my hip and placed her palm right on top of my chest. She grumbled something low in her sleep and pushed her face against my throat. My arms trembled as I pressed my hand low on her back and pushed her into me, pulling her closer against me.

My eyes watered, a shaky breath escaping my chest as my heart settled. Because for the first time in my life, a woman had slept in my arms, and I finally felt at home.

CHAPTER 22

A door slamming jerked me awake. My heart pounded in my chest at the unknown surroundings as I forgot where I was for a second. My eyes snapped to Dominic, who stood at the door of his bedroom, and the previous night flashed through my mind.

I looked down and found myself in a fluffy white robe that was nearly open. Quickly, I clutched it closed as Dominic walked up to me.

I didn't even remember falling asleep. The last thing I remembered was feeling Dominic's large hands moving through my hair as he blow-dried my hair and my heart feeling so full I got tears in my eyes.

I was lost in memories when Dominic loomed over me, his eyes frighteningly worried as he pulled off my blanket. "Oh my god, Dominic. Are you okay? What is going on?"

He clutched his hair and pulled the strands as he paced the room. "I am so, so sorry, Samaira. But we have a problem."

My mind instantly prepared for the worst. I jumped off

the bed, my robe almost falling open. "Do I need a gun? Are there any intruders in your house?"

His steps halted, and he looked at me with his jaw hung open. "Uh…should've known you'd think the worst."

"You said we got a problem."

His shoulders curled, and he cringed. "Yeah. My parents. They're on their way here."

"What?" I shrieked. Oh no no no no no no no. No.

I really wished it were the intruders. They would've been so much easier to deal with.

I looked down at my robe and ran to the washroom. My eyes fell on the wet clothes in the corner of the shower. "Dominic," I shrieked. "All my clothes are wet. I can't meet your parents in a robe."

I was officially freaking the fuck out. I'd met his parents once. As a professional Wildcat on a mission to bring their daughter and their family justice. Not sleeping with their son. I looked down the large window in the washroom.

Was it possible to survive a fall from the 120th floor? Probably not. Next time, I was going to have a parachute set here.

Dominic barged into the bathroom with a pair of sweatpants and a large sweatshirt clutched in his hand. "Okay, no need to panic, baby. I have some clothes that you can wear."

I grabbed his clothes from his hands and pushed him out of the bathroom. "They're going to know we slept together, Dominic," I shouted from behind the door, putting on his clothes.

Fuck, they smelled so good. His sweatpants fit me perfectly around the ass; I only had to fold them a bit from the bottom.

I heard him stepping behind the door. "They might. Can't deny that. But they wouldn't mind."

My head popped out of his sweatshirt as my eyes rounded at the door. "Of course they're going to mind. You *hired* me to find your sister's rapists. And here I am, sleeping with you. Oh god, what was I thinking?"

"You have one minute before I'm coming in, so you better finish getting ready, baby."

"Ugh. I'm never staying over at your place again, Dominic," I shouted and quickly peed, washed my face, and brushed my teeth.

My hair looked soft and slightly rumpled. I quickly brushed the strands with my fingers and was putting my hair in a ponytail when Dominic barged through the door. He walked up to me and pulled me into his arms. "You, Maira, do not get to regret last night. We weren't a mistake. I will not stop taking care of you. Is that clear?"

His eyes were burning with ironclad determination, and I knew nothing I said would change his mind. If I were being honest with myself, last night was the first time in years that I'd felt like the Samaira from thirteen years ago. The young girl who'd dreamed of falling in love, of finding a man who would treat her like a princess, who'd lay the world at her feet and dance with her under the stars. Dominic had made me feel soft, like a woman who was more than just a killing machine, like a woman who needed to be cared for.

I hated admitting it, but I loved how he pampered me.

I looked at Dominic, who was waiting for my answer. He held my face with so much care I wanted to melt in his arms. "Crystal clear."

A relieved smile came over his face, and he pulled me into a quick kiss. "Good girl. Now, let's hurry."

He grabbed my hand and rushed us out the door. I couldn't help but giggle as my stomach twisted with nerves. I felt like we were teenagers sneaking into our rooms to make out. Not a man who managed a billion-dollar empire and a woman who killed and tortured men for a living.

A loud doorbell chimed somewhere overhead, and Dominic let go of my hand as he rushed to the door. I stood near his wide couch, preparing myself for the look of shock—and maybe disappointment—on his parents' faces.

The moment the door opened, Dominic's mother slammed into Dominic, pulling him into a hug. She wore a blouse and loose-fitting pants and carried a large bag in her hands. Dominic and his father ran behind her as she pulled out of the hug and entered the house. "Dominic Park. When were you going to tell your parents that you were attacked? Do you have any idea…Oh, dear."

His mother's words trailed off as her eyes finally landed on me. They scanned over my body, taking in my clothes, and I was tempted to run upstairs and lock myself in Dominic's room. Instead, I gave her a small wave, my stomach cramping with nerves. "Hello, Mrs. Park."

I was prepared for her to be disappointed. But a downright gleeful smile came over her face, and that just managed to terrify me even further. "Oh, Samaira, dear. Didn't expect to find you here. And didn't I tell you to call me Hana-eonni?"

"Oh…uh…Sorry, Hana-eonni. I was just leaving."

"Oh, nonsense, dear. I'm so glad to see you here. Sophie told me all about you saving both my babies and taking a bullet for them." She quickly handed off the bag in her hand to Dominic and came rushing to me.

In the next moment, I was pulled into a hug, her arms wrapping around me so tightly and with such motherly warmth that my eyes filled with tears. I glanced at Dominic from above her head, and his eyes widened with concern. "Eomma, we don't want to scare Samaira."

She quickly let me go and held my cheeks. I had to bend lower due to our height difference. "I don't know how I could ever thank you for saving my children, dear. But you must stay so I can feed you breakfast. Okay?"

I sniffled and gave her a jerky nod. There was a reason I had left my own family. They made me so weak. So terrified. If something were to happen to Dominic's family because of the work I did, I would never be able to forgive myself. Hana-eonni clutched my hand and dragged me toward the kitchen and dining space and sat me down at the dining table.

Dominic went to the kitchen and placed the large bag on the countertop, which seemed to be packed with food. She went to the kitchen, where Dominic was emptying the contents. "Dominic, let's get the food going, shall we?"

"I can help." I got up from the chair but was quickly stopped by just the look in Hana-eonni's eyes. "Absolutely not, dear. You need to rest. You were shot."

"It was just a graze," I mumbled, but Dominic and his mother both glared at me to sit back down.

While the mother-son duo got busy in the kitchen, Dominic's father sat across from me. "I'd like to thank you as well, Miss Samaira. You are very brave."

"It's no problem, Mr. Park. It's my job to protect your children and find your culprits."

We talked about where the interrogation had reached and the possible suspects when Dominic walked toward the entrance. I was almost off my seat to get the door when he waved a hand. "It's just Sophie and Sloane."

Sophie came and hugged her parents, and her dad handed her a suitcase. While the Park family caught up with all that had transpired, Sloane came to sit beside me. She deliberately and very slowly dragged her eyes from my sweatpants to the sweatshirt I wore. "Stop it or I'm going to punch you, Sloane."

Her smile turned devious as she mumbled slowly so only the two of us could hear. "Oh, I thought a good dicking down would put you in a better mood."

I kicked her feet under the table. "Shut up. His parents are right here."

She quickly raised her hands in surrender and bumped my shoulder. "I'm happy for you, Sami. He looks at you as if you're the only person to exist in the world."

Blood rushed to my cheeks, and I couldn't help but turn around in my seat to look at Dominic, only to find him staring at me. I was so fucked. His mom gave him a tap on his head, dragging his attention away from me. I couldn't help but get lost in how warm and homely the Park family looked.

Sloane pressed her chin to my shoulder. "Some of us don't have the option, Sami. But you do. Give them a call."

I sighed. I didn't want to get into my parents right now. "Please tell me you brought me clothes."

She was used to this, so she didn't call me out for changing the topic. "Yep. I got you a whole new personal assistant wardrobe. You're gonna love it."

"Please tell me it's not pencil skirts."

She scoffed. "As if you could handle pencil skirts."

"I absolutely could. They're just not practical if I have to fight in them."

She rolled her eyes. "Relax. You're going to love what I got you."

We were talking about how Sophie was settling in when Dominic, Sophie, and Hana-eonni brought all the food to the table. There was an abundance of food—a large pot of soup, rice, stir-fried tofu on the side, kimchi, pickled radishes, and rolled omelets. Sloane moaned dramatically after tasting bites of each food item, making everyone laugh. Sophie talked about the den and how she was settling in, whereas Dominic sat directly across from me and held my leg between his the entire time we ate.

Once we'd had the early breakfast and cleaned everything up, Dominic's parents left with strict instructions to keep them posted on every little update. Sophie and Sloane also left after bringing in a brand-new wardrobe.

Since Dominic was already running late for his meeting, he pulled me into the shower with him, insisting that it would help us get ready quicker. One orgasm later, where he came between my ass cheeks after eating me out, we rushed around to get ready.

The moment I stepped out of the bathroom in a professional blouse and large flare pants, with my golden necklaces and choker and half of my ear piercings pulled out to give me a slightly less edgy look, Dominic halted from where he was putting on his tie. "How do I look? Do I fit the bill as your personal assistant?"

Slowly, he tightened his tie and made his way to me. He tucked a stray strand of hair behind my ear and gave me a soft kiss on the cheek. "If we don't leave my house in the next minute, I won't be responsible for what happens next."

I couldn't help but chuckle. "You do know that my only job here is to keep you safe. And you're the safest in your house. You won't hear any objections from me if you'd prefer to stay in."

He pulled me into his arms with a loud groan. "We need to go. I have an important client from London coming in an hour."

I clutched his tie and started walking downstairs. "Let's get moving then."

In the next five minutes, we were seated in the back seat of his car, and Maxim drove us to the office. Dominic updated me on the arrangements Kai made for settling me into his office. While he would attend the meetings, I'd stay busy catching up on the recordings from the state attorney's office.

Maxim dropped us at the entrance, where I got out before Dominic. I checked for different vantage points and let Dominic walk in front of me, keeping an eye on the surroundings. Once we were inside the large lobby space of his office building, Dominic directed us to the private elevator reserved for executives working on the top floor of the building.

We entered a large, open office space. Dominic was a powerhouse as he walked along the length of the aisle separating the working space with purpose and power. People paused what they were doing as they stared at him. While Dominic's focus was on greeting everyone around him, my focus was on him.

I kept my eyes trained on the surroundings, taking note of the exits, the kitchen space, the lounge areas, and the conference rooms. All the spaces were separated by glass partitions, flooding the entire office space with morning light.

Dominic stopped in front of Kai, who stood smiling at the door to what was Dominic's office. Before Dominic could get a word in, Kai turned to me. "I can tell you today's going to be amazing."

I chuckled. "Is that right?"

He shrugged. "I'm pretty sure Mr. Park here will be in a very good mood. And every one of us would breathe a little easier."

Dominic sighed beside me and walked into his office, with Kai and me following. I met Kai's eyes, and he gave me a see-what-I-have-to-deal-with-everyday look, making me chuckle. "He's a hard-ass, huh?"

"Don't you think so?" Kai asked, his eyes scrunched in genuine curiosity.

I glanced at Dominic, who stood leaning against his desk, staring at us, and I could just imagine him meticulously checking everybody's work and snapping at every little mistake he caught. The man seemed to demand perfection from the world around him. But with me, I'd only ever seen him smile. Except in the bedroom. He was a bossy fucker there, but that just made him hotter.

I shook my head at Kai though. "He's alright."

Kai snorted. "Pretty sure he's too scared of you."

A chuckle burst out of me at the same time Dominic scoffed. "Fuck off, Kai. I'm not scared of Samaira."

Our eyes met, and I raised my eyebrows at him.

He simply rolled his eyes and grumbled something low in his throat.

Kai nodded, looking at Dominic with a ridiculously mischievous smile on his face. "That's right, Hyung. Totally not scared of her. I see it."

Dominic sighed, clutching the bridge of his nose. "Why the hell do I keep you around?"

Kai righted the tie he wore and cleared his throat. "Everything's been set as per your instructions in your office for Miss Samaira. Mr. Thompson would be here in five minutes. I've already set up the presentation on the screen in the conference room along with the refreshments."

Dominic's lip curled on one side. "Hmm. Sounds about right. Thank you."

Kai gave me a wink and turned to Dominic. "If there wasn't anything else, I'll be in the conference room."

With that, he left the office, closing the door behind him.

I took in Dominic's office. His desk was situated in the center of the entire space, with two maroon rolling chairs facing his sleek yet comfortable chair. To the right of his desk, along the adjacent wall, a chair and a small white desk were set up, clearly for me.

I could see everything from his full-facade glass windows, from the Empire State Building to the One World Trade Center. While Dominic sat at his desk, I placed my purse—something I rarely used—on my desk and pulled out my laptop.

Once I sat down in my chair, I turned around to find Dominic staring at me. "You good, baby?"

My eyes widened. "You can't say that here. I'm your fake personal assistant and your very real bodyguard. We can't... We can't be together like that out in public."

His eyes slightly dimmed, and I instantly regretted it. I knew I was right, but he looked like I'd kicked his puppy. Still, he gave me a nod and a small smile. "I understand, Samaira. You're right. Now, I have a meeting in five and just want to make sure you're all set?"

I stood. "I'm all set. But I'd like to see the London associates for myself."

He pressed his lips together as if suppressing his smile.

"Alright. They should be here soon. Umm…are you planning to pat them down?"

I shook my head. "I'm just an assistant, remember? Can't exactly go full bodyguard on them. I just want to see and get a general vibe on them."

"Alright. Let me know if something feels off."

"I will."

In the meantime, he walked up to the small pantry on the other side of the room and said, "I have a personal coffee machine here. But feel free to get whatever you want from the kitchen area. We get fresh snacks delivered every day."

He led me to the kitchen and dining space, and I could feel the eyes of everyone from his office.

"Are you planning to tell them who I am?" I asked him softly.

He grabbed a plate and placed a blueberry muffin on it, then nodded. "Kai already sent out an email that I've hired a personal assistant. They're just curious."

I nodded and took the plate he handed me. "Makes sense."

Right then, the elevator doors pinged open and five men stepped out. I placed the plate on one of the empty tables in the dining area and walked beside Dominic as he made his way to welcome the associates. Kai arrived at the same time and stood right beside me.

They looked like typical suit-clad businessmen. The slightly older man in the center wore a jolly smile on his face as he shook Dominic's hand. Clearly, he was the boss. The remaining four stayed a step behind, following their boss's cues. Dominic shook everybody's hand and introduced us. "Gentlemen, these are my personal assistants, Samaira and Kai. Kai will be joining us in the meeting."

Once we exchanged pleasantries, Kai led them all to the conference room while Dominic led me back to his office.

Once we stepped inside, he turned to me, his eyebrows raised in question.

"They don't look like a threat. You should be fine."

Dominic nodded, and I could see in his eyes that he wanted to step closer to me. His hands clenched into fists as he asked, "You'll be fine?"

I pressed my lips together, stopping myself from getting too giddy, and nodded. "I'll be fine, Dominic. You go do your thing. I'll see you later. I'm a big girl. I can handle myself."

He ran his hand along his hair, being careful not to mess it up. "I know you can, Maira. Well, see you in a few hours. This meeting might run a bit long."

Once he was gone, I grabbed a coffee and an energy bar from his pantry and got to work. I plugged in my headphones and started listening to the state attorney's office recording at twice the speed, needing to catch up. I surfed through the hit man's phone on the other side, checking to see if he'd gotten any calls. I couldn't believe it had only been yesterday when we were attacked.

So much seemed to have changed in the past twenty-four hours. Dominic finally kissed me. Dominic made me come on his tongue, calling me *baby, Maira, sweetheart*. Dominic dried my hair, and we slept together in his bed. I was still not sure what this meant.

Did I want him to fuck me and fulfill all those filthy promises he made in my ear? Yes, absolutely yes.

Was I terrified of putting a label on what we were? Also, yes.

He seemed to have made up his mind that we belonged to each other. However, he also lived in a world where there were no consequences for one's actions. He didn't have to sacrifice a part of himself to be with the person he loved. It wasn't true for me, though.

I was extremely aware of my life choices. Being with him would only lead to danger and disaster. He made me weak.

He made me paranoid. He made me forget the world around me. Every time he looked at me, I forgot who I was. I forgot all the sacrifices I'd made to become a Wildcat.

Last night had been the first time I'd been taken care of like I was precious. Someone delicate. He was filthy and careful. He was full of rage, but he also had that loneliness shining in his eyes, which tugged at my heart. His eyes always softened when he looked at me but also churned with the darkest of desires when he touched me.

And I wanted more of his touch, more of his deliciously filthy words. I wanted his eyes on me—*only me*—all the time. I hated it when other women came closer to him and laughed with him. The thought of Dominic having gone down on some other woman made my blood boil.

His tongue, his cock, his heart, his attention, his thoughts, his smiles—they were all *mine*.

The only problem was that being mine might just put him in a constant state of risk and danger, and I wouldn't let anything or anybody harm Dominic. Not even me.

CHAPTER 23

Dominic had returned to the office after four long hours and was busy working on his computer. I grabbed lunch from the kitchen and flagged a few conversations from the state attorney for the Wildcats to review. That man was shady as fuck. Even if his son was found innocent of the crime against Sophie, these were not innocent men. There was something in his occasional conversations with the "boss" that raised my hackles. I needed Tara to put some sort of tracker on them.

I chatted in my Wildcats group, asking about updates on other cases. Lena had decided to pause on taking up a new case until we found the person who ordered a hit on Dominic. She was fairly certain that I'd also become a target if the person discovered I'd saved the Park siblings.

I was looking into the phone when I felt Dominic's eyes on me. I turned to him and gave him a quick glare, then looked around the glass walls of his office. Without moving his eyes off me, he clicked a button under his desk, and the glass walls turned opaque.

"Fancy." I looked at him, finally not worrying about people's eyes on us.

"Necessary." He winked at me.

"You have any more meetings?"

He shook his head. "No. Just some work to finish before we leave. You bored?"

I dragged my eyes over his suit and his broad chest. "I have a nice view."

A growl tore through his chest. "Careful, Maira. The office door has locks too."

Heat rushed to my cheeks at the nickname. "Have you ever done it here?" The question slipped from my lips before I could stop myself.

His eyes widened for a second, and an infuriating smile came over his face, making me regret asking the question. "You jealous, baby?"

I scowled. "No. Why would I be jealous? It would've been in the past."

His finger lightly rubbed his lips as if trying to hide the smile. "Hmm. I've never done anything sordid in my office, Maira. You'd be happy to know that you're the first woman I've slept with in three years."

"Three years?" How was that possible?

He chuckled and looked away as if embarrassed. "I've never seen you smile wider, baby."

I tried to school my expressions, but it was impossible. My heart was skipping to a stupidly jolly tune and dancing in delight. "How? Why? Look at you, Dominic. You're fucking hot."

His lips lifted in a smile as he shook his head. "Well, I guess, as years passed by, sleeping with someone just for the sake of a physical release stopped being fun. I felt even emptier and lonelier after sleeping with a random stranger, so I just stopped. I prefer to connect with someone emotionally first. I've dated long enough, and I've never found someone with whom I genuinely connected, someone I wanted to share my life with. So after a point, I just stopped trying."

My heart squeezed in my chest at the thought of Dominic feeling empty and lonely. Not everyone understood the loneliness that plagues your soul in the middle of the night when there is nobody to wrap their arms around you. Nobody to whisper secret nothings in your ear, nobody to share a laugh with, nobody to hold you when you cried. "Believe it or not, I understand better than most."

His eyes widened at that, and he instantly straightened in his chair. "Maira, I've been meaning to ask you. When you came to meet Sophie that first time, you said something very similar to Sophie. *Believe it or not, I understand better than most.* Did…uh…did something happen?"

My heart stopped. Fear paralyzed my body as my mind was transported to the past. To a time when I was a different Samaira. To a time when I lost everything. Memories flashed behind my eyes, one horrendous moment after another, striking my heart with vicious blows. I could see Dominic move across the room to sit on his knees, but I was somewhere else. I thought I was over it. I thought I'd fought through that time.

I knew I would have to share my history with Dominic someday.

I just didn't know it had to be today.

A strong grip on my knees and soft murmurs of my name in my ear pulled me out of my spiral, only to find Dominic's worried gaze on me. His eyes were rolling clouds of thunder. "Maira, baby. I'm so sorry for bringing this up out of nowhere. I should've been sensitive."

I squeezed his hand on my knee, my own hand trembling. "It's okay. Uh…it was a very long time ago."

"What the fuck happened?" he gritted out, his words dripping with fear and borderline anger.

I caressed his hand with my thumb, trying to stay in the

present with him. He looked at me with so much worry that it made me want to protect him from further pain. But for once, I knew he would be able to handle it.

I looked at him and gently caressed his cheek. "It was thirteen years ago. I was a nineteen-year-old college student in a small town in Texas. My parents were immigrants from India. They'd moved to Texas on a work visa. My younger sister, brother, and I were born in America. We grew up moving a lot. My dad was a software engineer and worked contract jobs. So, every few years, we would change towns and cities until he finally landed a permanent job when I was seventeen. We'd moved around so much that I accepted admission to a community college to live in the same town as my family. I wanted to have a steady life with my family for once, you know?"

When he nodded, I continued, "Anyway, life wasn't always easy when you were a brown girl in a predominantly white small town in Texas. Especially not when you're interested in dance and drama school."

Dominic's eyes widened, and I couldn't help but chuckle. "I know, right? Young Samaira was obsessed with Bollywood and wanted to become an actress in Hollywood. Can you imagine that?"

His eyes were serious, but he had a small smile on his face. It was that smile that softened the jagged edges of my old wounds. "I can imagine it, baby."

My cheeks warmed, and I rolled my eyes playfully. "Anyway, it wasn't easy. I was already dealing with a few mean girls in the drama club. I wasn't this well-built and strong then. I was just a tall brown girl with too many curves in a class where the standard was white girls who were a size 0. But I danced well. And not all boys thought curves made me fat.

"It sucked that it was the wrong kinda boys who noticed me. Being a naive fool who was finally getting some attention from a popular boy, I couldn't tell right from wrong. I was just happy to have the attention of the football jock. But as much as I loved the attention, my parents had drilled into me that I wasn't allowed to have a boyfriend until I graduated. So I was terrified of being intimate. I'd never even kissed a guy before the jock. But with each passing day, he grew increasingly impatient, and his impatience made him irritable. His words became harsh. Every word started to sting my soul. I was fat one minute, and I was sexy another. Word started to spread around that I was a prude. An uptight bitch. That I thought I was too good for him. So I obviously broke up with him. But…"

"But what?" Dominic's voice brought me back to the present. His voice was the warm honey to the open wound that Jack's words had inflicted.

I gave Dominic a soft smile and clutched his hand, reminding myself of the man that he was. "But weak and insecure men can't handle a girl's rejection. They especially can't handle rejection from a brown girl, an outcast. Well, things just got worse for me. He turned the entire college against me. He labeled me a slut. A bad lay. A frigid bitch. Girls bullied me while boys called me the worst names. Words that sliced away so much of my self-confidence, severely affecting my performance. Be it drama club or dance, I just couldn't perform.

"It was my birthday. I still remember I'd gotten a new dress. It wrapped around me so well that my curves looked perfect. My mom had prepared my favorite breakfast for me. Dad had booked a family vacation trip for us for the next weekend. I was thrilled at the thought of getting away from everything and spending time with people who loved me. I was running late for some reason and was walking to the bus stop. I still don't remember whether the streets were empty or not, but three guys grabbed me from behind and pushed me into their car."

Dominic's hand tightened on me as an anguished whisper escaped his lips. "No."

My eyes filled with tears as I whispered back, "Sound familiar? You want me to keep going? It's all more or less the same."

"Keep going, baby." His voice trembled, and his eyes glistened with tears.

"I won't go into much detail because I can't. But they raped me. Multiple times. I was missing for two days. I don't think they planned to kill me. They were trying to teach me a lesson. But they did kill that Samaira. I was in a coma for three days, then in the ICU for seven days after that. I read Sophie's medical reports. It was all the same and more. I have uterine scarring as well, which might impact my fertility."

A lone tear dropped down Dominic's cheek. I wiped it away. He was as still as a statue, not breathing, not moving. For some reason, that gave me the strength to keep talking. "They were rich white kids. One was the son of the college dean, another was the son of the police commissioner, and another was the son of a lawyer. Not only did we not get any justice, but they also made our lives hell. They got my dad fired from his work and bullied us into leaving the city. I never graduated. I lived with my parents for a year, depressed and broken. And it wasn't just me who broke. They broke my family. My parents were utterly defeated. My own father couldn't look me in the eye. My mother constantly cried and worried about my future. My little sister was terrified to go to school. She was afraid of her own classmates. My younger brother got into so many fights. We were all just so fucking broken. So one day, I just packed my bag and left my house. I couldn't watch my family suffer. I couldn't handle what I'd let happen to my family. Every time they saw me, their faces dropped. They forgot to smile. They forgot to live. And I couldn't take it. I…"

"You…what, sweetheart?"

I looked into his eyes and found nothing but kindness. Compassion. No pity. And I was grateful. "I miss them," I whispered in a broken voice. "I miss them so much."

Dominic's chest heaved. Pure anguish tore through his chest. "You haven't seen them since then?"

Tears rolled down my cheeks freely. I quickly wiped them off, loath to give my past power over me. "I couldn't before. But after I got my revenge, I became a Wildcat. And if...if something were to happen to me, I couldn't put them through that kind of suffering again. I did send them a letter that the rapists were taken care of. That I was alive. That it was time for me to move away for a while. I check in on them often, just to see if they're okay. And it seems they are. I just can't risk their lives. I can't be that selfish."

A hundred words seemed to be on the tip of his tongue. His eyes burned with red-hot rage as helplessness like never before appeared on his face. But only four words escaped his lips. "Tell me they're dead."

My mind flashed with the memories of the sweet, sweet revenge I'd exacted on those three scums. I still remember their tortured screams, their whimpering apologies, the warmth of their blood on my fingers, the coldness of their dead bodies. I met Dominic's eyes, and mine were filled with the memories of cold vengeance. "They're dead."

His chest expanded as his fist clenched tightly on my thigh. "Tell me they suffered."

A victorious smile came over my face. Softly, I held his face. "They're the first three dicks I chopped off."

"That's my girl. My vicious fucking tigress." He rose on his knees and pulled me into his arms, tucking my face in the crook of his neck. "I'm so fucking sorry that happened to you. It kills me, fucking guts me, that two of my favorite women had to suffer. I want to bring those fuckers back to life and kill them all over again."

I nuzzled into his chest, breathing in his spicy sandalwood

scent. Warmth spread through my body, thawing the coldness that had seeped into my bones. He gently ran his fingers through my hair as he kept apologizing.

I pressed a light kiss on his neck. "It's okay, Dominic. It was a long time ago."

I felt him shake his head over me. "It's never okay." All of a sudden, he froze. He pulled me out of his arms by my shoulders and looked down at me. A severe frown line ran between his eyebrows as he clenched his jaw. "Maira, I wasn't exactly gentle or kind while we were intimate. Did I hurt you? Was I too rough? Too blunt?"

I loved that he worried. I gave him a small, consoling smile. "You were perfect. For a long time, I didn't have sex with anyone. However, over time, I began to learn about my own body. What I liked. What triggered me. What made me soar."

"And?" He sat back on his knees near my feet and took my hands in his. It seems like he needed the touch more than I did.

I caressed the side of his face, playing with the strand of hair that fell over his forehead. "With the right person, I like to give up control. I like rough sex. I love to be mishandled a little under my explicit consent. Makes me feel like I'm reclaiming a part of me that I lost."

"I would never do anything without your consent. Please tell me you know that."

I pressed a kiss on the line between his eyebrows. "Dominic, maybe it's the way we met or the circumstances that brought us together, but I've never felt wary of you. My mind and my body have never, not even for a second, considered you a threat. There is nobody I trust more than you to not only ask for my consent but also give me exactly what I need. Your one kiss was better than all my past experiences combined."

"Fuck, baby. You're going to be the death of me. And

please don't talk about your past experiences. It makes me want to punch something."

I chuckled. "On the contrary, I'm here to protect you from a certain death. Don't you forget that."

"Hmm. Can't even try." He pressed his lips to my forehead, breathing me in. Goose bumps raced across my skin with the way he was being soft and careful with me. Like he needed to just hold me and didn't plan on letting me go.

How was I ever going to let him go? Dominic was slowly burrowing his way into my heart, making himself fucking vital for my happiness. With every conversation, with every kiss, with every soft smile, I was turning greedier and more obsessive. I wanted his laughs. I wanted his early morning kisses. I wanted to sleep with him buried inside me. I wanted to wake up with my nose pressed against his throat. I wanted to cook him my chai. I wanted to eat breakfast with him and his family. I wanted to ride my bike with him. I wanted to watch a movie with my head in his lap as he caressed my hair. I wanted to protect him. I wanted to please him. I wanted to kill for him. And I would.

My heart knew I wouldn't let anybody else have him. My body knew it would jump in front of a hundred bullets before they ever reached him. But my brain, the logical, practical part of my mind, the part that had seen and experienced the cruelties of this world, that understood the consequences of actions and the price to be paid to love someone, refused to claim him. All it wanted to do was keep him safe.

Dominic stood from where he sat, pulling a wounded sound from my chest. He pressed a kiss to my head. "Just give me a minute."

My hands tightened into fists as I watched him walk back to his table. He pressed a button on the phone, and Kai's voice came over the speaker. Dominic's voice was straight to the point when he said, "Kai, I'll send you my report by tonight.

I'll be leaving now. If you get any calls for me, please take a message and email me the transcripts."

"You got it. Have a good evening."

He turned his computer off and looked at me. "You ready to go?"

I got up and packed my laptop in my purse. "Where are we going?"

He moved closer to me and held my neck. "Home, baby. I need to hold you and feed you cake in bed. That's the only plan I have for us."

Laughter burst out of me. I flexed my biceps. "You think I got these muscles by eating cake in bed?"

He grabbed my hand and moved it over his rock-hard abs. "I've eaten many a cake in bed and kept these. You won't lose those guns if you eat it once."

"You're spoiling me, Dominic. This bodyguard gig is starting to sound more and more like a vacation."

He pressed a soft kiss on my lips as if he couldn't help himself. "First, feeding you cake in bed is hardly spoiling you. Second, if you want, we can fight it out in the ring after."

Now that had me smiling like a fool. "Sounds perfect."

He mock-gasped. "Wow, so beating me up sounds better to you than eating cake in bed, huh?"

I lightly jumped and wrapped my arm around his throat in a headlock. "Gotta toughen you up, baby."

I quickly let him go as he tickled my ribs and said, "Let's go. I'll text Maxim to pull the car around to the entrance."

I led the way from his office to the car. While he answered some of his emails, I realized how Dominic had managed to pull me out of the darkest memories of my past with his warm hugs and soft kisses. And I knew there was nothing I wouldn't do for this man.

Whoever dared to harm him was going to pay.

CHAPTER 24

DOMINIC

The only thing keeping me from turning into a raging lunatic was the fact that Samaira had opened up to me. That she'd deemed me worthy enough to share her past and her trauma with me. Also, the fact that her rapists had died after suffering at her hands, rightfully so.

Samaira was the strongest woman I'd ever met in my life, and to think that she had been raped and abused made me want to wrap her in my arms and protect her from the world. Sadly, that woman had the exact opposite idea. She now hunted men—predators—and brought women justice.

Except for right now.

Right now, she was wrapped up in my arms under the blanket, and I was feeding her chocolate cake, just like I'd promised. She wore my T-shirt and her panties, our legs tangled in each other as I fed her a bite and pressed a kiss to her forehead. "How did you get into the Wildcats?"

She swallowed her bite. "Well, like I said, those three men came from too much money and power. All we could afford was the lawyer that the government provided us. And that lawyer was Lena. She saw my condition and the brutality of those monsters. She saw how my family was harassed and the way those three walked free with no charges on their records. And she offered to take justice into her own hands. She asked me if I'd like for her to take care of them. She's the one I called after leaving my family."

She chuckled as she closed my jaw. I couldn't believe that the leader of the Wildcats was a lawyer. "Lena's a lawyer?"

She nodded, a delighted smile on her face. "Yep. How do you think we find cases where women don't get justice?"

I shook my head in awe of these women. "That's amazing."

She got a wistful smile on her face. "Yeah, she is. At that time, she was a frustrated lawyer and a rage-filled woman who was tired of seeing women suffer at the hands of men and never getting justice. So when she offered to take those men out for me, I agreed. But I was so furious, so fucking enraged at seeing what my rape did to my family, I wanted to be the one to dole out the justice."

"So she trained you?" I asked, feeding her another bite of the cake.

She nodded, chewing and moaning at every bite. "She actually refused at first. She didn't want me involved in a murder. But I hounded her and wouldn't stop stalking her until she agreed to train me. And then, she helped me kill them all with no traces. She was the one who had helped us relocate after my father was fired."

I pulled her into my arms and pressed a kiss to her forehead. I rubbed her arms and kept pressing my lips to her hair, her neck, her cheek. I hated that she had to go through so much in her life at such a young age, but I was so proud of her fortitude. I kept touching her and kissing her, reminding myself that she was all right now, that she'd exacted revenge on those fuckers and they were rotting in hell while my girl was being hand-fed cake by her fucking man. That she was the most powerful woman in the world, and no one would ever be able to harm a hair on her head.

A hint of loneliness and guilt appeared in Maira's eyes, and I knew what it was. "Maira, you miss your family, baby."

She bit her lip as her eyes softened. "Of course, I do."

I softly pushed a lock of her hair behind her ear, pressing a soft kiss there. "Then I'm sure they miss you too."

She shrugged her shoulders, not looking at me. "Maybe."

Slowly, so she wouldn't get spooked and pull back from me, I took her hand in mine, pulling it onto my lap. "You should call them, meet them, baby."

Instantly, she shook her head in denial. "I can't. It's too dangerous to be associated with me or the Wildcats. We might be vigilantes, but we're still murderers." She looked me square in the eyes, as if challenging me. "You have no idea how many men I've mutilated, tortured, and killed, Dominic. People don't kill so many people and get away with it. One day, it's going to catch up to us, and I don't need my family to be condemned with me. It's better they remember their daughter as the innocent girl I once was."

"Samaira," I sighed, pulling her closer to me and pressing my forehead to hers, trying to soothe her.

She grazed her fingers along my jaw. "I should leave you alone for the same reason. We shouldn't be doing this. *You* shouldn't associate yourself with me. As proud as I am of being a Wildcat, I can't have you incriminated because of me. It would kill me if something were to happen to you or your family because…"

I pressed my lips to hers, shutting up her bullshit once and for all. I kissed her with everything I had, showing her the raw need pumping in my heart for her. I pulled her on my lap, her legs on either side of my hips, and crushed her to my chest. Her breaths were heavy in my mouth as I brushed my tongue against hers, tasting the delicious chocolate and the mind-melting sweetness that was all her. "I." *Kiss.* "Will." *Kiss.* "Never." *Kiss.* "Leave." *Kiss.* "You."

My cock was raging hard as anger and protectiveness and obsession overpowered all my other thoughts and senses. Every time she talked about putting distance between us, my heart urged me to pull her closer. I refused to let her live a life of solitude, one where others could not love and care for her. She might have her girls, but something told me she would sacrifice herself if it meant saving them. I wrapped my fingers around her neck and pulled back from the kiss. I rolled my hips while pressing her down on my lap, pushing my cock against her panty-covered pussy, making her moan. "You will not push me away, Maira. I forbid it."

A shaky laugh escaped her. "You forbid it, huh?"

With my hand still wrapped around her throat, I rolled us and pushed her down on the bed, looming over her. "Yes. I won't let you talk about leaving me. You're not allowed to take a bullet for me, then put a wall between us." I climbed on top of her, my legs on either side of her waist, and bent lower so our lips touched. "If you ever talk about leaving me, I'm going to stuff your mouth with my cock."

Her eyes gleamed with hunger. "Dominic …"

My heart thundered, and all I wanted was to do just that. But before I could proceed, we needed to have a little conversation. I pressed my thumb on her lips, pulling a gasp out of her. "Before I feed you my cock, I need to know your soft and hard limits, baby."

She gulped but her eyes darkened. "Alright."

I squeezed her throat lightly. "This okay?"

She licked her lips and nodded. "Yes."

I loosened my grip and ran my thumb along her cheek. "Spanking?"

"Yes, please."

"Calling you my slut?"

Her eyes darkened. "Yes," she whispered with hooded eyes.

"What if I spit in your mouth?"

Her back arched and a moan slipped past her lips. "Then I'll open my mouth wider."

"That's my girl." I leaned down and pressed a kiss on her lips, giving her a sharp nip.

Her moan caressed my lips and I wanted to devour her. My cock pulsed with need and I couldn't help but press into her stomach harder.

My voice was like gravel when I asked, "Would you get on your knees for me, Maira?"

Her eyes were liquid fire. "You know I will."

"What if I degrade you?"

"Feel my pussy, Dominic. See how wet you make me."

I did just that and a growl shook my chest. "You're soaked, baby. But I need your words."

"Yes, Dominic. Degrade me. Call me names. Spit on me. Shut me up with your cock. Spank me. Fuck me in the ass. I'm all yours to please."

My cock jerked and precum leaked in my sweats. I was hanging by a thread. "What's your hard limit?"

Her answer was quick. "No water sports. No canes. No whips. Nothing that actually hurts. Pain isn't my kink."

"Understood. And if there is ever a time you need me to pull back or stop, just tell me."

"I will."

"Promise me, baby. Because it will destroy me if I ever hurt you."

"I promise, Dominic. Now get on with it. I'm begging you."

I now squeezed her throat tighter and rolled my hips on her stomach. "You want this cock in your mouth, don't you, baby?"

Her neck arched, and she licked my lips. "Please, Dominic."

I removed her T-shirt, leaving her in just her panties, and got out of all my clothes. I sat across her chest and pulled at my aching, hard cock, stroking it slowly, running the wet head along her lips. "Is this what you want, baby?"

She nodded, swiping out her tongue to get a taste, and I quickly pulled my cock away. "Not yet, Maira. Hold the headboard with both hands. And do not let go."

She quickly obeyed, and my cock throbbed in my hand. I moved forward so my legs were on either side of her chest and placed another pillow under her head. Slowly, holding my cock upright, I brought my balls closer to her mouth. "Lick my balls, baby. Worship them, show me how much you need my cock in your mouth, and I'll feed it to you."

I didn't have to tell her twice. She pushed her tongue out and swiped it all the way from my perineum to the base of my cock, sending jolts of electric pleasure racing up my spine. A loud moan vibrated up my chest as I clutched the headboard, my knees shaking from the pleasure. She sucked my balls into her mouth, swallowing around them, and making my eyes roll back in my head. Her eyes were hooded with pleasure, her fingers tightening around the slat of the headboard as she moaned around my sack. As if she loved sucking on my balls. My sack tightened, and my cock leaked so much precum that it ran down the length of it. My hips jerked of their own volition, chasing the staggering pleasure threatening to tear apart my mind.

I ground on her face as I threw my head back, and my eyes snapped to our reflection in the overhead ceiling mirror. The sight had me groaning out loud, my cock on the verge of exploding in my hand. Samaira's face was stuffed full of my sack, saliva sliding down her cheeks on both sides, tears streaming down her face, and her hips arched up high, seeking pleasure. And I was a writhing mess on top of her, my one hand grabbing the headboard like my life depended on it, and another entirely unable to let go of my cock, pleasure so intense spreading through my veins, I felt like I'd died and gone to heaven.

The sight was so fucking erotic, I pushed my balls deeper into her mouth and growled, "Look up in the mirror, Maira. Watch your mouth stuffed full of my sack. You're a dirty little slut for my cock, aren't you?"

Her gaze snapped to the mirror above, and her eyes rolled back in her head. Her lips clamped around me harder, pulling out a rough grunt from my chest. I stared up at the mirror and watched her legs spread-eagle behind me, moving restlessly, hips undulating, seeking that friction only I could give her.

I pulled my balls out of her mouth. A string of her saliva dripped down her chin, making my vision turn dark with need. I reached back and cupped her pussy, stroking her clit through her soaking panties. "You've ruined your panties, baby. Do you want me in here that bad?"

Her eyes begged me to slide my finger in her sopping wet cunt. She widened her legs and arched her hips, trying to get my fingers to move deeper. And I couldn't help but spank her wet pussy. She whimpered as she clutched my waist. I spanked her harder between her legs, causing her to shriek. "Did I tell you to let go of the headboard?"

Immediately, her hands were back in position, her muscles bunching. "Good fucking girl. Now open your mouth." Her lips parted at my command, her eyes darkening at my praise. I tapped my cock to her lips, spreading my precum along the bottom one. "Wider."

As soon as her lips opened wide enough, I pushed my cock inside her mouth in one deep thrust. My vision turned white, and my back arched as pleasure shot from the tip of my cock all the way to my balls. I had to squeeze my balls to stop myself from shooting down her throat with the first thrust.

Heaven and hell wrapped around my length, the painful

need to move, to thrust, battling with the unbelievable plea-sure racing down my spine. And the little wildcat that was my Maira, ran her tongue along my cock, making precum spurt down her throat. "Maira, baby. Look at me."

Her eyes snapped to my face. I grabbed the side of her throat and squeezed. "Do I look like I'd survive without you? Do I look like I'd let you fucking go?"

She swallowed around my cock, making me growl, and slowly shook her head.

"Good," I growled. "You better remember it, baby. You're all mine, and I'm not letting you go."

Saliva dripped down the side of her lips as I started thrust-ing, turning feral for my wildcat. With one hand clutching her throat and another holding the fuck on to the headboard, I fucked her mouth like I'd fuck her pussy. I pushed in deep, stopping there for a second, challenging her breathing before pulling out. She melted underneath me, her fingers clutching the headboard and taking everything I gave her like a good girl.

I looked behind to find her legs squeezed together, trying to ease her ache. I met her eyes and ran my thumb along her jaw, slowly fucking her mouth. "You feeling empty, baby? You need this cock filling your pussy?"

She nodded around my cock, the motion pushing me too close to the edge of coming in her mouth. I pulled out before I lost all my control. I moved down her body so our faces were closer. "You want me to fill that aching fucking emptiness in your heart, Maira?"

Her eyes glittered under the warm light, her need like a beacon for my aching heart. I moved down her body and pulled off her panties, spreading her legs for my view. She was a filthy, glorious mess. Her thighs glistened with her need, and a large wet spot was spread on the bed sheet. I pushed her leg with my shoulder, opening her up wider, looking at her slick pussy pulsing with that aching emptiness and need.

I rubbed my thumb at her wet opening, making her whimper. "You know how I know how much your heart aches with loneliness?"

She shivered, her chest heaving and hips jerking wildly. She shook her head, looking at me with so much need, so much desperation. I wanted to pull my beating heart from my chest and drop it at her feet.

I moved over her, nestling my hips between her legs, looking deep into her eyes. Softly, I pressed my lips to her forehead and dragged them closer to her ear, making her shiver along my chest. "Because mine aches the same, baby."

Her fingers pushed into my hair, desperately pulling my head so our eyes met. A tear rolled down the side of her face as she sniffled. "What if I only bring destruction to your life?"

I pressed a kiss to her lips, gliding my aching cock to her opening, drenching it in her wetness. My body burned with the need to push inside her, my cock dripping with so much precum I was afraid of coming between her legs. At the same time, my heart pounded with so much affection, so much fucking wonder at the way she constantly wanted to protect people around her from herself that I had to catch my breath.

But she needed to know that she was wrong. "You've only ever brought hope to my life. You've brought strength and fortitude. You've brought excitement and wonder and the brightest sunshine to my dark, empty life. If being with you will bring me destruction, I'd happily lie in the ruins with you in my arms."

She pulled me closer and pressed her lips to mine. She kissed me with surrender and hunger. She wrapped her legs around me, arching her hips to pull me into her. "Condom, baby."

She gasped and pushed at my chest. "Hurry."

Without breaking the kiss, I opened the drawer of my bedside table and found the packet. I quickly got on my knees, opened the packet, and rolled it down my aching cock. I gave it a slow stroke as Samaira's hungry eyes followed my motion.

She widened her legs and cupped her pussy, arching her neck. "Need you, Dom."

Her words turned the simmering heat into a raging inferno. With a roar that echoed in the room, I grabbed her hips and pushed my cock inside her in one solid thrust. Thunderous pleasure raced down my spine as I fought my body from moving, giving my girl the time to breathe. Our eyes met, and a maelstrom of emotion flooded between us.

She wrapped her legs around my hips, urging me to move, squeezing her pussy around my cock. A growl vibrated up my chest, my nostrils flaring to breathe down the pleasure trying to erupt. I cupped her cheek and pressed my lips to hers as I thrust hard, capturing her whimper in my mouth.

Her sweet sound hitting my tongue and her tight warmth enveloping my cock had deafening pleasure exploding inside my veins. I rocked hard into her body, slamming my cock inside her. With each thrust, her pussy tightened around me. My hips lost their rhythm as they thrust inside her with wild abandon, the sound of the headboard banging against the wall colliding with our moans and grunts. I wanted to consume her, brand my name on her soul, and shout out to the world that this woman was mine.

Her nails dug into my back sharply, causing pain and pleasure to splinter the thin thread of control I had over my body.

I grabbed her hips and tilted them up, angling her body so I hit her at the right spot, causing her to thrash in my arms. I rose on my knees and grabbed her throat, blocking her airway. Her eyes widened as her cheeks flushed. I slammed into her as I kept her airway blocked. She clutched my hand at her throat, her nails digging so deeply into my skin, I knew she'd leave marks. The need to leave some part of myself inside her had me gritting my teeth. "Open your mouth, Maira."

With her throat in a chokehold, her mouth dropped open.

I bent lower and spit in her mouth. Loosening my tight hold around her throat, I growled, "Swallow."

She immediately closed her mouth, and I felt her throat bob as she swallowed my spit. My blood roared in my veins, and I pumped into her like a man possessed. "You ready to come for me, baby?"

Her face was turning impossibly red, and I let go of the pressure around her throat. She keened low in her throat as air rushed through her windpipe and her orgasm wracked through her body. The walls of her pussy clamped unbearably tight around my cock, squeezing it and pulsing around it. "Yes, good girl. Come on my cock, Maira. Come for me, baby. Need to feel you squeezing me. Fuck, I want to come inside you and watch you dripping with my cum."

Her eyes rolled in the back of her head as her hot cunt started to squeeze and milk my cock once more, tears running down her cheeks and her nails digging so deep in my back, I knew I'd have marks on them for the next few days. "Come inside me, Dominic. Want to feel you."

Her words splintered my mind, and a tsunami of pleasure rushed down my spine. My control snapped, and my body was just a mindless beast, thrusting into her with the unending need to consume her. I wanted to be buried so deep inside her that she'd never be able to rid herself of me. She owned me wholly and completely, my body hers to command, my heart hers to break. My hips snapped with the need to fuse myself to her, to leave my mark on every inch of her body, reminding her of this bond between us.

Her lips sucked at my neck, her whimper muted by the wild moans escaping my throat. The moment her teeth bit the tendons of my neck, burning hot pleasure erupted from my cock, my hips mindlessly pushing into her, marking her as mine forever.

I breathed her in as I let the orgasm roll over me.

The ensuing silence had me dropping onto my back beside

her and pulling her closer into my body, wrapping her in my arms. I pulled off the condom and threw it in the trash can beside my bedside table, wishing I could've come inside her.

She ran her fingers down my chest as sweat clung to our skin, leaving cool tendrils of air washing over us. My heart pounded in my chest as she ran her fingers along my body, tucking her head in the space between my neck and shoulder.

Her hair was a beautiful mess, her throat had the imprints of my fingers, but her eyes had never shone brighter. She looked well and truly fucked, and all fucking mine. I held her hand and placed her open palm on my thundering heartbeat. When her eyes met mine, I pressed a kiss on her forehead as I pressed my own palm over her hand. "This heart, it's all yours. You hear it thundering like a wild beast? It's only for you. There has never been and there never will be another person to own it. You can love it, care for it, stomp on it, or break it. It will only ever be yours."

"Dominic," she whispered, her eyes flooding with tears.

"I know you're afraid that being with you would destroy me. But, sweetheart, being without you would destroy me first."

She pressed a kiss to the spot on my chest where my heart was trying to break out of my skin. "I'll never be able to forgive myself if something happened to you."

I held her cheek in my palm, treasuring how much she cared about me. I pressed a soft kiss on her lips. "You're Crimson fucking Tiger. Nothing and no one could harm a hair on my body if you're the one protecting me."

Fire blazed through her eyes, her lips lifting in a savage smile that had my cock getting hard again. "Damn fucking straight. I will tear apart anybody who would dare lay a finger on you."

I pulled her naked body on top of me, pushing my cock back inside her, warming it in her sweetness. "And I will destroy anybody who dares to take you away from me.

Nobody is allowed to separate us. Not even you, baby. You got that?"

I thrust into her bare, groaning into her mouth. She bit my lip and moved over my hips, pulling me in deeper. She gasped at my thrust. "Got it. Now fucking pull out of me when you're close because nobody would save you from me if you accidentally got me pregnant."

The visual of my girl pregnant had me coming too close to the edge. I quickly pulled her off my cock, grabbed another condom, and had her back on my cock, riding me into oblivion.

For the entire day, and throughout the night, we were a writhing mess of passion and hunger. She was my every meal. I memorized every one of her dips and curves, her strength and her muscles, all with my fingers and my tongue. I claimed her body and her heart, reminding her over and over again to not dare put up a single wall between us. Because I would tear them all down over and over again. No matter how long and how many times it took to get through her stubborn head.

She had sealed her fate, and I was her only destiny.

CHAPTER 25

SAMAIRA

The *ding-ding-ding* of notifications on my phone jerked me awake. I found myself enveloped in Dominic's warm heat, his arms holding me close to his chest, his leg wrapped over my hips. His heavy weight and hot skin along my back made me want to forget the world and just lie there, basking in the warm glow of hope that he unfurled in my chest. That cold, aching loneliness that had plagued my heart for thirteen long years was filling up with his soft smiles that I wanted to protect.

Early morning light lit up the bed in golden hues as my phone, once again, pinged with a notification.

Dominic grunted from behind me and wrapped himself around me tighter. "Shut that noise off, Maira."

I picked up my phone from the side table and found two missed calls and six messages from Tara.

Tara: I have something.

Tara: Wake up.

Tara: Call me back, bitch! You're gonna want to see this.

Tara: Come to the Den.

Tara: Bring Dominic and breakfast.

Tara: I swear to God, Sami.

I quickly started replying to her texts as I kicked at Dominic, making him grunt.

Me: We'll be there in an hour. With breakfast.

Dominic groaned as I shook him, nuzzling his face in my throat like an adorable puppy. My body melted into him, as his sleep-roughened voice groaned in my ear. "Maira, baby. You feel so good in my arms."

I turned around in his arms and wrapped my leg around his hip, feeling him throbbing at my aching core. My entire body zinged with electric pleasure as his bare chest rubbed against my aching nipples. His hand moved over my back in rough, heavy strokes until he cupped my butt and pulled me closer.

"Who was that?" His sleepy tone and hard cock rubbing against me had me dripping wet already.

I rubbed myself against his cock and held his face in my hands so his eyes met mine. "You have five minutes to make us come. We need to go to the Den."

He pulled me into a rough kiss and dragged me under him. "I only need three."

With that, he grabbed a condom from the side table, put it on, and pushed his hard cock inside me in one deep thrust. I was already soaking wet, and my back arched with the blinding pleasure shooting down my spine from the way his cock created friction at my opening.

I was so, so close already as his thrusts turned deeper. He

pumped into me in hard strokes, his cock hitting me at the right spot, making me see stars behind my eyes.

Dom grunted into my neck, his body shaking under my palms. "Fuck, Maira. I want to be buried in you forever. Want to feel your hot cunt bare and fill you with my cum."

My pussy throbbed at his filthy words, needing to feel him coming inside me. I moved my hands lower, squeezing the perfect round globes of his ass, and pulled him deeper.

Pleasure and need danced under the edge of my skin. Dominic's deep thrusts made me so full of him that I was afraid I was going to burst out of my skin. Needing to feel him deeper, needing to make Dom lose all shreds of his control, I moved one of my hands and dragged my finger along the tight little rosebud of his ass, causing him to moan into my neck and push his ass out. "Push that little finger inside, baby. Let me feel you inside me."

If I thought Dominic Park couldn't get any hotter, I was wrong. The way he pushed out his ass, begging for my finger, had my pussy turning wetter and needier. I dragged my finger to his cock that was wet with my juices and slid around it to lube up my finger. I bit his lip and massaged his perineum, making him grind into me with a desperate ferocity that had pleasure hitting my G-spot. I whimpered and slowly pushed my finger into the tight ring of his ass. His incredible tight heat clamped around my finger as a loud groan escaped his throat.

With a gentleness that had him slowing his thrusts, I pushed my finger in deeper. He let out a long moan that had blood roaring through my veins. "Hmm…deeper, baby. I won't break."

My pussy clenched tight around his cock at his words, and I obeyed. I pushed my finger deeper. He moaned into my neck and thrust hard into me, instantly pulling out and fucking himself on my finger.

I twisted my finger, trying to find that little spongelike part that would make him lose his fucking mind. And I knew I found that little nub when Dominic Park fucking whimpered in my arms and started to pound into me.

I looked up in the overhead mirror, and my body went up in flames at the way Dominic's round globes looked clenched around my finger as he slammed inside me. I pushed inside him deeper, loving the sensation of him squeezing around my finger, the way his back arched and his body heaved over me. "You look so fucking hot, Dom. I could lie here forever staring at your beautiful fucking ass. Fuck, Dom. Fuck me harder."

A loud groan rumbled from his chest as his thrusts turned feral. It felt like he didn't know whether he wanted to fuck me harder or get fucked deeper. His mouth sucked at my neck as his whimpers grew, and his thrusts lost their steady rhythm.

He was all animalistic grunts and vicious roars as he pounded into me. My fingers pushed into his ass, pulling every whimpering pleasure and wild hunger from him. "Need you to come, Maira," he growled. "Can't hold back. Come on my cock, baby."

And like every fucking time, my body obeyed. My orgasm ripped through me in a wave of blinding-hot pleasure, squeezing unbearably tight around his cock, my hand pulling him deeper and deeper, my voice screaming his name in ecstasy.

As my orgasm subsided, I twisted my finger and pushed two of them inside him, rubbing along his prostate, finally giving him the pleasure with a clear head. And what a magnificent beauty it was to witness Dominic Park shedding all of his control and being a mindless, whimpering beast, taking his pleasure in my pussy while being impaled on my fingers.

His orgasm tore through his chest as he ground into me, his hands squeezing the life out of the pillow by my head, his ass squeezing and pulsing around my fingers while his cock erupted inside me, throbbing and pounding as he moaned and shivered over my body. He was devastatingly stunning with his rumpled hair and his wet lips. His large body shook with the force of his pleasure as his eyes looked dazzlingly lost in mine.

My fingers were still inside him, and I gave him a light rub, pulling another sexy grunt out of his sinfully pretty lips. "Next time, I'm going to take my time here."

He pushed his tongue inside me as he slowly pulled out of me. "Next time, I'm going to ruin your ass. And then let you ruin mine."

I pulled out my fingers and ran my hand along his back, feeling his strong muscles. "I have a lot of toys," I said, waggling my eyebrows.

His chuckle hit my lips, and I pulled him in for a taste. He kissed me once. Twice. Thrice. "Good. And if I'm not wrong, that was four minutes."

He held me and pulled us out of the bed with me in his arms. I couldn't help but giggle at the way he was able to lift me so easily. "What is it?" he asked, looking at me with so much tenderness I wanted to stay in his arms forever.

I ran my hand through his hair. "I love how you can lift me in your arms. But how shit you are at defeating me in a fight."

He quickly dropped me and tickled me, making me shriek with laughter. "Apologize, baby. Say you're sorry."

"I'm sorry," I screamed. "Stop, I'm gonna pee."

He stopped and let me go. He pulled us into the shower as I informed him about Tara's messages.

Dominic instantly turned serious and became a man on a mission. We rushed through the shower and tore through the streets.

As I promised Tara, we reached Thunder Claw in fifty minutes along with breakfast.

As we walked down the stairs to the basement, Dominic looked at me, carrying the large bag of bagels and spreads in his hand. "I'm excited to see the infamous Den."

He genuinely looked excited, his eyes glittering, and he

had a bounce in his step. Or maybe that was the high of a fantastic fucking. "If you must know, no man has ever seen the Den. And the unfortunate souls who have haven't come out alive."

His jaw opened as he stared at me in shock. "Should I be afraid?"

I chuckled, dragging him to the trapdoor in the far corner of the basement. "You should always be afraid, baby."

As soon as I opened the trapdoor, the well-lit, wide stairwell welcomed us. I took a step in, and Dominic quickly followed, closing the door behind him. We stepped down about twenty steps when the pretty Wildcats logo wall with all our lockers opened in front of us. Dominic let out a low whistle as he took everything in. He stood in front of the locker with the gold, crimson, and black tiger mask and turned back to me. "You are a fantasy come to life, Maira."

Red blush rushed to my cheeks. Before I could say anything, a loud "Aw" came from the living area. Dominic chuckled and yelled, "Am I right?"

I gave him a playful roll of my eyes and walked to the living area, where we found Sophie and the rest of the Wildcats in different seats. The moment Dominic stepped foot behind me, the loud bark of Shadow was the only warning we got before his rushing form was upon us.

I quickly jumped in front of Dominic, bearing the weight of Shadow in my arms. "Down, Shadow baby. He's one of us."

Shadow's barks were earsplittingly loud as he kept jumping on me and around me, trying to get to Dominic. His snarls were vicious, and saliva dripped down his tongue.

I stood strong, trying to grab Shadow's collar when Dominic stepped to my side and sat lower, holding Shadow's collar in his hand. All the Wildcats were nearly on their feet as they saw Dominic give him a treat.

When did he get that?

Shadow hated men. He hated if they got closer to one of us. And he did not hesitate to bite their hand off. And Dominic was no different.

Before I could pull him back, Shadow chomped down the treat from Dominic's hand, gave a sniff to his fingers, and—*was I seeing this right?*—gave him a long, wet lick, making Dominic laugh.

"What the actual fuck?" Tara stole the words right out of my mouth.

"I can't believe it," Lena mumbled, looking at our big black Doberman being putty and playful in Dominic's hands.

Dominic turned to look at us. "What's wrong?"

Sloane was the only one who had words for him. "He likes you. He actually fucking likes you."

Dominic rubbed Shadow's head, caressing his ear, getting a ridiculously low whine of pleasure from him as he jumped into his lap, pushing him down on the floor. Dominic's loud chuckle filled the room as he happily petted Shadow, giving him another treat and cooing at him. "Who's a good boy? Who's my new best friend?"

"Marry him," Naomi said, and I turned to find her looking at me with gleeful eyes.

"Maybe next year," Dominic answered casually, getting loud cheers from all the ladies.

"He's kidding," I told them, glaring at Dominic.

He only gave me a flying kiss and turned to the girls. "Not kidding."

I turned to Tara, who was still sitting shell-shocked at Shadow's display of affection for a man. "Tara, you called us. What did you find?"

Her eyes were glued in shock at Shadow on the floor, on his back, giving happy little grunts at Dominic's petting. "My dog likes a man."

Tara had always felt unsafe around men, especially after she was attacked. Ever since she'd found Shadow, she relied on

Shadow's hatred of men to keep them away. Every time they went out for a walk or a run, Shadow was quick to bark at any man who got too close to them. Never had he shown an inkling of trust or affection for a man. To find him so enamored with Dominic seemed to have shaken her trust in Shadow.

I bent closer to her face. "Dominic must smell like me. That's the only reason Shadow would trust a man."

Her eyes turned to me and widened in understanding. "Yes. That's the only reason."

"Now, can you please tell me what you found?"

She straightened in her chair and turned on her monitor, getting serious. "Did you bring the hit man's phone?"

I pulled it out of my pocket and handed it to her. "I checked, but it was dead. And neither Dominic nor I had the right charger for it."

She plugged the phone into the charger. "Thought so. Otherwise, you'd have definitely reached out to me."

"Why? What happened?" My heart started to beat faster at the way Tara's eyes glinted with excitement.

Dominic must've sensed my impatience because he was right next to me. Shadow jumped to Sophie, where she sat on the couch between Sloane and Naomi.

She pulled up the recording software that we used to listen to the conversations. "Well, I was going through the conversation of the state attorney from where you left off. And I heard him talking to his son in yesterday's recording, telling him that he had a plan. That he'd hired someone to get rid of the problem. He also called him again later in the day, frustrated that his phone calls and messages were going unanswered. Now, they're planning to bring his son into the media spotlight by announcing that he's going to be joining the state attorney's office tomorrow. He's reaching the city tonight."

My temper flared. "Fuck. He can't go out in public. It would make kidnapping him much more high-profile."

Dominic thrummed with anticipation beside me. "Did the phone switch on?"

Tara pressed the button on the side of the phone as we all waited for the phone to turn on. Before she could even tell us it was on, the *ping-ping-ping* of the notifications on the phone told us all we needed to know.

Tara handed me the phone before I even had to ask.

I opened the Messages app and found several messages.

> Unknown number: Status update?
>
> Unknown number: You said the job would be done in 24 hours. It has been 72 hours now.
>
> Unknown number: You are fired.

I went to the recent calls and found four missed calls at intervals of a few hours.

Dominic was right beside me as I went through the phone. His jaw was clenched tight as he gritted out, "It's the state attorney's son, isn't it? He's our culprit. We've got all the proof we need."

I held his jaw and gave him a small smile. "Let me just check one more thing."

I looked at Tara. "Wear your headphones and turn on the live audio feed of the state attorney's office." I handed the phone to Dominic. "I want you to talk to Thomas Cooper. I just want to confirm he's the one who picks up the call. This is all the confirmation we'd need."

A savage smile came over Dominic's face as he hit call on the phone and pressed the speaker button.

The dial tone rang three times before we heard the click. Before Dominic could even speak a word, a voice from a modulator came over the speaker. "I fired you already. You've obviously not finished your job. Consider our deal over. Don't call this phone again."

The call dropped without Dominic having to utter a word.

We all turned our eyes to Tara, and she played the recording from the attorney's office of the last two minutes. The sound of Thomas Cooper saying the exact words played on the screen, and we finally got all the proof that we needed.

My eyes turned to Sophie, and I walked up to where she sat. Her eyes glistened with tears, yet she got up and stood strong in front of me. I cupped the side of her face and gave her a reassuring smile. "You ready to rain down hell upon the motherfuckers that dared to touch you?"

Dominic came and stood beside her, his face shrouded with a dangerous lethality that only managed to turn me on. He wrapped his arm around Sophie, pulling her close to his body.

Sophie simply looked at me and nodded. "I'm ready."

Dominic pressed a kiss to her head and gave her a small smile, rubbing her arm in comfort. "I'm right here with you, Soph."

With a sigh, she leaned her head against him. "I know."

Dominic looked at me and then turned to the girls. "What's the plan?"

Lena and I shared a look, and she gave me a nod. I stepped forward so I faced everyone and looked at Dominic. "We get Tommy and his two friends tonight. He would have plenty of security on his way from the airport to his house. We kidnap him and his friends from their homes. My priority is Tommy. His friends wouldn't have as much security protecting them, nor would they be under the public eye. If we don't get them today, we can get them tomorrow when they're out looking for him. But if I were a betting woman, I'd bet on his two friends staying with him for the protection they'd get by staying close to him. Men like Tommy need a lot of scape-goats to keep them safe. We'll need to confirm if the two men we've seen hanging around with him are indeed the ones who assaulted Sophie."

Everyone nodded. Dominic met my eyes, and they were

dark with the need for violence. "What do you need me to do?"

This was the hardest part. I looked at Sophie and then at him. "Nothing. I need you and Sophie to have a solid alibi. Both of you should go to a high-profile bar and be there way past midnight. Ask Kai and other friends to join you. Sophie goes back to her parents' place for the night after the party since your parents have a full security detail."

As expected, Dominic let go of Sophie and took a step closer to me. "Absolutely not, Maira. You can't put me off the case. We're supposed to be working on this together."

I folded my arms at my chest and stood toe-to-toe with him. "I promised you the rapists. We'll be delivering them to you tonight. None of us will touch the three men aside from the kidnapping. Their fate belongs to Sophie. And then you. But we won't risk the two of you getting targeted by the cops. Our mission is to get them to you without putting you or Sophie in danger. You both need to get out of this unharmed and undetected. You will get to do what you please with them tomorrow. Tonight, you and Sophie need alibis."

Dominic was still breathing hard, probably processing, when my eyes met Sophie's. She stepped closer to her brother and clutched his arm. "You know she's right, Dominic. As much as I want the rapists punished, I'd never forgive myself if it came at the cost of losing you. Let the Wildcats do their job, Oppa."

I gave Sophie a big smile and looked at Dominic. "Sophie is definitely the smarter sibling."

A light chuckle escaped him as he looked between the two of us. "Fine. We'll party tonight. What's the plan for you all?"

Lena got up from the couch and moved to stand beside me. "Now, we get to the safe house and plan every minute of the mission. We don't have much time, but I want every minute planned for each of us. Naomi, you're joining the mission as well. We need a fighter more than we need a medic tonight."

Naomi nodded. "Cool. Silver Jaguar's gonna be in the fucking house."

Dominic raised his eyebrows at her, a small smile on his lips, while the rest of us cheered loudly.

Lena turned to Dominic and Sophie. "Both of you are welcome to join us at the safe house and be involved in the planning. But I want you both out of there by late afternoon. The more you're seen out in public places for the evening, the stronger your alibi."

When they both nodded obediently, we all sprang into action.

We packed our cars with all the necessary gear and equipment and arrived at the safe house within the next hour.

Tara located the state attorney's and his son's houses. Looking at the activity happening at Tommy Cooper's large, vacant house, it was evident that his father was putting security in place for his arrival. The audio recordings in his office and Tara's hacking into Thomas Cooper's computer and phone also gave us Tommy and his friends' flight information.

We monitored the area continuously, keeping a close eye on the security measures being implemented at his house. Every camera they installed, Tara hacked. Every new car that arrived at either of the Coopers' houses, Tara kept track of it through the street cameras. Every new person who entered Tommy's place was accounted for. We were dealing with twelve security operatives, each carrying a semi-automatic gun. Each of us had our targets set and marked. Every move was planned and plotted to the point where we could recite it in our sleep.

Every *i* was dotted and every *t* was crossed as we planned out the mission.

We were ready to get these motherfuckers.

It was late afternoon, and Dominic and Sophie were ready to head out.

I walked them out to the car after getting teased mercilessly by the rest of the girls. Sophie sat in the passenger seat as I stood close to Dominic near the driver's side door. "It's going to be okay, Dominic. I promise."

He clutched my hand and pulled it to his chest. I felt the rapid pounding of his heartbeat against my palm. I slowly caressed the spot, trying to calm it down. "You have to trust me, Dom. I'm going to get those bastards for you and Sophie."

His warm palm held the side of my neck as his thumb grazed my jaw with an aching tenderness. "I trust you, Maira. You're my tigress. Fierce and strong and a warrior."

I nuzzled into his palm and gave him a wink. "Damn right."

He pulled me closer and lowered his forehead against mine. He took in a deep breath as if he was breathing me in and opened his eyes. He tightened his hold on my neck, his thumb stopping on my lip, forcing me to meet his eyes. "Not a single scratch on you. You understand?"

I gave a slow lick to his thumb, my heart clenching painfully in my chest at his protectiveness. "Yes, sir."

His eyes darkened to dark pools of hunger, and he pushed his tongue into my mouth, kissing me hard and fast until I was breathless. "Go get 'em, Tiger."

My heart bloomed in my chest at his encouragement. He said the same thing the last time he was on a mission with me. This time, I knew it was deliberate. It felt like it was his little slogan just for me. And I loved it. Maybe a little too much.

I was his tigress, and I was going to love hunting the bastards who dared to harm my man and his sister. Let the fucking hunt begin.

CHAPTER 26

DOMINIC

asked Kai to make a reservation at the most happening bar in Manhattan and to invite as many people as he could. He would meet us at my place to get ready and bring Sophie some party wear.

Sophie and I were silent as I drove us to my place, each of us lost in our thoughts. On one hand, my blood thrashed against my skin at the thought of finally getting my hands on Sophie's rapists. But on the other hand, my mind fretted with worry for Samaira. If something happened to her because of this case, because of my need for vengeance, I would never forgive myself.

That thought took me by surprise because before Samaira, nothing was more important to me than bringing justice to Sophie. But if something happened to Samaira, then I'd have failed not only Sophie but Samaira as well. I didn't know if I had the strength to bear the brunt of that pain.

The moment we walked into my apartment, I went to the minibar and poured myself a stiff drink. I turned to Sophie, who'd snuggled into my large couch, and asked, "Would you like a drink, Soph?"

She shrugged and nodded. "I could use one. Thanks."

Once I'd poured us the drinks, I placed them on the coffee table and sat across from Sophie.

Before she could take a sip, I cleared my throat and raised my glass in a toast. "To getting you justice."

A small smile came over her lips. "To getting me justice."

As big of a deal as finding her rapists was, Sophie looked subdued. "Hey, Soph. You okay?"

She took a small sip and shrugged. "I'm fine. I just thought I'd feel happy or raging mad or emotional at the thought of being so close to capturing those monsters."

"But?" I prompted.

"But I don't feel much different. And I just realized that even if we capture those men, even if we kill those men, I'm still going to feel like shit. My life isn't going to magically go back to the time before I was raped. My nightmares might not stop. My fears might not disappear."

My heart ached at the thought of Sophie suffering so much. I placed my drink back on the coffee table and moved to sit beside her. "No, it might not. But you're not alone. As much as I regret not picking up your calls, I'll never let you deal with everything alone."

"And this is another thing, Dominic," she screamed, slamming the drink on the table. She clutched her head and looked at me with tears in her eyes. "You need to stop blaming yourself. I can't deal with the guilt."

No matter what she said, how could I ever stop feeling guilty? "I don't know how, Soph. I wish I had picked up your calls."

"But that's just it, Dominic. I had called you after my confrontation with that man during the charity. After I got him thrown out of the event. I had only called you twice to tell you about it, just because I was so mad. Only twice. If I had actually felt threatened, I'd have called you more. I'd have gotten in touch with you somehow. The rest of the calls were from Ashley, who had used my phone after the incident."

"Still, if I'd just picked up, I might have come to the party."

She shook her head, tears streaking down her cheeks. "You need to let it go, Dominic. I don't blame you. I've *never* blamed you. Don't you see? Even if we catch those guys, even if you kill them, you won't stop feeling guilty until you forgive yourself."

I knew she was right. Catching those bastards and killing them would bring Sophie justice, but I didn't think I would stop feeling guilty. That guilt had somehow embedded deep inside my soul, constantly punishing me with the reminder of my failure to protect my baby sister.

My eyes pricked at the way Sophie looked at me with tears in her eyes, and I shook my head defeatedly. "I don't know how to forgive myself, Soph."

She wrapped both her arms around mine and laid her head on my shoulder. "I forgive you, Oppa. You forgive yourself by accepting that there's nothing you could have done even if you'd picked up my calls. You forgive yourself by realizing that you've never left me alone after what happened. You forgive yourself because you never gave up. You never stopped looking for those bastards even when the rest of the world did. You forgive yourself because you found the Wildcats, and now they're going to bring those rascals to our feet."

She looked at me, her eyes red and cheeks puffy. "You forgive yourself because you will bring me the justice you promised."

She grabbed my hand and squeezed it with both of hers. "You forgive yourself, Oppa, because I'm asking you to." She only called me Oppa when she got really emotional or when she wanted to convince me of something. And right now, it was both.

The thread of control I had on my emotions snapped. My eyes flooded with tears as I pulled Sophie into a crushing hug. "I'm so sorry I couldn't stop it, Soph. So fucking sorry. If I could take your place, I'd do it in a heartbeat."

Her soft sobs tore my heart open. "I know, Oppa. You're the best big brother a girl could ever ask for. Now promise me, you'll forgive yourself."

I squeezed her to me. "I promise I'll try."

She sniffled. "I'll take that."

Right then, the door to my apartment slammed open. "I'm here, people," Kai boomed.

What was I thinking, giving him access to my place? *Fucking hell.*

We quickly jumped away from each other, wiping our cheeks and grabbing our drinks.

The moment he reached us, his feet stopped, and his eyes widened.

I could only imagine how we looked. Eyes red and cheeks puffy. Sophie gave Kai a bright, teary smile. "Hey, Kai. You're early."

As if Kai knew we needed some distraction, he sat next to Sophie and pulled her into his side by her shoulders. "Soph, you must tell me this secret on how to make Hyung cry. Usually, it's always the other way around. Spill, girl."

Sophie burst out laughing while I got up and dumped my drink on his head, making him screech like a banshee. "Not my hair."

He turned to Sophie. "See, this is what I'm talking about. He's a menace."

I pointed at the door farther to the left. "Washroom."

He turned to step to the washroom, but in the next moment, before my mind could send my body the message to move, Kai launched himself at me, rubbing his whiskey-soaked shirt and hair all over me, making me jerk my whole body to get him off me. "Let go, you little fucker."

"No. Join the fucking party, Hyung," he screeched in my ear, ruining my hair and clothes in retribution. Sophie now had tears *of laughter* running down her face. That was the only reason I didn't punch the little fucker.

"You have three seconds before I make you spar with me in the ring."

The next thing I saw was his back running to the washroom as he shouted, "I'm getting a new suit and sending you the bill."

I turned to make myself and him a drink with a sigh. In five minutes, Kai had pulled a laugh out of Sophie and brought a lightness to my chest. As chaotic as he was, he fucking knew how to read a room and put people at ease.

The three of us hung out at my apartment for the next two hours, where Sophie updated Kai about the Wildcats' plan for tonight, and we got ready for the party.

Kai seemed to have invited half of Manhattan's young population. The bar was packed. Drinks were flowing, people were dancing, and I'd said *Hi* to at least a hundred people.

Sophie's and my alibi was fucking set.

Now, everything was up to the Wildcats.

CHAPTER 27

SAMAIRA

Lena, Sloane, Naomi, and I were en route to Tommy's mansion. Tara was at the safe house, serving as our lookout for the evening. She loved to be in the field with us, but she was our best hacker. Sloane usually could handle most of it, too, but Tara was the one who could multi-task between being our eyes on top and keeping a watch on disabling cameras and traffic signal lights at the right time.

The four of us were decked out in our gear, our masks in place as we drove in our van. Tommy lived in a large, beach-front mansion on Long Island. Tara had hacked into every traffic signal on our way so as not to draw any attention from passersby or the cops on our way there. Considering we left Thunder Claw at midnight, there wasn't any traffic en route to his mansion. It was a long two-hour drive, since the asshole lived all the way in Southampton.

"Ladies, you'll be arriving at the house in five minutes. There's a turn right around the corner with five large trees. You'll need to park there. One of you can get the van closer to the mansion once you've dealt with the hired security team."

We all heard the instruction, and Sloane slowed down the van while Lena, on the passenger side, replied to her, "Copy, Shadow Panther." Naomi and I were in the back seat with the rest of our weapons and equipment.

You never knew where people would place a recording device. Whether she was with us or not, we only used code names. Sloane saw the trees and slowly parked the van between the canopies, making it as inconspicuous as possible.

We grabbed our weapons and slowly exited the van. Thankfully, the streets were empty at this time of night. None of us made the slightest of sounds, knowing where we were supposed to go.

While Sloane and I took the ocean-facing backyard, Naomi and Lena would breach the property from the front. We parted ways in an alley, and Sloane and I made our way to our positions.

Tara's voice chimed into my ear. "Crimson Tiger and Cherry Cheetah, you've got five people guarding the back-yard. Cheetah, you jump down from the tree into the yard. Tiger, you jump onto the balcony that directly opens into Tommy's bedroom."

"Copy," we both mumbled as we climbed into the trees twenty feet apart.

"Tiger, while you incapacitate the targets, Golden Lioness and Silver Jaguar will take care of the four men at the entrance."

"That's a lot of security for the son of a state attorney. They're clearly spooked about something," Naomi mumbled low in my ear. I didn't respond, considering I was on a tree and looking down at two men in black suits with guns.

Adrenaline ran high in my system, my heart pumping a mile a minute. No matter how many times I did this, there was always a risk of getting caught. It didn't matter whether I succeeded a hundred times or a thousand times. It only took one failure to ruin it all. But today wasn't that day.

I looked to my side to find Sloane sitting in another tree, tracking the men she was going to have to discreetly incapacitate.

"Cherry Cheetah, go." Tara's voice came over the headset.

Sloane silently dropped into the large backyard. It had ten lounge chairs around a large pool and five large statues of animals. She got one man down when Tara's voice came in my ears. "Crimson Tiger, your turn."

I jumped over the balcony railing about four feet from the tree and landed on my feet. The night was still completely silent, not a hint of panic from the security detail. *Idiots.* I crept to the door leading inside the house and silently turned the knob. Lucky fucking me, the three idiots were deep asleep.

Wouldn't want to disturb their beauty sleep. The last fucking time they got to sleep in a bed. Or fucking ever.

I got the chloroform and napkin from my pocket. In the next five minutes, all three were unconscious while the entire security detail was none the wiser. Quietly, I opened the bedroom door to inspect if we needed to take care of any personnel, only to find Naomi's silver jaguar face right up against me.

I lightly punched her and whispered, "You almost got yourself killed."

She scoffed. "As if."

"All good downstairs and at the front?"

She walked to find three unconscious men and nodded. "Yep. The entire security detail is unconscious. Golden Lioness and Cherry Cheetah are checking through the house and the yard."

"All clear," Lena piped into the headset. "Cherry Cheetah is bringing the van to the front. Crimson Tiger, Silver Jaguar, grab the targets and meet us in the front."

We nodded at each other, and I lifted one of Tommy's

friends and placed him on Naomi's shoulder. A sharp exhale burst out of her. "Damn, he's a pig."

I scoffed as I placed the other two on each of my shoulders. "You're just rusty. Need to get on the field more often."

"I'd rather play doctor."

Naomi was one of the least bloodthirsty among the five of us. She was a healer first and a fighter after. So I was grateful that she'd joined today. "Thanks for coming, Silver."

"Don't mention it, Tiger."

Just as we reached the front door, Lena pulled it open as Sloane rolled down the van at the front gate.

Tara's voice chimed in. "No vehicles within a half-mile radius. No lights or any movement in any neighboring house. Keep your head down and run, Wildcats."

We rushed to the back of the van. Lena pulled open the door, and Naomi and I dropped the men on the floor of the van and dove inside. By the time we'd closed the door, Lena was already seated in the passenger seat.

None of us removed our masks as Sloane pulled out of the Southampton neighborhood. Tara kept clearing the street signals for us and leading us away from the streets that had cops patrolling.

I removed my mask as soon as we were out of the Southamptons and into our familiar area. My face was dotted with sweat as adrenaline slowly started to leave my system.

Naomi removed her mask from across me and met my eyes. Her lips curled in an exhilarating smile. "Did we just do it? Did we kidnap the son of the state attorney?"

"Shh," Lena shushed her. "Don't you jinx it. Let's reach the safe house first."

I gave Naomi a wink and an exaggerated nod, mouthing, "We totally did it."

We burst into a giggle, and just to add to the fun, I chloroformed the three motherfuckers at my feet once again.

Once I knew they were completely unconscious, I

inspected Tommy's two friends. We still needed to confirm if these were the two fuckers who raped Sophie, or if it was someone else.

Remembering what Sophie had told me about one of them being really hairy, I pulled up the shirts of the two, and lo and behold, one of them was wearing a sweater of hair. The fucker didn't need a shirt to cover his chest. Fucking disgusting. I'd still need to pull out a confession from him, but he was a definite suspect.

I'd have to interrogate these two fuckers tomorrow morning. Hopefully, before I asked Dominic and Sophie to come to the safe house.

After driving for over an hour and a half, as instructed by Tara, we reached the safe house. The moment Sloane turned off the van, Lena looked behind us with a gleeful smile on her face. "We did it," she shrieked. "Let's get these bastards tied up in the basement and celebrate."

After we did just that, the five of us congregated in the primary bedroom. Tara got a tray of hot chocolates, cookies, and some chips. We'd converted the primary bedroom of the safe house into a cozy hangout space with lush carpets so you could sleep and sit on the floor itself with about twenty thick, fluffy pillows. We joined two California king-size beds along the wall to make a mother of all beds so we could all fit together and hung a giant TV screen across from it.

It wasn't often that we all stayed over at the safe house at the same time. So when all five of us got to be here together, it almost felt like a vacation, except for the three men who were tied up in the basement.

I grabbed a hot chocolate and called Sophie's office partner, Ashley. We'd decided not to have any calls from either Dominic or Sophie at least ten hours before and after the kidnapping time. The call rang twice before Sophie's voice came over the call.

"Oh my god, Samaira, did you guys do it?"

A smile came over my face at her nerves. "We did it, Sophie girl."

Her voice broke on the other end as if she was choking on a sob. "I…I can't believe it. Thank you."

"Hey," I cooed. "You're good, Sophie. Everything's going to be alright."

She sniffled. "I believe you. Thanks, Samaira. Here, talk to Dominic. He's been hovering over my head."

A chuckle escaped my lips at the thought of Dominic glaring over Sophie's head with impatience. A small shuffling sound came on, and Dominic's voice filled my ears. "Maira, baby. You alright?"

The fact that that was his first question to me had my heart in a fucking puddle. To my unfortunate luck, every single girl around me saw my face the moment Dominic asked me the question.

Sloane was the first to hold both her cheeks in her hand. "Aww. Sami's blushing."

"What did he ask?" Naomi followed.

"Did he say something dirty?" Tara asked, a smile on her face sans her half mask.

Lena nudged her shoulder playfully. "I bet he said something sweet."

The way they were all looking at me, I knew I wasn't getting out of this one without sharing. I rolled my eyes and muttered, "He's just asking if I'm alright."

Four different variations of awws surrounded me, making me groan and hide under the comforter to talk to Dominic in peace. I could hear his chuckle on the other end. "I like your friends."

"They're all right."

It seemed like he was walking, with the way the noise in the background kept changing. "Just hold on a second, Maira. I'm going somewhere quiet." After some shuffling sounds,

Dominic said, "Okay, I'm in the office of the bar's owner. Now, tell me everything that went down today."

There wasn't much to tell except that the mission went pretty smoothly. He kept giving encouraging hmms as I relayed the entire night to him. "By the way, tomorrow, you will just go to work like every other day. I'll be there with you as your personal assistant. I'm pretty sure the state attorney might visit you."

"Let that bastard come," he growled, the sound sending a shiver up my spine.

"Easy there, Dom. The goal is not to have him suspect you. You're not to antagonize him."

He sighed, and I could just imagine the man getting upset and pouty. "Fine. What about your alibi?"

"We've got plenty of fabricated footage of me at the bar. I've also got plenty of friends and patrons to confirm my presence in the bar, if you know what I mean."

"Perfect. And when do Sophie and I get to come down to the safe house and deal with those motherfuckers?"

I chewed my lip, thinking over the next steps. I'd have to sit with the girls to brainstorm. It could be too risky to keep these three men kidnapped for an extended period. The longer they're alive, the greater the chances of the cops or private detectives finding them. But I was fairly certain that starting tomorrow, Dominic and Sophie would have eyes on them, depending on whether the state attorney would involve cops or hire goons. "Let's see who the state attorney brings to your office. We'll make a decision then."

"Alright. I'll trust you on this. Are you all going to stay at the safe house till then?"

"Yep. Pretty much. Again, I might not come to your office if I get tailed tomorrow."

"Makes sense. You'll come to my place, then?"

A smile came over my face. "You're just trying to get me back in your bed."

He chuckled, the soft, breathy sound sending shivers down my spine. "Tell me you don't want to get back in my bed."

"Go home, Dominic. And go to sleep. I'll most likely meet you at your office in the morning. Do not give access to your place to anybody other than you and Sophie."

"Yes, ma'am. And you be careful."

"Yes, sir."

A growl came over the line, and I quickly ended the call before he made me blush any further.

I turned around to find four sets of eyes staring at me with their jaws hanging open and their eyes shining with glee.

"Not a word," I muttered, picking up my hot chocolate.

"Fuck that," Sloane said, jumping beside me and wrapping herself around me like an octopus. "Look at you smile, Sami," she shrieked in my ear, swinging me side to side. "I've never seen you so cute and soft. I wanna cuddle you."

Before I could get myself out of her clutch, Tara jumped on my other side and wrapped around me. "He makes you blush, and I love him for you."

Lena and Naomi, thankfully, stayed put on the floor, sipping their hot chocolates while looking at us with wide smiles on their faces. Lena lay down on the carpet, placing her head on Naomi's lap, and asked, "So are you guys officially together? Is Dominic Park your boyfriend?"

With the two ladies clinging to me like octopuses, I shrugged. "I don't know. You might get a very different answer if you ask him. But I feel guilty being with him."

"Why?" Naomi had a look of pure disbelief on her face. "That man worships the ground you walk on. He'd literally lay the world at your feet."

I looked down at my lap, not able to meet anybody's eyes. "We literally have three men kidnapped in our basement. One day, we're gonna get caught. What if somebody harmed Dominic to exact revenge on me? What if associating with me puts his life in danger? How can I be so selfish?"

Lena got back to a sitting position in a snap. "Samaira. Enough with the protective bullshit. There's a chance we won't get caught. You know why? Because we're targeting the people who deserve to be taken off the face of this earth. We're targeting the vilest humans who get away from being held accountable because they've got money and connections. Your boyfriend has given us fifty fucking million dollars. That money will keep us out of a lot more scrutiny. Add in the internal connections we've built everywhere. There is a reason we haven't been caught in the past thirteen years. I understand you wanting to protect your family. They're helpless. But Dominic is a fucking billionaire. He's got enough money and power not only to protect himself but also to get you out of sticky situations if they ever arise."

I felt Sloane nodding her head against my arm. "You need to let others support you and protect you. You need to let him love you. Don't you want your own person to go home to and cuddle up to after killing and torturing vile monsters? Someone who makes you believe in the good of humanity?"

Tara squeezed me on my other side, nodding along with Sloane. "Someone who brings lightness to our dark world? I know we have each other. I get all the love I need from the four of you. But, Sami, you can never have enough love when we're surrounded by so much hatred."

Naomi nodded and walked closer on her knees to the bed that the three of us sat on. "Just because we fight for justice and truth doesn't mean we're not allowed to live this life that we've been gifted. Lena gave you a new life, a new purpose. You did that for me. Wouldn't you want me to live my best life? Grab the little piece of love and joy with both of your hands."

Lena came closer and finished our little huddle, placing her hand on my thigh. "You're ruthless. You're my warrior. You're strength. You're the motherfucking rage of all women. And we're all so proud of who you are. But we want you to be a little more greedy. A little more selfish. A little more happy. We love seeing our Crimson Tiger blush and giggle. We love seeing love in your eyes. I need you to cherish and treasure this love. What good are we as Wildcats if we live in fear and with constraints? Be fucking wild, Sami. We're all with you."

Tears streamed down my face as all my girls bundled me up in their arms. Why was it so easy for me to rage and torture and kill people but so fucking terrifying to give my heart to a man? A man who was soft and powerful, a man who I was protecting but who made me feel cared for, a man who wasn't afraid of laying out all his feelings on the table and refused to give up on me.

"What if he breaks my heart?" I whispered, the question haunting me.

Tara squeezed me tight into her arms, laying her cheek on my shoulder. "Then we break him."

"Tara," I chided, but I wore the biggest smile.

"So how big is his dick?" Sloane asked, a devious smile on her face.

I shook her off my arm. "Go to sleep. I have to leave too early tomorrow."

"C'mon, did he fuck you hard or was he gentle?"

Once again, all four sets of eyes looked at me as if they deserved the answer to the questions. I stared back, but I was only one girl against four besties. I raised my hands in defeat and sighed. "Fine. He fucked me just right. And he ate me out."

All four groaned in appreciation. "Twice," I added, getting squeals and nudges.

"I knew he was a giver." Sloane had literal heart eyes.

Of all five of us, she was the only one who'd never experienced the love of parents. She'd grown up being passed around in the foster system. She had no idea who her parents were or what her heritage was. She'd grown up fighting for survival. She was only seventeen when Lena and I found her. We were literally her only family.

I pulled her back into my arms and lay down on the bed, cuddling her. "He is. You'll find a giver too someday."

"We all will," she said, her voice wistful.

Someone turned the lights off as my eyes shut down, my mind finally a little more at peace and ready to claim Dominic Park.

CHAPTER 28

DOMINIC

Samaira pretended to be working on the laptop she'd set up on her desk while I was reviewing a proposal when Kai's voice piped up on the intercom. "Mr. Park, the state attorney is here to see you with two men."

My eyes met Samaira's as she pulled out a gun from her purse and tucked it in the back of her pants. Her eyes were razor sharp as she gave me a nod. She tucked a stray strand of hair behind her ears, sitting with her legs crossed, curling her shoulders inward to try to appear nonthreatening.

I pressed the intercom button. "Kai, please send them in."

I hit the button under my desk that made the glass walls of my office opaque just as the door to my office burst open. A red-faced State Attorney Thomas Cooper Sr. barged in, two of his men flanking his sides. One of them locked the door to the office behind him as Thomas stood right against my desk, looking down at me. "Where is my son, Dominic?"

I raised my eyebrows. "What are you talking about, Mr. Cooper?"

His round face turned red, and spittle flew out of his

mouth as he pointed an accusing finger at me. "You damn well know what I'm talking about. You've kidnapped my son."

I sat on my chair perfectly still as if I didn't want to bash his skull into my desk. "Mr. Cooper, why would I want to kidnap your son? I don't even know the guy. I've never even met him."

His eyes blazed with cold fury. "You know why."

My eyes met Samaira's for half a second, and I saw her warning there. My fist clenched tight under my desk while blood roared through my veins. The fucker knew but refused to admit it. "I assure you, I don't."

"Where were you last night?" he asked.

I acted bored with the questions. I picked up my pen and rolled it around my fingers. "Not that I owe you anything, but I was at a bar. Some of us were having a party well into the night. And then, I went home to sleep, and now, here I am."

He shook his head, as if not believing a word out of my mouth. "I'll need proof."

I got out of my chair then and buttoned my suit, causing him to take a step back automatically. "Mr. Cooper. First, I have no idea what happened to your son or where he is. Second, you're not here with the cops. You're here with goons. So I'd need you to get a formal warrant before you ask me anything. If you're planning to visit me again, I'd appreciate it if you could book an appointment with my secretary. Then I can have my lawyer with me. Now, if there isn't anything else."

"Do you have any idea who you're dealing with here?" he hissed, leaning over my desk.

I leaned across from him, looking him in the eyes, letting some of my brewing rage slip off the leash. "Do I look like I give a fuck?"

His eyes narrowed at me as he kept shaking his head. "I know it's you. You're the one who's got my son. I need him back, or I'm going to rain down hell on your little life." He gave me a slimy fucking smile that made me want to rip his tongue out of his mouth. "I've heard your sister is a pretty successful interior designer. How's she doing these days?"

My knuckles cracked with the force of restraining myself from punching the shit out of him. "I don't appreciate being accused without any proof. Next time, you'll be talking to my lawyer. I'd like you to take your leave. Now."

He stared daggers at me, trying to intimidate me. But weak men didn't intimidate me. They irritated me. When I stared back at him with sheer boredom etched on my face, he huffed and turned around. His eyes paused on Samaira, who stood with her shoulders curling inward, looking like a scared personal assistant.

He went and stood directly across from her. Samaira, being an Oscar-winning actress, turned to look at me with nervous eyes and then stared at the floor. Thomas crossed his arms in front of her and asked, "What were you doing last night?"

She widened her eyes at him, and her jaw silently opened and closed, as if she were too nervous to answer. "I...I went to a bar with some of my friends in the evening and went home. Why, sir?"

He raised his finger to her face, and I instantly saw red. "Careful, Mr. Cooper. I don't know how you treat the women in your office, but I will not tolerate you disrespecting my employee. Put. That. Finger. Down. Now."

His eyes flashed to me, and they widened impossibly further with fear. He immediately pulled his finger away from Samaira and waved his hand at both of us. "I know it was you who did it. I'll be watching you. Mark my words. If my son is not returned to me, you will not like what happens next."

I walked around my table and stood in front of him, my head looming about half a foot over his short frame. "I will not be blackmailed in my own office. If you have any substantial accusations to make, contact my lawyers. Now, leave."

His eyes dripped with menace as he stared at me for a few seconds, and with a huff, turned around and walked out of my office, his two goons trailing him.

Samaira instantly checked under and around the table for any recording devices or camera implants, and gave me a nod when she didn't find anything.

I stepped closer to her and held her cheek. "You okay?"

She pressed a quick kiss to my palm and nodded, giving me a smile. "You handled yourself well. I was afraid you were going to pounce on him, and I'd have to kill those two goons in the middle of your office."

Even when my body was roaring with dark, black anger and a need for violence, Maira had a way of pulling me out of it. I raised my eyebrows at her. "You'd have killed those goons, huh?"

To my utter shock and a very delightful surprise, she stepped closer to me and pressed a kiss on my jaw. She'd never initiated a loving touch before, and I instantly wrapped my arm around her waist, pulling her closer. She murmured in my ear, "I'd kill, torture, and maim anyone who threatens your safety."

"Stop talking dirty to me, baby, or I'm gonna have to fuck you on my desk."

Her cheeks flushed a delicious red, and I was damn near tempted when she took a step back. "As much as I would love that, we have other priorities."

"What are our next steps?"

Samaira walked back and forth across the office. "You heard him. He's looking for his son. I don't think he'd wait more than twenty-four hours before involving the cops. You ready to get your revenge for Sophie?"

I wrapped my hand around her throat and pulled her into me, crushing my mouth against hers. "You wonderful fucking woman. You are giving me and my family the justice we need, and I'm forever going to be your puppet."

Her lips stretched into a smile against mine. "A controlling, bossy puppet, you mean."

I bit her lip playfully. "A loyal, devoted puppet committed to every one of your whims and pleasures."

She shook her head and looked at me with so much affection, it caught me off guard. Something had happened between yesterday and today. Samaira from yesterday did not look at me like that—with so much softness, so much warmth, and such an openly affectionate gaze. Samaira from yesterday snuck glances at me from the corner of her eyes, growled at me when I argued about not needing her protection, and hesitated in pulling me closer to her. But, I liked this new Samaira. I liked her a lot.

She pulled out of my embrace and packed her purse. "Let's get moving. We need to get Sophie and your parents to the safe house. I promised them vengeance, and vengeance they will get."

Once I informed Kai to postpone all my meetings for today, Samaira led the way to the basement of the office building. I had asked Kai if he wanted to join us at the safe house when I killed those fuckers. But Kai was a gentle soul. He said he'd rather be there for Sophie afterward. So he'd be going to my parents' place after work.

While Samaira drove us to the safe house, taking a hundred wrong turns to lose anybody tagging behind us, I called up my dad and gave him the precise route to take to reach the safe house. He promised to be there with Mom and Sophie in the next hour. While I did that, Samaira called the Wildcats to update them on Thomas's visit and his threats. She also let them know we were on our way there.

We were silent in the car as Samaira drove, occasionally slowing down and inspecting the cars behind us. "I think we're good. We had at least two cars tagging us, but we're good now."

"Good."

"You okay?" she asked, giving me a quick glance.

I leaned against the door so I didn't have to turn my neck to see her. "Yeah. Just a little worried about Sophie and my parents. I don't know how much violence they would be able to handle. I don't know how far I'd go. I've seen plenty of shady deals and dealt with certain dangerous clients and politicians. But I've never had to kill or torture anyone. I've been so angry for months, I've envisioned so much violence, inflicted so much pain and torture to those scums in my head, I feel like I'm about to burst at the seams here."

She nodded and gave me a soft look. "I completely understand where you're coming from, but there's one thing you must remember. This justice belongs to Sophie first. She is the only one who gets to decide the fate of her rapists."

My heart gave a sharp squeeze in my chest at the thought of Sophie, the memories of her in the hospital, suffering through surgeries and recovery over months, the way I saw our parents break down at seeing their daughter suffer, and I knew it in my bones. Even if Sophie chose to spare them their lives, *I* won't. It wasn't up for debate.

I heard a sigh and realized I had been lost in my own thoughts. Samaira shook her head, and I saw her lip curling. "You're going to kill them all, aren't you? Even if Sophie decides otherwise?"

"Sophie doesn't need to know."

She snorted. "Alright."

Her one word took me by surprise. "Alright? You don't think I should spare their life if Sophie asks us to?"

She gave me a glance for merely half a second, but it was enough to show me the lethal edge in her eyes. "Not my decision to make, Dom. But I am not a very forgiving person. I think raping a woman, abusing a woman in any shape or form, is the most dehumanizing act a man can commit. It not only strips a woman of her power and her choice but it permanently breaks something inside her. No man has the right to do that to a woman just to satisfy his ego. And that's what this is. It's purely an ego trip of a hateful person. There is never a motive to commit atrocities against women except a bruised ego. And I love nothing more than stomping the fuck over it. Men like them *never* learn. They never stop. They never repent. They always find new victims. I'd rather eradicate such men before another innocent woman has to suffer."

I fucking loved how sure Samaira was of herself. There wasn't really much of a gray area for her. For something as heinous as rape and abuse, I unequivocally stood with her. "Let's kill those bastards then."

The moment we walked into the safe house, Samaira took me downstairs to their basement, which was a large open room with a big cage in the center. The three rapists were held behind the cage and sat on chairs with their hands tied to the back and duct tape to their mouths. Their cheeks ran with tears as they kept screaming from behind the tape.

Sloane and Tara sat outside the cage, Tara working furiously on her laptop with Sloane licking a lollipop and shooting darts inside the cage. Now that I looked at the men properly, each of them had two to three darts sticking out of their bodies, streaks of blood sliding down the hit area.

Tommy's two friends were in slightly worse shape than Tommy, and I glared at Samaira. "You started without me?"

Samaira stood beside me and shrugged her shoulders. "I needed a confession from them before I handed them over to you. What if they weren't the ones who raped Sophie? Can't have you harming an innocent person."

I cracked my knuckles. "And?"

She smirked, her gaze stuck on them. "Eh. A little roughhousing, some blackmail, a few white lies, and they broke. Confessed everything. They thought putting the entire blame on Tommy would get them out. Save them. Fucking idiots."

My eyes narrowed at the three bastards as they stared back at me. My body automatically rushed to the cage as I slammed against it, my fingers crushing the wires of the cage. My vision tunneled in on the man in the center as his eyes turned mocking, and I could feel his pompous arrogance pouring through them, despite being tied to a chair. Thank God his mouth was taped shut, because if I had heard him speak, I wouldn't have had the control to wait for Sophie and my parents to arrive.

Tommy and his friends' fate belonged to her first.

"You know me, don't you, Tommy?" I asked between gritted teeth.

He simply rolled his eyes at me. I banged on the cage. "Answer me, you pathetic fuck."

I turned to the men on his sides; one of them was whimpering like a fool, while the other kept trying to loosen his hands from behind the chair. My blood boiled inside my veins, and fury coursed through my body in an endless wave. I wanted to bash their skulls in, pull their beating hearts out of their chests and feed them to them.

The sound of a gasp from behind me had me turning around. There, at the bottom of the stairs, stood Sophie, with my parents on either side of her.

Her feet were frozen in place as she stood clutching my mom's hands, her lips trembling and eyes shining with unshed tears. I walked toward her, hiding the view of the three men behind me, and stood in front of her. Softly, I held her cheek and turned her face to look at me. "Hey, Soph. I'm right here."

I could feel Samaira, Sloane, and Tara's eyes on us. But I kept my gaze on Sophie, as she whispered, "Is it them?"

I turned to look at Samaira, and Sophie followed my gaze. Samaira met Sophie's eyes and nodded. Perhaps it was the confirmation from Samaira, or perhaps it was looking at the three powerful women, each of whom had gone through something similar and emerged stronger, that gave Sophie the strength to take a step forward. Keeping her hand in my mom's, she said, "I want to see them, Dominic."

I stepped aside from her line of vision and let her take a step toward the men who changed her life forever, who tried to break her down with cruelty, who took from her what wasn't given freely. But my sister had fought back. She'd pulled through and now stood across them with fire burning in her eyes.

Her eyes glistened with tears as she stood still, staring each man in the eye for long minutes, her fingers tightening around the wires of the cage, her jaw clenched with tension.

She kept her eyes on the man in the center and, in a soft, silver-edged tone that sent shivers down my spine, said, "Open the cage."

My eyes snapped to her, and then to Samaira, who instantly obeyed Sophie. My heart pumped harder as fear for my sister had blood rushing to my ears. I softly clutched Sophie's hand. "Maybe it's not the best idea."

Her eyes snapped to me, and rage unlike anything I'd ever seen in my sister's eyes collided with mine. It made me immediately shut up. Sophie turned to walk to the cage door, and my eyes met Samaira's over her head, only to find her giving me a smirk. She raised her eyebrows at me, as if reminding me of our conversation in the car, and I took a deep breath and stood beside my parents.

Once Samaira opened the door to the cage, she walked in front and let Sophie enter. She kept the cage open, as if leaving Sophie the option to get out whenever she wanted.

Sophie was silent as she walked up to the guy in the center, who looked at her with the sadistic cruelty that made me want to gouge his eyes out. She moved closer, and that had me instantly taking a step forward. She ripped the tape off his mouth, making him hiss in pain.

"Why did you do it?" My sister's voice was so soft, so sad,

it made my heart bleed. It made me want to pound into this fucker's face that much more.

The fucking audacity of Tommy, he simply shrugged. "Didn't you disrespect me first?"

Sophie's fingers clenched into a tight fist, her knuckles turning white. "You slipped something into my colleague's drink. You were going to take advantage of her."

The fucker simply rolled his eyes as the two men beside him started to scream from behind the tape, shaking their heads. "You should've minded your own fucking business. This was never about you."

"So you raped me just because you couldn't rape my colleague?"

He sighed and rolled his eyes as if Sophie was exhausting him. "Trust me, I'm regretting it now." He, then, sneered. "Your pussy wasn't even worth all the hassle you've put me through."

A loud crack rang in the air as Sophie slapped Tommy across the face, her body heaving. The fucker's eyes gleamed as he spat blood on the floor. "Fuck."

"Do you regret it?" My sister's voice was deathly calm, as if the answer to that one question would change everything. But the dense fucker didn't pick up her tone or actually didn't give a fuck. He had the audacity to look upon her, dragging his gaze from top to bottom, his eyes glinting with the demented darkness that made my stomach curdle. "Nope. Should've fucked you harder."

Her pubic bone had fractured. Her body had scars to prove the fucker's brutality. A growl rumbled out of my chest at his words while Tommy looked at me with a bored expression on his face. As if he truly didn't realize that he was living the last moments of his life.

Sophie turned her head to look at Samaira and asked loud enough for all three men to hear her clearly. "What do the men do when you chop off their dicks?"

Samaira looked at the three fuckers and winked at them. She pulled a knife from her back pocket and twisted it around her fingers. She looked Tommy straight in the eyes and said, "They squeal like the pigs that they are."

Samaira looked at Sophie and asked, "Whose little chopped-off dick do you want?"

Now, the fucker's arrogant smile faltered. "Uh…what… what nonsense is this?"

Sophie stood in front of the fucker, her shoulders squared. "Vengeance. Revenge. Justice. Retribution. Retaliation. Payback. There are plenty of words for it. To put it simply, say bye-bye to your dicks, motherfuckers."

She looked at Samaira. "All of them."

Before Samaira could take a step forward in their direction, I walked to the cage door. "I'd like to volunteer."

Sophie looked at me with her eyes wide open, whereas Samaira gave me a surprised smile. "You'd like to chop off their dicks?"

I placed my hands in my pockets and looked down at the three fuckers who were now starting to realize the severity of their situation. Not looking away from them, I nodded. "Among other things."

I looked at Sophie then. "Is that okay with you, Soph? I'd like to do this."

She frowned with worry. "Are you sure?"

I gave her a nod. "More than anything."

She nodded and stepped closer to me. In a voice the men couldn't hear, she said, "And Dominic?"

"Hmm?"

"Kill them for me."

I pressed a quick kiss to the side of her head. "With pleasure."

She then walked out of the cage, her head held high, and stood outside it with Mom and Dad. I turned my head to

Samaira, who stood in the corner waiting for me, and gave her a nod. "Lock the gate from outside."

She smiled and walked up to me. She handed me her knife and her brass knuckles. "You'll need it later. I recommend chopping the dick *after* you beat the shit out of them. Otherwise, they just die before you're done with beating the fuck out of them."

Even at a time like this, my lips curled in a smile. "Noted."

She kissed my cheek and walked out, shutting the door of the cage behind me with a loud clang.

CHAPTER 29

The first thing Dominic did after being locked in the cage was open all the bindings that held the three men immobile. The second thing he did was stand in front of Tommy and punch him with the brass knuckles so hard that two of his teeth fell out.

After that, it was a no-holds-barred attack. It was three against one, but there was no competition. It was cold-blooded revenge. Pure and simple, and fucking beautiful.

Dominic was poetry in violence. Every punch was a punishment, every kick was a catharsis. Every scream was a cry of retribution. Every drop of blood that he shed of his enemies was proof of vengeance. Dominic was beautiful in his brutality. He was a man who cared deeply about his family, whose dedication to their happiness and well-being was the driving force behind his need for revenge.

Dominic's sister, mother, and father stood outside the cage, watching him beat the ever-living shit out of Sophie's rapists. None of them blinked. Not even once. None of them got squeamish. None of them asked him to stop. This was as much their fight as it was Dominic's. Sophie's face was streaked with tears as she held the crisscross wires of the cage like her life depended on it.

She flinched when one of them punched Dominic hard in the stomach, causing him to fall on his knees.

"Get up, Oppa," Sophie screamed, shaking the walls of the cage.

My fist clenched with the need to go inside and chop off the hand of the fucker who dared to touch Dominic. But I stayed put. This was his fight. His revenge. I was here, and nothing was going to happen to Dominic under my watch.

The three of them tried to restrain Dominic. They punched him; they kicked him. But a brother's wrath wasn't something you ever won against.

Dominic got back up every single time. His lips dripped with blood, his one eye was swollen shut, his knuckles were bruised, the brass knuckles dripping with blood, but he had a vicious smile on his face. He wiped his lips with the back of his hand as he stared at Tommy with murder in his eyes. "How does it feel to know you're never getting out of here?"

Tommy snarled. "You have any idea who you're dealing with?"

Tommy's friend came at Dominic at the same time as Tommy spoke, and Dominic punched him in the nose and then kicked him in the knees so his leg twisted and cracked. The guy went down with a whimper.

Dominic turned back to Tommy. "The state attorney. I'm aware. But you know what? I don't give a fuck."

Tommy laughed as if he found Dominic naive. "Oh, Dominic. My dad and I are just pawns in a vast game of chess. If anything were to happen to me, my dad would destroy you. All these real estate contracts and clients you get, they'll disappear. All those partnerships you're involved in, they'll pull out. The Park family will be on the streets with one word from my father. Are you sure you want to risk it all for one night of my mistake?"

Dominic's body heaved, and with a loud snarl that shook the cage, he threw the nearest chair at Tommy, slamming him against the cage. He lunged at Tommy, grabbing him by the collar and landing a punch on his nose. "A mistake is making a wrong investment." *Punch.* "A mistake is spilling your coffee on someone." *Punch.* "A mistake is trusting the wrong person." *Punch.* "If what you did to my sister was your *mistake,* it was the last mistake you will ever make in your pathetic excuse of a life."

By the time Dominic was done letting out all his anger, the three of them were a writhing, groaning mess on the floor.

Dominic turned to look at his family as he removed the bloody brass knuckles and put them in his pocket. He then pulled the knife from his back pocket that I'd handed him. "You might want to go upstairs. This is not gonna be pretty."

Dominic's mom took a step forward and stood beside Sophie. "These three men brutally raped your sister. Every time I close my eyes, I see my daughter beaten and broken and fighting for her life. Go ahead, Dominic. My eyes have been waiting for the day to replace that image with something better."

"As you wish, Mom." Dominic's face was splattered with the blood of his sister's rapists. He held a knife like an amateur, but the smile on his face was death incarnate.

As Dominic turned around to face the three men, his father stepped up to his daughter and wife, holding them in his arms, his gaze unwavering as he looked at Dominic.

I had no idea if Dominic had ever held another man's dick before, especially a tiny, soft one, soaking in piss. But Dominic did not hesitate for a second as he snapped open Tommy's friend's pants and pulled out his cock as he kicked and screamed to no avail.

"Like slicing an apple, Dom," I said, my eyes glued to Dominic.

He looked back at me, holding down the fucker, and gave me a sharp smile. "I usually bite into an apple. Haven't really sliced one before."

I snorted. "Just put us out of our misery and do it, Dom."

Sophie cleared her throat, turning all our eyes to her. "He's the one who asked Tommy not to do it. But when Tommy told him that he'd let him fuck me if he kept his mouth shut, he very happily obeyed. He raped me not once but twice. He's the one who drove the car around till they were all done."

Dominic's eyes darkened with fury, and he turned to the man whimpering beneath him, screaming his apologies. With one sharp motion, Dominic sliced off the man's penis. Fucking nasty business, but he turned around and dropped the tiny, bloody dick on the floor near Sophie's feet. "One down, two to go."

His screams echoed in the room, causing the remaining two to lose their shit. They kept trying to hit Dominic, but they were already too weak. He grabbed Tommy's other friend and climbed on top of him, raining down punches.

He paused after pulling down the guy's pants, and I realized he was waiting for Sophie.

Sophie realized it too, and she cleared her throat. "He's the one who tore open my ass. He beat me so hard, my cheekbone cracked. And he spit on me."

Dominic's body heaved as he did the same thing to the man underneath him. He spat on him, sliced his dick off, and then, without mercy, without a single pause, slammed the knife inside his ass, tearing it open. The guy died instantly. He then placed the chopped dick with the other mutilated dick near Sophie's feet.

Watching two of his men get their dicks chopped off was the perfect way to traumatize Tommy into madness. Once

Dominic descended on him, Sophie, for the last time, said, "He's the one who ordered for me to be raped. He's the one who orchestrated the whole thing. He slapped me. Bit me. He's the one responsible for most of my injuries. He's the one who stole my chance to be a mom someday."

With that last sentence, Dominic cut off Tommy's dick and then stabbed him in the heart, stealing his last breath.

In two more flicks, he killed the last man alive who was busy writhing in his own pool of blood, finally claiming justice for his sister.

He dropped to his knees at Sophie's feet from inside the cage, placing the last dick at her feet. I quickly unlocked the cage. Sophie and their parents rushed in and dropped to their knees beside him, tears streaming down their faces.

Dominic looked at his sister, his cheeks streaked with blood and tears, and cupped her face. "Soph, I'm so sorry I couldn't protect you from these assholes."

Sophie pulled Dominic into a hug, her shoulders shaking as he held her. "It's okay, Dominic. Thank you for finding them for me. For killing them for me."

"They didn't deserve to live."

She cried into his chest as their parents caressed Dominic's arm and patted his hair.

My heart squeezed in my chest at watching their family get the justice they'd been waiting for for four long months. It might not magically make everything all right and heal Sophie, but it would certainly help them put the culprits to rest. My eyes met Sloane's and Tara's, knowing that each of us remembered the day we found our own justice. The relief. The sense of peace. The transcendent feeling that felt like a rebirth. A new beginning.

That moment when my rapists breathed their last breath. It was seared in my brain forever. It was a memory that I clung to when the monsters in my brain surged to swallow me whole. That one memory helped me keep them at bay. The cold, hard fact that the real monsters had ceased to exist that day. That nobody was coming to get me. Watching them bleed out on the floor, their warm blood soaking my hands, had given my mind the ammunition that it needed to pull out of that spiral of doom and helplessness that had paralyzed me.

And I knew from the bottom of my soul that Sophie was feeling all those emotions right now. That tomorrow, she would wake up knowing that her assailants were wiped out from the face of the earth.

Leaving the Park family to cope with what happened with some privacy, I moved to Sloane and Tara. Tara had been on her laptop the whole time Dominic had been busy. I sat beside her, looking at her laptop. "You find anything?"

Her lips curled in an arrogant smile. "I found a lot of things."

"Think it can get us the state attorney out of the picture?"

"Look at this." She turned the laptop to me. "This man might be worse than his son. I dug deep into his records, his past, his cases. And there's a pretty common theme here. This man might have killed his wife. Not just that, there have been a few reports of missing women where his name has been a suspect. Of course, his name was cleared every time, but if it's a pattern, there has to be some truth associated with it."

"Fuck."

"Exactly. So I dug deeper. And found that all these missing women were quite young. Definitely under twenty-five. All of them were immigrants. Some of the families were paid off to retract their complaints, and three entire families are now missing. I went digging through his personal properties, and voilà. He's got a property near the Catskills, and the fucker has a propensity for recording his activities. Lucky for us, I was able to hack into all the security footage till about four years ago. And the fucker has had too many parties with barely legal girls. The recordings feature high-profile individuals engaging in illegal activities to the extent that they could potentially dismantle the state's justice system. If this footage were released to the public accidentally, it could ruin the lives of many high-profile individuals. The state attorney could avoid accusations from ordinary middle-class people. But you don't mess with the reputation of high-profile people. Those sharks would eat him alive."

Finally, my heart started to settle. Dominic was getting out of this mess. "So what's the plan? Are we releasing the footage or blackmailing him?"

Sloane, who had been listening to the conversation, asked, "How about eliminating him altogether?"

Tara's lips curled into a satisfied smile as if she'd been thinking the same. "We've killed people for less."

My eyes met my girls, and my own smile slipped through. "You know it's my favorite way to tie up loose ends."

Sloane's eyes looked behind me for a second before she met my gaze. "You go with your man. We'll take care of the attorney."

I had never *not* taken care of loose ends before. I hated feeling like I was slacking off or taking advantage of my girls. That somebody else was taking priority over finishing the job. "Are you sure?"

Tara gave me a warm smile. "He needs you more, Sami. We're fine. It's just one guy. He'd be frazzled right now. It wouldn't take much to get him alone and slit his throat. It would take even less time to blast all his crimes on the internet to see. Cops will think someone from his close network came to finish the job. Dominic would be off the suspect list soon after."

Sloane waggled her eyebrows. "See, Tara's got it all figured out. Don't worry about us. Your man needs you. Looks like it was his first kill."

I looked at my man and found him talking quietly with his family. They finally had small smiles on their faces even though each one looked mentally wiped. I got up from the couch, thanked the girls, and made my way to the Parks.

I stepped into the cage and asked softly, "You all want to get out of here?"

Dominic turned back to look at the now cold, dead bodies of the three men and cringed. "Yeah. Definitely."

The moment he was up on his feet, he rushed to me and pulled me into a crushing hug. I could feel his hands shaking at my back and his heart racing against my chest. I ran my hand down his back, soothing and caressing him to try to calm the adrenaline flooding his system. "Let's go home, Dom."

"Thank you." His voice was a whisper, but I still heard the bone-deep gratitude in his two little words.

Once we stepped out of the cage, I turned to Sloane. "I need you and Naomi to go and drop Sophie and her parents off at their house safe and sound."

"On it." Sloane was up and leading the way upstairs while I followed the Park family at the back, keeping my hand in Dominic's.

Once we were out of the basement, Dominic's dad stopped in the living room where Naomi and Lena sat at the large table. He turned and walked toward me. I immediately let go of Dominic's hand as his father took both my hands in his. "Thank you, Samaira." He looked at all the girls. "Thank you, all of you." He turned back to me, and with tears shining in his eyes, said, "You girls are family now. You need anything, you call me. Or Dominic."

I gave him a nod and squeezed his hand. "We will. Although Dominic has done enough for us, as it is."

Dominic gave my waist a light squeeze as his dad nodded, and we all slowly moved toward our cars. While Dominic and I got into one car, Sloane, Naomi, Sophie, and her parents got into the other. After promising to call them once we were home, we made our way to Dominic's place.

This time, I took the wheel. Dominic was in no condition

to focus, let alone drive. He had taken not one but three lives today. No matter what crime someone had committed, it never felt *normal* to take someone's life. The world was filled with the most depraved monsters, and somebody had to be the one to slay them. Dominic had killed three of those monsters today, extinguishing the lives of living, breathing creatures. No matter how cruel those men were, no matter how much they deserved it, killing them still took away a part of your soul. As if it were a punishment for deciding their fate rather than letting fate come to them.

I hated that he had to listen to Sophie recount those nightmares, that she had to look at her culprits and know that she was just a victim of a bruised male ego. For her to bare those ugliest truths in front of her whole family took balls of steel and a shit ton of trauma. Those men deserved to die. And I was so proud of Dominic for not shaking, not stumbling, not hesitating, for even a second before doling out justice.

I looked beside me to find his hands shaking on his lap as he stared outside the window. In my personal experience, I was always left on a huge high after a kill, leaving me desperate for a fuck or an hour or two in a hot bath. Those were the only two things that combated the violent paradox of the chill that seeped through my bones and the volcanic blood roaring through my veins. It was a clash of adrenaline trying to escape my body, while my mind struggled to hold on to it, seeking a sense of control.

Slowly, I reached forward and grazed my fingers along his chilled hand that was still caked in dry blood. His eyes snapped to me, his face was streaked with blood splatter, and I gave him a small smile. I moved my hand in his and slowly brought it to my lap. "You okay?"

His palm squeezed my thigh hard as if that was the only thing holding him up. His eyes were a storm of darkness, violence, and *need*. "Park the car to the side."

We were still closer to the safe house and way too far from

the main highway or any population. Just a long stretch of road, swallowed up by trees on both sides, the only light coming from the car's headlights. Knowing that we could easily get the privacy we needed, I slowed the car and drove it to the side. I moved his hand from my lap to the apex of my thighs, at the burning hot spot that ached for him. "You need me right now, don't you, Dom? You can't hold on till we get home?"

CHAPTER 30

DOMINIC

I couldn't hold on for a minute longer, let alone all the way home. I felt like I was flying, or more like jumping off a plane and free-falling to the ground. My heart was racing, my blood was roaring in my ears, and my cock was rock fucking hard.

I grabbed her crotch and felt the warmth at her apex, pulling a rumble out of my chest. I felt unhinged. Untethered. Like a wild fucking animal. All I needed was Maira's skin against mine. To feel her beating heart against my chest, her wet, warm pussy soaking my cock. I rubbed at her covered pussy, uncaring that she was still driving, trying to park on the side of the road. "Fuck, Maira. Need you."

My hands shook, and my body trembled. An ache bloomed under my skin as my chest felt a kind of emptiness that I'd never felt before. I clutched my heart and squeezed, trying to stem the pounding heartbeat. I felt like I was stuck in a free fall through the freezing winds and being swept in a blazing tornado in the desert. My body wanted to run, to fuck, to scream, to punch. But my mind was frozen and achingly alone. It was only my hand touching Samaira that kept me barely tethered to the present.

The moment I felt the car turn off, I snapped open our seat belts and dragged her on top of me before she could even blink. "Fuck, you're so warm, baby. So fucking soft."

Her legs were on either side of me as I pushed my face against her throat. An animalistic sound escaped my lips as I breathed in her soft, feminine scent mixed with a hint of sweat. My hips moved of their own accord between her legs, trying to get inside her.

Need so deep ran in my veins, my chest heaved as I clutched her to me, her tank top bunching in my fists. I kept breathing her in, pulling in deep gulps of her scent as I felt her fingers running through my hair. I realized she was trying to soothe me. My lips moved lower, down her neck, to the top of her chest, licking and biting her skin, feeling the warmth of her skin on my tongue. My body shook with the aching emptiness and cold that seemed to be slowly thawing the more I touched Samaira.

I was about to tear open her tank top when she quickly grabbed both of my hands at her chest. "Shh...Dom. Give me a second, baby."

Warmth bloomed in my chest at her endearment, and I halted my movements as I watched her remove her tank top. The moment she snapped open her bra from the front, I lunged. I ran the flat of my tongue on her breast, pulling a long moan out of Maira that echoed in the car. My ears rang, and my cock pulsed in my pants as I pulled her nipple in my mouth and sucked.

"Dominic." My name on Samaira's lips had my blood thrumming in my veins and my mind relishing in the soft warmth of her breast on my tongue. Precum oozed from my cock as Samaira ran her fingers in my hair and pushed her nipple deeper into my mouth with a whimper, urging me to suck harder. Her hips rolled on my lap, and all my senses focused on sucking and nipping and licking at her breasts, pulling out moans from her lips.

She pulled me off her tits with a sharp tug on my hair. Her chest heaved as her dark eyes met mine. I grabbed her jaw and noticed the deep red spatter of blood on my fingers. "I'm going to mess you up, Maira. Tell me to stop now."

A wide, vicious smile stretched across her face, and she ran her tongue over my lips, giving a sharp bite to the bottom one. "Mess me the fuck up, Dom."

Arousal and adrenaline roared a battle in my body as all thoughts escaped my mind except one. Samaira.

I clutched her hair at the back of her head and slammed her mouth to mine, swallowing her moan and tasting her need. My tongue swiped between her lips with the urgency to taste her sweetness, her warmth, her life. I sucked and nipped at her lips and kissed her like it was my last breath.

The bone-chilling cold that had seeped into every pore of my body melted as the warmth of the woman in my lap seeped into my soul, into my very essence.

She clutched the back of my neck as she pushed her tongue deep into my mouth, fucking it the way I wanted to fuck her pussy. She bit my lip and murmured in my ear, "The moment you chopped off those dicks, I soaked my fucking panties. You were so fucking hot."

With a growl, I wildly dragged her pants and panties down, causing her to gasp in my mouth as she helped me undress her, and then opened the zipper of my pants. My cock sprang up as I pulled it out of my briefs and shoved my clothes down my hips.

Her lips ran along the side of my throat, causing goose bumps to erupt down my back. "I fucking loved that you didn't hesitate for even a second. I'm so fucking proud of you."

Her words were gasoline to the fire erupting in my chest. My cock pulsed with need, and I pushed it along her soaking wet pussy. I was so hard, arousal drumming through my blood so fucking viciously, I was afraid I'd come just by her words. Samaira was proud of me for killing three people. A laugh rattled in my chest and escaped my mouth.

Samaira brushed a quick kiss on my mouth as her lips quirked in a smile. "What's so funny?"

I couldn't bear not to have my lips on her skin for even a second. I licked her throat, feeling her pulse on my tongue, and said against her neck, "You're proud of me for killing three men."

Her neck arched with a delicious moan, and she rubbed her pussy on my cock. Rising on her knees and slowly, so achingly, punishingly slowly, she sank down on my cock in one stretch.

I roared as her soft, wet heat engulfed me, enveloping me so thoroughly, I rammed into her again and again, needing more of her heavenly warmth. Blinding pleasure replaced the harrowing emptiness.

I wasn't free-falling anymore. I was flying. I was swooping. I was fucking soaring into her wild heat.

Maira pulled my hair and stared down at me, our chests heaving, our breaths fogging up the windows of the car. "I'm even more proud that you used *my* fucking knife and *my* brass knuckles. You marked my knife with your first kill." Her teeth clenched as she pulsed around my cock, her eyes rolling back in her head with a moan. "Fuck me, Dominic."

My mind obliterated. Red-hot arousal pulsed in my veins as I slammed into her with the desperation of a dying man. I sank deep into her, dragging my cock along the walls of her pussy, making her shriek along my jaw.

With every hard thrust into her heat, one truth crystallized in my mind. I held her throat with one hand and held her still above me with another on her waist. She moaned with need and looked into my eyes with a wild desperation as I halted all our movements. "I'm glad you're proud of me for killing those men because if anybody puts a single scratch on you, I'd flay them open and skin them alive. I'd kill for you. Bleed for you. Burn for you. Fucking die for you."

My words ended on her lips. "Like I said before, Dom, death would have to get through me first before it ever grazed you."

Like I'd ever let that happen. She wanted to protect me, and her protectiveness only made me want her more. Protect *her* more. I'd let her keep her promise. But if ever death came knocking on our door, if anybody tried to take Samaira away from me, I'd fucking tear them apart. Samaira was mine, and I refused to exist in a world without this woman.

I grabbed her hand and sucked two of her fingers into my mouth. I kept them pressed along my lips as I said, "This." I thrust into her. "Yours."

I dragged her hand lower and pressed her palm against my chest. "This." *Thrust.* "Yours."

I moved her hand lower so she touched the spot where my cock entered her pussy. "This." *Thrust.* "Only fucking yours."

She whimpered and rubbed her clit in time with my thrusts. My pulse pounded as my balls tightened, and that familiar heat unfurled at the base of my spine. My rhythmic fucking faltered, and my body lost all its control as my balls slapped at her ass. "Samaira. Be a good girl and come on my fucking cock, baby."

With a keening cry, Samaira tightened unbearably around my cock, her pussy pulsating around me, and she flooded my lap with her orgasm. Before I even knew it, she pulled off me, making me roar like an animal in heat as she held my cock.

Her dark eyes met my wild ones. "No condom. Come on me, Dom. Soak my pussy."

Her words were my undoing as my vision whitened and my orgasm barreled down my spine. I snarled and bucked my hips as she jerked me off, my mind splintering and my cum shooting all over her pussy and stomach.

Our foreheads touched as we looked down at the mess I'd made on her. She panted against my lips as I moved my fingers in the mess and spread it even more on her body, rubbing my cum on her skin. "I like you dripping with my cum."

"Me too." Her whisper touched my lips, making me smile.

I pulled her into a whisper-soft kiss. "Let's go home."

She quickly donned her pants sans panties. She handed those to me for safekeeping. And I held on to them like a life-line. I stared down at my blood-splattered hand, clutching her delicate lace panties. My cock stirred in my pants at the beautiful paradox.

She pressed the switch on the car to get the fog out after she started the car. Once we got back on the road, I turned in my seat so I could look at her. "Can I ask you something?"

She nodded. "Anything."

"Are you on birth control pills?" I'd fucking love to come inside her. Just the thought had blood stirring in my cock.

She bit her lip and shook her head in denial. "I've always gotten normal periods. After my assault, I didn't have sex for a few years. I started to have more positive sexual experiences after I got some toys, which made me want to have some dick willingly. So I hooked up once in a while but always with protection. I wasn't going to put my body and my hormones through the side effects of birth control pills when I had normal periods and was occasionally having sex with condoms. I had no desire to feel a man coming in me."

A growl rumbled in my chest at the thought of another man even touching my girl. "Good. And now? Is that something you want?"

Her hands squeezed the steering wheel as she bit her lip. "Honestly, I don't know if we really need condoms. After my assault, I was told that I'd most likely never conceive. I've made my peace with that. I don't want to risk a pregnancy on the off chance though, you know. But I'd love nothing more than to feel you come inside me."

"Hmm. Me too, baby. And if you'd like to have children in the future, I'll have the best doctors to help us out."

Her lips curled in a shy smile, and I loved it even more. She shook her head and asked, "Do you want children?"

I turned to her and found her biting her lip as if nervous about my response. I brought my hand to the back of her neck and squeezed. "There are always options when it comes to having a kid. But when it comes to a life partner, there is only one option and choice for me. You."

She rolled her eyes, but her lips were stretched in a wide smile. "I don't mind going to an ob-gyn to discuss my options for birth control." She softly muttered, "Fucking never stood a chance."

My throat dried up, and I had to swallow before my words came out in a hoarse voice. "Only if you feel comfortable, Maira. You discuss it with your doctor first."

"Alright then."

"Alright."

Our smiles were wide, and we looked like fools, but I was happy.

Even though I'd killed three men less than an hour ago, I was happy.

Once we reached home, Samaira turned on the shower to high heat, helped me remove all my clothes, and followed me in naked. My body was trying to shut down, the adrenaline starting to leave my system.

Samaira patiently and thoroughly cleaned and washed every part of me until the water flowing in the drain went from red and bloody to clear and full of suds. She washed until every single speck of blood was removed from my body. She washed my hair, my armpits, my rock-hard dick, and even the crack of my ass. Which, again, only managed to ramp up my arousal. But another emotion was flooding my heart even more than the arousal.

Warmth.

Warmth of her care.

Warmth of her smile.

Warmth of her fingers gently washing me.

Warmth of her love.

We hadn't said those words to each other, but this overwhelming feeling of warmth that settled in my heart down to the marrow of my bones was nothing but love.

When she pulled me into the bed, under the warm blanket, her bare skin against mine, all I could think was I wanted *this* every day for the rest of my life.

Technically, Samaira and the Wildcats had fulfilled their job. She was free to leave me any time now. She had no obligation whatsoever to me.

I could only hope that she, too, wanted to *stay*.

I slept with her in my arms, feeling her chest move against my front, my cock nestled in the cleft of her ass, and a decision was made.

Make Samaira fall in love with me. Because I was completely and irrevocably in love with her.

CHAPTER 31

I woke up alone in Dominic's bed, feeling the cold bedsheet and emptiness along my back. I grabbed my phone from the nightstand for any updates from the Wildcats.

I found a long string of messages from the girls in our group chat.

Tara: Threat resolved.

Tara: Congratulations, the mission is successful and complete.

Sloane: Fuck yeah.

Naomi: That means Sami shouldn't be back for days.

Lena: Yes. You need to claim that man, Sami. Follow your heart.

Sloane: Yes, please. We all know you want him. He clearly is obsessed with you.

Naomi: Yes

Tara: Yes

Lena: Yes

I couldn't help but smile at their enthusiasm. I sprawled on the bed and messaged in the group chat.

Me: What if being with him puts our entire existence in jeopardy? Are you all okay with a risk like that?

Sloane: Fuck yeah. I'd die for you, bitch. Getting exposed at the cost of your happiness is nothing.

Lena: Same.

Tara: Same. And you'd say the same for any of us. So don't give us that.

Naomi: Like Tara said.

Me: What if being with me puts HIS life in jeopardy? What if something happens to him under my watch?

Tara: Don't you be a chicken and ask us such stupid questions. You're the motherfucking Crimson Tiger.

Sloane: Laughing emoji

Naomi: Laughing emoji

Lena: Any other excuse you have that makes you want to put more walls around you?

Me: Fuck you guys.

Me: Also, love you guys.

Sloane: <3

Lena: We love you too <3

Naomi: <3

Tara: <3

I placed the phone back on the side table and went to the restroom to freshen up. I stared at myself in the mirror while brushing my teeth and looked into my eyes, remembering Tara's words. I *was* the motherfucking Crimson Tiger. Was I genuinely afraid that I wouldn't be able to protect him, that the Wildcats would be better off without involving a public figure billionaire, or was I just terrified of being hurt?

Did I truly believe Dominic could hurt me? My heart knew he was safe. My body knew he was safe. But my mind was a scaredy cat. After pushing everyone away for years, keeping my family at bay to protect them, not accepting any long-term relationship, I was too used to taking care of myself. Of not having to worry about someone. Of not having to think about someone day in and day out. Of not having a smiling face to welcome me home. Of not having someone to laugh with while watching a movie. Of not having a warm embrace on cold nights.

Once I went downstairs, the smell of freshly brewed coffee pulled me to the kitchen area. A smile instantly came over my face as I watched a shirtless Dominic cooking an omelet. How was I ever going to let this man go?

My feet automatically led me to his back as I wrapped my arms around his waist, resting my head between his shoulder blades. His chest expanded as he held my hands at his waist. "I was hoping to wake you up with breakfast in bed."

Oh, this man. I tightened my arms around him and pressed a kiss to his back. "You can just feed it to me now."

"Of course, my tigress. Coffee?" He turned halfway and pressed a kiss to my head. My heart gave a little thump as if telling me, *See how good it feels to be cared for?* My body definitely noticed the way his biceps were bulging as he held me.

I squeezed his arms and raised my eyebrows. "Did you work out this morning?"

He chuckled and flexed his muscles. "Of course. You see, my girlfriend is fucking jacked and built like a tigress. I have to work out twice a day to build enough muscles to be able to throw her down on the mat in a fight."

Blood rushed to my cheeks as I tried to stop the ridiculous smile on my face by biting my lip. "Girlfriend, huh?"

He turned off the stove and pulled me into his arms, his face scrunching in a frown. "Feels too casual, huh? How about my lover? My life? My woman, whom I'm so fucking obsessed with, I could write poetry about her?"

Fuck, he was going to make me cry. What was it about him that I had no control over my emotions? That I couldn't hold it together? That I fucking blushed and stammered and melted? The thought of something happening to Dominic terrified me to my bones. I clutched his waist and felt the warmth of his skin. "What if being with her puts your life in danger?" My voice was a mere whisper, too terrified to hear his answer.

His eyes turned soft, and a small smile tugged at his lips. He brushed a strand of my hair behind my ears and pressed a kiss to my nose. "My life, as it is, is over if I don't get to spend it with you."

A tear slipped down my cheek, and I pressed my face to his neck. "I'm scared," I whispered.

He tightened his arms around me. "Tell me something, baby."

"What?"

"If there was no risk, if you knew for certain that nothing would ever happen to me if we were together, and the Wild-cats would never ever get exposed, what would you do?"

The sheer possibility of both of those things coming true had me praying to the gods that I'd stopped believing in years ago. But I knew what he was asking, and I fucking knew what

I would do. I met his eyes and cupped his jaw. "Then I'd tie you to my bed and my life forever. I'd give you all my days and my nights. I'd wake up in your arms and have breakfast in bed. I'd train with you and slam you in the boxing ring, and I'd take you for rides on my motorcycle. I'd cry in your arms when life got too tough. I'd celebrate my wins with you by my side. I'd fuck you every night and go to sleep with you buried deep inside me."

He pulled me into a kiss so full of passion, so full of hope and need, my knees almost gave out. He rested his forehead against mine and held me like I was precious to him. "Then give us a chance, Maira. Let's live that life. Because I'd rather have a month of what you described than fifty years of a miserable existence without you."

"I'd never be able to forgive myself if something happened to you."

He clutched my face with both of his hands, his eyes looking at me with fierceness and frustration. "I'm going to tell you this one thing, Samaira. You do not have the right to make decisions on behalf of others. You need to let people love you. You need to let people decide if you're worth risking their lives for. You need to let people be in your fucking life if they want to. You don't get to shut them all out because you're afraid to feel the pain of losing them. Be it me or your parents. Let people love you, baby. Let *me* love you. Because even if you don't, I'm afraid it's too late. I'm in love with you, baby. I'm in love with every inch of the crazy, jealous, protective, soft, powerful, kinky parts of you. And I refuse to stop. You understand?"

My lips trembled, and my throat closed up. All I could do was nod as tears streamed down my face.

With a groan, he pulled me back into his arms. "I thought I hated seeing you hurt. But tears? Baby, these can kill me."

I sniffed. "Shut up. You're a dork."

He chuckled as he swayed me in his arms. "A dork you

love," he singsonged. "And don't you fucking deny it. You don't have to say it for me to know it in my heart. You can take as much time as you need. I'll wait."

He was right. The words were on the tip of my tongue, but my mind was terrified to let them out. "Thank you."

He let me go and pulled me to the dining table. Then he went back to the kitchen in all his shirtless glory and prepared me breakfast while I ogled him to my heart's content. We ate across from each other, our legs entangled under the table, with Dominic feeding me an omelet and toast.

He looked at me, his face resting on his palm, a faint smile on his face. "Do you have anything planned today?"

I shook my head. "Nope. The girls handled the state attorney. He's dead. So the case is officially complete and successful. I've been asked to take a bit of a break."

Dominic's eyes rounded. "When did you decide to kill him?"

I shrugged. "Tara uncovered the thousands of skeletons that Thomas was hiding in his closet yesterday, right before we arrived. He made his son look like an innocent little puppy. We've executed men for less. Tara would release some very incriminating evidence of his crimes on the internet, and you'd be off any suspicions."

"Fucking perfect. Thank the ladies for me, would ya?"

When I nodded, Dominic reached across the table and held my hand. "Let's go on a date today."

Excitement fluttered in my stomach. "I have nothing to wear."

"Don't worry about it. Just say yes. I'll set everything up."

"Okay, then. Yes. Let's go on a date."

"Perfect. Now off you go to work out or rest or get ready. Give me an hour to set things up."

"An hour? We'll leave in an hour?"

He chuckled and got out of his chair. With a quick press

of his lips on my forehead, he started to walk out backward. "Tick tock, Tigress. Big plans today."

By the time I'd worked out for an hour in his home gym and stepped out of the shower, I found a large shopping bag on his bed with a card that read, "Wear me, please."

I opened the bag to find three boxes of varying sizes inside. The biggest box revealed a dark red dress made of the softest material I'd ever touched. Another box had matching heels with a very distinct red sole. A gasp escaped me as I opened the last box, the smallest one, which revealed a stunning diamond choker necklace.

Dominic had gone all out and was apparently sparing no expense. And boy, did I love it. I felt like Cinderella now.

I pulled off my towel and held up the strapless gown. As soon as I pulled it on, it draped over every one of my curves and muscles like magic, turning me from a fighter to a fairy. One side of the dress had a long slit all the way up my thigh, and it just made me look fucking hotter. I stood in front of the mirror, loving how beautiful I looked. My eyes were suddenly looking at those of a young Samaira. She wasn't jaded. She wasn't a survivor. She wasn't a fighter. She was a dreamer. She was a dancer. She was a girl full of hopes and yearning for a life of love and beauty. She was innocence and laughter. She was grace and giggles.

This dress was bringing the young Samaira back to life, and I only had Dominic to thank for it. I never thought I'd enjoy feeling like a princess before, but my entire body was tingling, and a million butterflies fluttered in my stomach. There wasn't a pair of panties in sight, and I was all but delighted to forgo them. *Devious, devious Dominic.*

The material of the gown was so smooth, it glided down my body, caressing all the right places and sending tendrils of arousal to dance along my skin.

I removed my necklaces and choker and put on the thick diamond choker with five teardrop-shaped rings dangling at equal spacing, with one big hollow teardrop at the center. It felt cool to the touch, and it rested at the base of my collarbone. I stepped into the black high heels with a red sole and finally twirled in front of the mirror.

I also found a bag of makeup at the vanity. Living with Sloane had its benefits. That woman was a genius at applying makeup and had given us countless tutorials on how to get ready and look like a fucking queen. With a silent thanks to her, I was ready with my hair and makeup in another half an hour. As I made my way downstairs, my heels clacked against the wooden stairs.

The moment I turned around the spiral staircase, my eyes fell on Dominic, who stood near the dining table, sipping from a glass of water. He wore a dashing black suit over a black shirt and black pants. His hair was styled to perfection, and his jaw seemed to be cut from glass. He looked so fucking hot, I almost missed a step.

As soon as his eyes landed on me, the glass of water slipped out of his hands and shattered on the floor at his feet into hundreds of pieces. He didn't even react to the glass breaking because his eyes were glued to me. They roved from the top of my head to the tip of my toes, a red blush coating his cheeks.

He met my eyes and clutched his chest, acting as if his heart couldn't handle it, making me giggle. Was this what life would be like if I were to be with Dominic forever?

He stepped over the glass and walked to me. Taking my hand in his, he pressed a small kiss on my fingers. "You look breathtaking, baby."

Blood rushed to my cheeks. "Should we clean up the glass?"

"What glass?"

I chuckled and turned his face to the shattered pieces of glass on the floor. "That glass."

"Huh. How'd that happen?"

It only made me laugh harder.

He held my waist and pulled me into him, grazing his jaw along mine, placing a kiss on my bare shoulder. Then he bit me right there, pulling a moan out of me as my pussy throbbed. "You didn't give me panties."

"Hmm." He grazed his finger on the choker. "I didn't."

I leaned my head back, letting him pull his finger under the choker. "It's going to cause a very sticky situation."

His hand moved lower and cupped my ass, his fingers squeezing my cheek to the teetering point of pain and pleasure, making me whimper. "I'm counting on it."

With one last kiss at my throat that made me want to push him on the couch, pull my dress up, and put his cock inside me, he straightened. "Let's go, Maira. Long day ahead of us."

We made our way to the elevator, and instead of pressing the parking floor button, he hit the button for the roof. "Where are we going?"

He kept my hand in his and winked at me, popping off his dimples. "It's a surprise."

The moment we reached the roof, a motherfucking helicopter waited for us, the sound of the blades beating through the air around us. The noise was deafening as the wind blew my hair and dress, making me tighten my hold on Dominic's hand.

We were quickly seated inside the helicopter, and the pilot took off.

I couldn't stop staring at the city of Manhattan below. Dominic's voice filtered into my ear through the headset. "Have you been in a helicopter before?"

I wooted loudly as it swooped low and took a flight up. "Never. I've never even been in a plane."

"Well, you're in for lots of new experiences, baby."

Before I could ask him more about it, the helicopter leaned sideways, and I felt like I could almost plunge onto the roof of a building. It was magnificent. It was thrilling. It felt like I was living a dream I never knew I had.

It wasn't more than fifteen minutes before we arrived at a large empty lot. I turned my head around the space and found a number of small planes, and my eyes snapped to Dominic. "What are we doing? Where are we going?"

He turned his eyes all innocent and shrugged. "You just said you haven't ever been in a plane."

My eyes widened. "You didn't say where we're going."

He helped me down from the helicopter. "Just enjoy the ride, baby. I have your passport and anything else that you might need."

"H…How? When? This is getting too much, Dom." My heart was beating so loud I was afraid he would be able to hear it over the helicopter blades.

He looked at me, his eyes staring down into mine. "Are you having fun?"

"But…"

"Yes or no? Be honest."

"Yes."

"Then let's go."

I shook my head as he took my hand and led us to a small plane with its door open, featuring three steps leading up to it. He held my dress as I climbed. I entered what appeared to be the luxurious living room of a billionaire. I turned to find his eyes trained on me. "You like?" he asked.

"You could live here," I said, looking at the plush couch and two cozy leather chairs.

We walked in farther, and he opened the door at the back to reveal a bedroom with a massive king-size bed, covered in the softest bedsheets. "For later," he whispered in my ear, making me snort.

We were soon seated on the couch, my dress spreading along the surface as we sipped on some sparkling champagne. Once we were high up in the sky, I turned to look at Dominic, who had my bare feet in his lap and was slowly massaging them, making me moan every few seconds. "Are we going to a gala or something?"

He frowned. "No."

I gave him a look and turned my eyes to my dress. "Then why the dress?"

A boyish smile came over his face, his dimples a beacon to my senses. "I wanted to see you in it."

My jaw dropped. "That's it? That's your reason? What if I'm overdressed for wherever you're taking me?"

He scoffed. "You're perfect. Believe me, you're the hottest woman in the world in your tank tops and cargo pants, fighting and killing assholes. But right now, you look like an angel of death."

I couldn't help it. I climbed on his lap, my dress trailing me, and held his face in both of my hands. Slowly, I pressed the softest kiss on his lips. "You make me feel like an angel. I never thought I'd be into wearing gowns and diamonds. But I've never felt more stunning in my life. You're helping young Samaira reclaim all her wild dreams."

He pulled me closer by the tear-shaped ring at my choker and deepened the kiss. "I'm going to shower you in diamonds and silks. I want to fulfill every one of your desires, no matter how big or small. You name it, and it's yours, baby."

This man. This dress. This feeling. All of it had arousal thrumming through my veins. "All I want right now is your cock inside me, Dominic. Or my pussy on your mouth."

His cheeks flushed, and a loud groan escaped his lips as he grabbed my ass and got up from the couch. "How about both?"

I pressed my lips to his, tasting the champagne on his tongue, as he carried us to the bedroom. "Sounds perfect to me."

———

We spent a few hours on the plane fucking, eating, watching a movie, then fucking again. Dominic had packed my passport, but he really didn't pack me any panties. So even after coming multiple times, I was still extremely sensitive every time I walked or moved and was getting aroused embarrassingly fast. It wasn't often I went without underwear, and now I knew why. Thank God he was using a condom. Otherwise, my legs would be streaked with his cum.

A shudder went through my body at the thought, and I had to admit, it didn't sound bad at all. Maybe after I got an IUD, we could do this again.

The moment the plane touched the ground, Dominic turned to me with a smile on his face. "Welcome to Barcelona, baby."

It was dark when we got off the flight. There was a limousine waiting for us at the airstrip. Dominic handed me another glass of champagne as we got into the limo. "You ready to dance?"

My eyes widened. "Dance?"

He turned to face me and grazed his finger along my jaw. "You told me you used to love to dance when you were a kid. When was the last time you went to a club for dancing?"

"Never."

"Do you still dance?"

I bit my lip before I nodded. "Sometimes. Usually when I'm home alone."

"Why'd you stop, Maira?" His face dropped as if it hurt *him* that I stopped dancing.

I shrugged. "Well, with the things that I see every day, the things that I do every day, I don't find many reasons to dance, or even the mood, to be honest."

He placed a soft kiss on my cheek and murmured softly in my ear, "And now? Will you dance with me, Maira?"

"Yes. I'd love to."

"That's my girl."

Dominic took me to the most happening club in Barcelona. According to him, nobody in the world had a better clubbing scene. Since I'd never stepped foot outside America, I took his word for it. The club had amazing beats, the lighting shrouded everything in bright purples and reds, the drinks kept flowing, and we danced till our feet ached. I didn't even remember when I'd shed my heels and didn't even care that I was totally overdressed for clubbing. But under the purple lights of the club, Dominic looked at me as if all he saw was me. His hands never left my body, his lips never stopped smiling, his dimples never disappeared, and I'd never been happier.

At one point, he changed our drinks to mocktails and water. When I gave him a quizzical look, he only said, "I need you to remember this. Also, I need you not to be drunk for later. I have a special surprise."

I was having so much fun that I simply shrugged and let it go. All I needed was Dominic's hot and hard body against mine as I swayed to the music.

I spread my arms wide, embracing the moment.

I dipped down low with Dominic holding me to him, getting lost in the tunes.

I laughed when he stepped on my toes.

I loved when he pushed other guys off me.

I wished my girls were here with me, but for once, I refused to feel guilty for having fun.

Because that was what I was doing—having fun with the man I loved.

———

As the night turned to dawn, Dominic rushed me into our hotel room and slammed me against the back of the door, his lips devouring me with a ferocity that had me mewling. My body was on fire, and every inch of me wanted to be consumed by the man holding my ass with both of his hands and sucking my neck, leaving bruises.

I clutched the back of his head, my fingers pulling at his lush hair, moaning with abandon. "Dominic, fuck me. Please."

Dominic carried me farther into the room, his voice rumbling from his chest. "Soon, Tigress. I want you to do something for me first."

My back was arched deep, pleasure from Dominic's kisses running rampant through my veins, clouding my vision into a hazy fog. "Anything."

Instantly, Dominic's heat disappeared, and my eyes snapped open, taking him in. He'd taken a step back and had his hands in his pockets. His face tilted slightly to the side as his eyes clouded with dark desire. "Do you trust me?"

With the way his eyes darkened and his chest stopped moving, I realized that this was more than just a sexual question for him. So I looked him in the eyes and gave him a straight answer, filling my voice with pure conviction. "Yes. You know I do."

His lips pressed together with a hint of a smile, and his eyes softened the tiniest bit. "Close your eyes, Maira."

Without hesitation, I followed his instructions.

"That's my girl." His words were gasoline to the fire erupting along my skin. I was so fucking turned on that my thighs were streaked with my arousal.

I could hear some movement, but I didn't dare open my eyes. Dominic wanted to know if I trusted him, and I was going to show him. I stood there with my hands clasped behind my back. My breathing was so erratic that my chest was heaving, and my core pulsed with the need to be filled.

The sound of footsteps moving closer had me straightening my posture further before I felt the heat of Dominic's chest against mine. I kept my eyes closed as I felt the brush of his fingers along my cheek before he pressed the softest kiss on my nose. "Good girl."

I bit my lip to stop the moan from escaping my throat.

He pulled both of my hands in front of me and placed what felt like a stack of clothes in my hands.

"Open your eyes, Maira." His words were a whisper against my ears, sending crackling pleasure slithering down my spine.

I opened my eyes to find my hands holding my Wildcats suit, with my mask and the brass knuckles. *Oh, Dominic. You dirty dog.*

My lips stretched into a smile as my gaze met his. I found his eyes burning with heat. "Suit up for me."

I bit my lip and gave him a quick salute. "Yes, sir."

I turned to walk to the restroom when his voice stopped me. "And Maira." When I turned to meet his eyes, he said, "Keep up with the *sir.*"

Heat flooded my belly, and an embarrassing amount of wetness flooded between my legs. "Yes, sir."

With that, I locked myself behind the restroom, the heat of his gaze following me all the way.

The moment I slid the suit up my body, another surprise awaited me. I bent over my waist and stared down at the very big slit right at my crotch. *Did he cut up my suit?*

I zipped up my suit, pulling my brand-new diamond choker on top of it, not wanting to hide it underneath. It was a gift from Dominic, and I knew, deep in my bones, that he'd enjoy watching his present on my body.

My body flooded with excitement and want. The need to please Dominic—*sir*—started to ride my body hard, my knees shaking with desire. I'd always wanted to be fucked in my suit. I would be lying if I claimed to never have fucked myself with my favorite vibrator while suited up. But this. This was my own fantasy coming to life.

I swiped a finger along my wetness, running it around my aching clit, a desperate moan escaping my lips.

A loud bang crashed against the door. "Don't you fucking dare touch what's mine. You have ten seconds to come out."

Oh fuck. Need thrummed in my veins, and I rushed to put on my mask and slide on my brass knuckles.

Quickly, I pulled the door open and was immediately met with Dominic's large chest right at my face. He'd gotten out of his shirt and had removed his belt. His hands were behind his back, his wide chest expanding as he took in a sharp breath.

His eyes darkened as he stepped back and took me in. His gaze slowly traveled from my mask to my tits to the apex of my thighs. They lingered there for a moment longer, his nostrils flaring, before he walked to me, stopping right in front of me.

He slowly moved his hand up and, to my utter surprise, pushed his finger in the teardrop opening of my choker pendant. With a slight flick of his finger, he pulled me closer to his lips, making me whimper from behind my mask. His next words had my toes curling. "Kneel."

With his finger still holding me by the choker, I lowered to my knees and leaned at his feet. The evidence of how much this pleased him stared right at my face, his erection pulling his pants taut. I clenched my fingers on my lap, stopping myself from running them over it.

Just because he'd asked me to kneel didn't mean I'd stare down at his feet. I turned my masked face up to meet his eyes, making him look down at my crimson tiger mask.

His chest heaved, and he ran his fingers along my mask, caressing it. There was a reverence in his eyes that made me feel as if he were the one on his knees, worshipping me, rather than the other way around. "Good girl."

My body trembled, and I widened my knees farther, just to feel the cool breeze at my core. I felt so empty that I ached. I needed him. Needed him to push his tongue inside me or slam his cock in that one deep thrust the way he always did.

He tightened his finger in my choker, drawing my attention to him. "Give me a safe word, baby."

Even in the heat of the moment, when I was dying for a taste of him, when I was ready to do just about anything for this man, he cared about my safety. And if that wasn't just one more reason I'd trust him with my eyes closed. "Red."

He jerked the collar and growled. I remembered. "Red, *sir.*"

He gave me a pleased nod. With another graze on my mask, he reached behind his back and pulled out a long—very long—diamond chain. Before I could ask him what the hell he was doing when I was damn near losing my mind, he removed his finger from the choker and latched one end of the chain to it.

A *fucking* leash.

Dominic Park had put a diamond leash on the Crimson Tiger.

My mind exploded as I watched him wrap the entire length of the leash around his palm, the veins of his arms popping as he clutched the thing. His cock visibly throbbed behind his pants, and his hand tightened around the leash.

He paused for a moment, and I looked up at him. His face slightly tilted to the side as if asking me for permission. I mirrored his motion and nuzzled at his hand holding the leash. A rough growl escaped his lips as he took a step backward. Then another, unspooling the sparkling diamond leash between us.

He moved back until he sat on the armchair behind him, his hand still wrapped around some more of the leash. *How long was the fucking leash?* It must've cost him a fucking fortune.

He sat on the chair as if it were his throne, his back resting lazily on the backrest, his legs spread open, showing off the wet spot that was forming where his cock was trapped behind his pants. He jerked the leash, snapping my head toward him. "Crawl to me, Tigress."

Oh, he wanted the Crimson Tiger. The Wildcat. He *would* get a Wildcat.

"Yes, sir." I got on all fours and pushed my ass up in a deep arch, getting a loud growl out of Dominic. With one hand in front of the other, I crawled as if I were a tigress on a hunt. I crawled with my ass swinging behind me, arching it back. Not just because every time I did it, Dominic's hold on the leash tightened. But because I was aching for it. I was dripping wet, soaking my suit. He was fulfilling my deepest, darkest fantasies, the kind that I never dared to dream about.

I crawled slowly, needing it to last longer. Needing to see the storm of pleasure swirling in Dominic's eyes for longer. His chest heaved, his hair fell over his eyes, and his lips were parted as if breathing was too difficult for him right now.

The wet spot on his pants kept growing larger, and I was dying to lap it up.

"Hold." His voice rang loud and clear in the room.

I stopped mid-crawl and tilted my head.

"Get rid of the mask." His voice was raspy, as if he could barely get the words out.

Now the fun really begins.

I sat back on my knees and pulled off the mask. Cool air touched my sweat-soaked face, and I all but whimpered in relief. But I held my expression together. All I showed him was the tornado of pleasure riding my body, all because of the damn leash.

I bit my lip and, with my eyes staring back at him, got back on all fours and arched my back. My hair fell over one shoulder and grazed the floor. "Please ask me to crawl to you, sir."

His jaw clenched hard, and his nostrils flared. With a growl, he pulled at the leash. Without a word uttered from his mouth, I crawled. Keeping my eyes trained on him, I watched how his chest heaved as I put one hand in front of the other. I watched his other hand clenched in a deathly grip on the armrest.

A needy whimper burst out of my mouth as he pulled me harder by the leash, making me crawl faster, winding the leash around his hand the closer I got.

When I finally reached him, my hands stopping at his feet, he pulled me even closer, only stopping the leash when my lips brushed his covered cock.

"You're dying for a taste, aren't you?"

My jaw ached with the need to lick his throbbing cock. But I didn't dare. I simply nodded. "Yes, sir."

His hips jerked with a growl. "Then lick, Tigress. Make a fucking mess on my lap."

I didn't have to be told twice. I pushed my mouth against the wet spot that I'd been eyeing and fucking sucked. I licked him through his pants, the scent of his sex making my pussy leak. I spat on his pants and sucked his thick cock in my mouth, licking and searching for his taste. While his one hand kept the leash wrapped in his hand tightly, his other hand grabbed the long locks of my hair and pushed me deeper into his crotch.

"Yes, Tigress. Use your fucking teeth."

When I bit him hard, he pulled me off by the leash, his eyes dangerously hard. "Not so hard."

When I nodded, he pulled me back again, and I grazed my teeth along his length. Lightly. Thoroughly. His hips ground on my face, and I was in fucking heaven. If I could, I'd spend the rest of my days leashed and chained to Dominic, feeling treasured and cherished at his feet, just like this.

When he snapped his pants open, I keened. I was hungry for his taste finally hitting my tongue, and I could only whimper when he pulled out his cock from his underwear and swiped it along my lips.

I opened my jaw wide for him and arched my hips back, begging him for his cock. He stroked himself once, twice, and finally, pushed it in my wide-open mouth. My eyes rolled to the back of my head as his wet cock flooded my mouth with his taste. My fingers bit into my lap as my pussy clenched tight, my hips jerked, and a sudden orgasm slammed into my body, rendering me shuddering at Dominic's lap.

His hips jerked sharply, and he quickly pulled out of my mouth and grabbed my jaw. His eyes were wide with shock and arousal. "Did you just come without my permission?"

My mind was still in a fog from the residual orgasm, but I gave him a small nod. "It came out of nowhere, sir. I need you so much, I could come again and again."

Dominic's cock had precum sliding down his length as he stroked himself once again. "Get up."

He loosened his leash, and I immediately got back on my feet, obeying him.

He jerked his head at the bed behind us. "Climb on all fours. Now."

I walked to the bed, swaying my hips, feeling the wetness between my legs, soaking my entire pussy. I wasn't lying to Dominic. I felt like I was flying. All the chaos that usually plagued my mind was in a state of complete calm. Not a single thought churned in my mind except one. Dominic.

All I had to do was do as he said. Obey him. Pleasure him. Be his little Crimson Tiger on a leash. I fucking loved every second of it.

As soon as I was in position, I felt movement behind me. A large hand pushed my neck down so I was ass up in the air. In the next moment, a large slap rang in my ears as my ass stung like a motherfucker.

A moan escaped my lips as pain spread around my ass.

Another spank hit the other cheek as Dominic growled, "This was for coming before you got permission."

Dominic didn't hold back. His spanks hit my cheeks hard, the impact making me slide forward. But he kept me in position by the leash, refusing to let me slide forward. Pain and pleasure spread across my cheeks, and I could feel Dominic's hand getting wet every time he swiped his fingers across my opening.

Tears sprang in my eyes as he hit my ass really hard, and a sob escaped my chest. Before I could brace myself for another spank, Dominic's tongue swiped through my slit, pushing into my soaking wet pussy. And I screamed.

My hips automatically arched and ground on his face, and he let me. His groan vibrated through my opening, and I flooded his mouth. He bit my ass and swiped his tongue on the spot when I moaned. "You either come in my mouth or on my cock. Are we clear?"

When I didn't respond instantly, he spanked my pussy. Hard. I screamed, "Yes, sir. Very clear."

He pressed the softest kiss on my pussy. "Good girl."

In the next moment, he slammed his cock inside me with one deep thrust. A loud groan echoed in the room, slamming into my heart. His cock throbbed inside me, and his large hands grabbed my hips in a deathly grip. And then, he started pounding into me. His thrusts were wild and deep. He unashamedly groaned in my ear with every snap of his hips.

He grunted as he pulled me up by my leash so his chest pressed against my back, and he grabbed my neck with his large hand. He held my waist with the other and bucked his hips like an animal unleashed from a cage.

He was a writhing beast of a man, growling and grunting as he rutted inside me. He dropped us on the bed, and suddenly, I was on my back and had my legs wrapped around his hips as he slammed into me. He pushed his tongue into my mouth, and I pushed my fingers into his hair, holding him to me. "Who do you fucking belong to, Tigress?" he asked, his words hitting my lips with every thrust.

My neck arched as his cock dragged along the walls of my

pussy, hitting me at just the right spot. He bit me and thrust into me hard. "Answer me, baby."

I keened, waves of pleasure exploding from my core all the way to the tip of my toes, my body going taut with the impending orgasm. I squeezed my pussy around his cock, pulling out a loud groan from him. "You. Only you," I answered, slamming my mouth on him, swallowing his grunt.

With every hard thrust, he groaned in my ear. "Tell me I can come inside you, Maira."

I whimpered, my pussy squeezing around him involuntarily at his words.

He pushed into me again and again, his cock dragging along the walls of my pussy, sending blinding-white electric pleasure skittering down my spine, as he clenched his jaw. "Tell me, baby. Tell me to fill you up with my cum. I'll get you a morning-after pill."

My mind splintered at the thought of Dominic coming inside me and marking me, and I nodded. "Fuck, okay. Yes, fuck. I'm gonna come, Dominic. Come with me. Fill me up."

His hips bucked, and he rutted into me. My orgasm barreled into me as my mind exploded into a thousand bursts of light. My spine arched and my toes curled as Dominic didn't stop—*couldn't* stop—thrusting inside me. His body started to shake over me as his eyes rolled back in his head, and he let out a loud roar as his cock pulsed inside me, flooding me with his cum.

He kept rolling his hips inside me as if trying to push his cum deeper and dropped his entire weight on me. And because I was Crimson fucking Tiger, I removed the brass knuckles from my hands and pushed them to the side, wrapped my legs around him, and ran my hand in his sweat-soaked hair, carrying his weight—fucking *loving* his weight—on me.

When a few minutes passed with both of us catching our

breaths, Dominic pushed himself on his elbows and looked down at me. It didn't escape my notice that he was still inside me. He pushed a lock of my hair behind my ears and, with a soft smile, asked, "Did you like that?"

And because he was still inside me, I squeezed tight around him, pulling out a grunt from him. Dropping a quick kiss on his lips, I nodded. "I loved that."

He slowly started to move his hips inside me again, making me gasp. "Good. I plan to do this often."

My breath hitched, and I tightened my legs around him. "Works for me. But don't you fucking dare tear apart the crotches of my gear. Or else, I'd actually go on a mission in this suit."

He thrust hard at that, growling at me. "I have ten more suits ordered for our personal use. Your actual suits are safe in your locker for the actual mission. And don't you dare think about wearing these to your actual mission."

I gave him an obedient smile. "Yes, sir."

With a rough groan, he started to slam into me once again, bringing me to the highest of the highs, showing me just how much he enjoyed fucking the Crimson Tiger.

We made love in our beautiful hotel from dawn to early morning. We slept in each other's arms till late morning. Dom later took me to his favorite restaurant and had me try paella and escalivada. We walked the streets of Barcelona sharing churros. We kissed in corners and walked with his arm around my waist.

I sent a hundred pictures to our group chats, and I received a variety of messages from the girls that made me laugh. I purchased souvenirs for them, and Dominic promised me that he'd bring us all here next time.

I never wanted the day to end. I wanted to just keep walking hand in hand with this man. Every time our eyes met, he placed a kiss on my nose. And every time he did that, I fell a little more in love with him.

We basically slept on our way back to the city. When we were back in the helicopter, Dominic held my hand and pressed a kiss on my fingers. "I have one more surprise for you, baby."

"Absolutely not, Dominic. This was already too much. I can't handle any more surprises."

He ran his hand through his hair and shook his head. "This is the last one."

I shook my head and looked outside the window as we started to lower down on the helipad of a building that wasn't Dominic's house.

I quickly turned to look at him. "Where the hell are we landing? You don't live here."

"Patience, Maira."

"Dominic, I swear to God…"

He simply winked at me and looked ahead. We had just landed on the tallest building in Manhattan. Once we were out of the helicopter, Dominic clutched my hand and pulled me to the elevator.

He pressed the button to the 130th floor. This was a 135-story residential building, according to the latest news around the city, which reported that it was the up-and-coming tallest residential building in Manhattan, overlooking Central Park.

The moment the elevator door dinged open, we stepped into a massive open space. I turned to Dominic, my eyes full of unspoken questions and bubbling anticipation and anxiety.

He gave me a bashful smile and rubbed the back of his neck. He actually looked nervous, and that ended up making me nervous. "You're scaring me, Dominic. What is all this?"

He released a breath. "Alright. Uh, so I wanted to gift you and the Wildcats a more secure and spacious headquarters. I don't mean to imply that Thunder Claw isn't already a great place, and you all haven't made it secure. It's perfect as it is. But I wanted you all to have the kind of access and facilities that would help you take down even bigger criminals."

I looked around the massive open space.

Dominic stood beside me and kept talking. "Uh. I've bought out the top ten floors of this building. They're all yours. You can convert it to holding cells, workout areas, your den, an armory, tech space, rooms for women in need, anything. The top floors have separate elevator access. You get a private helipad and, of course, a helicopter. The building features a top-notch security system. The glass of the facade is bulletproof. The possibility of somebody attacking your place of work would be minimal, if not zero. I was also hoping that you would convert a few floors into private apartments so you could all live here. Together. Safely. Of course, you can choose to live in your own homes. It's just a thought."

My heart was beating out of my chest as I looked around at the bright city lights from the glass facade. A million possibilities ran through my mind. We'd all be able to live closer together. We'd all be safe. Tara wouldn't have to stay in the basement all the time while she hacked and tracked perpetrators. Sloane could have an entire floor of undercover costumes and weapons. Naomi could turn a floor into her own hospital. Lena and her son would have a safe space to live. Given the work we did and the consequences she already suffered, she worried about her son.

But how could I accept so much from Dominic? This wasn't his fifty-million-dollar payment, which also felt too fucking much as it was.

My silence must've worried Dominic because he came to stand in front of me and held my cheeks. "Baby, say something. I know you worry that being with me would mean that you'd be putting the Wildcats at risk. Or that you'd have to sacrifice your work, your passion, the very thing that makes you *you*. But Samaira, *I* want to be a part of the Wildcats. Not as a fighter, of course. I'd be shit at that, as you know. But let me contribute the best way I know how. As proud as I am of all that you've accomplished, as much as I want you to go out there and kick some ass, I also want to care for you and your friends. You all deserve the best headquarters, the best weapons, the best technology, and the best location so you can give your best to the world. There is nothing that I wouldn't give you women to make you happy and safe."

"It's too much, Dominic." My voice was a whisper.

He pressed his forehead against mine. "It's not enough, Samaira. You and your friends put your lives at risk. You fight for a better world. You fight for women's safety and justice. There is no one else who deserves this more. I have money. That's all I have and all I can offer. Allow me to do my part in helping you soar. We would be stronger together."

I couldn't resist a moment longer. I jumped on him, and he immediately caught me in his arms before pulling me in for a heated kiss. I tasted my tears on his tongue, I felt his pounding heart beating against mine, and I knew I would never let him go. I knew I loved him. Not because he was being foolishly extravagant but because he wanted to join me. He wanted to be a part of *my* life, not the other way around. He wasn't expecting me to change. He was aware of every threat imaginable, and instead of wanting me to stop, he was providing me with the ammunition to go bigger.

I held both of his cheeks as he lifted me in his arms and looked at the prettiest fucking face in the world. I looked into his eyes, and I wanted to lay my heart at his feet. Because I knew in the marrow of my bones that he would never ever stomp on it. He would hold it in the palm of his hands and cherish it. "You love me?"

He gently put me on my feet and held my waist. "Always and forever."

My voice broke when I clutched his shirt. "Good. That's

good. Because I've fallen so deeply in love with you that you'll never be able to get rid of me. I'm gonna love you so hard…"

My words were swallowed by his lips as a deep moan rumbled out of his chest. He crushed me in his arms and lifted me off my feet as he continued to steal my breath. He held me by the back of my neck in the most possessive grip and stared at me with the most beautiful dimple-popping smile on his face. "Say it again."

My heart burst with happiness. "I love you, Dominic Park. I'm in love with you, and I'm never letting you go. And if someone dares to take you from me, I'll tear them to pieces."

He growled. "That's my fucking tigress."

He pulled me into another kiss, pushing me against the wall. With a quick grunt, he lifted me off my feet, and I wrapped my legs around his waist, never once pulling off his lips. My brand-new dress that Dominic got me just this morning pooled at my waist as Dom quickly undid his belt.

"I'm so glad you never packed any underwear, baby." I moaned in his mouth as he pushed inside me in a single, powerful thrust with a grunt.

My pussy was dripping down my thighs as he plunged into me like a man possessed.

He moved his mouth lower and sucked at the junction of my neck and shoulder, nipping and biting at the exposed skin, pushing me against the wall harder and harder with each powerful thrust that pushed me toward the peak.

I clutched at his hair and moved over him, squeezing tightly around his cock.

He pulled my dress down, exposing my breasts. He sucked my nipples hard, making my back arch and pulling a whimper out of me. I grabbed the back of his head and pulled him into me harder.

"Say it again," he growled.

I let out a broken moan and clutched him to me. "I love you, Dominic."

A growl escaped his chest, and he moaned so loudly that it echoed off the empty walls around us as he lost all control. He pounded into me, hitting that spot inside me that had my orgasm barreling down my spine, and my mind and body shattered into a million white lights as my toes curled and my back arched. Pleasure unlike anything pulsed through every neuron in my body as my pussy contracted around his cock. Dominic shook around me, his hand clutching me to him, and I felt his cock jerk inside me as he kept thrusting, my name a chant on his lips.

Something deep within my heart settled. It was as if Dominic had locked himself inside my heart, filling that aching hole that always persisted painfully. Now, I felt achingly, happily full. Warmth bloomed in my chest as Dominic twitched inside me, refusing to pull out of me. "You going to stay there all day?"

He nodded into my neck. "As long as I can. Leave me alone."

I clutched him in my arms and shook my head. "Literally just promised you that I'm never leaving you alone again."

His warm breath kissed my neck as he sighed. "Sounds perfect to me."

"Ugh. You're so cheesy."

"Fuck you."

"Hmm. That's better."

He bit my neck, and I laughed. "I'm leaving you."

He scoffed. "No, you're not. You love me too much."

"Doubtful."

He spanked my butt cheek. Hard. "Tell me you love me." And I couldn't help it. My pussy clenched as a wave of arousal rushed through me.

I kept my lips sealed shut, and a devious smile came over his face as he twitched inside me. "Say it, Maira."

I bit his lip. "Make me."

He slammed his mouth over me as he started to move

inside me again. He bit my jaw and grunted in my ear. "Gonna fill you up with another one of my loads."

I only dug my heels deeper into his ass, pulling him into me deeper, as he did exactly that and had me screaming my love for him all over again.

CHAPTER 32

DOMINIC

Maxim stopped the car right across the entrance to her building. We left my place early in the morning since I had work, while Samaira needed to shower and reach Thunder Claw. While I was dressed in my suit, Maira had borrowed my T-shirt and sweatpants. To her utter dismay, they fit her perfectly.

I looked at her as she still sat beside me with a slightly miffed expression. I'd have to get some extra-large T-shirts. "Are you still mad at my clothes, baby?"

She only grumbled something under her breath, making me chuckle. "What was that?"

She narrowed her eyes at me. "I'm going to beat your ass in the ring, that's what."

My cock twitched in my pants at the thought. I already wanted to cancel all my meetings for the day and get right into the ring, but I had some very important calls today. So I held her cheeks and squished them, puckering her lips, and placed a soft kiss on them. "I'll see you tonight at Thunder Claw. Get ready to lose."

She snorted. "Sure." She stopped smiling and bit her lip. "Um…I'll talk to the girls about the apartments."

"You do that. It's all yours. Tell them there are no restrictions. No limits. You all can decorate them, furnish them, and make them into whatever suits your needs. All ten floors are yours."

"You're crazy."

I kissed her. She didn't know it, but I'd actually bought the top twenty floors. I knew she'd lose her mind if I gifted her twenty. "Only for you. Now, off you go before I ask Maxim to turn this car around."

She laughed and launched herself out of the car.

I pushed my head outside the window and yelled at her retreating form. "I really thought you'd have chosen to turn the car back around."

"Go to work. Leave me alone, you fool."

"Ouch."

She blew me a kiss. "Miss me."

I caught it in my hand and showed her putting it in my jacket pocket. "I already do."

Once she got inside the apartment and came to her window, I blew her one last kiss and asked Maxim to take us to work.

Maxim looked at me from the rearview mirror with a smile on his face. "Tell me you're gonna marry that woman."

My heart burst out of my chest as I pulled out the ring from my pocket and raised it in my hand so he'd see it in the rearview mirror. "Already got the ring."

His eyes widened, and he almost turned around. "Holy… Holy fuck. Congratulations, Dominic."

I ran my hand through my hair as my heart pounded in a nervous beat. "She hasn't said yes."

Maxim shook his head, a wide smile still etched on his face. "You haven't asked."

"She literally just said she loved me last night. She'd run off if I showed her this ring."

He scoffed so loudly, it actually made me feel stupid. "You gifted her ten floors in the tallest building in Manhattan. She didn't run off. And you think a ring would scare her off?"

I chewed my lip as I stared at the ring in my hand. "You think she won't?"

He sighed as if I were the stupidest person he'd ever met. "She would take a bullet for you. Pretty sure she'd marry you."

My heart pumped so loudly in my chest I was sure Maxim could hear it. "Fine. I'll ask her..." He whooped, and I quickly finished my sentence, "In six months."

He groaned. "Dominic. That's too long. Do it in six weeks."

I scoffed as my heart started to pound harder. "No chance. She'd bail."

He shook his head and met my eyes from the rearview mirror with a smile when we were suddenly flung to the side.

My head crashed into the window, and my mind went hazy. "Maxim," I groaned.

My vision was blurry when I heard the car door open. A loud gunshot, followed by Maxim's groan, had adrenaline shooting through my system. My eyes widened. My body scrambled only to find a gun pointing at Maxim. Before the shooter could take another shot at him, I slammed my car door open and stepped outside.

That had the shooter turning his gun from Maxim to me. Before I could even attempt to fight him, three more cars came screeching to a halt, surrounding us. Five men from each car came rushing out, their guns pointed at me. The man who'd shot Maxim kept his gun pointed at me. "Come with us, or I'll kill the driver."

I raised my hands in surrender. My only goal was to keep

the attention of these men off Maxim. I just had to hope someone would call 911 for him. I simply nodded at the man in front of me, and with his gun pointed at me, he led me to a large black SUV.

The moment I got inside, I was hit on the head with something heavy and blunt.

My vision once again turned hazy, and my last thought was Samaira, of what she'd do to these men if—no, *when*—she found out. Darkness soon enveloped me, but I had a smile on my face.

———

I woke up to the sharp sting of ice-cold water hitting my face, my body jerking against the restraints I didn't remember being put on me. My body automatically pulled against the restraints, and I slowly realized that my arms were tied at my back, and my feet were tied to the chair I sat on.

My muscles burned as I pulled against the restraints harder, my teeth gritting against each other.

"Now, now, Dominic. I wouldn't have put restraints on you if you could pull them open."

My head snapped to the voice. A man I'd never seen before walked toward me, flanked by two huge fuckers who looked like they could smash my skull with their fist. I stared at the man, his six-foot, lean frame less than intimidating on its own. "Who are you?" My voice was a croak. I didn't even realize how long I was unconscious.

One of the men grabbed a chair for him and placed it a few feet away, right across from me. "Mr. Dominic Park, I am the man whose business you interfered with."

"Could you be any more vague, Mr. Whoever the Fuck You Are?"

His eyes narrowed to slits, and he gave a mirthless chuckle.

It was too late before I noticed that the fucker had a gun in his hand, because in the next second, he raised his arm and pulled the trigger. Blinding pain shot through my leg, and my ears rang like a motherfucker. My chest heaved as I felt the wet trickle of blood rolling down my calf and ankle.

As if I were a huge inconvenience, the asshole in front of me sighed. "Now, let's keep the attitude to a minimum, shall we?"

With gritted teeth and hazy vision, I stared at him, trying to remember if I'd ever seen him before. "Who are you?"

"Now, was that hard?" He cocked his head at me. When I continued to stare at him, he continued, "You killed four of my very important men."

"State Attorney, his son, and the two friends?"

"Precisely, Mr. Park. You and your little girlfriend, or was it assistant? Both of you have proven to be extremely inconvenient for my business."

"What business do you have with the state attorney?"

He laughed and turned to his bodyguards. "This man doesn't get it." He turned to me with eyes that screamed danger and volatility. "Like I said, it's none of your goddamn business. It took me fucking years to get that stupid Thomas Cooper appointed as the state attorney. Even more fucking time to train his fucking incompetent son and his friends."

"They raped my sister," I spoke through gritted teeth, the pain from the bullet wound making me dizzy.

The fucker waved his hand like it was nothing. "Did she die? That one girl has cost me millions, you prick."

My body rattled against the restraints, the need to jam my fist in his mouth overpowering the shooting pain spreading through my calf. "Fuck. You."

My vision turned darker, and I swayed forward. I heard the fucker tell his lackeys to tie up my wounds. "I need him alive to call his little girlfriend. A real powerhouse, that one."

I grunted as one of the men wrapped a fucking cloth

around my calf and tightened it to the point where I stopped feeling blood in my leg. Despite that, I couldn't help but chuckle.

"What's so funny?" he asked.

"My *little* girlfriend is going to kill you."

CHAPTER 33

t was a new day and a new mission. Tara, Sloane, and I had just returned to Thunder Claw from the safe house. The mission was quite straightforward. A woman had caught her husband sexually abusing her seven-year-old daughter, who was his stepdaughter. She'd found us through another one of our networks. It was an in-and-out mission.

Greg was an unemployed, alcoholic fuck. We'd found him drunk on his couch. It had taken Sloane half a second to slit his throat. She had a special kind of hatred reserved for abusive stepfathers and foster fathers. All Tara and I had to do was help her take the body to the safe house. Lena had already called the cleanup crew when we arrived there. Once they'd taken care of the body, we'd cleaned up there and returned when it was dark outside.

The moment I stepped foot inside the Den at Thunder Claw, I rushed to my phone. I hadn't even stopped to change into normal clothes and was still decked in all my Wildcat gear sans the mask. I'd dropped Dominic a message when I'd left for the mission, and I was sure I'd find at least a few texts from him. We never really carried our personal phones on missions, just in case we dropped them somewhere and got compromised.

So it was surprising when I didn't find a single message waiting in my inbox. What the fuck!

That wasn't like Dominic at all.

Immediately, I placed a call to his phone. Nothing.

Something ugly churned in my stomach. All my senses started to ping, and fear skittered down my spine. "Tara," I screamed.

She came rushing out of the bathroom in the middle of putting on her sweatshirt. "What is it?"

I dialed Dom's phone again, panic making my fingers shake. I looked at her as his phone rang in my ears. "Track Dominic. Now." I screamed the last word, which had her rushing to her setup.

Sloane, Naomi, and Lena rushed to the Den's living room, their eyes going between Tara and me. "What's going on?" Lena asked.

"I can't reach Dominic."

"Maybe he's in a meeting?" Naomi asked.

I shook my head. "He would pick up my call."

"Maybe his phone isn't with him," Sloane piped in.

I looked at her. "Why?"

She shrugged weakly and mumbled, "I don't know."

I glared at Tara as my heart started to pound so hard that I was afraid everyone around me could hear it. "Did you find anything? I last saw him when he dropped me at my place with his driver, Maxim."

Shadow apparently sensed my distress because he bounded to me and started running circles around me. I rubbed my hand lightly on his head, but it did absolutely nothing for me.

She bit her lip as her fingers furiously worked at her

keyboard. "I'm hacking into the system. Give me two minutes, Sami."

"Fucking hurry." Speaking of Maxim, I was glad I'd grabbed his contact number when I was Dom's bodyguard. I dialed his number, and after just three rings, the call connected. My heart dropped when it wasn't Maxim who answered. "Good evening, this is Dr. Brown from Downstate Medical Center in Brooklyn. Are you related to Mr. Maxim?"

My voice shook as my knees gave out. "I'm his friend. What's wrong?"

My eyes met Tara's, and her face was sheet white. My mind was frozen, but my body moved of its own volition. As my legs moved toward her desk, the doctor spoke, "He's been shot."

My step faltered as I reached her desk and looked at the screen. A man just shot the driver, and Dominic jumped out of the back seat of their car, which was surrounded by three other cars. The man who'd shot Maxim pointed his gun at Dominic, making my heart stop in my chest.

I threw my phone at Lena, who caught it midair and pressed her ear to the phone. Her conversation was a dull noise as my eyes zoned in on Dominic. It was mere minutes after he'd left my place, and I hadn't even known. I was busy watching Sloane kill a loser when the love of my life was in fucking danger.

"Location. Now," I barked, my vision turning into a red haze as I stormed to the locker to grab my mask.

A million thoughts circled my mind. I had just told him I loved him. How could something happen to the man I'd just given my heart to? How could I not protect him? How could I let him be taken away?

Lena immediately jumped off the couch. "We need to strategize before you storm out, guns blazing."

I pulled out my brass knuckles, jammed three guns in my holsters, and retied my shoelaces.

I stormed into the living room, where I found Sloane, Naomi, and Tara huddled around the computer.

"Where the fuck is he? And who the fuck took him?"

Tara's fingers were flying on the keyboard. "I'm following the street cameras to locate where they are. I ran a search on the guy who was pointing a gun at Dominic. They're Russians."

Lena turned to me. "Call Dominic again. Maybe his kidnappers will pick up."

I immediately dialed the call and put it on speaker. I stared at Lena as the call went unanswered. My glare moved to Tara. "Two more minutes and I'm going out to find him."

She didn't respond to me, just started clicking and typing faster, biting her lip furiously.

Sloane, Lena, and Naomi rushed to their respective lockers and started changing.

As they changed, Tara gasped.

"What is it?" I rushed and went to stare at her screen.

"They're at a warehouse in the Bronx." She zoomed in on the screen, and I was looking at the top view of the area. "There are about fifty men here."

My fist clenched, and my knuckles cracked. "Good. More for me to kill."

Tara glared. "It's five against at least fifty, Sami."

Lena came rushing out, righting her gear. "We need a plan."

I looked at her. "I have a plan. Kill. Maim. Bury."

I had no idea if Dominic was alive or dead, if he was being tortured or shot. I didn't have a minute to spare. I only knew one thing. Protect Dominic.

I plucked on my earpiece that connected me to them, plugged in the GPS on my phone, and, without a glance at the girls, stormed out of the basement. I knew they'd come. I just didn't have time to plan it.

My bike started with a roar, and I was zipping through the

streets of New York City. My heart raced, and my mind had absolutely shut the fuck down. If something had happened to Dominic, if there was even a single fucking scratch on Dominic, I was going to destroy the motherfuckers who dared to lay a hand on him.

I sped up the bike, the wind hitting my face and rushing through my hair, doing absolutely nothing to calm my racing heart. Fear was spreading through my body like a wildfire, the mere thought of losing Dominic making my limbs tremble.

Tears slid from my eyes and got swept away in the wind, my mind urging me to go faster and faster.

I was going at a flat-out speed, and every traffic signal "miraculously" turned green at the right time.

"Crimson Tiger, checking in." Lena's voice came through my earpiece.

I sniffled. "I'm here. What'd you find?"

"The warehouse belongs to the Russian mob. The only person you and Dominic have targeted is the state attorney. Seems like the attorney might've been involved in some shady business with the mob. They must've had some deal in place, and the disappearance of Thomas Cooper must've affected him in some way."

"Not for long," I said, imagining slicing the throat of the Russian fucker who pointed his gun at my man.

"You're not going to wait for us to catch up, are you?"

"Don't ask me to, Lioness."

"I understand. One order, though. Do not go in guns blazing. Take out as many as you can without getting noticed."

"So no guns?"

"For as long as you can."

"Thanks, Lioness. See you soon."

"Do not fucking get caught or injured. We're not far behind you."

"Yes, boss."

I parked my bike two blocks from the warehouse. It was

easier to conceal myself in the dark. I didn't waste any time climbing the fence of the warehouse.

With a swift snap of necks, I had two men down. I'd have only injured them if I could have shot them in the knees or something. But snapping necks was the easiest way to silence these men without alerting the others. I hid their bodies behind the car that was parked near the side of the building.

My only goal was to get to Dominic as quickly as possible. I didn't waste time in killing off whichever men came in my way. I looked up and around the building, trying to find an alternative entrance to the building other than the front one.

As I circled the building slowly, I killed off three more guys who had accidentally seen me.

There were ten other men circling the area around the warehouse, whereas three stood at the entrance with massive guns.

Every man in this building was an enemy.

Four cars had gone and kidnapped Dominic.

If I had to kill every single one of them to get Dominic out of here, I would do it without a stain on my dark, murderous soul.

I finally found an open window on the third floor at the back of the building. Before one of the men could spot me, I climbed up the pipe at the side of the building. Luckily, it was on the same side as the window opening. Considering I'd been climbing up trees and fences for years now, the pipe took me under a minute to climb. The darkness cloaked me in shadows, and I jumped through the window and inside the building without being spotted.

The moment I turned around to face the room, my feet came to a screeching halt. Eight pairs of eyes stared at me. Not one belonging to the men whom I was about to crush.

These were eight tearful sets of eyes of young women gagged and tied. They all sat in a corner on the floor, their hands and feet tied up, a cloth wrapped around their mouth.

Tears streamed down their cheeks, and a few of them had bruises on their faces.

Immediately, I turned to my earpiece. "Golden Lioness, Crimson Tiger here. You copy?"

"Crimson Tiger, copy. What is it?"

"There are eight women here. Kidnapped. Gagged and tied. On the top floor at the back. One of you will have to get them out."

"Fuck. Got it."

I put a finger over my mouth, asking them to remain silent. They all stared at me as I stepped closer and sat on my knees. "My friends will release you soon. Just stay put. I'm going to take care of these men."

One of them shook her head and tried to say something through the gag. I quickly shushed her. "If I release the gag, do you promise not to scream and tell me whatever it is silently?"

She quickly nodded, and I pulled down her gag. With a deep gulp of air, she whispered, "There are too many. And they're dangerous."

I gave her a smile. "Not as dangerous as me. Do any of you know the name of the boss here?"

All of them shook their heads. The girl whose gag I'd removed said, "Everybody calls him boss."

I gave her a nod and, before she could protest, put the gag back on her face. "Sorry, honey. I can't risk any screaming. One of my friends will be here soon to release you all."

With that, I got up and slowly opened the door. It opened into a long hallway with doors on both sides. Seeing nobody at the end of the hallway, I stepped out of the room. The moment I reached the end of the hallway, two men with big guns strapped around them stood at the stairs leading to the floor below.

Before any of them could raise an alarm, I jumped on them, snapping the neck of one while wrapping my legs around the other's neck, choking him until he passed out. I reached the second floor below to a lot more activity. I hid in the stairwell, taking note of the large boxes and columns that would help me conceal myself.

Finally, I put on my brass knuckles. Things were about to get a lot bloodier. The warehouse was much bigger inside than it looked from the outside. I started to make my way down the hallway, trying to find out if they'd kept Dominic in any rooms behind the closed doors.

I met the first guy the moment I rounded the corner. With three slams of my brass knuckles right on his mouth, I had him incapacitated. Blood coated my fingers, but I didn't give a fuck. I found an empty room and threw his body there. I kept moving forward and eliminated six men, throwing them all in the same empty room I'd put their friend in.

My hands were coated in blood, and my muscles burned after carrying all of them one after the other, all the while sneaking away from the men patrolling.

Time was running out, and I knew the Wildcats would be here soon. Not finding Dominic anywhere on this floor, I ran to the staircase leading to the ground floor. I was pretty sure I'd find him there. Or in the basement.

I was hidden at the base of the staircase when I saw a line of men standing in a circle. And I knew I'd found Dominic. I couldn't see anything with all the men blocking my view. But I knew he was there.

I took a few steps out and hid behind a large brown container. I bent around it slightly, and finally, from between two men, I found him.

Dominic.

My rage exploded in my chest as I found a pool of blood around him on the floor, his head bent lower, his hair hanging around his face. I moved my gaze to where a cloth was wrapped around his leg, and fear unlike anything skittered down my spine.

He was not moving.

Was he alive? Was he unconscious?

Violent rage exploded inside my chest, and I was about ready to launch myself at the thirty-something men in front of me when a loud shout from somewhere nearby had me freezing in my spot. "Boss, someone killed a lot of our men."

The men standing around immediately drew their guns and began shuffling around. In the midst of their panic, my eyes stayed focused only on one man. *My* man. And he finally moved. His chest shook as he laughed and let out a cough. My senses, my eyes, my ears, every part of my being was so fucking focused on him, so tuned to him, I heard him say, "I told you my girlfriend would come and kill you all."

My body screamed at me to move. To shoot them all and take him to the hospital. To prove Dominic right. Because of course I would come for him. There was no question I'd obliterate anybody who touched him, let alone shoot him.

Another man came into my view as he punched Dominic square in the face. I aimed a shot at him, but one of his men moved and stood in front of him. And I knew I'd kill that man in the suit with my bare hands. Not with a gun. He'd suffer. He'd face my wrath. He'd look me in the eye and know who took his life. He'd know he'd made a mistake by touching what was mine.

My earpiece crackled, and Lena's voice filtered in my ear. "We're inside the building. Naomi's got the girls. Tara's got the second floor covered. As soon as you start shooting, Sloane and I will barge through the front entrance. You're good to attack. Guns blazing, Tiger."

And I pulled the trigger at the lackey standing in front of the guy in the suit, spraying blood all over his shocked, frozen face, as the lackey's body slumped at Dominic's feet.

"Hi, Tigress." Dominic's voice might've been barely above a whisper, but I read his lips with perfect clarity.

Before the guy in the suit could even point his gun toward

Dominic, I shot the hand holding his gun. He screamed, clutching his hand. With guns in both of my hands, I jumped onto the box I was hiding behind and started shooting every man standing there. "Hi, baby."

More bullets started spraying on top of these men, coming from different directions. I knew my girls were here.

I walked toward the man who had dared to touch my man. I sprinted as I got closer, feeling a bullet zip past my head and lodge itself squarely in the head of the guy on my right.

I jumped and landed with my knees square on the guy in the suit while he screamed in pain as blood poured out of his shot arm. I pressed down on his chest, my knee digging deep into the rib cage. "Who the fuck are you?"

He coughed as he muttered in a hoarse voice, "Viktor Sokolov. You have no idea who you're dealing with."

"Correct me if I'm wrong. Russian mob. Drug trafficking. Women trafficking. Probably weapons trafficking. Am I wrong?"

He stayed silent. I punched him hard with my brass knuckles, his blood spraying on my face. "I asked you a question."

He spat out his blood with a cough. "Not wrong. You think there won't be others popping up if you kill me? This is much bigger than me. Than you. Than your rich boyfriend. You both messed with the wrong people."

I turned to look at Dominic, who was tied to the chair, his head hanging low. His leg was shot, and blood pooled at the soles of his feet. Anger coursed through every vein of my body. "Dominic," I called out his name, panic lacing my tone.

He grunted.

I punched Viktor square in the face once again, bashing his face with so much force that two of his teeth flew out. I looked at Dominic and shouted his name. "Dominic. Wake the fuck up."

He jerked, and his body moved as he raised his head to look at me. His eyes were bloodshot, but his body heaved in relief. "You're here, baby."

Tears stung my eyes. "Keep looking at me, Dom. You have to hold on just a few more minutes. Until I deal with this fucker."

Viktor's eyes widened under me. "You'll never be rid of what's coming to you. You'll constantly have to watch your backs. If you kill me or affect our base in any way, people far more dangerous than me will come after you." His head turned to the shot that rang. He looked at me and continued, "And your team."

I held him by the collar of his shirt and bent down. "We wouldn't even have known about you had you not come after my man. Nobody touches him and survives."

Before he could keep fucking talking and wasting my precious minutes, I pulled out my gun and shot him square in the forehead. I had no time to kill him with my bare hands.

"Great shot, baby," Dominic whispered.

I turned to him with a glare and slapped him hard as he was starting to conk out. "Stay awake, Dom. We need to put some serious tracking and monitoring systems in place for you."

He gave me a wide smile as his head lolled. "You can put a tracker under my skin."

I scoffed as I started pulling out the ropes holding him to the chair. "Oh, I'm most definitely gonna."

By the time I untied all of the ropes, silence ensued all around me. The rushing of footsteps had me looking up to find Sloane and Lena running toward me. "I need Naomi. Dominic's shot. I don't know how long ago. He's lost a lot of blood."

My voice was laced with bone-deep panic. Dominic was barely conscious enough to clutch my hand as I sat on my knees. "Shh…Maira. I'm fine."

He was delusional. He could barely keep his eyes open. It was only my grip on his shoulder that kept him upright in the chair. I held his cheeks and shook him until his eyes met mine. "If you fucking die on me, I'm going to follow you. I fucking dare you to close your eyes on me. You understand?" The last two words were a shrill scream that I didn't even realize I could let out.

His eyes finally widened as his grip on my hand tightened. Before he could attempt to say anything, I said to him, "Don't even try talking. Just shut up. Keep your eyes open. And do not fucking move."

I turned to Lena and Sloane. "Where's the car you came in? Where the fuck is Naomi?"

Lena and Sloane dropped down. Sloane was about to touch Dominic's wound, but red clouded my vision, and I fucking snarled at her audacity.

Sloane quickly raised her hands in surrender. "I'm just looking at the wound, Sami. We need to wrap the wound more if the cloth around his leg isn't wrapped tightly enough."

"Fine."

As Sloane inspected the wound, Lena said, "Tara is bringing the car to the front. Naomi is bringing all the women downstairs. We can't take all these women with us. We have no idea where they came from. I've called in an anonymous tip to the cops. They should be here in ten minutes. So we need to hurry the fuck up."

Dominic tried to move again, and I growled at him. "Do. Not. Fucking. Move."

His words were slurred. "Hurry. Get out. Here. Now."

The moment Sloane finished tightening the cloth around his wound, I clutched Dominic's arms and hauled him out of the chair. "Hold on, baby. Don't move." I bent lower and pulled him over my shoulder in a fireman's carry, making him groan.

"Stay still."

"Too heavy."

I slapped his ass. "You're not."

I clutched him tight to me and walked to the front. Naomi rushed down the stairs with all the ladies and asked them to stay near the front entrance. I ignored all of them and let the others handle the logistics of getting the women to safety. I stepped outside the front entrance.

Right then, our large van came screeching down the main gate of the warehouse and stopped right in front of me. Tara jumped out and opened the back door, and with a quick move, I had Dominic lying on the back seat of the van. I turned to her and barked, "The hospital."

Sloane and Lena jumped in beside me, while Tara took the driver's seat and started to drive like a madwoman. Good. Otherwise, I'd have to scream my lungs out at her to hurry the fuck up. I was still tempted, but Lena kept me focused on other things than the thought of losing Dominic to a fucking bullet wound.

I kept my eyes on Dominic while I heard Lena say, "Naomi is going to stay here hidden and make sure the cops get all the girls out safely. I'm sure once they find the big bust of the operation and fifty dead men, there will be an investigation."

I ran my hands through Dom's hair, soothing him as he groaned in pain. My eyes blurred with tears as the guilt of not protecting him sooner tried to pull me down. "We're on our way to the hospital."

He clutched my other hand. "It's okay. I'm...I'm right here."

I didn't look anywhere else as I heard Sloane asking Lena, "You think anything could get back at us?"

"I'm sure there were some cameras there that the cops might find. Since we were all in our gear and our masks, we should be fine. They might get a hint that the killers are all women. They might find Dominic. And he might be called in for questioning."

"Let's just hope they don't find any cameras."

Tara must have been listening to the conversation because her voice crackled in my earpiece. "No cameras. I stole the tapes from their IT room. And shot through all their systems. The cops wouldn't have the authority to go check the servers of the Russian mob, so we should be good."

Lena called Naomi on our device and asked her to conduct one final sweep of the warehouse and dispose of all the evidence.

When we screeched to a stop, Sloane opened the back door, and we jumped outside. By the time I moved Dominic forward in the seat, Sloane rushed to me with a stretcher and four nurses.

From there, it was a mad dash into the reception and a few violent demands from my end to get Dominic into the operating room. It was when the four of us got seated in the waiting area that I finally dissolved into tears. Three sets of arms wrapped around me as I cried for the man I almost lost. "This is what I was afraid of. To love someone so much and then lose them."

Lena cooed in my ear. "He's going to be just fine, Sami. You know it was a flesh wound."

I sniffled as my voice wobbled. "What if it's more the next time?"

"Then we protect him again. We get him bodyguards."

I nodded. "That's a given. If something happens to him, I'd never be able to forgive myself."

Tara ran her fingers down my back. "We won't let anything happen to him. He's part of our team now."

After about ten more minutes of losing myself to tears, I wiped my eyes. "I need to call Dominic's family."

Tara hummed. "They might get us out of this crowded

waiting room and bring us all to some good VIP section. People are staring at us."

We were still in our gear, and my fingers were coated in dried blood. "I should probably wash my hands," I muttered.

Sloane snorted. "You need a shower. You are covered in blood. You reek of it."

"Fuck you. Your hair is covered in dried blood."

She shrieked as Tara handed me my phone.

I dialed the call to Sophie, someone I knew would be able to handle the news. Sophie took the news fairly well and said they'd be here within an hour.

By the time I came out of the bathroom, one of the nurses called us and took us to the top floor of the building. She was extremely apologetic as she said, "Ma'am, you should've told us the man was *the* Dominic Park and you were his fiancée. We would've immediately moved you and your friends to the VIP rooms."

My jaw dropped open at that. But why did my heart give a happy little bounce at being called Dominic's fiancée? It certainly had a nice ring to it. Dom's family must've lied to the hospital to get us access.

Tara waggled her eyebrows at me while I turned to the nurse, trying not to dissolve into panic. "How's Dominic?"

She gave me a sympathetic smile that I instantly hated. "He's still in surgery, ma'am. The doctors will come speak with you as soon as they're done."

Lena cleared her throat as the nurse led us to a massive room with an empty bed and an attached bathroom. "Could we get some change of clothes?"

The nurse moved her eyes over all of us, wide with worry. "Um...sure. Do any of you need a doctor?"

Lena gave her a confident smile. "No need for a doctor. Also, if you keep this..." She gestured to all of our blood-soaked clothes and continued, "To yourself, we'd really appreciate it."

The nurse quickly nodded. "Of…of course, ma'am."

"That's wonderful. Thank you."

By the time we were all freshly showered and changed into scrubs, my patience had run extremely thin.

Sloane was handing me a cup of coffee from the coffee machine in the corner of the room when the door slammed open. Dominic's mother rushed into the room, her eyes moving over us. As soon as she found me, she rushed to me and pulled me into a hug. Her soft arms squeezing tight around me had me in tears. The guilt of her son landing in the hospital had me shaking. "I'm sorry I couldn't protect Dominic."

She pulled out of the hug and looked me in the eyes, her gaze stern. "None of that, Samaira. You saved my boy. Again."

"I should've checked in sooner. Or maybe kept being his bodyguard for another week. I would've been able to prevent his kidnapping if only I were there."

She held my cheek and gave me a stern motherly look. "It wasn't your fault. None of it has been your fault. Let's not take the blame for criminals, honey. We're above that."

My lips wobbled as I nodded at her, her words soothing a deep ache inside my chest that had been festering and festering. I wiped my eyes, and she handed me a bottle of water.

I'd just cracked open the cap when the door to our room opened, and a doctor walked in. Instantly, every person in the room forgot all that they were doing and rushed to the doctor, with me at the front.

Before I could even grab the doctor by the collar of his lab coat and shake some answers out of him, he raised his hands as if trying to calm a rabid animal. "Mr. Park is out of danger. We've removed the bullet from his leg. It will take some physical therapy for him to regain the strength in that leg, but he will be just fine. We'll be bringing him to the room in just a few minutes."

My legs gave out in relief. I forgot all about the water in my hands and accidentally spilled it on myself when I squeezed it too tightly. My chest heaved as air finally entered my lungs properly with what felt like the first breath I'd taken after hearing about Dom's kidnapping.

Someone took the ruined bottle and pressed another bottle into my hand, pushing it to my lips and making me drink all of it. Someone ran their fingers through my hair, softly coaxing me back to the present. "There, Samaira. You need to be strong. Who's going to take care of Dominic?"

Nobody but me, my mind answered.

CHAPTER 34

DOMINIC

A loud beeping noise hammered in my skull, disturbing my peaceful dream. Samaira was in my bed, wearing a beautiful red dress, her hair spread over the pillow, her neck arched as she laughed at something. But every time she tried to say something, the stupid fucking beeping noise came out of her mouth. It was getting infuriating. Her lips moved, but her mouth kept beeping. "What's wrong with you, Maira?"

"Me? You're the one in the hospital bed, you idiot." My ears rang as her voice came from somewhere close, and my eyes snapped open.

Pain exploded in my skull, and my eyes automatically closed at the bright white light that stabbed me in the head. It turned darker behind my closed eyes, and Samaira's voice touched my ears again. "Better now?"

Slowly, I opened my eyes again, and my heart jumped in my chest as my eyes fell on Maira. She had a scowl on her face as she looked at me, but her fingers were running softly through my hair. And suddenly, the events leading up to me lying here bombarded my mind. The beeping around me intensified, and I all but tried to get up to shut the fucking thing up myself.

But a strong hand held me to my bed, her eyes glaring daggers at me. "Calm the fuck down, Dominic."

My fingers grasped her arm, holding me down. "You okay, baby?"

She slowly rubbed my chest, and her eyes softened. Her lips slowly curled in a smile. "You're the one lying on the hospital bed, Dom. I'm not the one you should be worrying about."

"Don't tell me what to worry about. I'll worry about you if I want to."

She rolled her eyes as if I were being unreasonable. "I'm fine. You were the one who was shot."

Speaking of which, my leg throbbed a little, but I wasn't in too much pain. "I feel fine."

She gave me a soft smile. "You're on a lot of meds."

I tried to remember what had happened, but many pieces were still missing from my mind. I didn't remember how we got out. The last thing I remembered was Maira coming to my rescue, a lot of shooting, and…I looked at Samaira. "Did you slap me at some point?"

She bit her lip and bent closer to me. My lips went dry with the need to kiss her. "You kept going to sleep on me."

"So you slapped me?" I clutched her arm and pulled her closer.

Suddenly, her eyes filled with tears, and she bit her lip for an entirely different reason. "I couldn't lose you."

My heart squeezed tight beneath my chest, agony far more vicious than a bullet wound spreading through my veins at the sight of tears in her eyes. I pulled her into my arms, causing her to climb onto the bed with me. "Nothing can take me away from you, baby."

She sniffled into my chest as her body shook with tears. A

gnawing ache pierced my chest at every tear she shed for me. I squeezed her tight into my arms and pressed a kiss to her hair. "Please, don't cry, Maira. I can't take it. It's far more painful than that stupid bullet."

She wiped her cheeks on my chest and glared at me, her eyelashes wet with tears. She looked fucking adorable and like a little kitten. I couldn't help but smile at her. Her thumb grazed my lips, and I placed a soft kiss on it before sucking it into my mouth. Her eyes darkened, and she pushed her thumb deeper, pulling a groan out of my mouth and making my cock stir against her hips.

She immediately moved away, glaring at me. "You just got shot."

"In the leg," I countered. "My cock works just fine. And it needs you."

"Not until you're healed."

"I am healed."

"Let's ask the doctors, shall we?"

Right then, the door to the room slammed open and in rushed my mother, my dad, and Sophie.

Samaira tried to get off the bed and away from my arms, but I kept my hold tight on her. She slowly kept stirring around, but that just made me tighten my hold on her. If she thought she was getting away from my arms anytime soon, she was sadly mistaken.

My mom hugged me and smiled in Samaira's direction. And then launched into a heavy dose of rebuke as I kept nodding along at her words. "You will be keeping a team of bodyguards around you at all times, just like your father does. Are we clear?"

I scoffed and looked at Maira for support but found her staring me down just like my mother. My eyes widened. "Are you serious? You're with my mother on this?"

She put a finger under her chin. "Umm…let me think about it. Do I want the love of my life under constant protection, or do I want him susceptible to any harm? Hmm…tough choice."

Mom chuckled, and so did my dad. "Unbelievable."

She looked at my mom and said, "I'll be hiring a team for him myself."

"Good girl." Mom gave her a soft smile, the one she usually reserved for Sophie, and it just warmed my heart. Maira deserved to have a mom. Not just mine. But seeing how soft she got, how much she looked up to my mom, I knew she missed hers. I knew she'd never forgive herself if she never talked to her family. She deserved to have them in her life. They deserved to meet the strong, wonderful woman she'd become.

Mom kept scolding me till Dad brought in the doctor. Samaira, once again, tried to get out of my arms. I glared at her to stay put. The doctor simply gave us an amused smile and examined the machines as we talked about my level of pain.

"Everything looks good, Mr. Park. We would like to keep you here for two more days to monitor any infection. But everything seems fine as of now. I'd recommend that you rest a lot. Thankfully, the bullet didn't hit the bone. It will take some time for the wound to completely heal. We can schedule physical therapy to help you regain the full strength of your leg."

"Thank you, Doctor."

I turned to my parents and asked for coffee. At the doctor's nod, they left us alone.

Once they were gone, I turned to the doctor. "Do I need to wait to have sex?"

Samaira pinched me at my waist, making me jump. I turned to her with a pout. "I'm injured, baby."

I turned to the doctor and looked at him with pleading eyes. He gave me a small smile. "As long as you don't put any strain on your injured leg, you should be fine."

"Thank you, Doctor."

As soon as the doctor left the room, I quickly pulled Samaira on top of me, making her shriek with a laugh. "Dominic, put me down. You're gonna get hurt."

"I'm not putting any strain on my leg."

She simply shook her head and nuzzled into my throat, taking a deep inhale right at the junction between my neck and shoulder. "I can't live without you, Dominic."

I tightened my arms around her and ran my hand through her soft, wavy curls. "I'm not going anywhere, baby. I promise. I have a long, long life to live with you. Need to spend all my days loving you. Need to wake up to your adorable little snores. Need to feed you a healthy breakfast so you can kick proper ass. Need to fuck you. Deep and slow. Hard and fast. Need to show you the world. Need to spar with you and beat you at it."

That got me a snort and a wet chuckle. She turned in my arms and pressed her lips to mine. "I've never loved someone as much as I love you, Dominic. I never thought I'd allow someone close enough to me to become my weakness. My liability. But loving you made me realize that you're my strength. You're the light in my dark world. You're my reason to come home. You're the life I dreamed about but never allowed myself to pursue. But now that you're here, there's nothing I wouldn't do to keep you. No enemy I wouldn't destroy. No obstacle I wouldn't obliterate. You're mine. And before you even think about getting shot again or dying on me, you better know that I'll fucking follow you to the ends of the earth. You're never getting rid of me."

CHAPTER 35

SAMAIRA

Before I'd even finished the sentence, Dominic had his tongue down my throat, his groan sending tremors through my body. His kiss was all hunger and need and passion. His tongue swiped along mine, his taste a drug in my veins, making me soaking wet. His words touched my lips in a breathless whisper. "Lock the fucking door."

All my protests died in my mouth the moment he squeezed my throat and bit my ear. My chest heaved as my legs squeezed tight together to relieve the pulsing ache between them. I whimpered as he groaned. "Now, baby. Before I stop caring about privacy."

I made my legs move and ran to the door, locking it and checking it twice.

I turned around and found him holding up the blanket for me. For just a second, I tried to tell him no, to wait till he was healed. But the need in his eyes matched the one in mine, and I started to shed my clothes as I walked back to him.

His eyes flared with hunger and need. They devoured every inch that I revealed. His fist clenched the blanket, and he groaned so sweetly, so fucking desperately for me, my pussy pulsed with the need to be filled by his cock. I was completely naked by the time I reached him and climbed on his lap, knowing it would immobilize his leg. I looked at what he was wearing and gave him a wicked smile. "We need to thank the hospital for putting you in this gown."

He growled as I moved his flimsy little gown up his hips, exposing his thick, pulsing cock to me. Precum slid down his length, and I couldn't help but grind the heel of my palm to my aching clit, just to relieve that pounding pleasure racing down my spine. I moaned at the sight of his glistening cock that he now held in his fist.

A light day-old stubble lined his jaw as he clenched it, the veins in his forearms popping as he stroked his cock, precum glistening over his tip, making my mouth fucking water. I was fucking hungry, and he was waving my favorite candy in front of my face.

I pushed his hand away and moved farther down his legs. "I would've climbed on your cock, Dom. But you just had to show off. Now, you'll lie there without moving your fucking leg while I have my dessert first."

He fucking groaned as the beeping in the machine intensified. With a smirk, I held his cock in my hand and pushed the tip in my mouth. His taste exploded on my tongue, and my pussy ached with emptiness. My arousal slid down my thighs the more I sucked him down my throat.

Dominic was a live wire, thrumming with electric pleasure and want. His hand pushed into my hair and held it in his tight fist as he moved my head to direct me how he wanted me. He pushed my head down with a strong grip so my nose met the lightly trimmed hair at the base of his cock. I fucking inhaled him, and my hands clutched his thigh, my need to consume him pushing me to the edge of my sanity.

His essence, his smell, the feel of his skin on my tongue was so fucking intoxicating that I wanted to rub my face in the juncture of his thighs and balls and drown myself in him. He was sex and musk and mine. I moved off his cock and pushed my tongue right where I needed to, at the spot between his thighs and his balls, his taste exploding on my tongue.

Moans and whimpers clouded the air around us, and I realized they were coming from me. Dominic groaned as I rubbed my face along his balls and sucked one of them in my mouth. His hips moved, and I held his legs down with a scowl. "You move that leg, Dominic, and I'll stop."

"Fuck, baby. You're going to kill me. As much as I love seeing my balls between your lips, you need to be sitting on my cock. Before somebody comes knocking."

Urgency rushed through me. Dominic's cock was sopping wet, precum pooled on his abs. I swiped at it and rubbed my pussy with it, pleasure singeing every little nerve in my body. My hips pulsed of their own accord, uncontrollable need thrumming between my legs.

Hunger consumed me, and I moved over Dominic, reminding myself that he was here with me. He was safe. He was mine. I pushed my lips against his and aligned his cock at my soaking wet entrance.

He growled against my lips. "I fucking love how wet you get for me, Maira. Always soaking wet."

He bit my lip to the point of pain, his claim making me wild. I pushed his cock inside me in one uninterrupted thrust, taking him in all the way to the hilt. He groaned my name like a prayer, his large hands grabbing my ass hard enough to leave behind his fingerprints, and I loved that even more.

I moved over his cock, pulling him out right up to the tip. I sat back down, fully, capturing his wild groan on my tongue. His head arched back, the veins on his neck pulsing with the pounding of his heart.

I swiped my tongue on them and bit his neck, sucking it in time with my thrusts, whimpering as his cock hit the spot that had me seeing stars. Sweat pooled where our skin met as

Dominic clutched the back of my head and moved me so I met his eyes.

They were burning with desire, his jaw pulsing with raw possession. "How does this feel, baby?"

He slammed his cock inside me, holding me immobilized on top of him. "Your leg," I whimpered, trying to turn my head back to look at it. But he kept my head locked in his grip, and slammed into me once again, pulling a needy whimper out of my lips as spine-tingling pleasure erupted in my core. "I'm only using one leg. Now, tell me how it feels."

Another slam that had his balls slapping my ass and my eyes rolling back. "Incredible."

He pulled my face so his nose rubbed against mine, his breath hitting my cheek, and slammed into me again. "Now?"

"Fuck." My eyes burned, and my skin was on fire as pleasure coursed through my veins. My hips thrust in a wild motion, trying to pull him deeper into me, squeezing him tight to keep him inside me. "So good."

His thrusts turned slower but deeper; his lips touched mine with a softness that had tears sliding down my cheeks. His firm hold on my head turned lighter as he caressed my hair. His cock moved inside me so achingly slow, so punishingly deep, as if he was marking me as his from the inside. As if he could stay inside me forever and never be satisfied. His tongue swept along mine with so much passion, so much need, so much fucking care, every inch of me felt treasured. Tears slipped down my cheeks, and his tongue captured them, all the while thrusting inside me like a man devoted to my pleasure. "And now?" His rough voice caressed my throat as he tucked his head into my chest, sucking at the top of my breast,

My fingers laced in his hair as I pulled his head so his eyes —so soft, so achingly tender—met mine. "Love. It feels like love."

A blinding smile came over his face as he kept thrusting inside me in that same achingly slow manner, pushing me over the edge with his loving eyes and his rock-hard cock, shattering me into a million tiny pieces, pleasure ripping through my body in mindless waves. My pussy flooded with so much wetness, Dominic's eyes rolled back in his head as his cock thickened inside me. His hips lost all their rhythm, and he erupted inside me with a groan so loud I had to put my palm over his mouth.

His cock pulsing inside me had my pussy tightening around him, needing to keep him inside me. He was about to pull out of me, but I squeezed around him, pulling a grunt out of him. I pressed my lips to his and whispered, "Stay."

A small smile curled his lips, and he pulled me into a hug, his arms closing around me protectively. "As long as you want, baby."

His heart beat strongly in my ears, and I realized how close I came to losing him. I caressed his chest, right where his heart thumped in a strong, healthy rhythm. "I was worried." My voice broke on the last word.

His arms tightened around me as he laid his cheek on my head. "Me too. I kept thinking that I just got you, and I wasn't ready to lose you. What if our first date was our last? What if I only got to tell you that I love you once? What if I never got to see your smile again? Thank you for saving me, Samaira."

His hospital gown was wet with my tears as I turned my head to look at him. The light in his eyes. The smile on his lips. The warmth of his cheeks. "Thank you for finding me. Thank you for making me feel safe to love again. You thank me for saving you, but Dominic, you are the one who saved me from a lonely life when I was too afraid to love."

He pulled me closer to him, and his cock slipped out, making me feel empty and deliciously filthy wet. His lips pressed against my forehead. "Tell me you'll move in with me."

My heart soared and danced and sighed with relief. Because I did not want to spend a single night without being wrapped in his arms. I gave him a mocking, shocked gasp. "Dominic, what about that wonderful, large apartment you gifted me in that beautiful building?"

That had him scowling adorably. "Then I'll move in with you."

I wanted to squeal and giggle, but I kept my lips pursed in thought. "Isn't it too early in our relationship, though? What if we get in a fight? What if you realize that I'm not the best roommate or girlfriend and that it's impossible to live with me?"

He growled, and his eyes narrowed at me. "If we were at home, I'd spank you so fucking hard for every single one of your ridiculous questions, Maira, you wouldn't be able to sit on your ass for days."

I bit my lip to stop myself from laughing. "See, you're already mad at me, and we haven't even moved in together."

His glare turned into an adorable scowl. "Stop that. We're moving in together. Either at my place or we make a home in the brand-new apartment."

Every pore of my body bubbled with this overwhelming need to hold him in my arms and never let go. I wanted him. And he wanted me. And it was time to stop fighting myself. I'd spent every single day of the past thirteen years fighting and killing and surviving. I wanted to start living and loving my life, my dreams. I had a man who was laying the world at my feet, and it was time to take a step forward. I kissed Dominic and whispered against his lips. "Alright."

He kept talking. "Because I'm telling you, Maira. I'm not living a single day…" His eyes widened, and he stopped his tirade. "Did you just agree?"

My lips stretched into a smile so wide my cheeks hurt. "Yes, Dom."

He whooped, and he looked ridiculous and adorable for a thirty-eight-year-old man. "We're gonna live together."

I dissolved into laughter and hugged him. "I can't wait."

————

We spent the next two days at the hospital as Dominic recovered, to his utter dismay. For the life of me, I couldn't leave his side. We were watching a mindless fighting movie on his television when all four of my girls barged into the hospital room.

They each greeted me with a hug and a kiss on the cheek. Sloane handed me a big thermos container, and when I opened it, I found it filled with chai. I jumped on her and pulled her back into my arms. "Thank you."

Lena and Tara chuckled, whereas Naomi teased, "Now you look happy, Sami."

My eyes met Dominic's, and he raised his eyebrows, silently giving me the go-ahead to share my new living arrangements. I still hadn't talked to the girls about Dominic's ridiculously ostentatious surprise for us all. But I could share the most important bit. "Um…Dominic and I have decided to move in together."

All four of them shrieked and jumped on me, pulling me into a hug. Arms wrapped around me, and I was enveloped in a cocoon of so much love and warmth and acceptance and celebration, I felt like my heart was about to burst out of my chest.

Naomi quickly started to drag us toward the bed where Dominic sat. "We gotta welcome the new member of the Wildcats into the group hug, ladies. Make some room for the first ever boy member."

I giggled at the comical expression on Dominic's face as all five of us huddled around him and pulled him into a hug. "Umm, I'd prefer to be called a *man* member, not that it sounds any better."

"We'll call you a man member after you beat Sami in a sparring match," Tara piped in.

Once the hugs were done, the girls took a seat around the bed, while I climbed in to sit beside Dominic.

Lena opened her small notepad and looked at the two of us. "So after we all came to the hospital with Dominic, Naomi stayed hidden at the warehouse until the cops came. Like we imagined, they got all the women out. She also obtained basic information on all the women, just so we could check in and see if the cops had successfully sent them back home.

"It was a much bigger bust for them than they anticipated. The Russian man who had threatened Dominic was a big name in the criminal world for illegal smuggling of drugs, guns, and women. We actually shut down their New York operations when we shot down all their men. But…" She paused and sighed.

And I realized what had happened. "But now the cops are wondering who took them out."

Lena nodded. "I have a man on the inside. And the NYPD thinks it could be a rival gang who wanted to take the Russians out. They've got theories it could be a local vigilante group. Nobody suspects five women of managing to take down the entire base of operations of the Russian mob."

She then looked at Dominic. "There will be cops here to question you about the events." She looked at her watch, and her eyes met his as she continued, "In about fifteen minutes."

She handed him a stack of notes. "Here's the entire story on what you'll say. It's only going to be you and Samaira when the cops arrive. The four of us will go and grab some lunch in the meantime."

She got up along with the rest of the ladies and pointed at the notes. "It's not much. Read up."

Before they could all leave, Dominic cleared his throat, turning everyone's attention to him. He looked at all four of my girls and said, "I wanted to thank you all for coming to save me. You didn't have to do that. You're under no obligation to save my life. But I'm really grateful that you did."

Lena shrugged and glanced at me before turning back to Dominic. "Samaira loves you. That's reason enough."

Dominic held my hand and gave it a quick kiss. "I also truly appreciate you all being okay with me dating Samaira. I know how much she values each of your opinions. I'm glad we have your support."

My eyes misted, and I pulled him into a kiss. "I love you," I whispered against his lips, capturing his smile on my tongue.

"I love you too, Maira." His eyes shone with so much love, I could eat him up.

"Eww, stop it, you two. No need to make the single ladies jealous." Sloane slumped over Tara in an overly defeated expression that had us all cackling and Dominic sighing softly, even though he had the biggest smile on his face. "So this is my new life, huh?"

I pressed a soft kiss to his lips again, gaining more cheers and protests from the girls, and met his warm eyes. "Welcome to the Wildcats."

With that, they left the room, taking away all their cheers and chaos, leaving Dominic and me with Lena's meticulous notes.

By the time the door to Dominic's room opened, we were prepared. Dominic's doctor stepped in with two cops in NYPD uniforms in tow. The doctor picked up a chart from Dominic's side table and asked, "How do you feel, Mr. Park?"

Dominic gave him a polite smile and shrugged. "I feel fine. Just waiting to be out of here, honestly."

Dominic turned his head around the doctor and gave the two officers a nod. "Officers."

The man in front stepped forward to stand in front of Dominic. "Mr. Park. I'm Lieutenant Knox Steele. This, here, is Officer Brandon Sharpe."

Lieutenant Steele was a huge motherfucker with the coldest eyes I'd ever seen. Eyes that I didn't trust. At all. He was as tall as Dominic, maybe an inch or so shorter, but the man's biceps were as thick as tree trunks. His hair was cut short on the sides but slightly longer on top. His eyes moved between me and Dominic with a heavy dose of suspicion.

Dominic didn't get even slightly intimidated by his presence. He simply gave the lieutenant a nod. "Lieutenant. Pleased to meet you," he said and introduced me. "Please meet my girlfriend, Samaira."

Lieutenant Steele's eyes narrowed. "The doctor here mentioned that she's your fiancée."

Before I could interject, Dominic gave a relaxed smile with a shrug. "A little white lie to give her access to my condition. I'm sure you can understand."

Lieutenant Steele hummed. "If you don't mind, we have some questions for you and Ms. Samaira regarding your accident."

The doctor moved to the side, as if he couldn't stand the intensity and tension flooding the room. Dominic kept his cool and gave the lieutenant a nod. "Of course."

"How did you end up in the warehouse that belongs to the Russian mob?" he asked, his eyes accusatory. I did not like how he looked at us. It was as if he'd already made up his mind about us.

Dominic, following Lena's notes, said, "As you might know, or not, my sister was raped by three masked men about four months ago. Like any brother would do, I've been hunting for them for a while now with no success. I fear I might've gotten too close to the culprit. At least, that's what I believe."

"Did the officers on your sister's case not find any suspects?"

I guess these cops didn't know everything about everyone. Dominic sighed and shook his head in defeat. "Unfortunately not. They declared it a cold case. So I've been working on my own to find the culprits."

"And you think it's the Russian mob?" Lieutenant Steele's eyes were full of suspicion.

Dominic shrugged as if he were confused himself. "I don't know, lieutenant. I had just dropped Samaira at home and was on my way to work when four cars screeched around my car, shot my driver, and kidnapped me. This leads me to believe that I was getting close. What other reason could they possibly have for kidnapping me?"

Lieutenant Steele's eyes were narrowed on Dominic as he grunted. "What other reason, indeed."

"And how did you end up in a hospital with an injured leg? Who brought you here?"

Dominic, being the fantastic actor that he was—truly deserving of an Oscar—shrugged. "I have no idea, Lieutenant Steele. The last thing I remembered was being shot in the leg while tied to a chair, the Russian mob screaming at me for interfering in their business. I was dizzy and could barely make out my surroundings with the loss of blood, but I remember there being some sort of attack. There were a lot of gunshots and screaming and fighting. I don't recollect what exactly happened, but maybe somebody decided to spare me."

Before Lieutenant Steele could further question Dominic, I interjected, "Umm…Lieutenant Steele, if I may interrupt?"

The man's gaze slammed into me, and the power in his eyes had me straightening in my seat. The man exuded pure alpha energy, his eyes as dark and dead as a monster. And all my years of experience had trained me to never show weakness to a monster. "I was hanging out with my friends when I got a call that Dominic was shot, followed by a location pin."

Lieutenant Steele's eyes narrowed at me, but I continued, "I rushed with my friends and found Dominic's unconscious body around the corner from where the Russian mob's warehouse was attacked. Maybe someone was looking out for Dominic. Or maybe whoever attacked the mob didn't have any animosity toward Dominic and chose to spare him."

I hiccuped a sob and ran my fingers through Dominic's hair. "I'm just glad I found him alive. We rushed him to the hospital, and I've been here with him ever since."

Dominic clutched my hand in his and pressed his lips to my knuckles. "Hush now, baby. I'm right here. I'm alright. Nothing's going to happen to me."

I bit my lip and squeezed out a tear from my eye, all for Lieutenant Steele. "I'm worried you'll be lost to me forever if you keep trying to find Sophie's rapists. Clearly, it's someone very powerful."

Dominic sighed and turned to the lieutenant. "Lieutenant Steele, the officers assigned to our case didn't do shit. But if it's not too much to ask, I would love your help in finding my sister's rapists."

Lieutenant Steele gave him a polite smile. He was faking it. His eyes didn't soften at all and churned with that empty darkness that sent shivers up my spine. This man could be trouble. "Mr. Park. We will look into your sister's case. And if we can help out in any way, we will."

"Thank you, lieutenant. I appreciate it. Now, if you don't have any further questions, I'd like to rest up a bit."

His eyes sharpened, but he nodded. "Of course, Mr. Park. Please take care. I'll be in touch if I have any questions."

"Of course, Lieutenant Steele."

With another nod, both cops walked out the door with the doctor tagging behind them.

We both stared at the closed door in shocked silence.

I heard Dominic gulp when he asked, "How'd you think that went? Think he believed us?"

My eyes were stuck on the closed door, almost afraid that the lieutenant would come back. I could only shake my head. "I have no fucking idea."

Our eyes turned to each other, and Dominic shrugged. "Whatever happens, we'll deal with it together."

"Together."

CHAPTER 36

Samaira burst open the door to the brand-new apartment floor, leading the way, as the rest of the Wildcats followed her, exchanging furtive glances. I walked behind all of them, giving Samaira the chance to show them everything.

She turned to face them and spread her arms. "This is all from Dominic, and it was his surprise, so feel free to say no."

"Solid endorsement, baby," I piped in.

She smiled and winked at me. "He's gifted the Wildcats the top ten floors of this building."

"Happy to allot you more floors if you guys need," I added.

Their gazes ping-ponged between us as Samaira continued, "Each one of us can have an apartment, and we can convert the remaining five floors into our workspaces. There are two massive apartments on each floor. So we can pair up and each pair can take a floor. We could literally convert an entire floor into our personal training floor. We can move our main headquarters from Thunder Claw to here, keeping

Thunder Claw for client meetings or emergency operations. What do you guys think?"

Every woman looked around with a starstruck expression.

Lena, who had a slight inkling of what I was planning, turned to me and raised her eyebrows. "You said you were planning a *little* surprise."

I shrugged. "I own this entire 135-story building. I'm gifting you ten floors. It *is* a little surprise. So if you need twenty stories, just let me know."

Naomi bit her lip, her eyes shining with awe. "You think we could convert a floor or two into safe spaces for women who've got nowhere to go? These are huge apartments. At least ten people can comfortably fit in here."

Samaira nodded. "Definitely. We can do whatever we want with the space. Right, Dominic?"

I kept my hands firmly in my pocket, afraid I'd pull Samaira into my arms in front of all her friends. "Absolutely. I have a team of interior designers. You guys just need to let them know what you need, and they'll do it. No questions asked. I'll have them all sign an NDA to work on this with you."

Tara had Shadow tight on his leash in her hand as he tried to run around everywhere. Every time he got a glance at me, he gave me a vicious growl, which was the main reason his leash was firmly in Tara's grasp. One day, I was going to make him like me without needing any treats. Today wasn't that day.

Tara looked around the room with an appreciative glance. "We can have a high-end tech room and surveillance system set up."

I dropped to my knees and pulled out the treats from my pocket to give them to Shadow, earning a rough growl from him as he snatched them from my hand. I looked at Tara, who had an amused smile on her face. "Whatever machines, computers, security systems, internet speed, wiring that you need, just let me know. It's all yours."

Sloane and Lena kept smiling and giggling with Samaira.

Sloane turned to me and asked, "You sure about giving us all of these floors?"

"Very sure."

"What if you and Sami break up? Would we have to move out?"

I balked at her question as Samaira jabbed her in her ribs.

I walked to where they stood and wrapped Samaira in my arms, my chest meeting her back. I placed my chin on her shoulder. Pulling Samaira even closer to my chest, I smiled at Sloane. "We're never breaking up. This is a forever kinda deal."

That had Samaira turning and jumping into my arms. "You promise?"

I kept my hand under her ass as she wrapped her legs around my hips. "I promise."

I didn't know who moved first, but Samaira's lips were on mine, and everything was right in the world. We kissed as her friends cheered around us. But to my utter dismay, I had to put her down.

She turned to her friends and bit her lip. "So? What do you guys think?"

Lena nodded, looking around. "It's certainly safer and more private."

Sloane sighed. "Definitely. We can all live together but separately. We don't have to worry about each other's safety while we're away from the Den."

Tara walked along the wall of windows overlooking the sky and the entire skyline of New York City, bright sunlight shining down on her. "We can have a den with windows." As a person who preferred to stay inside because of her own trauma, having windows was certainly a huge luxury for her.

And all these apartments had light streaming through the glass windows as if we were floating under the sun.

Naomi pulled Tara into her arms. "And we can have an entire floor of your tech stuff. I can have an entire floor converted to a clinic. We can treat as many women as we want, give them a safe space, and train them to join us."

Samaira nodded and looked at all of them. "We can make the Wildcats bigger. We can do more. We can actively target gangs and mobs who're out there hurting and kidnapping women. We can be stronger together, more powerful. We can be unstoppable."

I stood aside and watched in awe as the five women talked about their goals. And I knew I'd give every single dollar of my wealth to helping them achieve every one of them. I knew these women could do anything they put their minds to. They were destined for greatness. These were the women whose suffering had turned them into ruthless protectors. The world needed more women like the Wildcats.

Once they'd hollered and cheered and decided to move here, I walked to where they stood. Every woman except Samaira knew where I was taking her next. So I gave them a nod as I pulled Samaira by the waist. "C'mon, I need to take you somewhere."

Her eyes twinkled as she wrapped her arms around my neck. "Ooh, is it a surprise?"

I tucked a lock of her hair behind her ear and pressed a kiss on her nose. "A big surprise."

A surprise she might hate. But something I knew she needed to do.

I led her to the roof of the building, and that had her chuckling. "Are we ever using a car to travel to this building? Or is it only accessible through the sky?"

My girl came and took a seat beside me in the chopper, and I pressed a kiss to her hand. "A car would take too long for where we're going."

Her eyes narrowed into a look of extreme suspicion. "Please tell me we're not flying out of the country. I'm not even dressed properly. And I need my girls to travel with me this time."

That had me chuckling. "We're not flying out of the country. And it's good to know that you still prefer the company of your girls over me."

The chopper was high up in the sky as we flew over the tallest skyscrapers of the city, and Maira pulled me into her arms. "Aw, you're my favorite person on this earth, Dominic Park. But none of us has ever stepped foot outside the East Coast, let alone the country. And I want them to see the world by my side, you know. We're a team. We're soul sisters."

How could someone so fucking caring be that resistant to letting other people care for her? She was a nurturer, my girl. She wanted to just protect and care for the people she loved. She was willing to leave the people she loved if it meant they were safer. She was selfless to the point of extreme stubbornness.

I pressed a kiss to her forehead. "I promise you, baby. We go anywhere, we take all the girls. I want nothing more than to see a smile on your beautiful face. Be it with your girls or me. You deserve all the fucking love in the world."

"How are you the way that you are?" Her eyes shone, and her voice trembled.

I bit my lip and looked around. "Keep that thought in mind when you see your surprise in a few minutes."

Before she could look around and get ideas, and probably run away from me, I put a blindfold on her, hiding her view of the surroundings. "What did you do, Dominic?"

"Hush now, baby. You'll thank me later."

"I have a terrible feeling about this."

My heart pounded as I walked her down from the chopper and got us in the car waiting for us at the helipad. I clutched Maira's hand in mine on the entire way to the destination, her questions and warnings making me terrified that I was making a big fucking mistake.

But the moment the destination came into view, determination raced through my heart. With a surety deep in my bones, I got out of the car and pulled Samaira out. Standing behind her, I pulled off her blindfold so she could see her surprise.

I kept my eyes on her as she took in the view in front of us, and her eyes widened to saucers. "No." She gasped.

CHAPTER 37

SAMAIRA

We stood across the street from my parents' home. My legs trembled as I tried to keep myself standing, with my eyes glued to the front door. It was only Dominic's arms wrapped around me that kept me from sprinting away or falling right here in a puddle. "It's time you let them in, baby."

My head shook, fear choking down my throat. "No. Dominic, it's too dangerous."

He pulled me around so I faced him. His eyes churned with so much anger and so much helplessness, my shoulders shrank within themselves. "Maira, they deserve to have you in their life. They deserve to see the strong, powerful woman you've become. I'm not asking you to tell them about the Wildcats. But they deserve to know that you're alright. They deserve to hug their daughter. They deserve to love their daughter."

My hands shook as I clutched his shirt. "They don't need me, Dom. They're doing fine with my younger siblings. They've got a nice little life set up here. I can't bring all the trouble here. You know how dangerous it is right now. If we're only going to aim for bigger criminals, you know I'd put their life at risk."

"I asked Tara to do some research. Your father has made donations to a charity that helps sexually abused women every month for the past thirteen years. Your mom talks to her sister about how much she misses you every single day. Your brother, Sameer, has googled your name every single day for the past thirteen years. Your sister, Arya, is learning computer science and goes to boxing. Her goal is to find her sister. You are wrong, Samaira. You are not protecting your family by staying away. You're hurting them. You're denying them the right to love their daughter, their sister, the way they want to. I know it hurt to see them suffering during your case, baby. But you got your revenge. You've got your purpose. But what about *their* purpose? I know you secretly go and watch them. I know you've seen the smiles on their faces. But you refuse to acknowledge the sadness in their eyes. Why?"

"I'm afraid," I whispered. "I wouldn't be able to survive if anything happened to them."

"Then we protect them. Together. I promise you. I'll never let anything happen to them. Their safety is my responsibility. When you're on a mission, they'll be protected. I'll do whatever it takes for you to feel secure in their safety. But don't punish yourself and them just to keep them safe. I know when you did that to me, and I'm telling you, it just makes me mad when you do that."

"What if they reject me after all these years?"

My voice was so broken, so scared, as my heart broke for my parents, for Sameer and Arya. They were so young when I left home. Tears slipped down my cheeks as terror unlike anything tried to pull me under. But suddenly, I was pulled into Dominic's arms as he pressed a kiss to my head. "Why don't we find out for ourselves?"

I nodded against his chest and mumbled, "You'll stay with me?"

"Couldn't get rid of me even if you tried."

He pulled out of my hug and dragged me across the street, closer to the house. "Let's go."

My steps faltered, but Dominic was having none of it. "I'm not going to run away, Dom."

He slowed his steps just a tad and raised his eyebrows at me with a smile. "I'm not risking it."

I bit my lip as I stopped my heart from bursting out of my chest and shook my head at him. "I'm going to kill you after this."

"I think you're going to thank me after this. On your knees, Tigress."

I scoffed, but the conversation stopped me from spiraling. Before I was even prepared, we reached the front door, and Dominic—the impatient asshole—pressed the doorbell.

My knees trembled, and my heart pounded in my chest as I heard movement on the other side. Suddenly, the door was pulled open, and a young woman with glasses perched on her eyes—eyes that matched mine—stood across from me. "Hey, Aryu," I whispered, using the nickname I always used for my sister.

A sob broke out on her face, and she launched herself into my arms, crying and screaming my name. Her familiar straw-berry-shampoo smell hit my nose, and I wrapped my arms tightly around her, lifting her off the ground. My sister's loud cries were like shards of glass tearing my heart apart, but her arms and legs wrapped around me and her mumbled "*I missed you*" were a balm to my soul.

A loud glass shattering had us turning. There stood my parents and my baby brother.

My lips wobbled as I looked at my mom and dad in the eyes for the first time after thirteen years. "Maa." I thought I'd never get to say that word again in my life. I didn't realize when my feet moved, but I was in my mother's arms as her tears slid down my neck. A solid, warm embrace, smelling of Old Spice aftershave, enveloped us, with two more sets of arms completing the circle, and I was finally home.

Tears and snot ran down my face as my dad held me in his arms, as Maa kept caressing my back and my arm.

I pulled Sameer into a hug, crushing him in my arms. "Oh my god, you're so muscular, Didi."

I laughed, tears sliding down my face, as my ears ached to hear Didi from his mouth again. I flexed my muscles at him and waggled my eyebrows. "Bet I can beat you in arm wrestling."

He was a pretty muscular twenty-two-year-old young man, and he immediately flexed his own muscles and turned to Arya. "Arya, who's got better muscles?"

Arya chuckled as tears slid down her own cheeks. "Didi, obviously. Just look how sexy she looks." I smiled mockingly at Sameer when she finished her sentence, "For a thirty-two-year-old."

My shocked, outrageous gasp had Sameer *and* Dominic chuckling.

I turned to Dominic. "What are you laughing at? You're older than me."

Arya gasped at Dominic, and I knew she was joking—she had to be—when she said, "No way you're older than my sister. You look so young."

The smile on Dominic's face at that moment could make a weak woman faint. He immediately stretched his hand forward to shake with Arya. "I'm Dominic. Your sister's boyfriend. Here, take this key."

Arya frowned and turned the key in her hands. "What's it for?"

"My Range Rover. It's yours now. I don't think I've

received a better compliment in my life. This is the least I can do to thank you."

My jaw dropped. My mother's jaw dropped. My father's jaw dropped. My brother's jaw dropped. Only, he quickly pulled it back up and rushed to Dominic and started shaking his hand. "You're the most beautiful person and the strongest man I've ever seen in my life."

That had Arya snorting and my dad physically pulling him away from a laughing Dominic.

Maa clutched my hand and pulled me inside the house. "Come on in, Mr. Dominic. Come on, beta, tell me all about where you've been. Are you alright?"

And then, with my mother's hand in mine, my family's warmth surrounding me, and Dominic's love in my heart, I let my family in. I told them all about my revenge. All about the Wildcats. Not in any gory details. But I shared my life's goals. I told them what I did for a living. I explained to them why I had stayed away from them.

We cried, and I apologized. After thirteen long years, I finally ate my mother's food. I sat with my father and watched television with him. I saw my sister's room and how she'd asked for two twin-size beds. "I knew you'd be back one day. And I needed you to have your own bed."

I burst into tears and apologized for abandoning her. She was twenty-six and refused to leave Mom and Dad to find a place for herself. It was the same for Sameer. Both of them knew how fragile my parents were after losing me.

I spent the entire day and the evening with my family, and the entire time, Dominic stayed by my side. He invited my parents to our home. He offered to move them into the brand-new apartment in the building we were moving into. My dad promised to consider moving at my insistence.

I sat on the floor as Maa applied oil to my hair, her fingers massaging my scalp just the way she used to. And when my sister sat in front of me to get me to put oil in her hair, I knew I was complete.

And I only had one person to thank for it.

My home. Dominic Park.

EPILOGUE - 1

SAMAIRA

Three months later

"Fuck, hurry, Dom." I gasped into his mouth as his thrusts into me turned frantic.

His large hand grabbed my thigh and wrapped it over his hip as he bit my lip, his cock slamming into my pussy. He growled in my ear, his other hand wrapped around my throat. "Why did you have to invite everyone over?"

Sweat from his hair dripped down my breast as he slammed into me with the power of a man possessed. I squeezed around his cock as pleasure raced through my body like electricity. My eyes rolled in my head as I remembered his question. I gasped at a hard thrust and answered, "It's called a fucking housewarming. More like houses-office-den warming."

I moved my hips in tandem with his, making him slide even deeper inside me as I slid across the fighting ring we had installed inside our apartment for our personal use. "Fuck, Dom. Harder. Need you deeper."

He groaned in my ear, squeezing my throat tighter, blocking my airway as the blood flow to my brain slowed down, and pleasure and suffocation started to build inside me in tandem, making me want to combust. "I'm going to defeat you one day." Dominic thrust hard into me between uttering every single word, his frustration at losing to me making me smile despite the restricted air flow.

Air burst out of me in a harsh exhale as I uttered between clenched teeth, "Never happening, sucker."

I whimpered as he snapped his hips harder, his hips moving against my clit in time with his pounding thrusts.

He kept releasing his tight hold on my throat for a small number of seconds, letting me breathe after every few thrusts, playing with my body, redirecting the rush of blood from my brain to my pussy and back and forth, until I was dizzy with pleasure.

I jerked my hips and twisted sharply, slamming him onto his back on the ring and climbing on top of him, trying to show him how easy it was for me to defeat him. His lips curled into an unhinged smile as he slammed into me from the bottom, jerking my body with dizzying pleasure. His arm snapped forward as he pulled me to his chest, holding me immobile to him with both arms as he moved inside me with powerful thrusts. "Take my cock, Maira. You don't get to control how I pleasure *my fucking pussy*. Look at how you're soaking my cock. Your juices are sliding down my balls."

I sucked at his throat as his arms wrapped around me, and he turned us back around, rolling me on my back so much more easily than he could two months ago. He was getting stronger and stronger each day. We had started training every day since we moved in, and every training session of ours ended exactly the same way.

I pound him during sparring, and he pounds into me after sparring.

As soon as I was on my back, he pulled out of me, making

a desperate whine climb out of my throat. Before I could protest loudly, Dominic climbed over my chest and grabbed the back of my head in his hand. He clutched his cock in his hand, stroking himself over me and spreading our wetness on my lips, his eyes burning with unrestrained desire. "You've made a mess of my cock, haven't you, baby? Look at this."

My pussy ached with emptiness, and I squeezed my legs together to relieve some of the pleasure as Dominic sat on my chest, his heavy balls resting at my neck, his hand painting my lips with his cum. My body buzzed with need and desire and pleasure, and I swiped my tongue along his cock, needing him to feed it to me.

"You don't get to suck my cock yet, baby. You need to clean up the mess you've made on my balls." He moved forward and slid his balls right to my lips, and like the greedy little slut I was for Dominic Park, I parted my lips and sucked them into my mouth.

His loud groan echoed in the room as his movements turned feral. My hands moved to his ass as I squeezed those perfect globes and sucked his balls deeper, my tongue swiping at his perineum, pulling a needy whine from his throat. "You look so pretty with your mouth full of my sack, baby."

His body shook over me as he stroked his cock right above me, his thick fingers moving over his length, making arousal pool between my legs. I needed him back inside me, flooding me with his cum.

I whimpered with need, his taste so potent in my mouth. I could come just like this if he kept this up. Before I could move my fingers to my pussy, Dominic pulled out of my mouth and moved down my body, pushing his tongue into my aching, wet pussy. My hips arched up, pulling him in deeper with a scream. "Don't stop, Dom. Please, don't stop. Love your tongue."

He was ravenous between my legs. His tongue moved from my back hole all the way to my clit, dipping into my pussy along the way. His groan had vibrations racing through my clit, unbearable pleasure building in my core, ready to burst out of me. His finger dipped into my rosebud as two of his fingers pushed into my pussy, making me feel so fucking full of everything Dominic. "Fuck, baby. You're squeezing me so tight."

His warm, wet tongue assaulted my clit with such well-timed precision. He was so in time with every thrust into my pussy and my ass that I exploded all over his hand, squeezing his fingers, pulling him deeper into me.

He groaned as he roughly pulled out of me and slammed his cock back into my pussy. He pulled me up by the loop of my diamond choker and pushed his tongue into me. With his harsh breath hitting my lips, he growled, "The only reason I'm not slamming into your tight little ass is because we've got a party to attend, and I don't want you aching. But I'm going to fuck this ass tonight."

I swiped my tongue on his cheek and pulled him into me deeper. "Need you to come inside me, Dom. Fuck, let me feel your cum. Breed me."

He groaned as his slams turned frantic. He fucked me with deep, rough strokes, his hips bucking into me with wild abandon, his balls slapping at my ass as his cock expanded inside me. With a loud groan, I felt his cock pulse deep inside me.

With a loud rumble, he dropped on top of me, his head nuzzling into my neck and his cock still nestled inside me. I fucking loved how he stayed deep inside me long after fucking me. I fucking loved feeling him harden back inside me, loved feeling full of him, as if he was leaving a part of him inside me. Only for me to keep.

He kissed my throat and licked my pulse. "Don't you wash away all my cum. I need my cum slipping into your panties all through the evening. I want you wet and aching when I fuck your ass tonight."

I moaned at the thought of feeling his cum dripping into

my panties and sitting in it the entire evening. Last time, he fucked me and left two loads of his cum and asked me to go on a mission. Every time I had kicked a target, the wetness trailing down my pussy had reminded me of Dominic. It had only made me more violent, more ruthless, and so fucking turned on, I had burst into Dominic's home office in the middle of his meeting and sat on his cock. He had quickly stopped his video call and muted his voice as I fucked myself on his cock as he continued the meeting.

Later, he'd fucked me and given me his cum over and over again throughout the night. Now, it was our pre-mission routine. He always fucked his cum deep into me before I went on a mission, leaving a very hot, very significant reminder of what was waiting for me on the other side.

I brushed his hair away from his eyes as his cock slipped out of me and gave him a kiss. "You need to train harder."

He groaned as we both climbed out of our boxing ring completely naked. "You're unbeatable."

I scoffed. "Lena can still beat me sometimes."

He grabbed my ass as we climbed the stairs to the bedroom. "Only because she's got more experience than you."

I yawned mockingly. "Excuses, excuses."

He laughed and pulled me into the shower with him. "Maybe I should train with Lena and learn how to beat you."

The way my heart rebelled at the thought, I pinned him to the shower wall, water sliding down our bodies. "You only train with me, Dominic."

His eyes were pools of warmth and love. "Yes, baby. Only ever with you. And get beaten every time."

I pushed into his arms, water raining down on us, our skin sliding against each other. "Aw, but I love defeating you. Gets me all wet."

He chuckled and pushed his two fingers inside me, swirling his cum over my clit. "I know."

He fucked me once more in the shower, leaving his cum

deep inside me and plugging me with our favorite plug before we got ready and climbed into the elevator to go downstairs to the brand-new Wildcats headquarters entrance.

Dominic and I had the topmost floor of the building, while Tara and Sloane had decided to grab the apartments across from each other on the floor below us. Naomi moved to the floor directly above the main Wildcats headquarters, converting the apartment across from hers into a personal clinic and research area.

Lena claimed the floor between Naomi and that of Tara and Sloane's, moving her and her son into one apartment. She had an empty apartment right across from her place, which found its perfect use.

It was now converted to our personal Den, fully equipped with the comfiest couch, a fully functioning kitchen, a large dining table with fifteen seats, indoor swings, a dedicated play area for Shadow, and a large bed where the five of us could sleep comfortably. This time around, the Den was a space completely dedicated to relaxing and comfort. We'd made it a rule to have Sunday lunches at the Den together. Last week, I'd invited my family for Sunday lunch with the girls and Dominic's family. Dominic's family officially met mine, and it was nothing short of miraculous.

I'd feared that our different cultural backgrounds would be an obstacle. However, our parents found common ground in the similarities between Korean and Indian cultures and traditions. Both our cultures value the importance of family, passing down traditions to younger generations, spicy foods, and a love for one's country of origin.

To think about the time before I'd met Dominic, my girls were my only family. To think I had closed myself off to the world so much that I'd refused to love others and let others love me. And now, Dominic had not only gifted me the love of his family but also opened my heart and given me the strength to let my own family back into my world. As awful as the circumstances were under which he'd entered my life, the life we were building with the love of so many people around us was something I'd never imagined in my wildest dreams.

Dominic and I walked into the foyer of Wildcats HQ and were welcomed by all the people we loved and cherished. In another time, in a world without Dominic by my side, that would've been just four of my girls.

But as the five of us cut the ribbon at the double doors to our brand-new headquarters, we were surrounded by my family, Dominic's family, and Lena's parents. My mom pulled me into a hug after we entered the new space, her blessings like a warm, protective blanket over my soul. Her eyes shone with tears as she held my cheeks, the feel of her soft fingers taking me back in time. "I'm so proud of you, beta. You're so strong. So brave. I know why you stayed away from us. But never again. I never want you to worry about our safety while you're avenging those who are suffering. You fight like a soldier. You must give us the honor of being the parents of a soldier. They don't cower. They aren't afraid for their life. Let us do the same. We love you. And we would die for you, beta. Just never push us away again."

Tears dripped down my face as I nodded and pulled Maa into my arms. "I promise, Maa. No more running. And I'm never going to let anything happen to you. We have a lot to catch up on. You need to move into this building quickly now so you can feed me all your food all the time. I miss your cooking."

I pouted at her, trying to convince her to move into this building already. But as proud parents of their daughter, their pride wouldn't allow them to move into a million-dollar apartment gifted to them by their daughter's life partner.

We kept trying to convince them, but my dad's pride wouldn't be swayed.

With Maa by my side, I looked around to find Arya deep in conversation with Tara. Apparently, they quickly formed a friendship when they came for Sunday brunch, as they share a common interest in computer science and are close in age. It was the first time I'd seen Tara in an animated discussion with someone other than the four of us, and it made my heart unreasonably happy. She still kept her mask on. But one day, I knew she would claim all parts of herself and live her life without any mask.

Sloane, Naomi, and Lena stood with Dominic, making him laugh as they all drank the champagne and ate the delicious appetizers being carried around by the servers. Despite this being a small, private event, Dominic had arranged for catering services with an extensive dinner spread. We had Korean food, Indian food, and a full bar with a bartender mixing up cocktails like a pro.

Starting tomorrow, Tara would send out mass alerts to all our contacts, all the ladies who used to come to Thunder Claw for training, with the new information on our location. Now that we had a bigger space, it was time for the Wildcats to grow. We were all ready.

And when I walked to Dominic, he pulled me into his chest as his smile touched my heart. The love shining in his eyes was so bright it made my heart glow. He looked at me like I was all he saw. He was the shore to my storm, he was the sun to my darkness. His love was his utter dedication to me.

It was in the way he laid his entire world at my feet.

It was in his commitment to the purpose of *my* life.

It was in the way he fought me for dominance but never disrespected my boundaries.

It was in the way he made me feel safe in a world full of darkness and danger.

His love was my strength, and I would demolish any danger that came his way, destroy any soul that dared to harm him, and raze the ground that his enemies tried to step on.

He was mine. To keep. To protect. To cherish. To love.

Forever.

EPILOGUE - 2

LIEUTENANT KNOX STEELE

At the same time, in a different part of NYC

Someone was killing off a lot of very bad men.
Someone was serving justice to women.
Someone was taking the law into their own hands.
Someone was playing judge, jury, and executioner.
Someone was hell-bent on doing *my job* in *my city*.
Someone was going to fucking pay.

AUTHOR'S NOTE

Thank you so much for giving my book a chance. I hope you continue with me and the Wildcats in their journey to their HEAs.

If you enjoyed Samaira and Dominic's story, please consider leaving a review. Every review makes a difference, and it would mean the world to me if you spare a few minutes for this baby author.

And yes, we're getting Lieutenant Steele, who will be falling for our beloved Tara and her Shadow baby. They're going to be AWESOME, and I can't wait for you to delve into their story.

ACKNOWLEDGMENTS

I've always wanted to write a romance where the traditional roles of the hero and heroine were slightly reversed. I wanted to see a morally gray heroine saving the hero at the end. I wanted a super strong and muscular woman who was swoon-worthy. I wanted to write about a group of women who other women fawned over. I hope I did the girls justice.

I would like to thank my fellow authors, Ruby Rana and Ava Rani, for cheering me on when I shared the idea for the book. Thank you, Ruby, for reading that first outline and encouraging me to write the story.

Thank you, Hannah, the best alpha reader in the world, for the superior commentary you left throughout my book. Every time I started to doubt myself, I went back to your comments and read through them. I'm never leaving you alone.

Thank you to my wonderful beta readers—Victoria Woods, Ankita, Apoorva, Malia, Saadia, and Kriti—for reading my book and providing me with your incredible opinions. Your hilarious and awesome comments and clarifying questions made the book a thousand times better.

Thank you to my sensitivity readers—Pearl, Teralyn Mitchell, and Giuliana Victoria—for your comments and insight. I am beyond grateful for your help.

Thank you to my mom for your constant support. She's not just a well-wisher, but she's the powerhouse who handles all the printing and shipping of my books from the website orders. I love you, Mom.

Last, but never the least, thank you to my husband for the constant support and encouragement. Thank you for making my website. Thank you for taking care of me when I'm too busy and lost in my books to do it myself. Thank you for letting me put real life to the side while I get lost in my fictional world for endless stretches of hours. Thank you for being the inspiration behind all my heroes. You're the Hero no. 1.

ABOUT THE AUTHOR

Nia Myst is a dark romance author. She loves writing strong, powerful heroines and alpha heroes who are obsessed with them. Her books are full of spice, action, humor, and heart-melting, swoonworthy romance.

You can reach her:
    Instagram: https://www.instagram.com/nia.myst.author/
    Tiktok: https://www.tiktok.com/@nia.myst.author
    Website: https://niamyst.com/
    Email: hello@niamyt.com